# Chi's Sweet Home

チーズ スイートホーム

# 6

## Konami Kanata

# contents
## homemade 93~110+

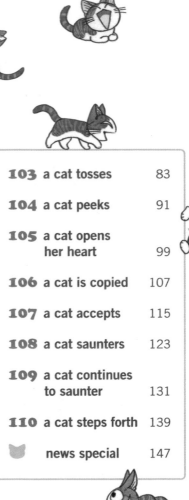

## homemade 93: a cat leaves her mark

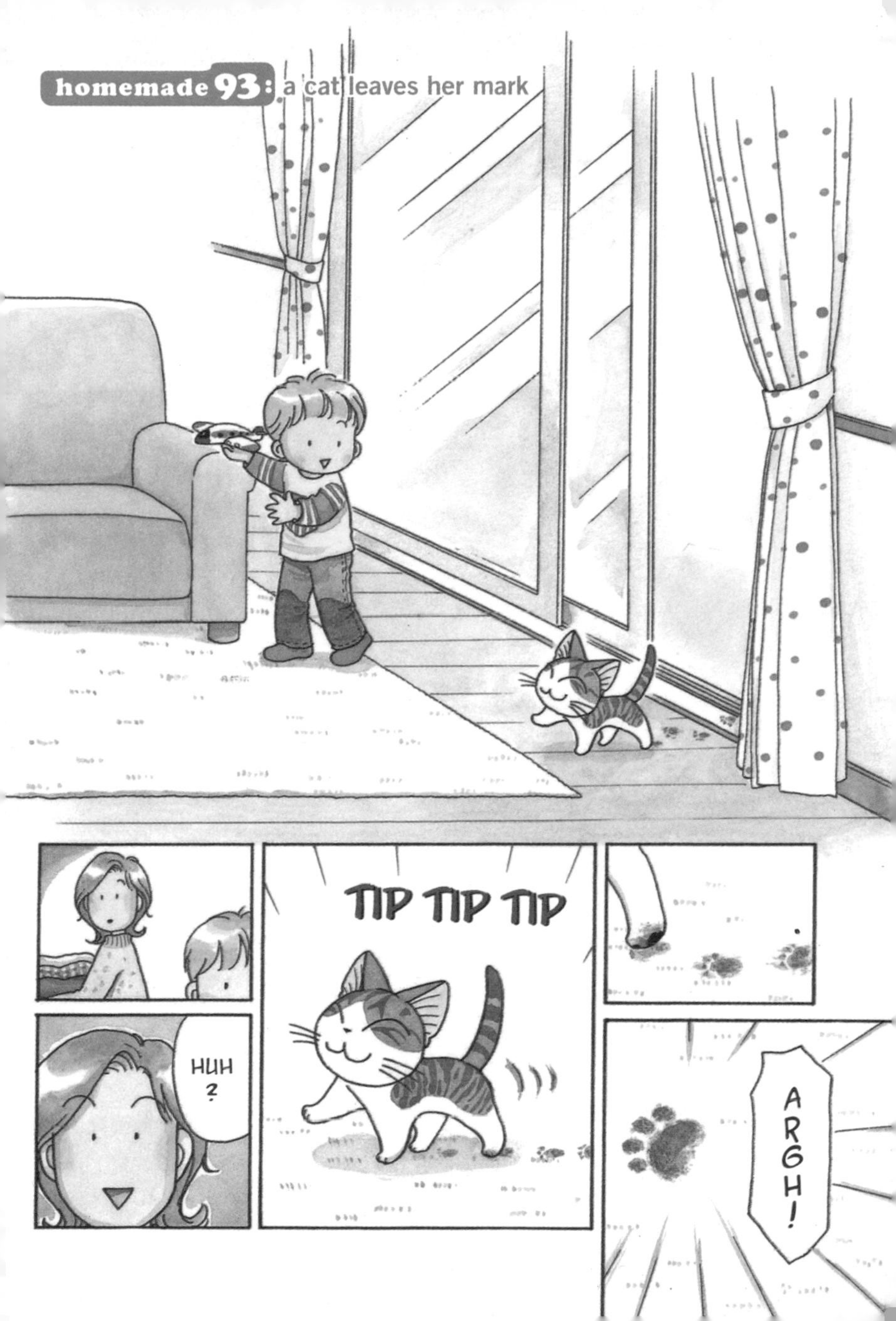
HUH?
TIP TIP TIP
ARGH!

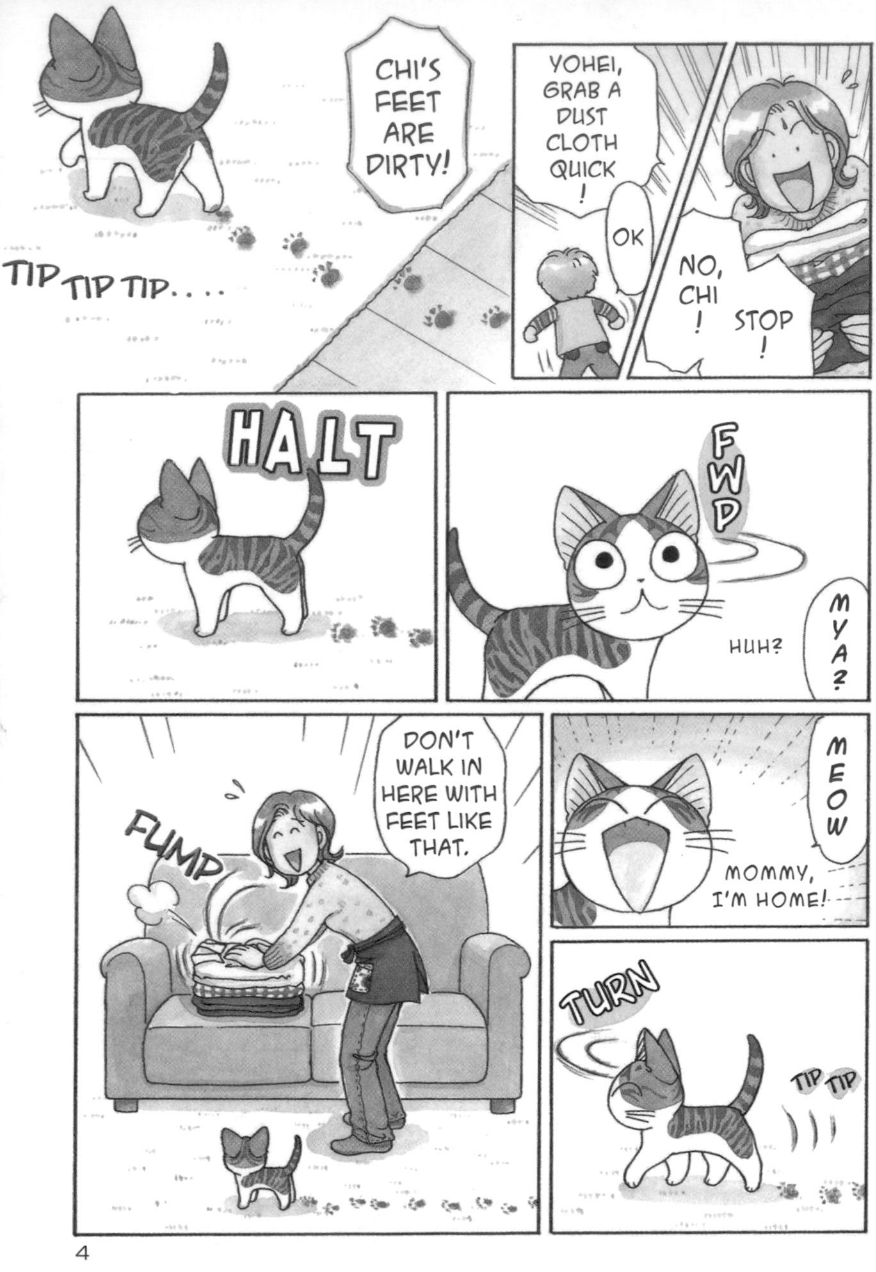
TIP TIP TIP....
CHI'S FEET ARE DIRTY!
YOHEI, GRAB A DUST CLOTH QUICK!
OK
NO, CHI!
STOP!
HALT
FWP
HUH?
MYA?
FUMP
DON'T WALK IN HERE WITH FEET LIKE THAT.
MEOW
MOMMY, I'M HOME!
TURN
TIP TIP

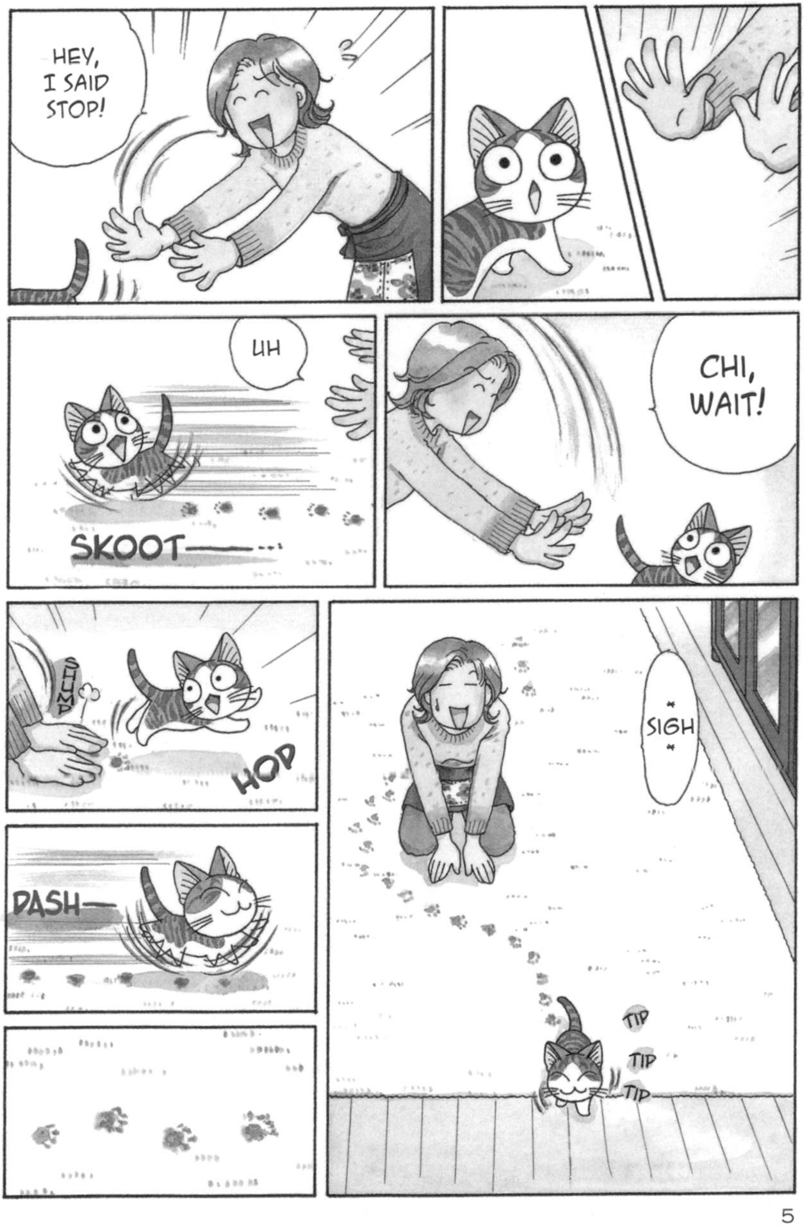
HEY, I SAID STOP!
UH
SKOOT
CHI, WAIT!
SHUMP
HOP
DASH
*SIGH*
TIP
TIP
TIP

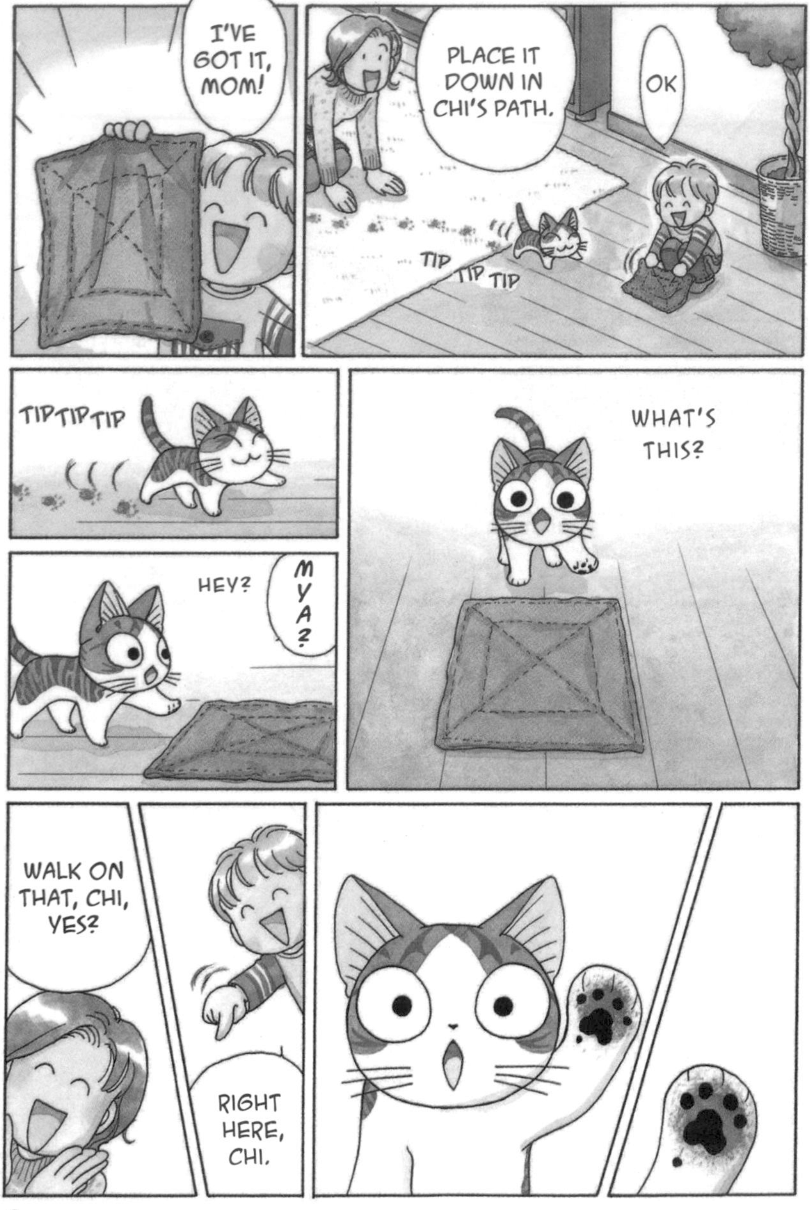
I'VE GOT IT, MOM!
PLACE IT DOWN IN CHI'S PATH.
OK
TIP TIP TIP
TIPTIPTIP
WHAT'S THIS?
HEY?
MYA?
WALK ON THAT, CHI, YES?
RIGHT HERE, CHI.

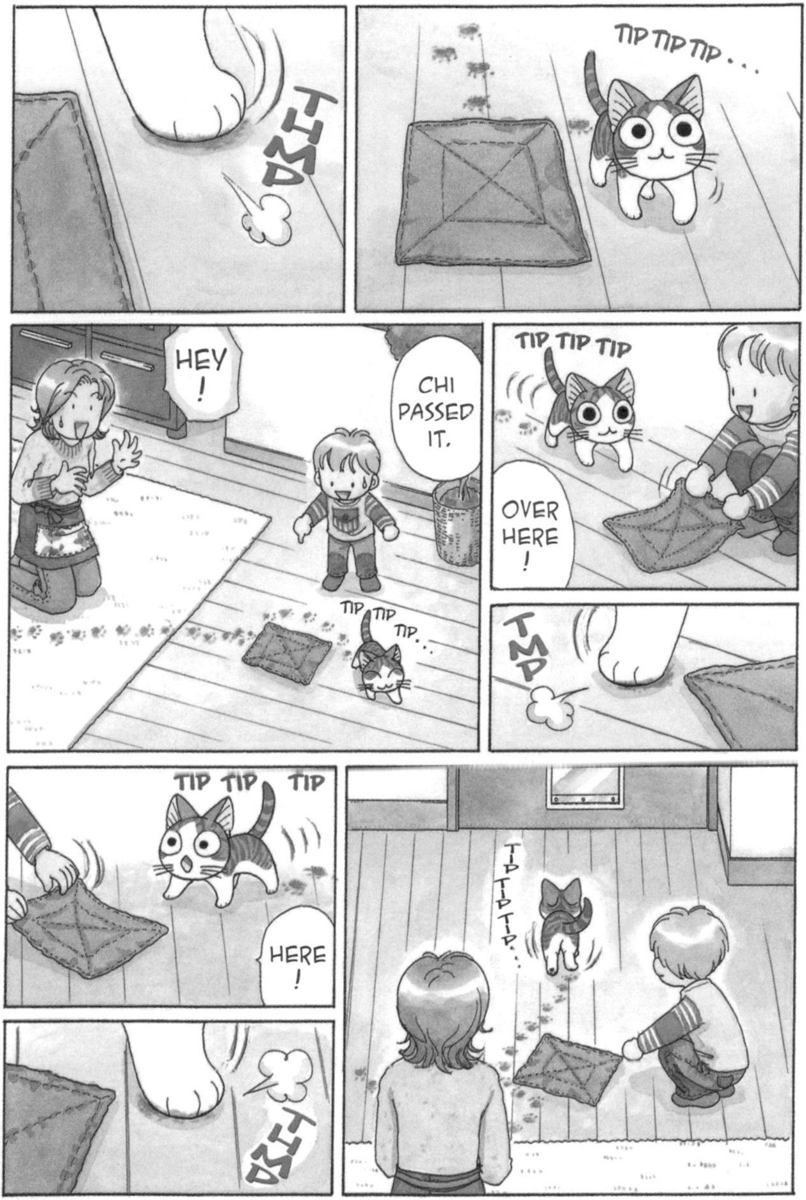
THMP
TIP TIP TIP . . .
HEY!
CHI PASSED IT.
TIP TIP TIP...
TIP TIP TIP
OVER HERE!
TMP
TIP TIP TIP
HERE!
THMP
TIP TIP TIP...

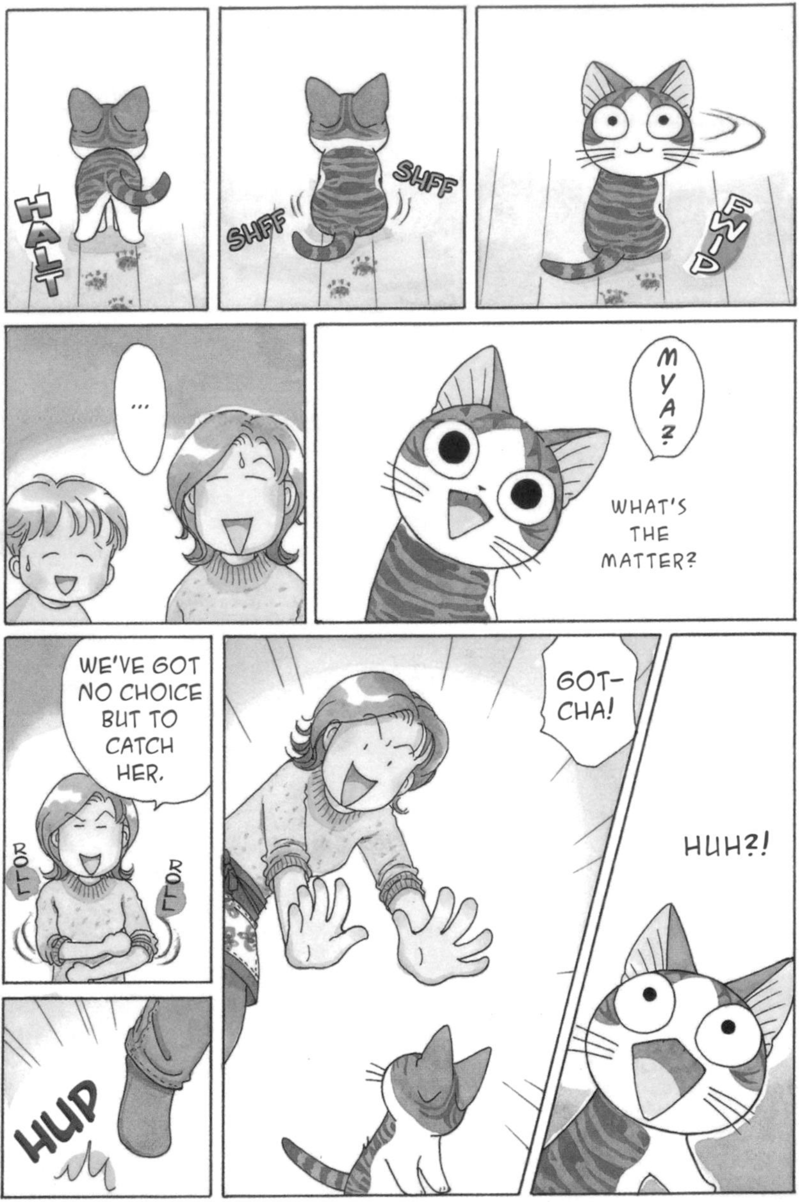
HALT
SHFF
SHFF
FWID
...
MYA?
WHAT'S THE MATTER?
WE'VE GOT NO CHOICE BUT TO CATCH HER.
ROLL
ROLL
HUP
GOT-CHA!
HUH?!

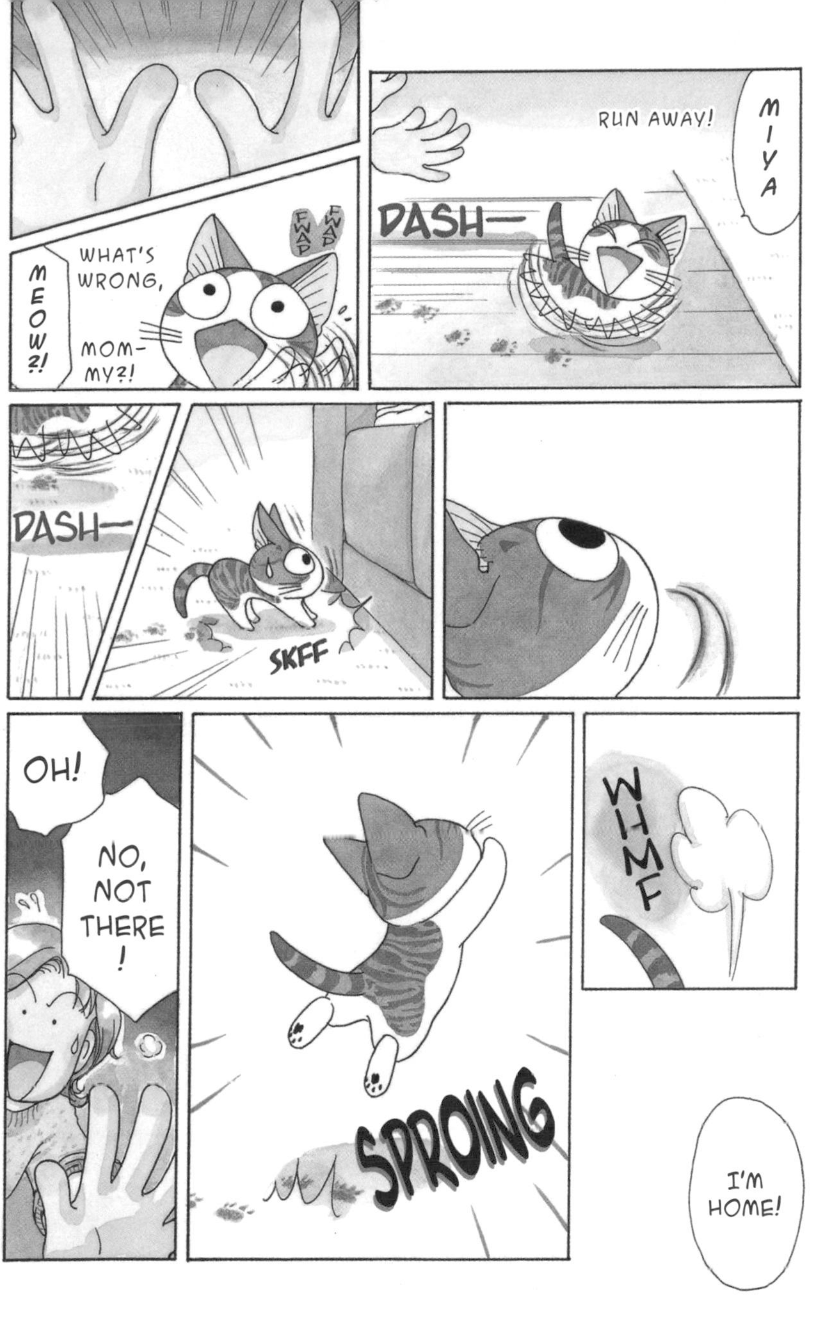
FWAP FWAP
WHAT'S WRONG, MOMMY?!
MEOW?!
RUN AWAY!
MIYA
DASH—
DASH—
SKFF
OH!
NO, NOT THERE!
SPROING
WHMF
I'M HOME!

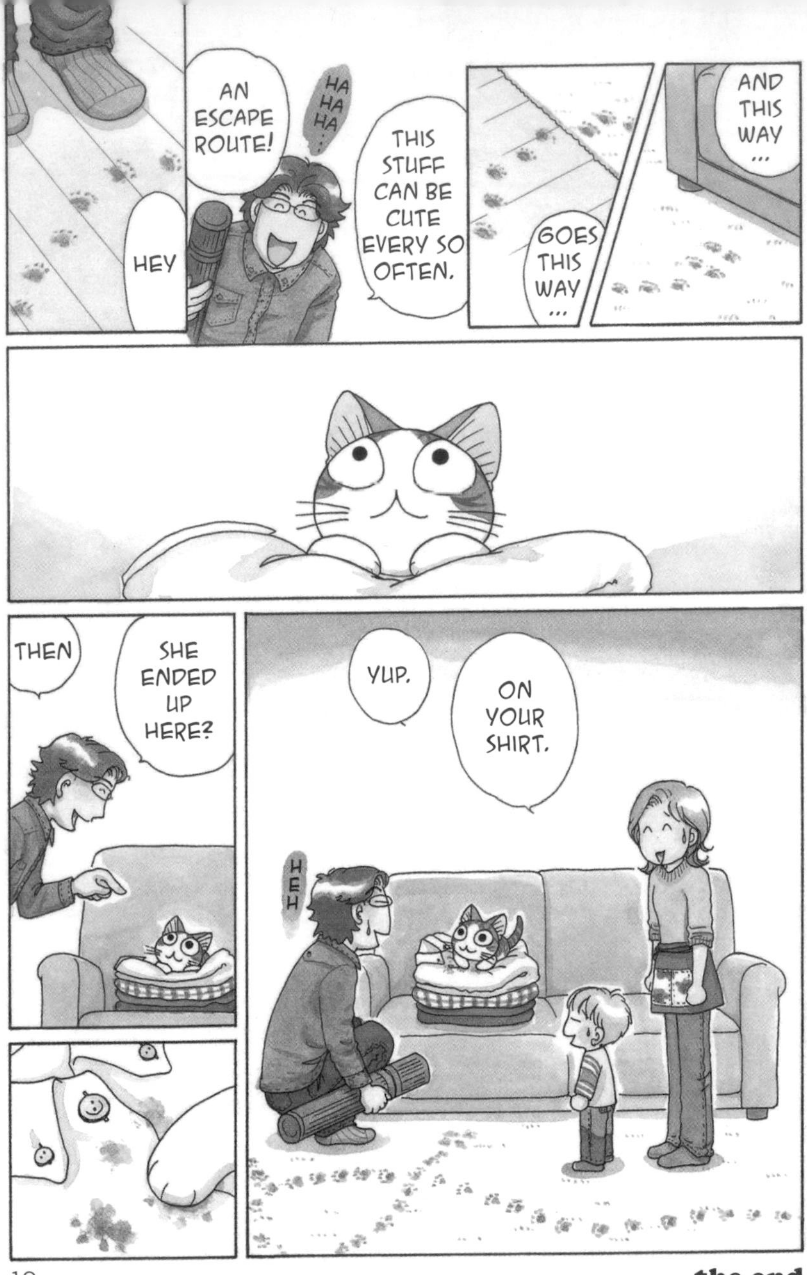
HEY
AN ESCAPE ROUTE!
HA HA HA...
THIS STUFF CAN BE CUTE EVERY SO OFTEN.
GOES THIS WAY...
AND THIS WAY...
THEN
SHE ENDED UP HERE?
YUP.
ON YOUR SHIRT.
HEH



**the end**

## homemade 94: a cat is stopped

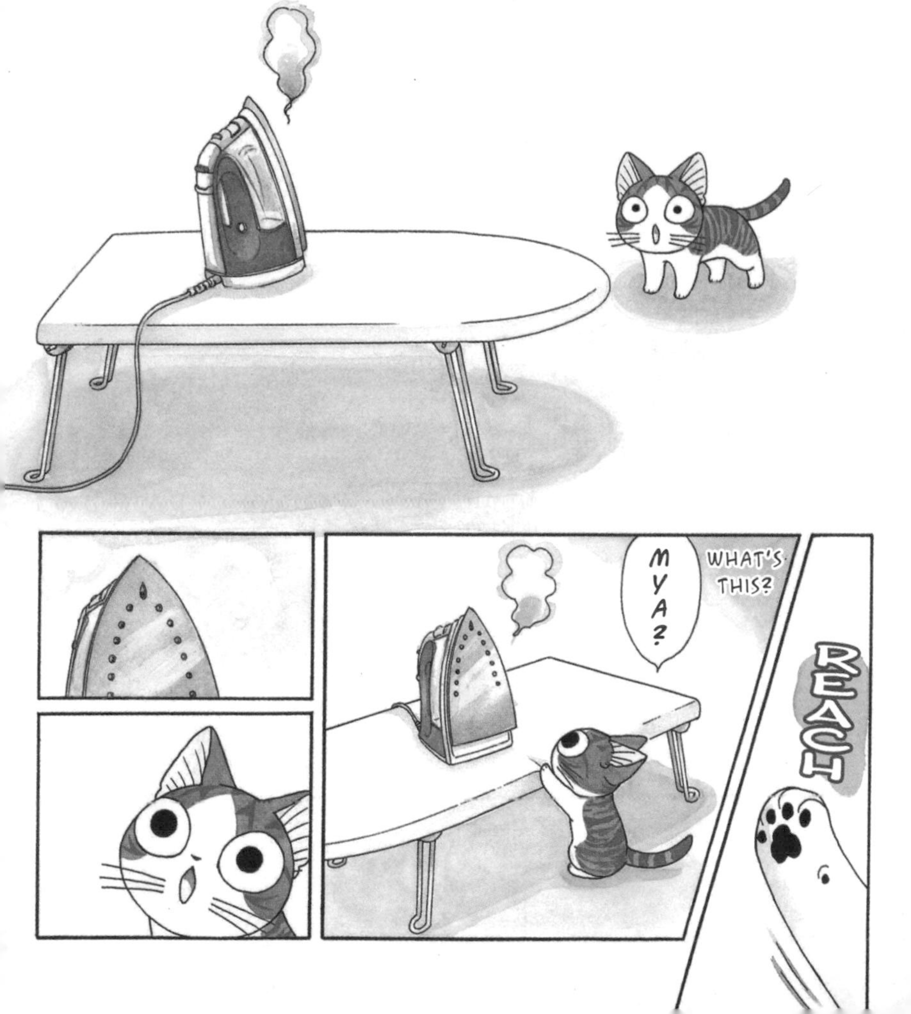
MYA?
WHAT'S THIS?
REACH

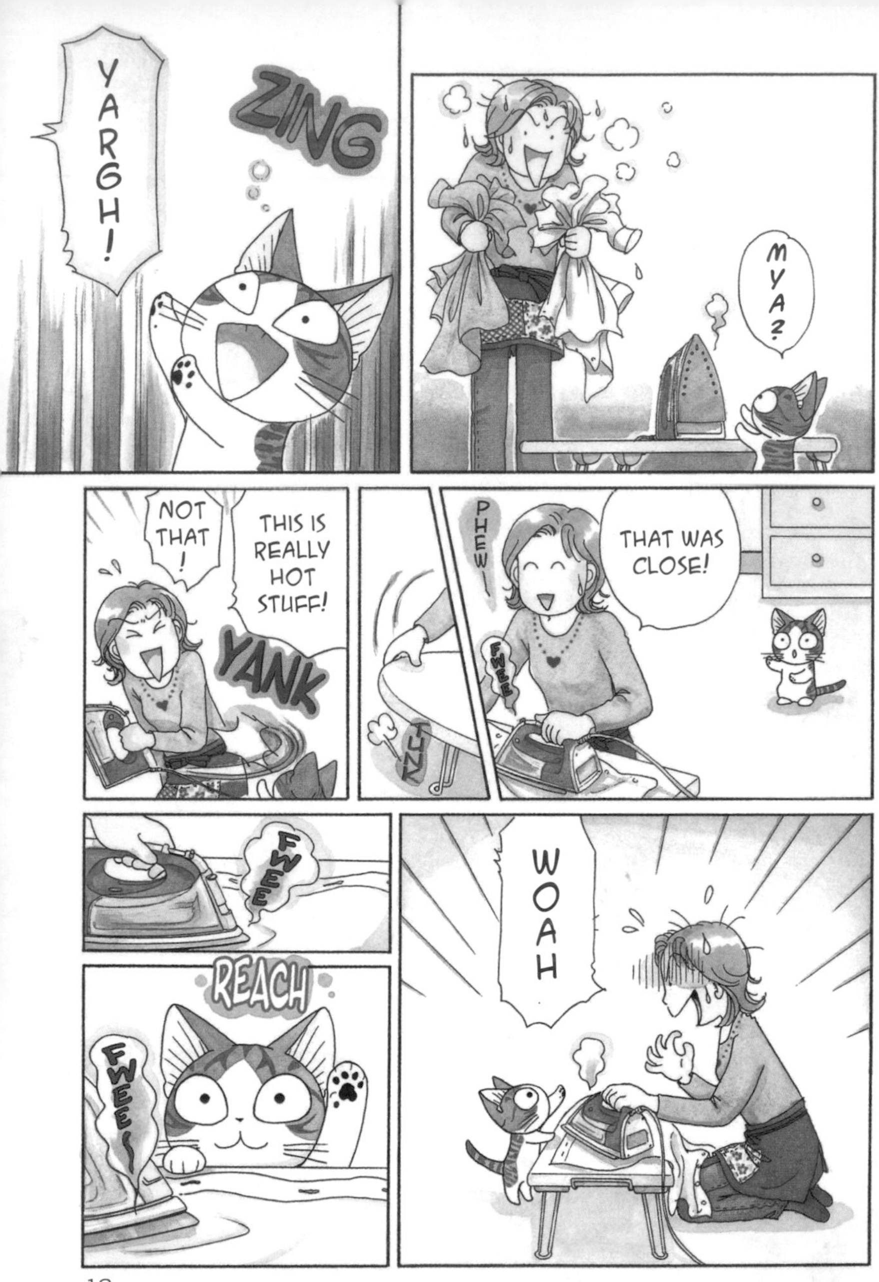
YARGH!
ZING
MYA?
NOT THAT!
THIS IS REALLY HOT STUFF!
YANK
TUNK
PHEW
THAT WAS CLOSE!
FWEE
FWEE
REACH
FWEE~
WOAH

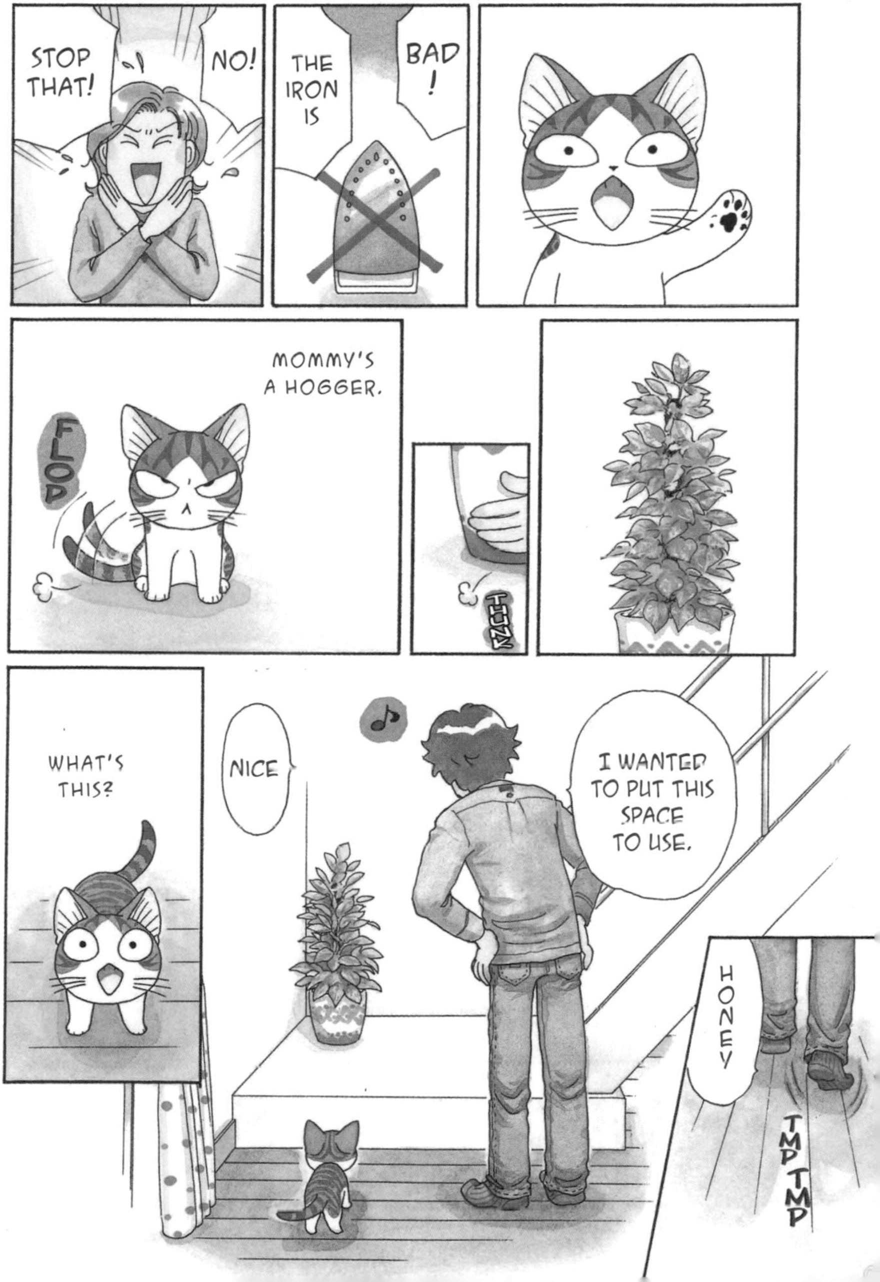
STOP THAT!
NO!
THE IRON IS
BAD!
FLOP
MOMMY'S A HOGGER.
THUNK
WHAT'S THIS?
NICE
♪
I WANTED TO PUT THIS SPACE TO USE.
HONEY
TMP TMP

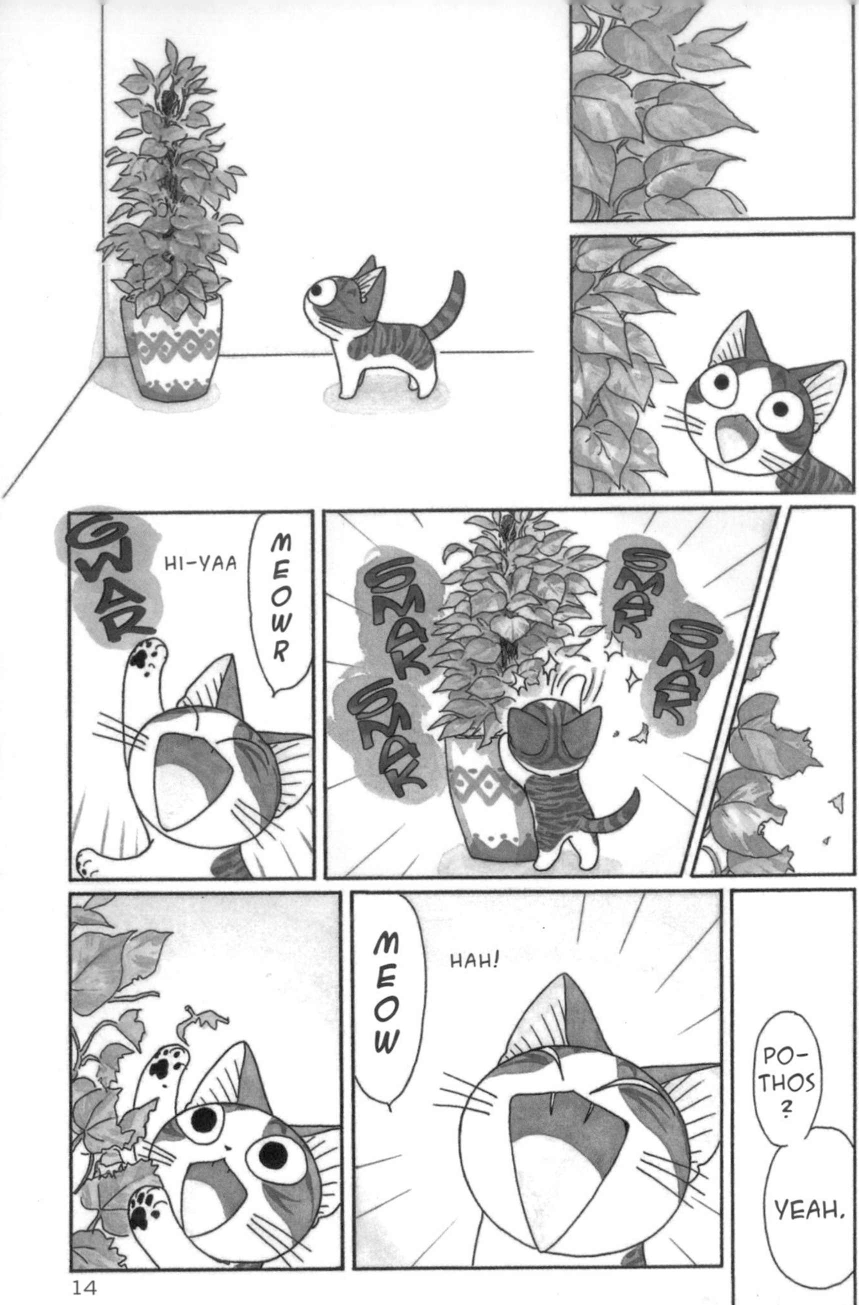
GWAR
HI-YAA
MEOWR
SMAK
SMAK
SMAK
SMAK
MEOW
HAH!
PO-THOS?
YEAH.

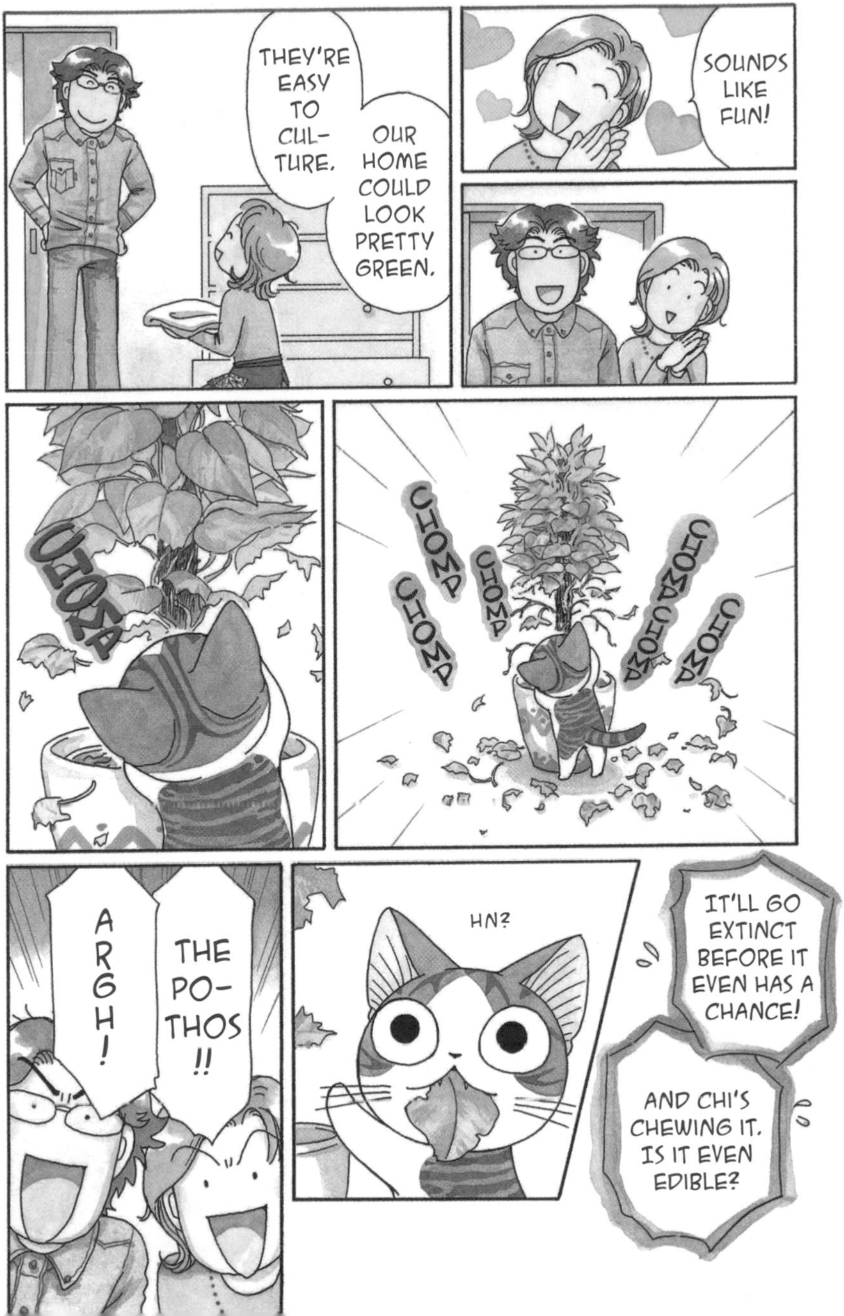
THEY'RE EASY TO CUL-TURE.
OUR HOME COULD LOOK PRETTY GREEN.
SOUNDS LIKE FUN!
CHOMP
CHOMP
CHOMP
CHOMP
CHOMPCHOMP
CHOMP
ARGH!
THE PO-THOS!!
HN?
IT'LL GO EXTINCT BEFORE IT EVEN HAS A CHANCE!
AND CHI'S CHEWING IT. IS IT EVEN EDIBLE?

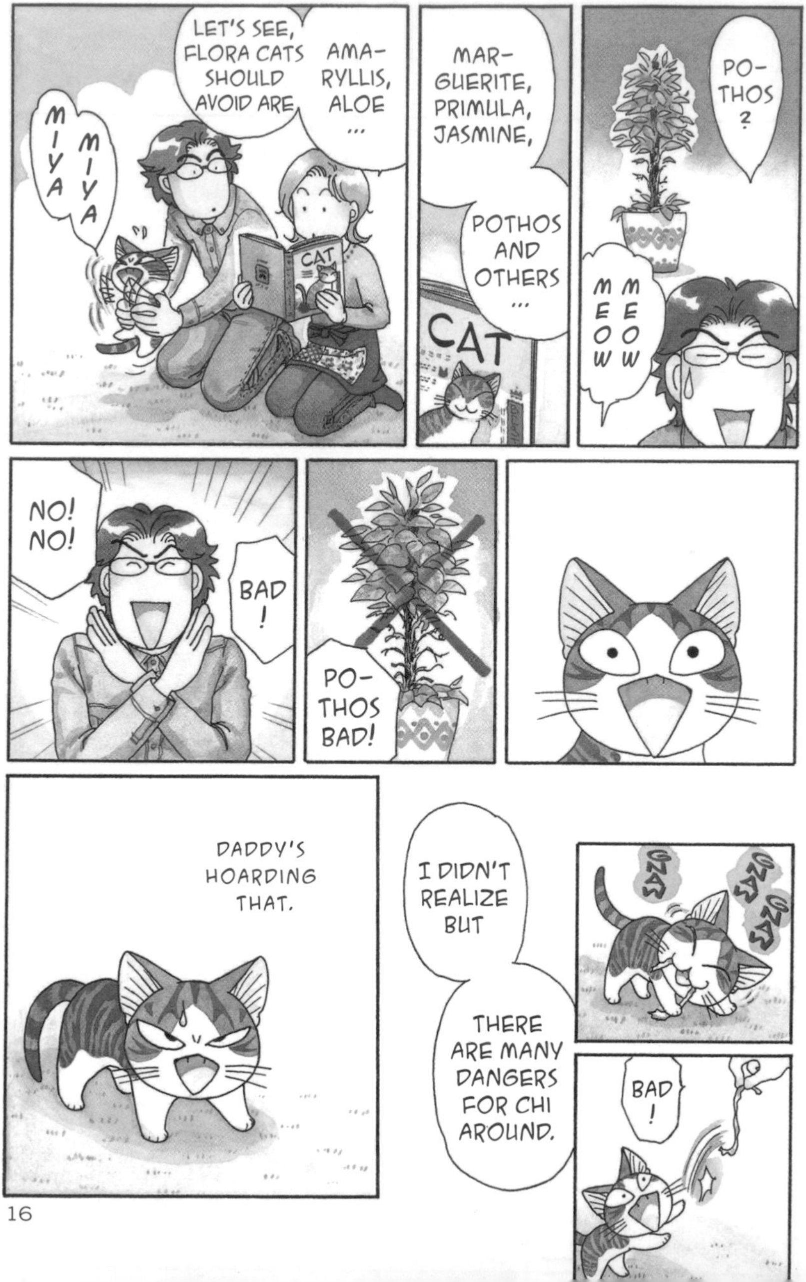
MIYA MIYA
LET'S SEE, FLORA CATS SHOULD AVOID ARE,
AMARYLLIS, ALOE ...
CAT
MARGUERITE, PRIMULA, JASMINE,
POTHOS AND OTHERS ...
CAT
POTHOS?
MEOW MEOW
NO! NO!
BAD!
POTHOS BAD!
DADDY'S HOARDING THAT.
I DIDN'T REALIZE BUT
THERE ARE MANY DANGERS FOR CHI AROUND.
GNAW GNAW GNAW
BAD!

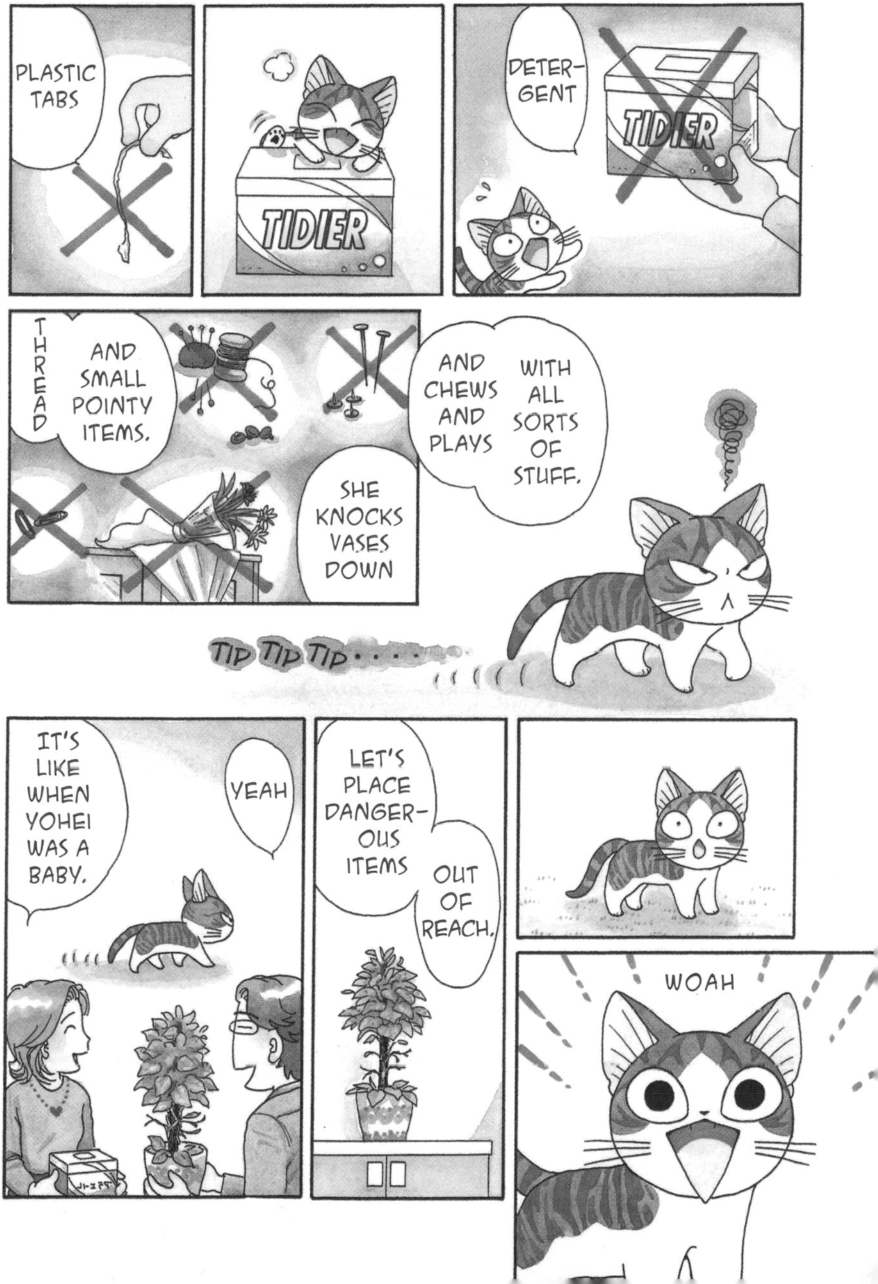
PLASTIC TABS
TIDIER
DETER-GENT
THREAD
AND SMALL POINTY ITEMS.
SHE KNOCKS VASES DOWN
AND CHEWS AND PLAYS
WITH ALL SORTS OF STUFF.
TIP TIP TIP....
IT'S LIKE WHEN YOHEI WAS A BABY.
YEAH
LET'S PLACE DANGER-OUS ITEMS
OUT OF REACH.
WOAH

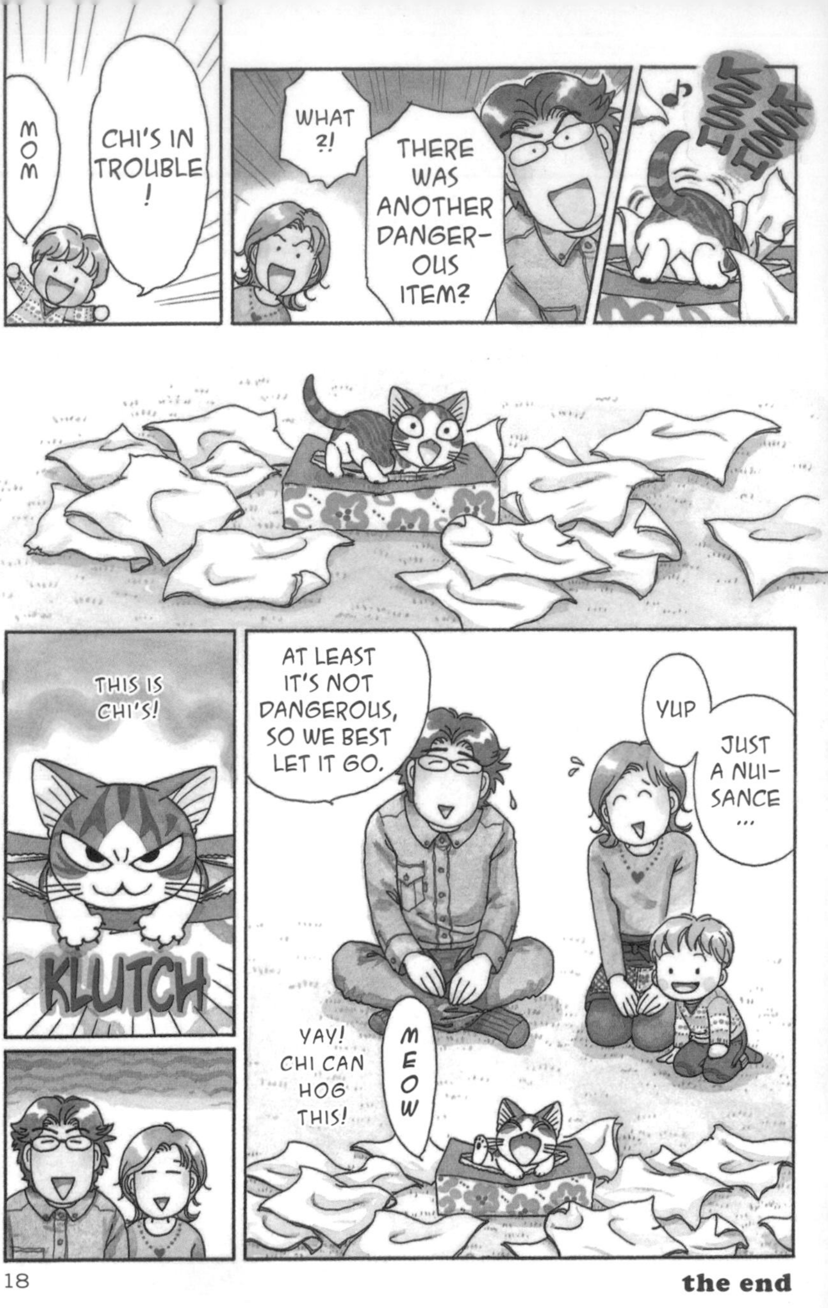
MOM
CHI'S IN TROUBLE!
WHAT?!
THERE WAS ANOTHER DANGER-OUS ITEM?
THIS IS CHI'S!
KLUTCH
AT LEAST IT'S NOT DANGEROUS, SO WE BEST LET IT GO.
YUP
JUST A NUI-SANCE...
YAY! CHI CAN HOG THIS!
MEOW



**the end**

# homemade 95: a cat battles

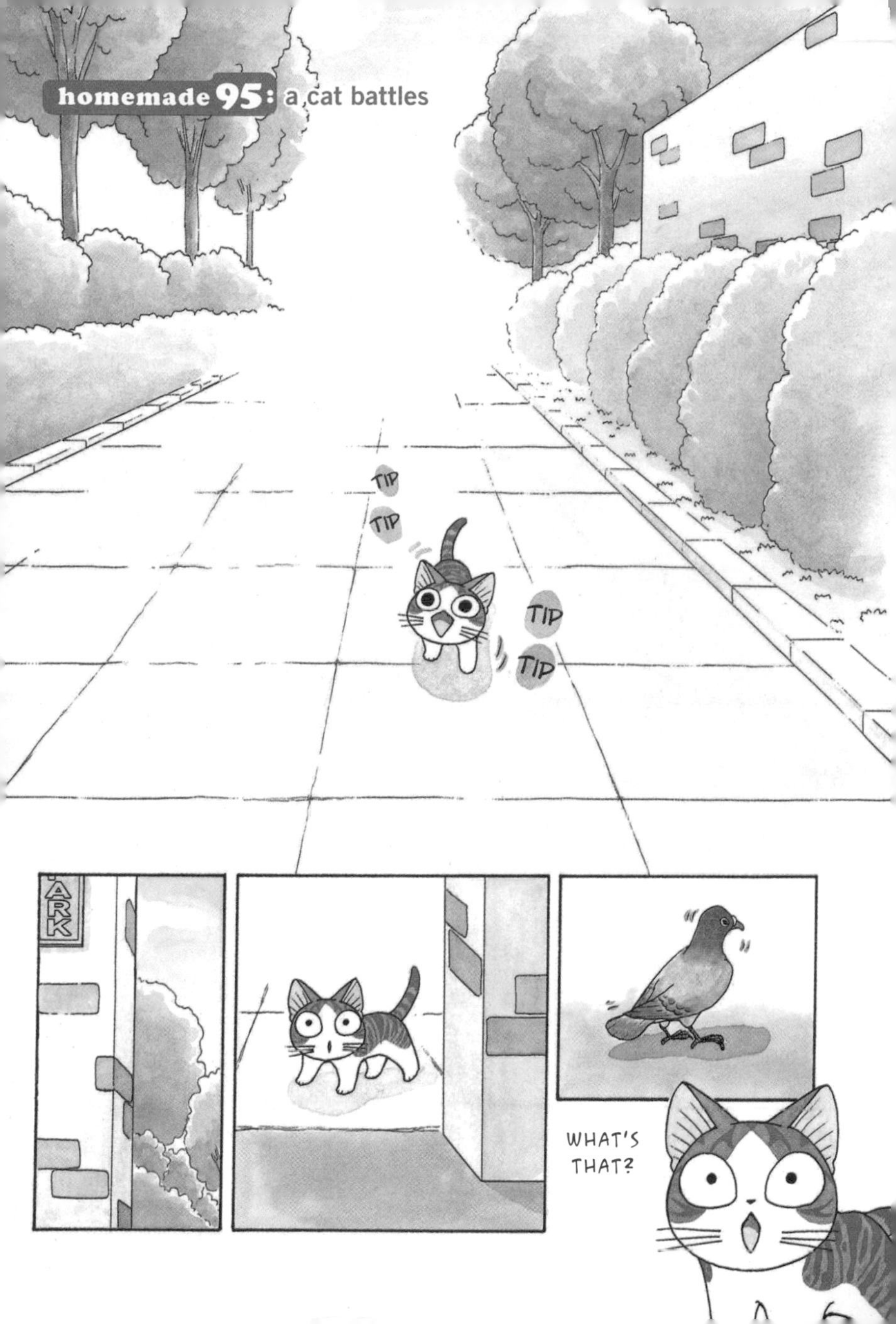
TIP
TIP
TIP
TIP
ARK
WHAT'S THAT?

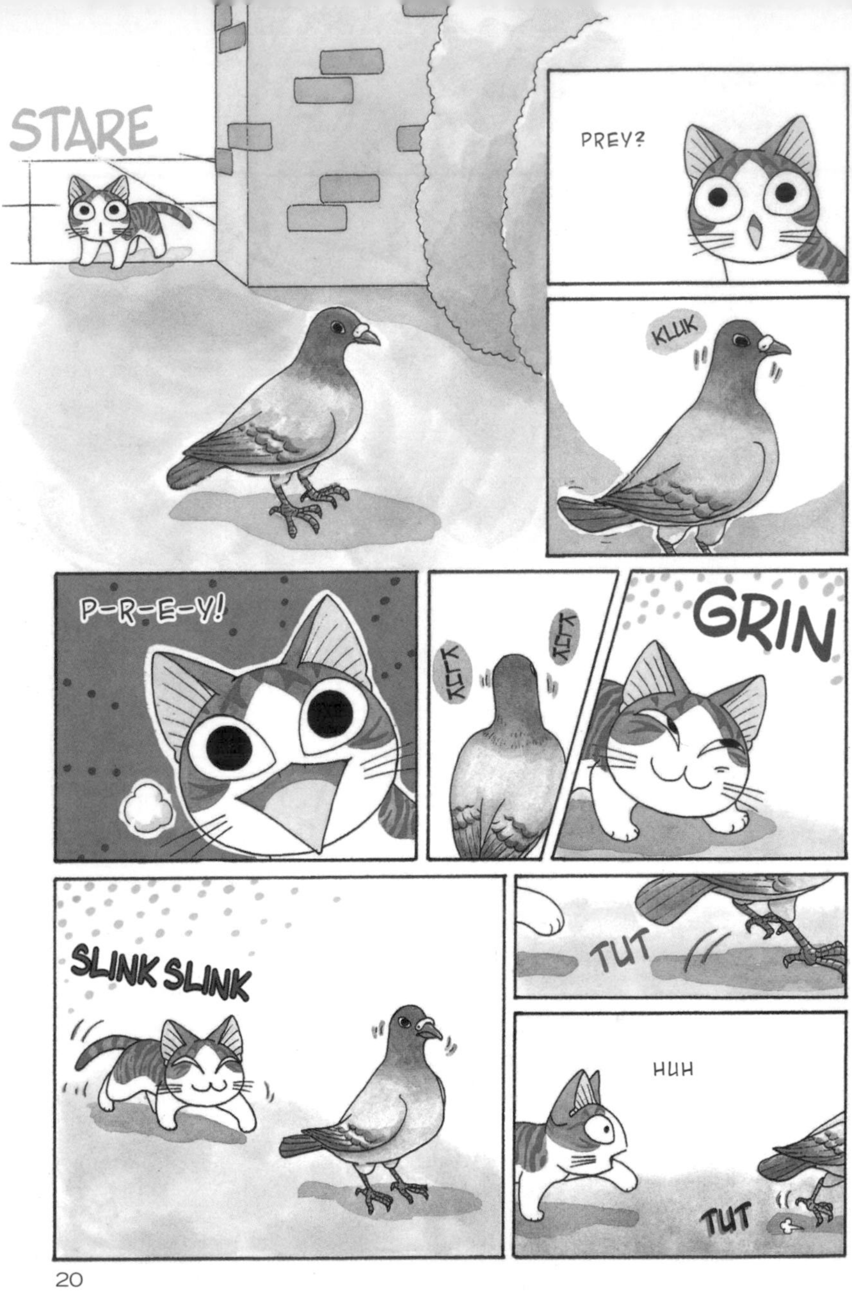
STARE
PREY?
KLUK
P-R-E-Y!
KLUK
KLUK
GRIN
SLINK SLINK
TUT
HUH
TUT

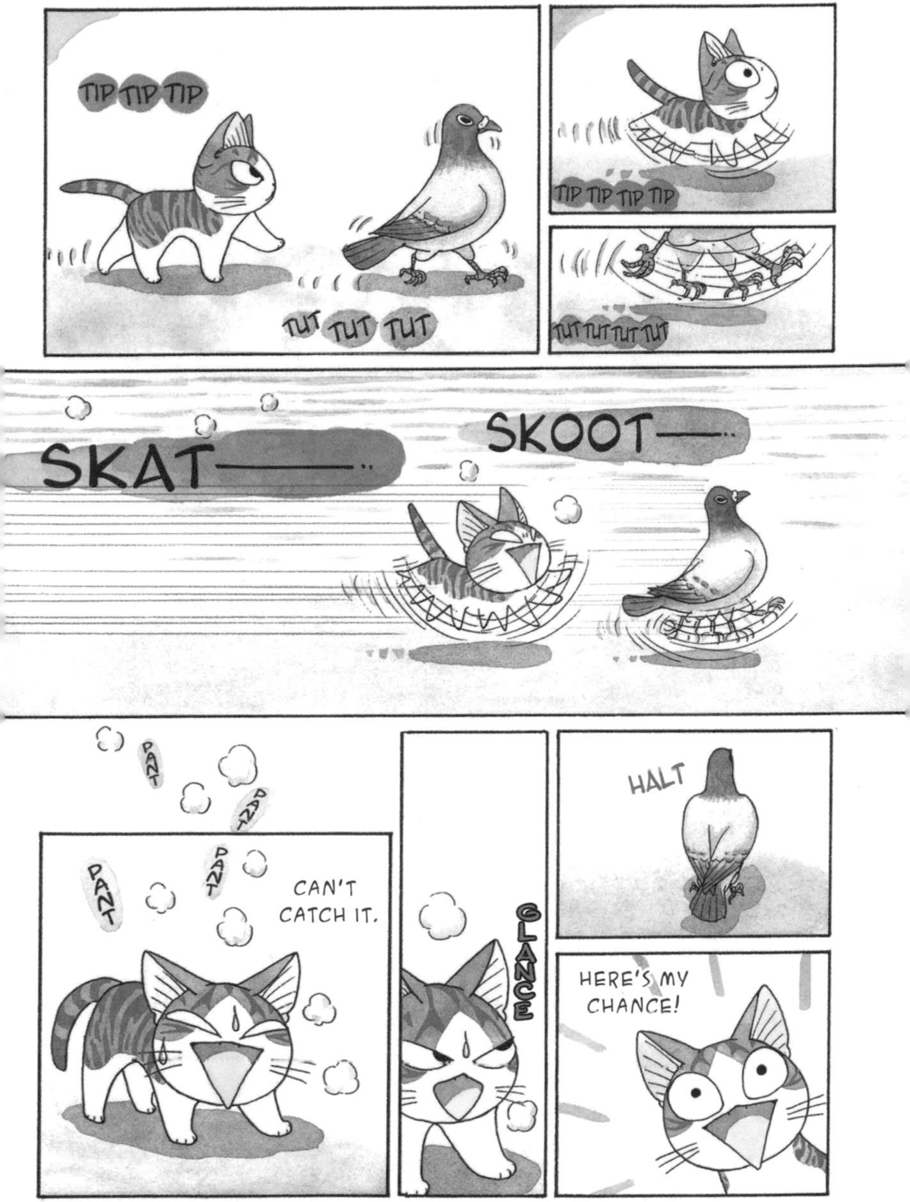
TIP TIP TIP
TUT TUT TUT
TIP TIP TIP TIP
TUT TUT TUT TUT
SKAT———..
SKOOT——..
PANT
PANT
PANT
PANT
CAN'T CATCH IT.
GLANCE
HALT
HERE'S MY CHANCE!

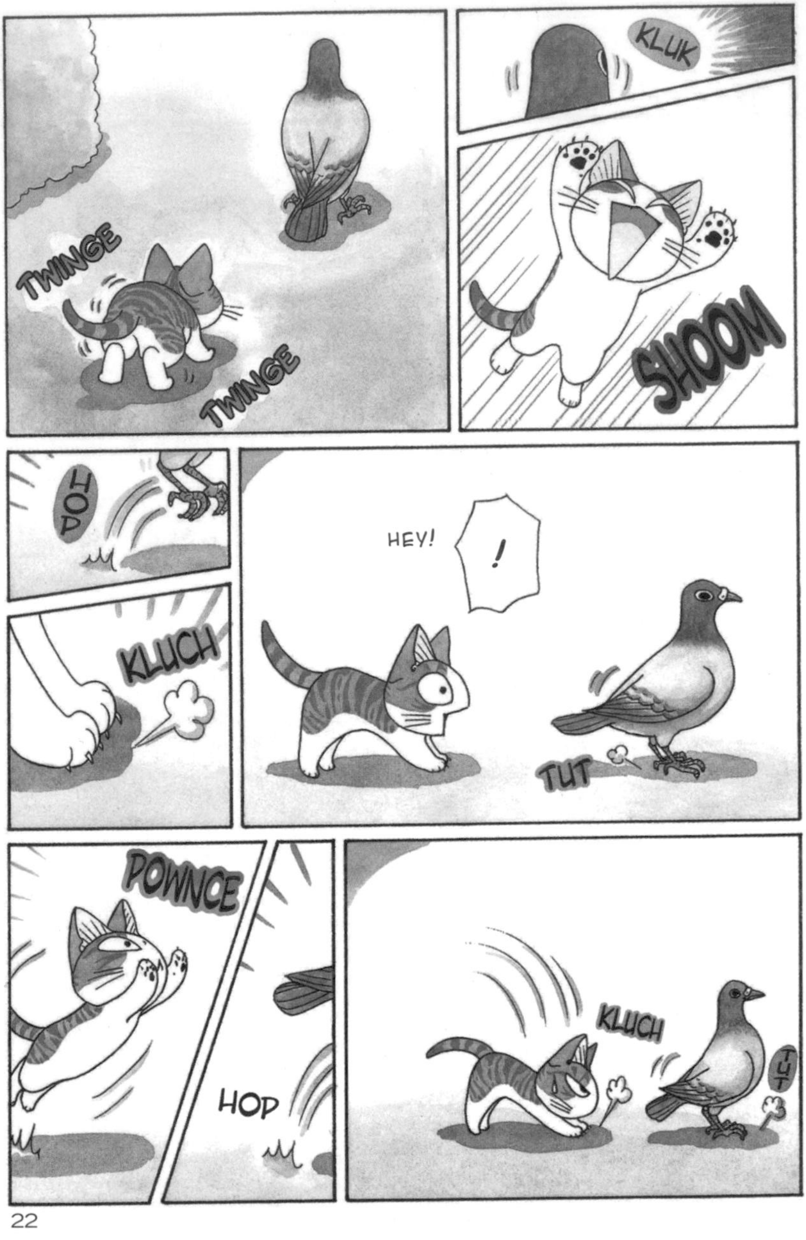
TWINGE
TWINGE
KLUK
SHOOM
HOP
KLUCH
HEY!
!
TUT
POWNCE
HOP
KLUCH
TUT

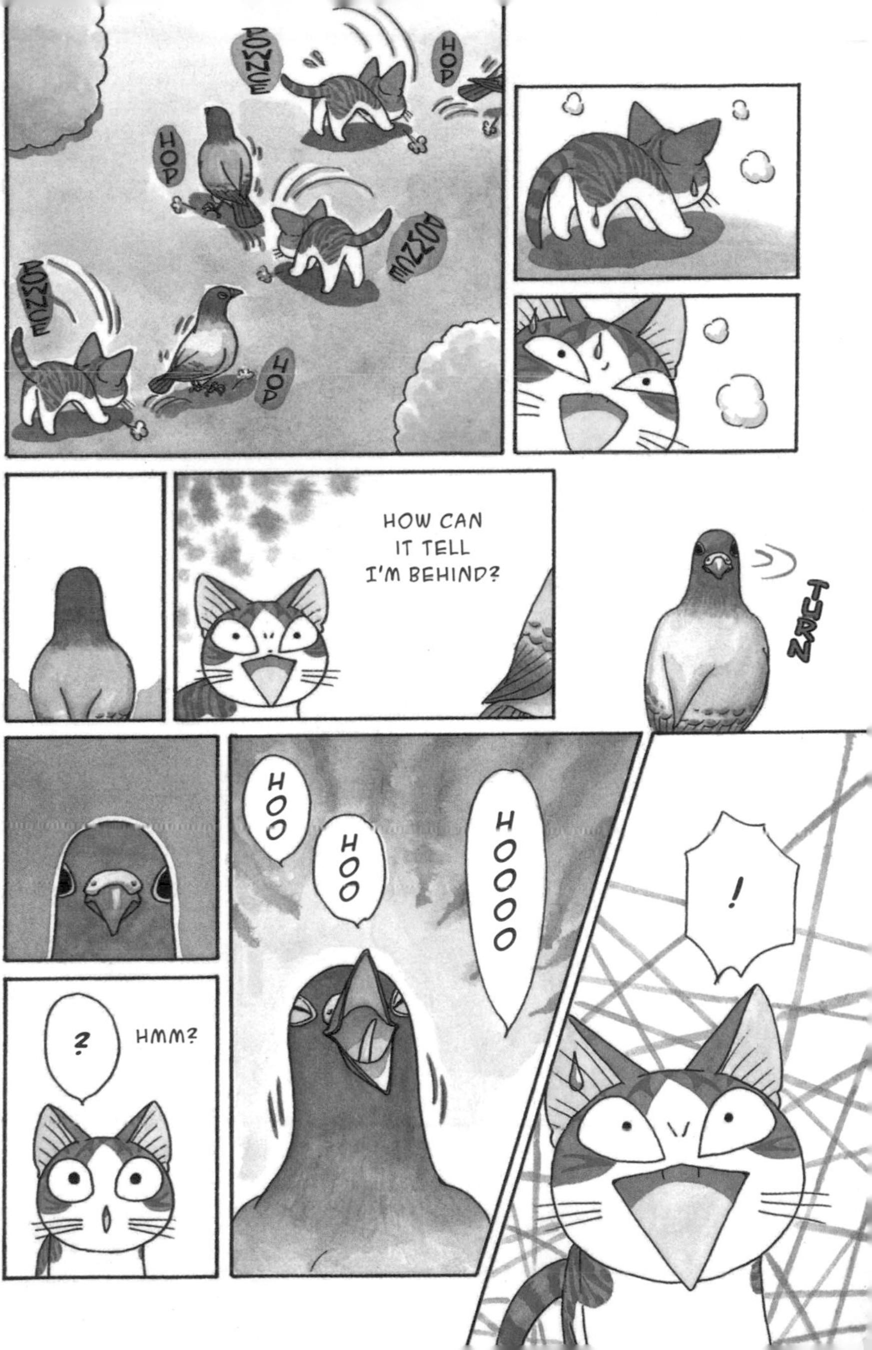
POUNCE
HOP
HOP
POUNCE
POUNCE
HOP
HOW CAN IT TELL I'M BEHIND?
TURN
?
HMM?
HOO
HOO
HOOOOO
!

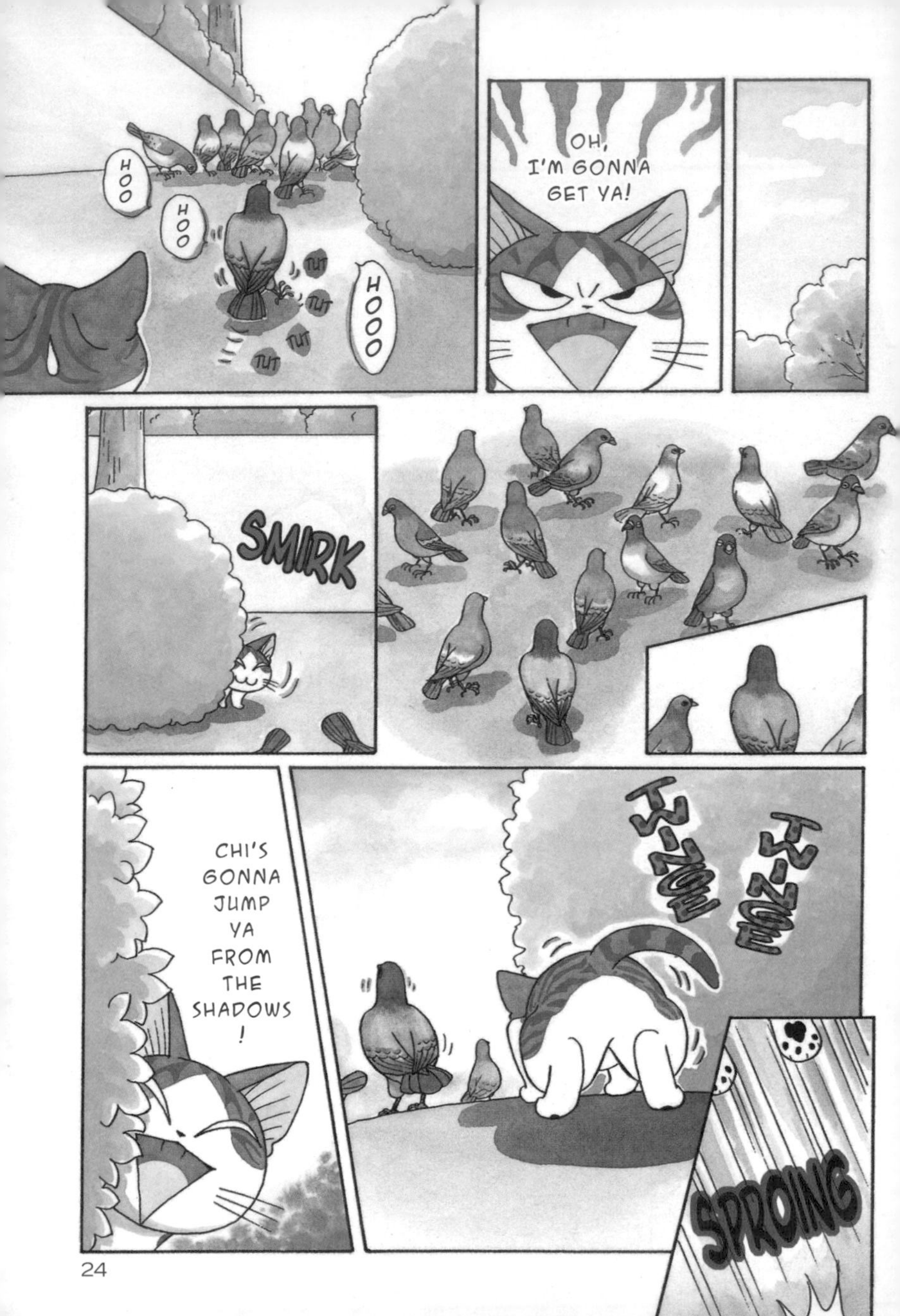
HOO
HOO
TUT
TUT
TUT
TUT
HOOO
OH, I'M GONNA GET YA!
SMIRK
CHI'S GONNA JUMP YA FROM THE SHADOWS!
TWINGE
TWINGE
SPROING

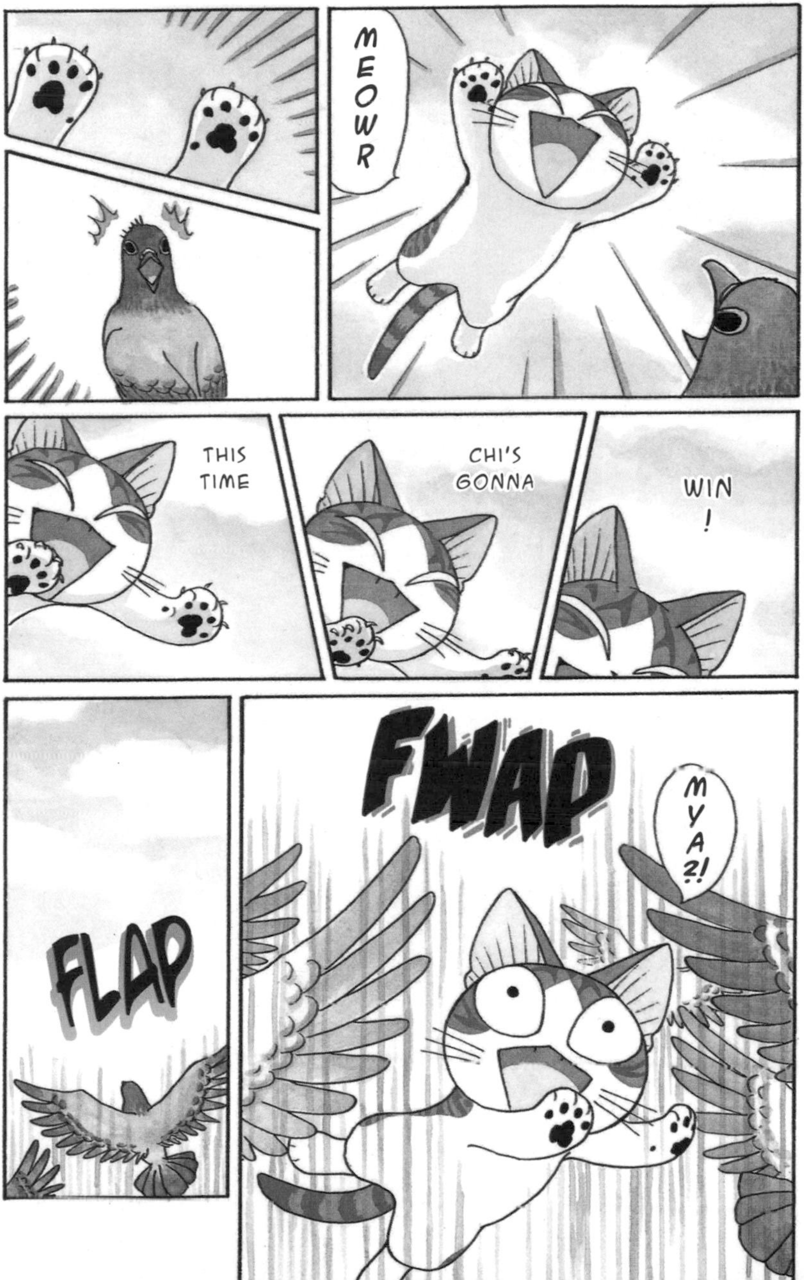
MEOWR
THIS TIME
CHI'S GONNA
WIN!
FLAP
FWAP
MYA?!

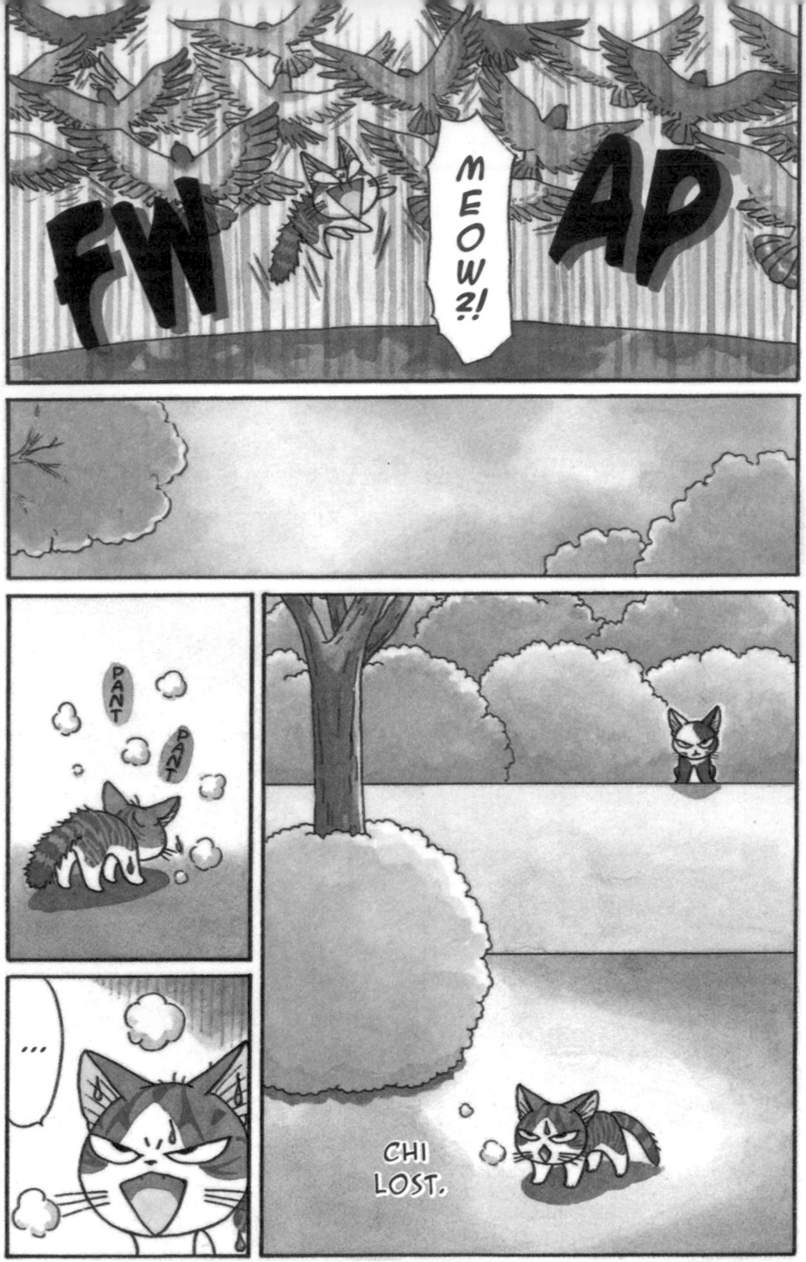
FW
MEOW?!
AP
PANT
PANT
...
CHI LOST.



**the end**

# homemade 96: a cat appears

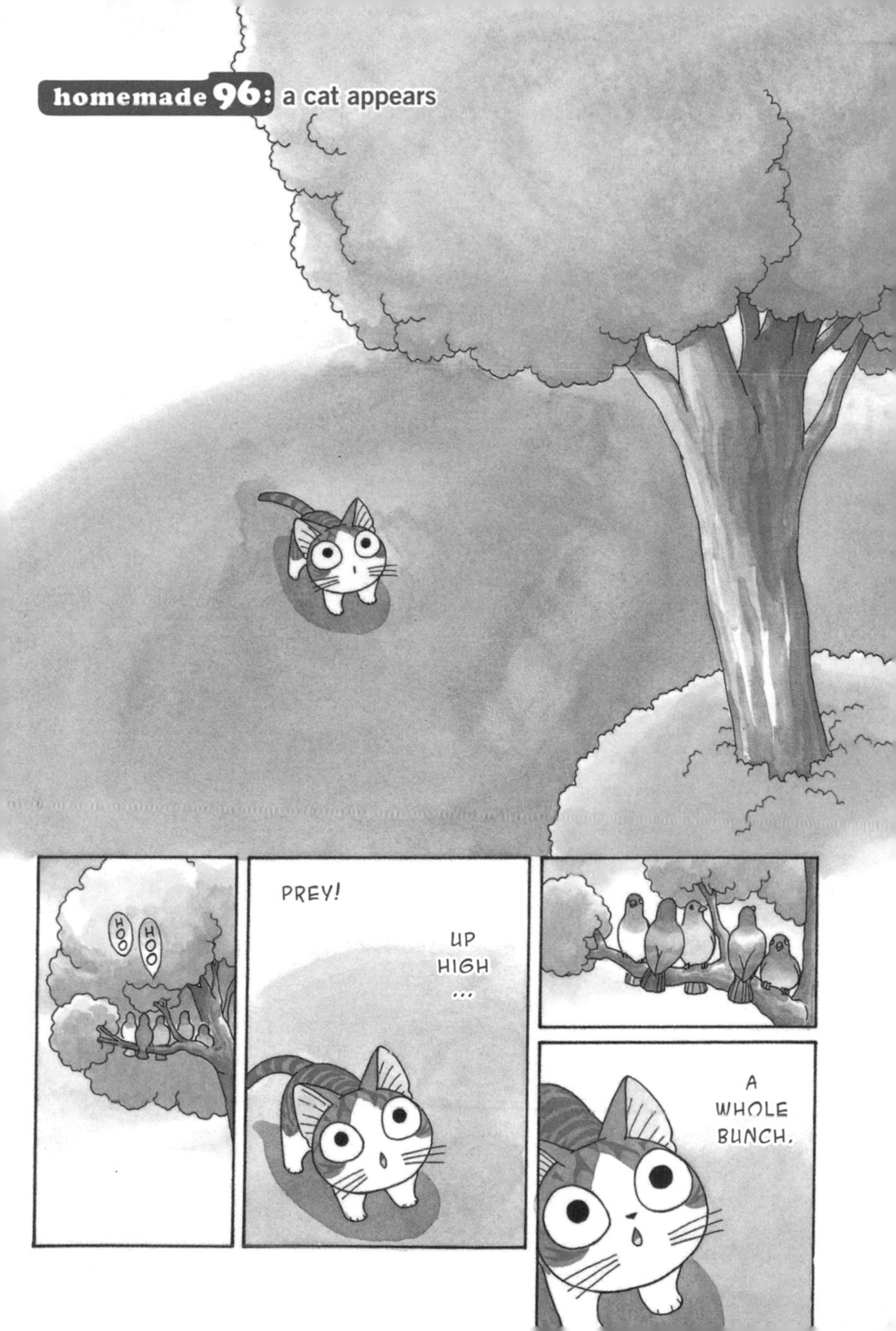

HOO
HOO
PREY!
UP HIGH ...
A WHOLE BUNCH.

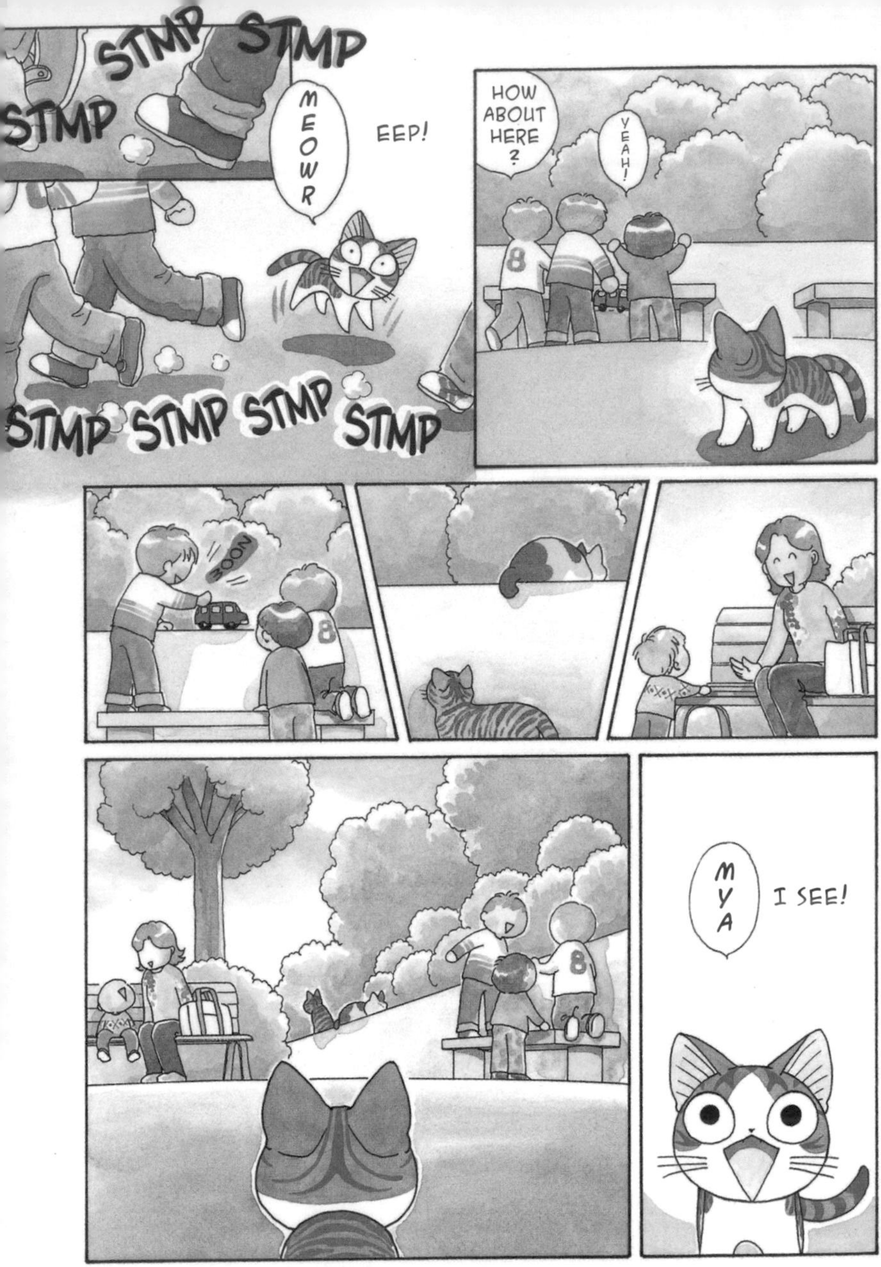
STMP STMP STMP
MEOWR
EEP!
STMP STMP STMP STMP
HOW ABOUT HERE?
YEAH!
BOON
MYA
I SEE!

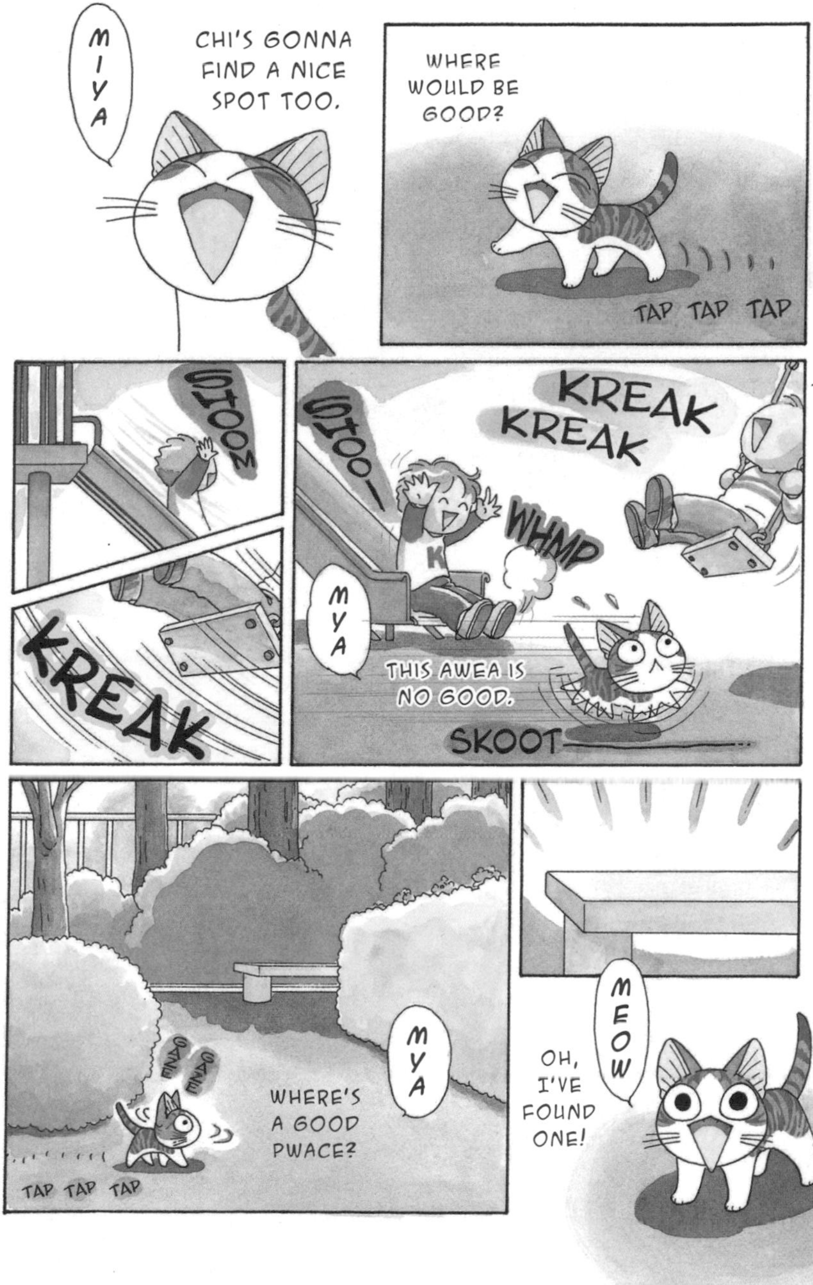
MIYA
CHI'S GONNA FIND A NICE SPOT TOO.
WHERE WOULD BE GOOD?
TAP TAP TAP
SHOOOM
KREAK
SHOOO!
KREAK KREAK
WHMP
MYA
THIS AWEA IS NO GOOD.
SKOOT
GAZE GAZE
TAP TAP TAP
WHERE'S A GOOD PWACE?
MYA
MEOW
OH, I'VE FOUND ONE!

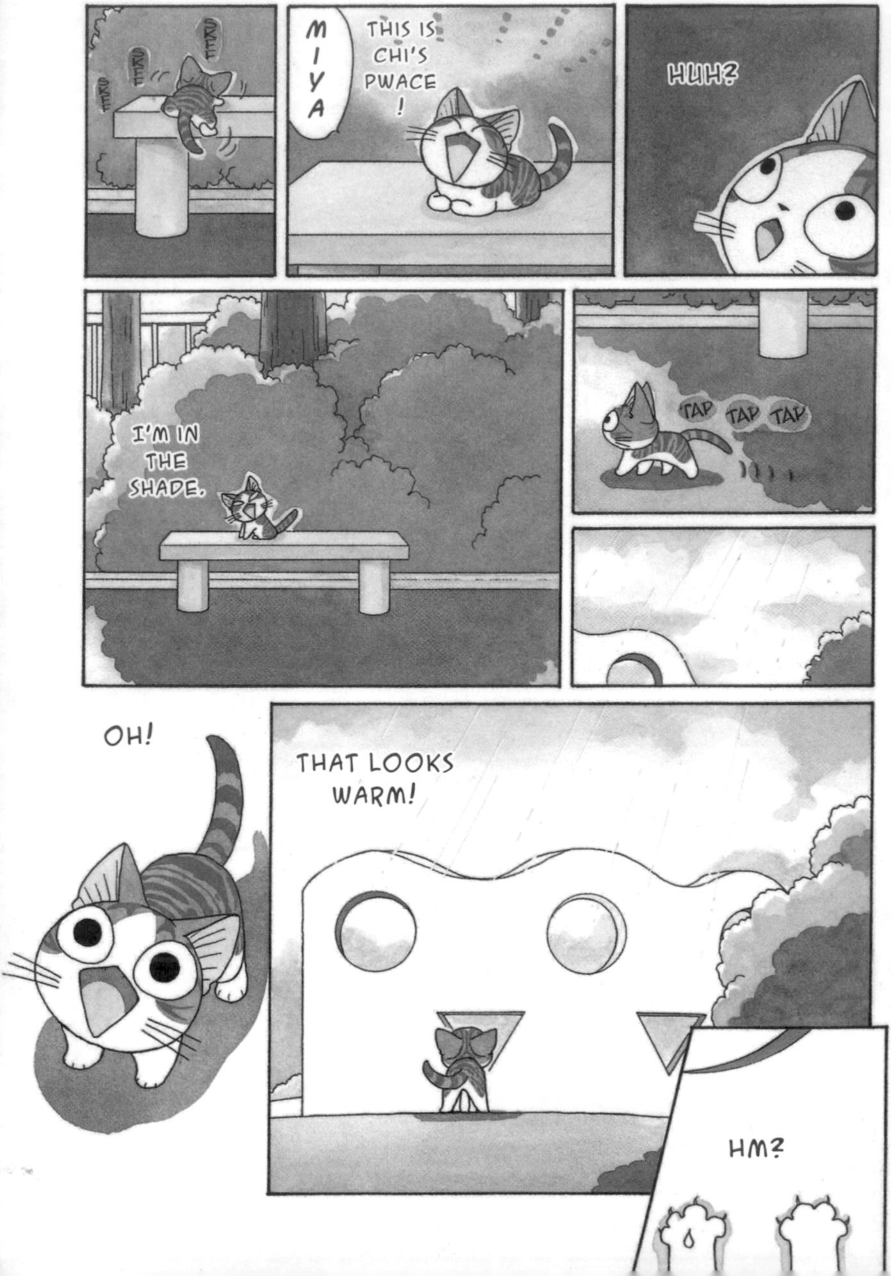
MIYA
THIS IS CHI'S PWACE!
HUH?
I'M IN THE SHADE.
TAP TAP TAP
OH!
THAT LOOKS WARM!
HM?

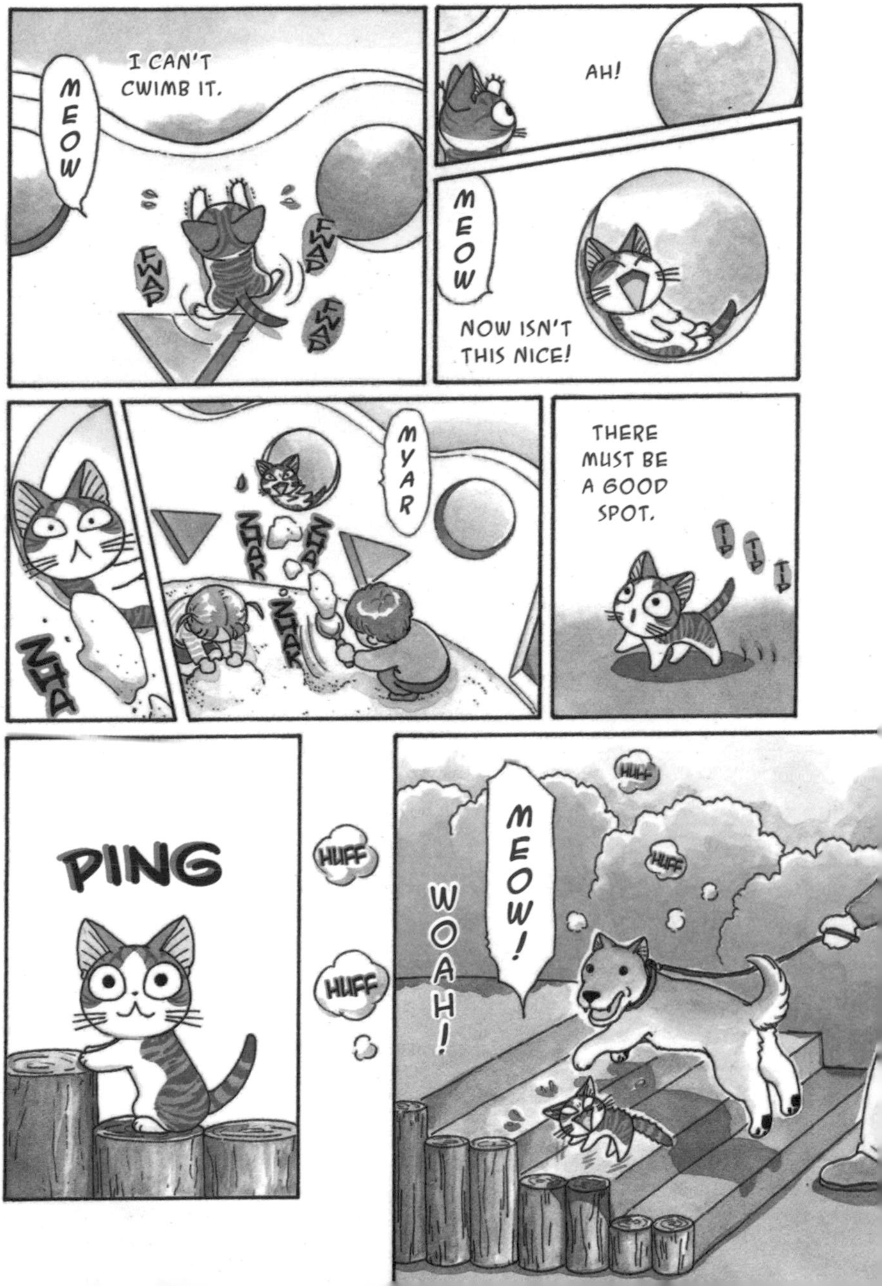
MEOW
I CAN'T CWIMB IT.
FWAP
FWAP
FWAP
AH!
MEOW
NOW ISN'T THIS NICE!
MYAR
THERE MUST BE A GOOD SPOT.
TIP
TIP
TIP
PING
HUFF
HUFF
HUFF
HUFF
MEOW!
WOAH!

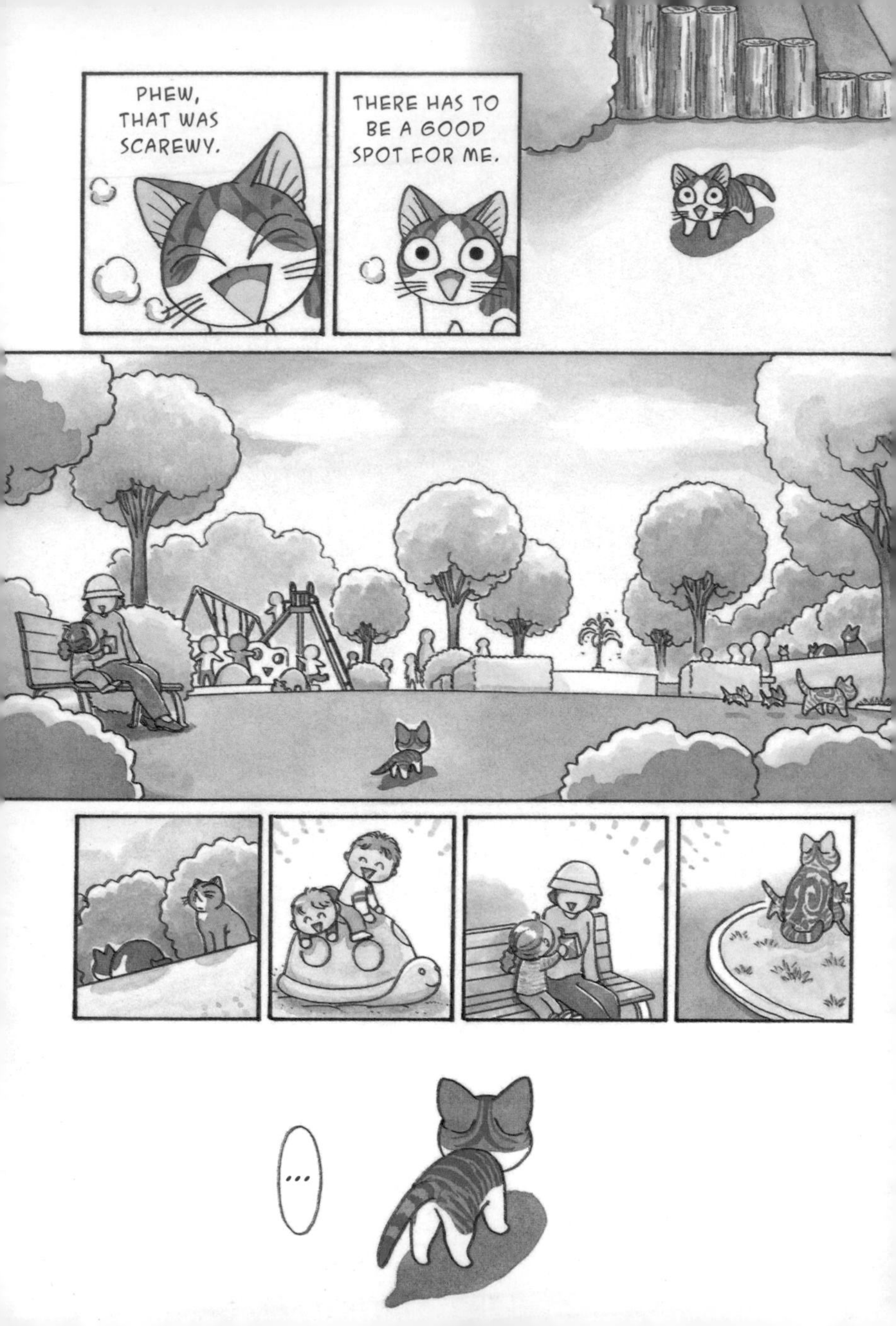
PHEW, THAT WAS SCAREWY.
THERE HAS TO BE A GOOD SPOT FOR ME.
...

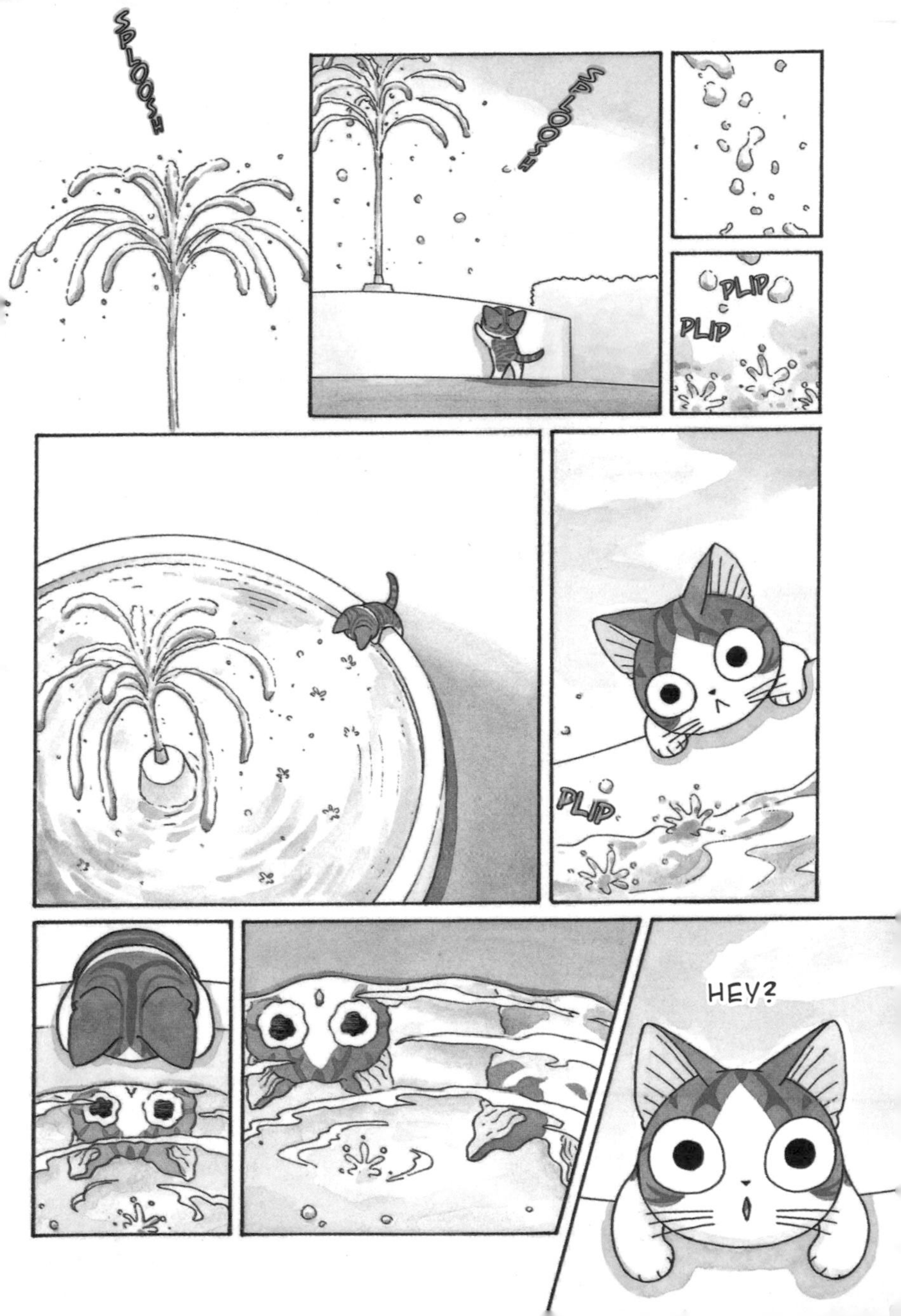
SPLOOSH
SPLOOSH
PLIP
PLIP
PLIP
HEY?

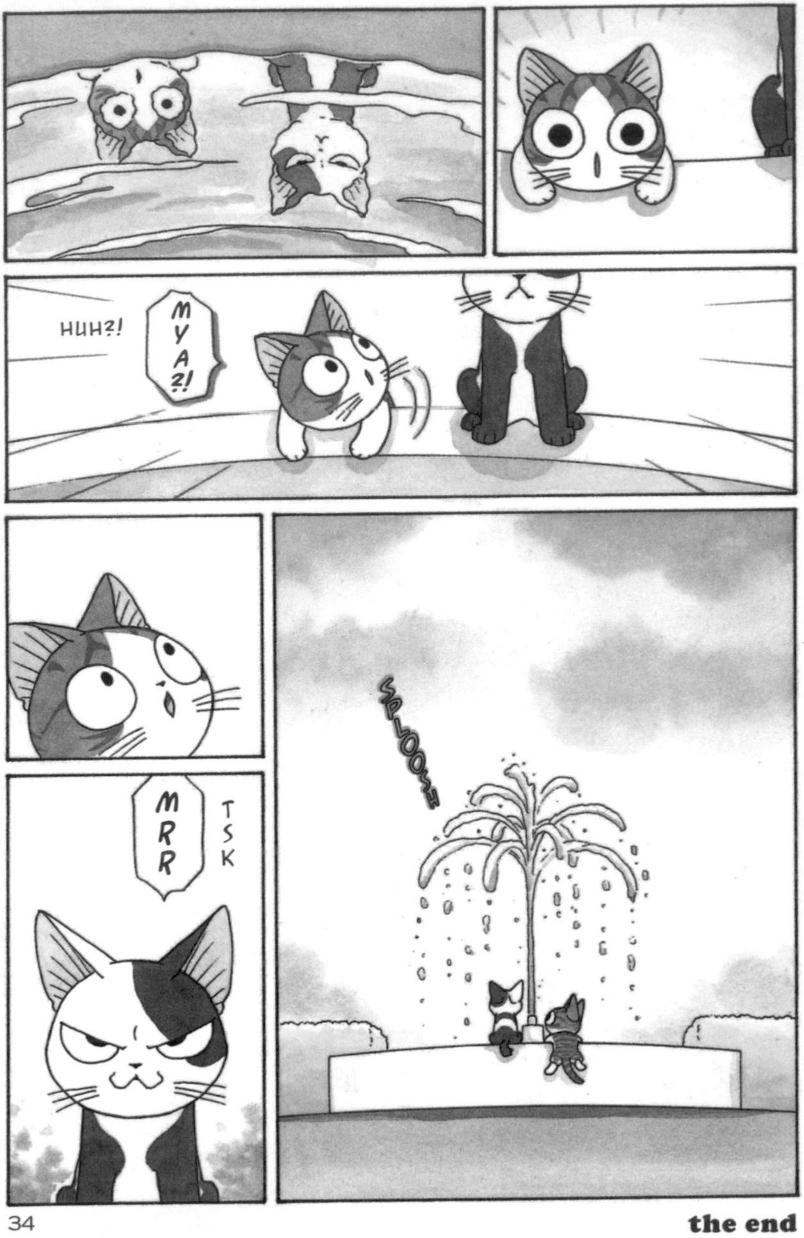
HUH?!
MYA?!
MRR
TSK
SPLOOSH



**the end**

## homemade 97: a cat beckons

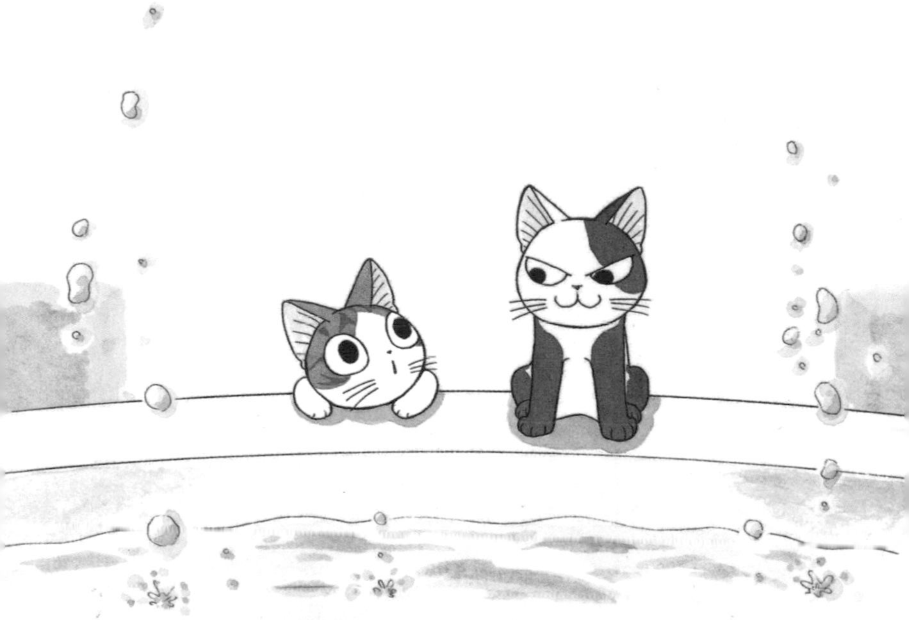

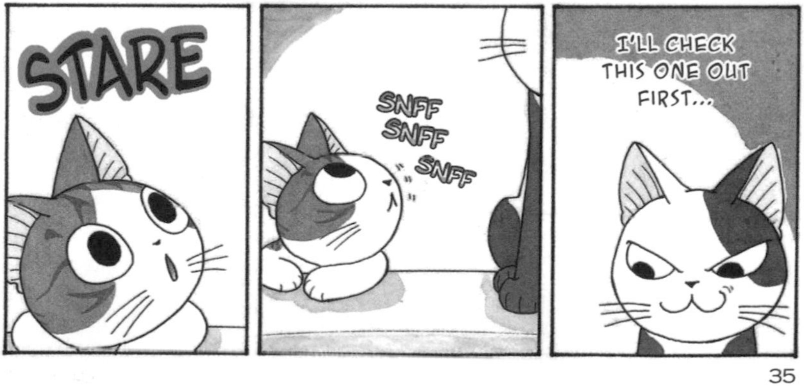
STARE
SNFF
SNFF
SNFF
I'LL CHECK THIS ONE OUT FIRST...

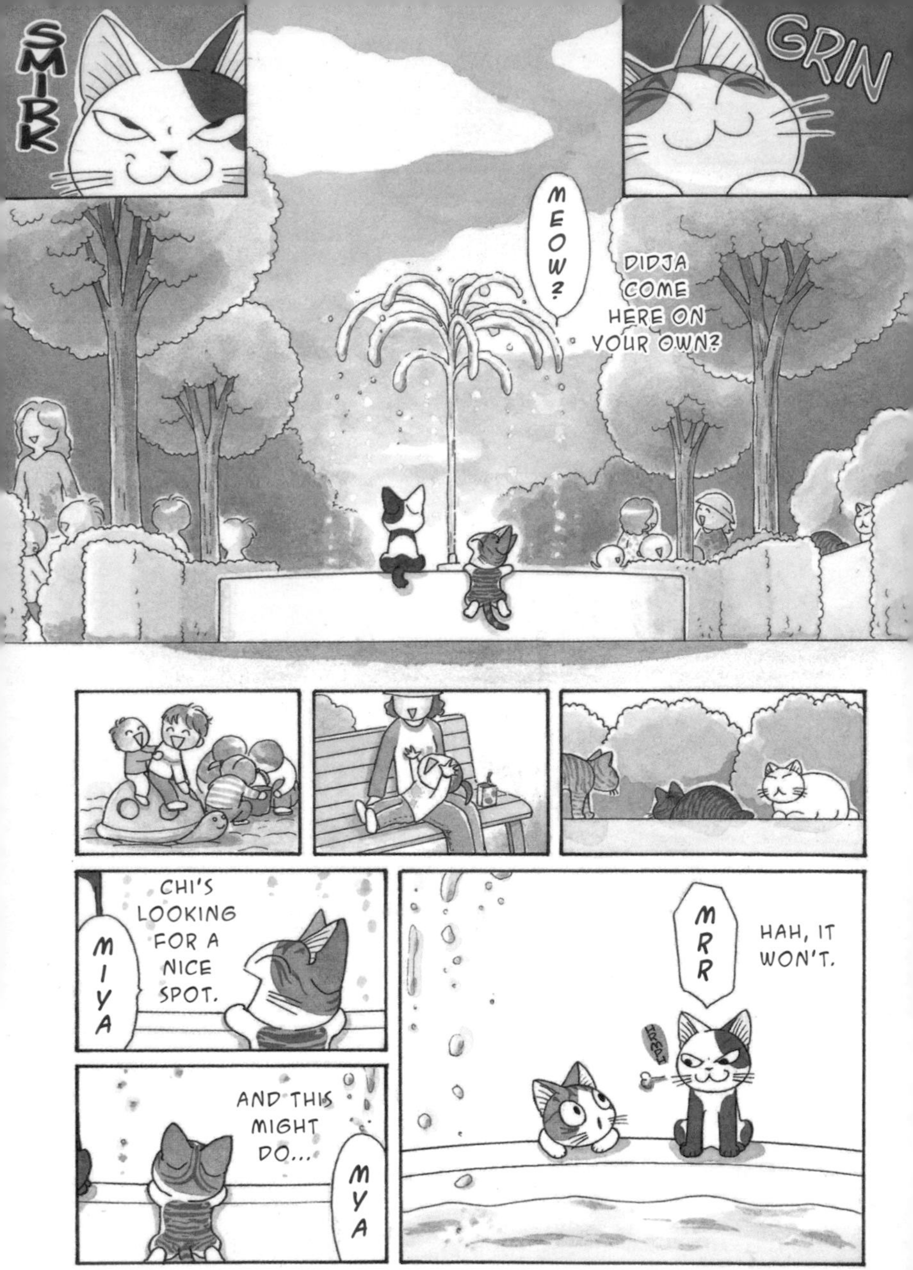
SMIRK
GRIN
MEOW?
DIDJA COME HERE ON YOUR OWN?
MIYA
CHI'S LOOKING FOR A NICE SPOT.
AND THIS MIGHT DO...
MYA
MRR
HAH, IT WON'T.

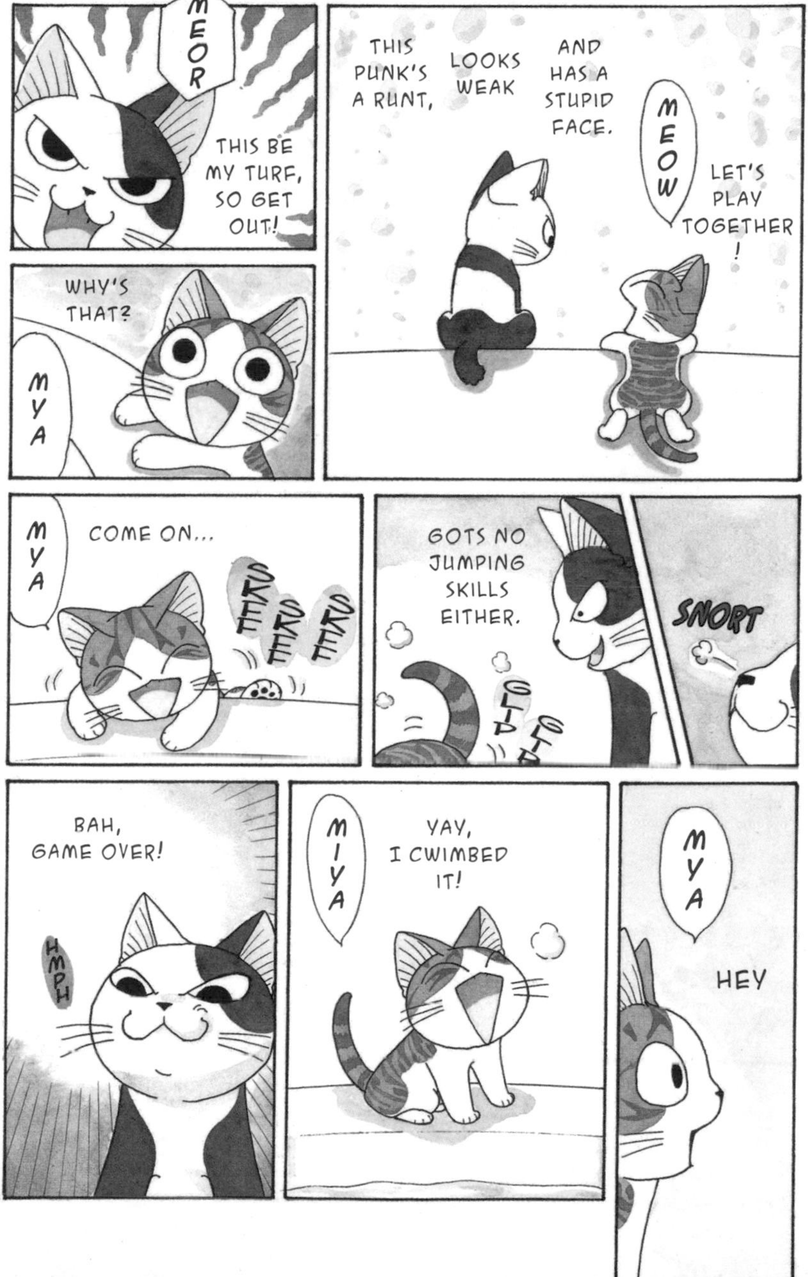
MEOR
THIS BE MY TURF, SO GET OUT!
WHY'S THAT?
MYA
THIS PUNK'S A RUNT,
LOOKS WEAK
AND HAS A STUPID FACE.
MEOW
LET'S PLAY TOGETHER!
MYA
COME ON...
SKREE
SKREE
SKREE
GOTS NO JUMPING SKILLS EITHER.
GLID
GLID
SNORT
BAH, GAME OVER!
HMPH
MIYA
YAY, I CWIMBED IT!
MYA
HEY

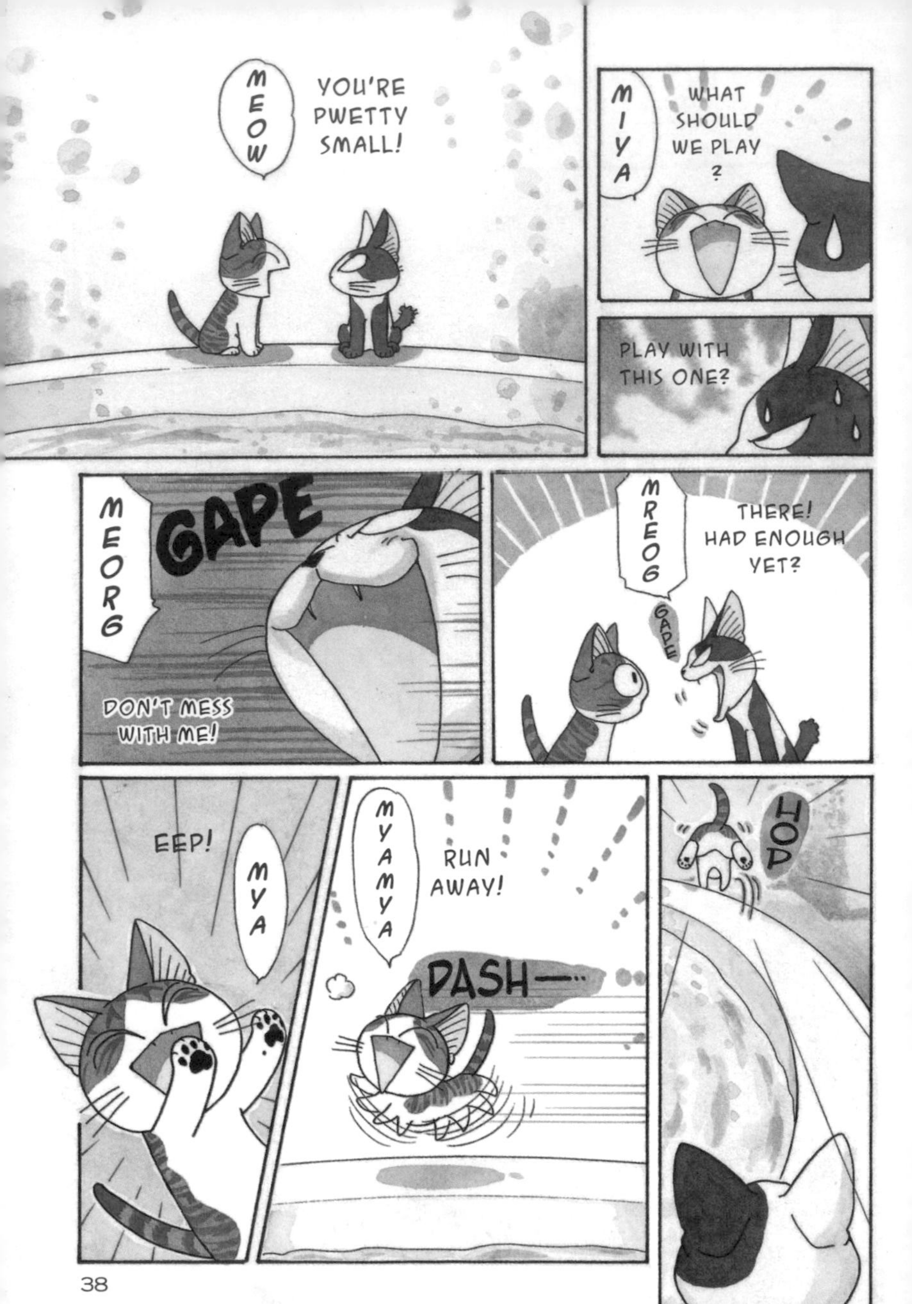
MEOW
YOU'RE PWETTY SMALL!
MIYA
WHAT SHOULD WE PLAY?
PLAY WITH THIS ONE?
MEORG
GAPE
DON'T MESS WITH ME!
MREOG
THERE! HAD ENOUGH YET?
GAPE
EEP!
MYA
MYAMYA
RUN AWAY!
DASH—
HOP

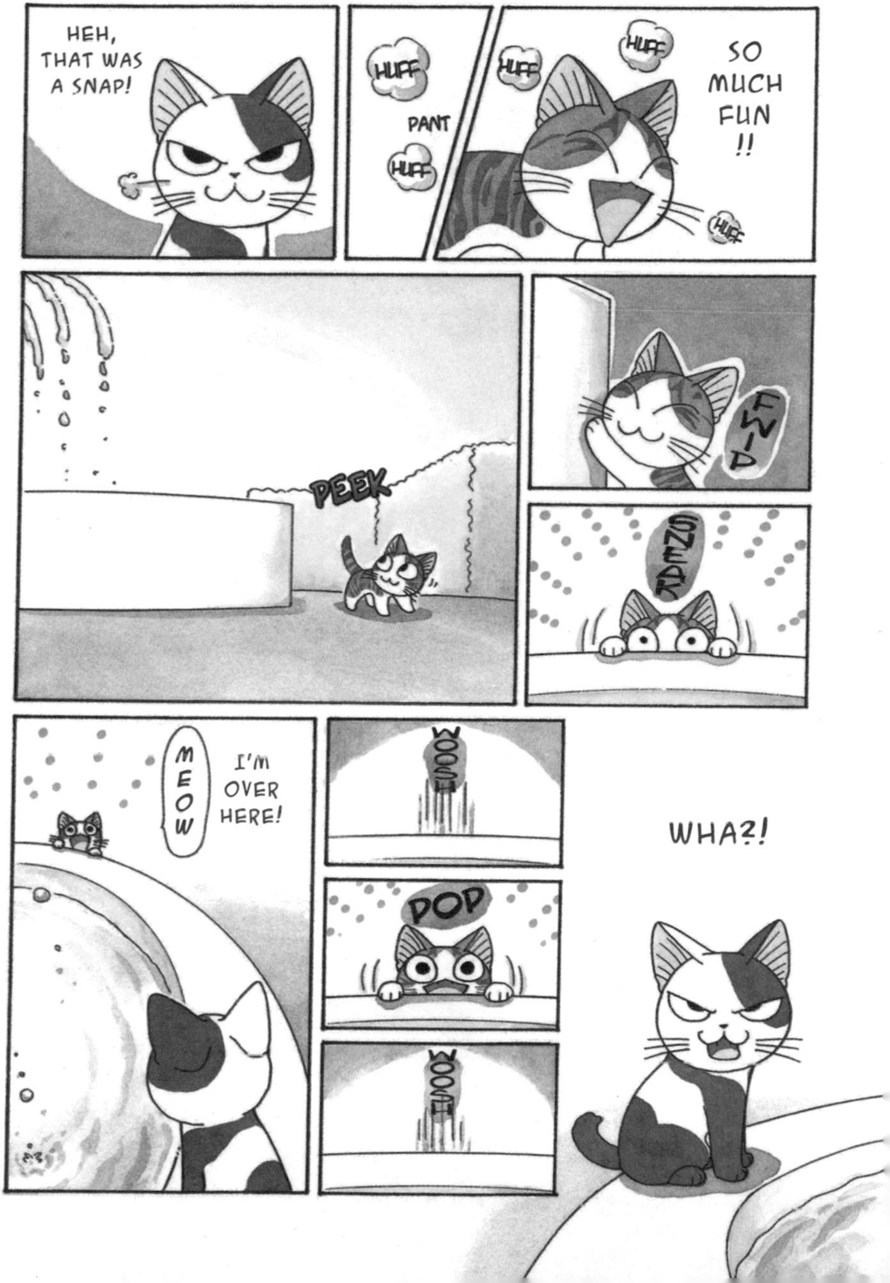
HEH, THAT WAS A SNAP!
HUFF
PANT
HUFF
HUFF
HUFF
SO MUCH FUN !!
HUFF
PEEK
FWID
SNEAK
MEOW
I'M OVER HERE!
WOOSH
POP
WOOSH
WHA?!

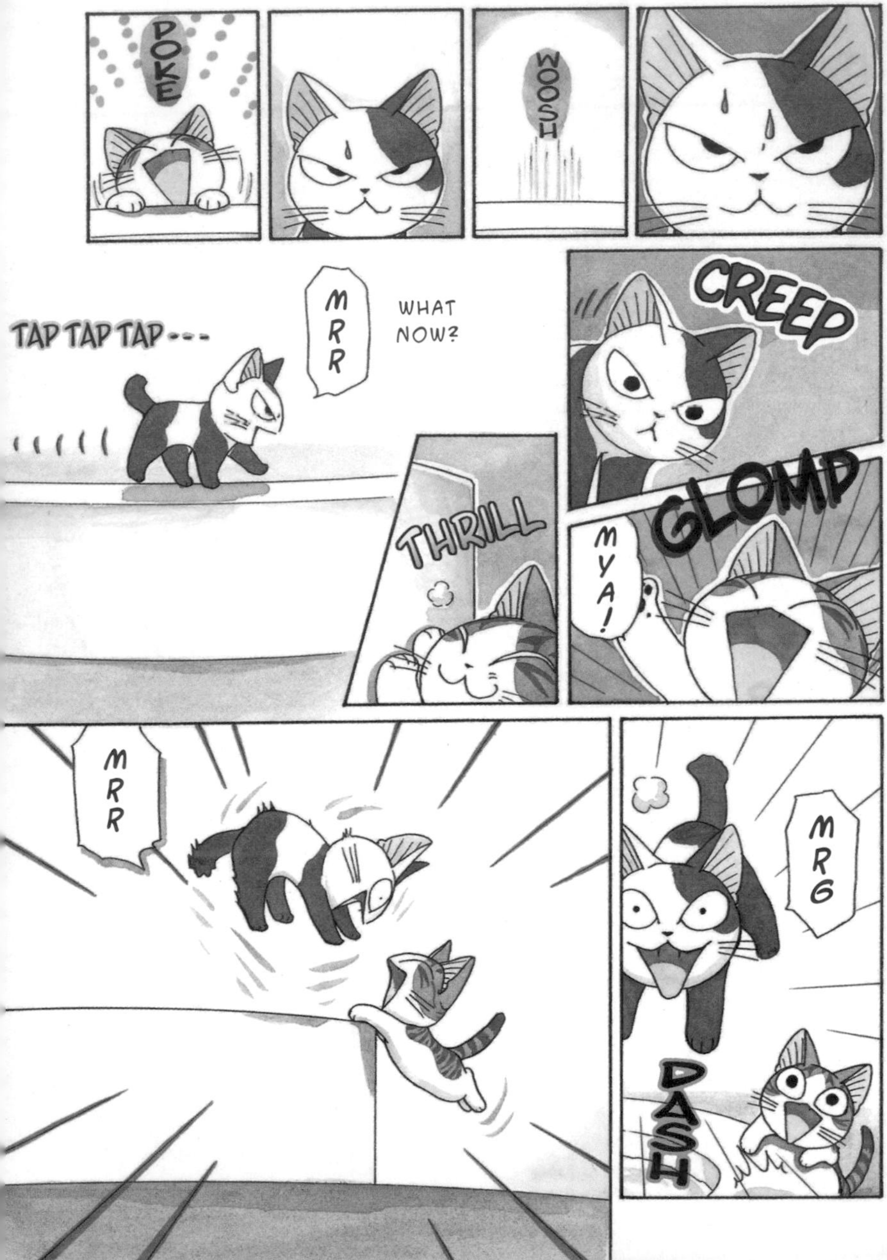
POKE
WOOSH
TAP TAP TAP...
MRR
WHAT NOW?
CREEP
THRILL
GLOMP
MYA!
MRR
MRG
DASH

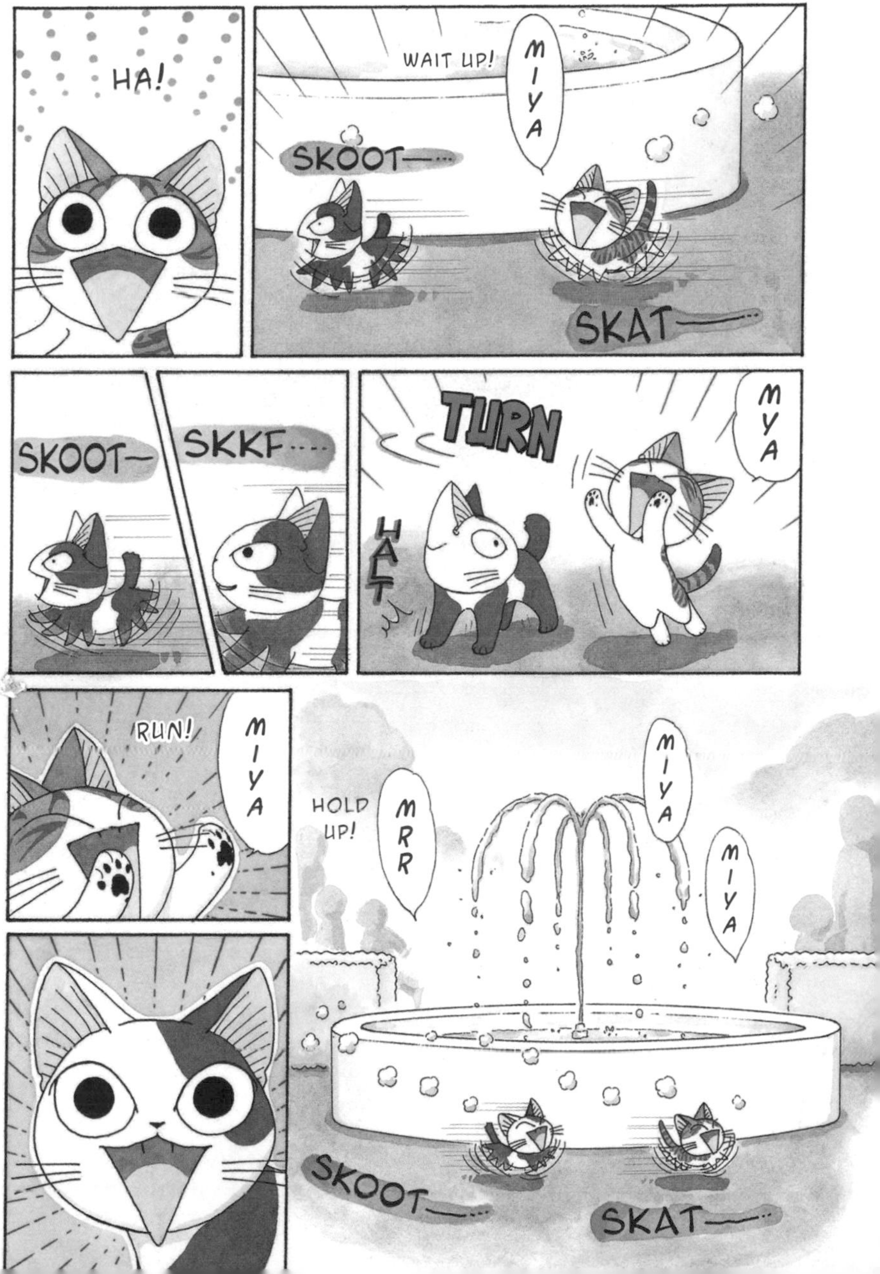
HA!
WAIT UP!
MIYA
SKOOT—...
SKAT—...
SKOOT~
SKKF....
TURN
HALT
MYA
RUN!
MIYA
HOLD UP!
MRR
MIYA
MIYA
SKOOT—...
SKAT—...

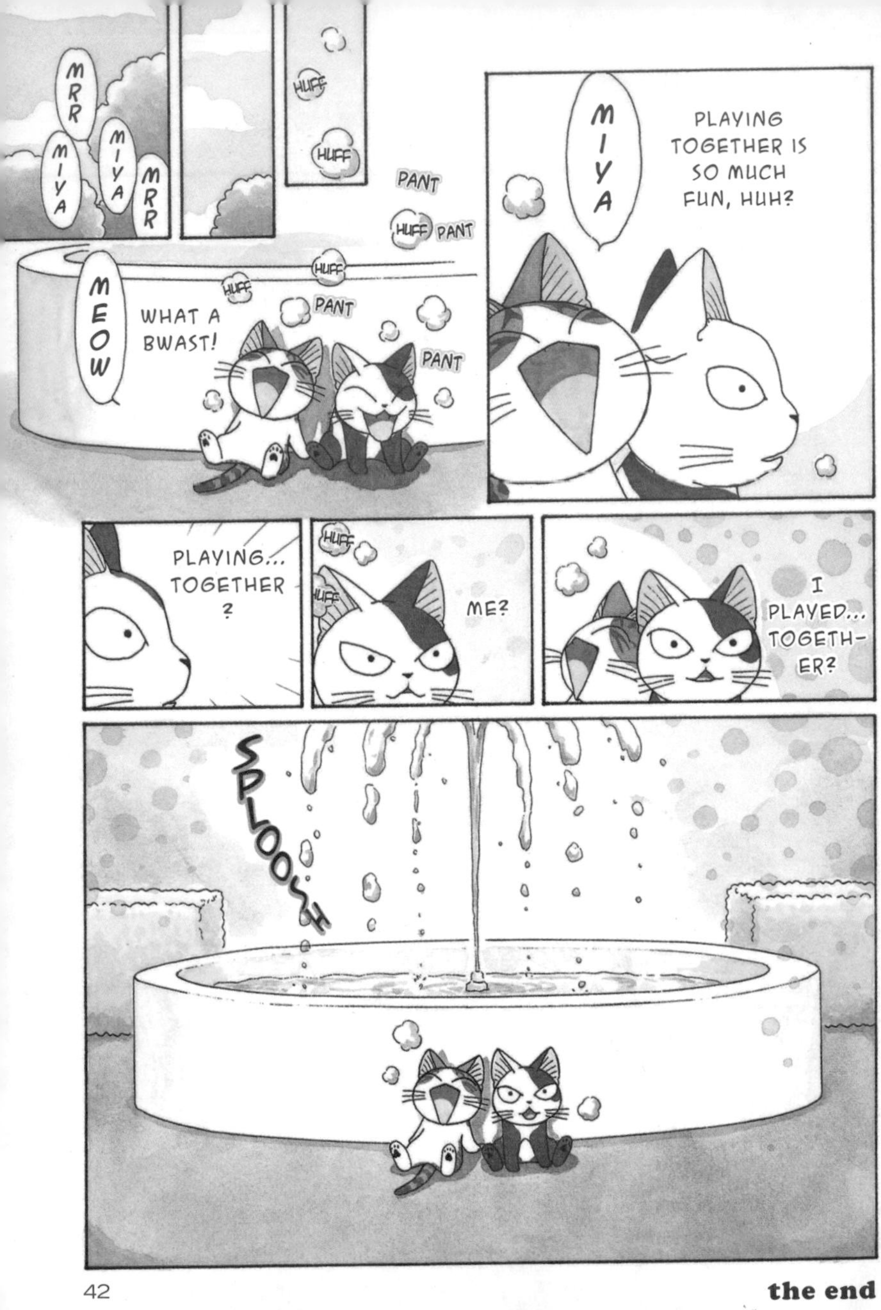
MRR
MIYA
MIYA
MRR
HUFF
HUFF
PANT
HUFF
PANT
HUFF
HUFF
PANT
MEOW
WHAT A BWAST!
PANT
MIYA
PLAYING TOGETHER IS SO MUCH FUN, HUH?
PLAYING... TOGETHER ?
HUFF
HUFF
ME?
I PLAYED... TOGETH-ER?
SPLOOSH



**the end**

## homemade 98: a cat is satisfied

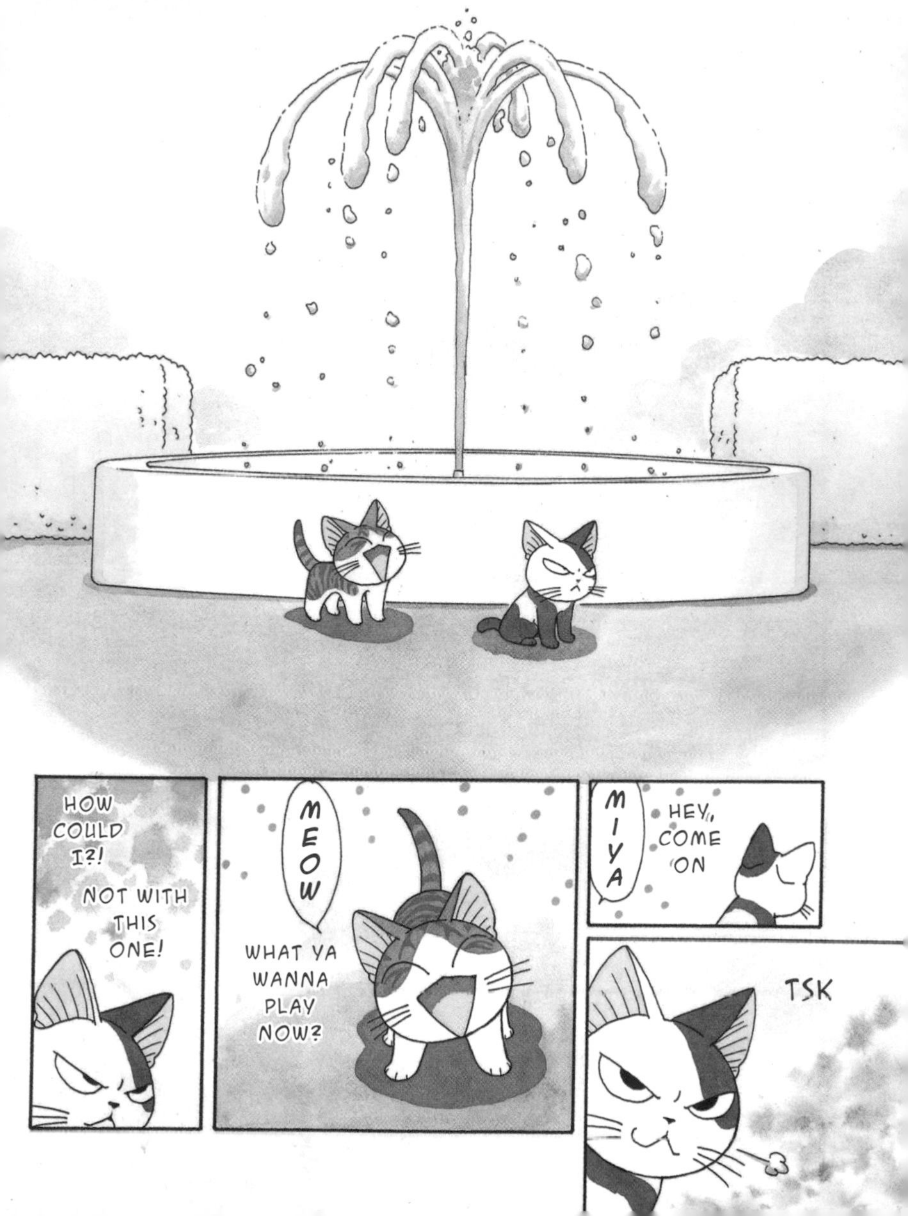
HOW COULD I?!
NOT WITH THIS ONE!
MEOW
WHAT YA WANNA PLAY NOW?
MIYA
HEY, COME ON
TSK

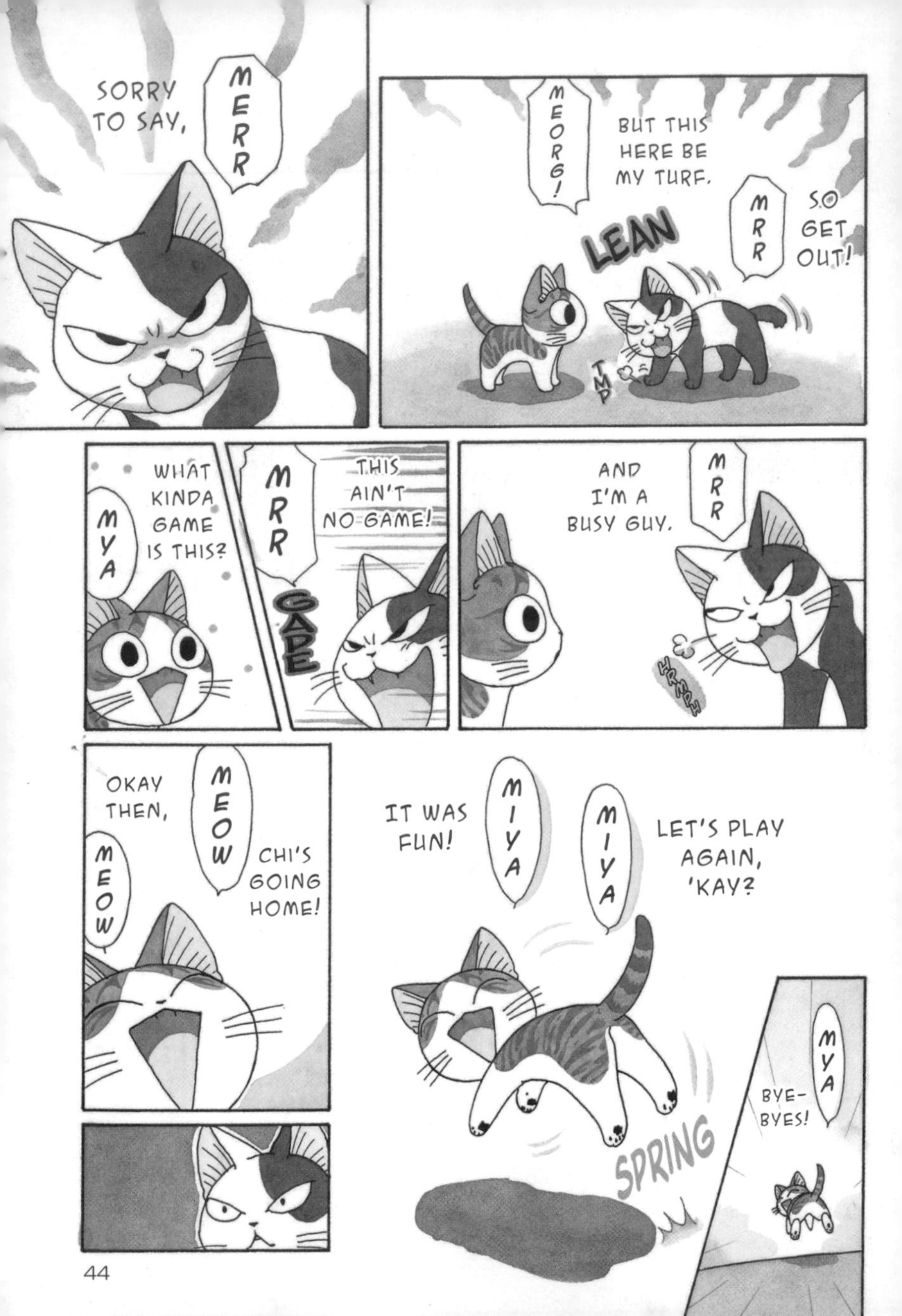
MERR
SORRY TO SAY,
MEORG!
BUT THIS HERE BE MY TURF.
LEAN
MRR
SO GET OUT!
TMP
MYA
WHAT KINDA GAME IS THIS?
MRR
THIS AIN'T NO GAME!
MRR
AND I'M A BUSY GUY.
MEOW
OKAY THEN,
MEOW
CHI'S GOING HOME!
MIYA
IT WAS FUN!
MIYA
LET'S PLAY AGAIN, 'KAY?
SPRING
MYA
BYE-BYES!

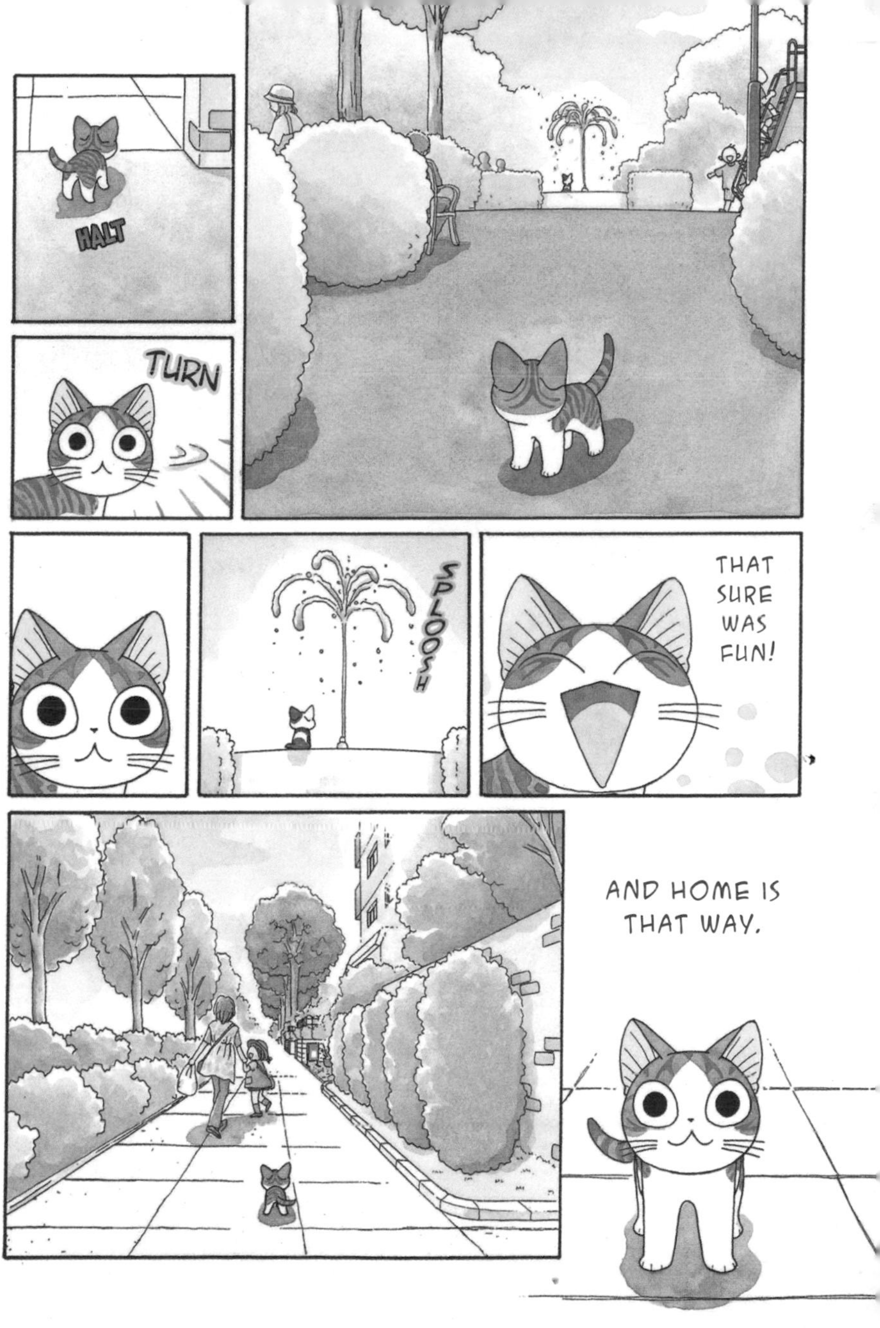
HALT
TURN
SPLOOSH
THAT SURE WAS FUN!
AND HOME IS THAT WAY.

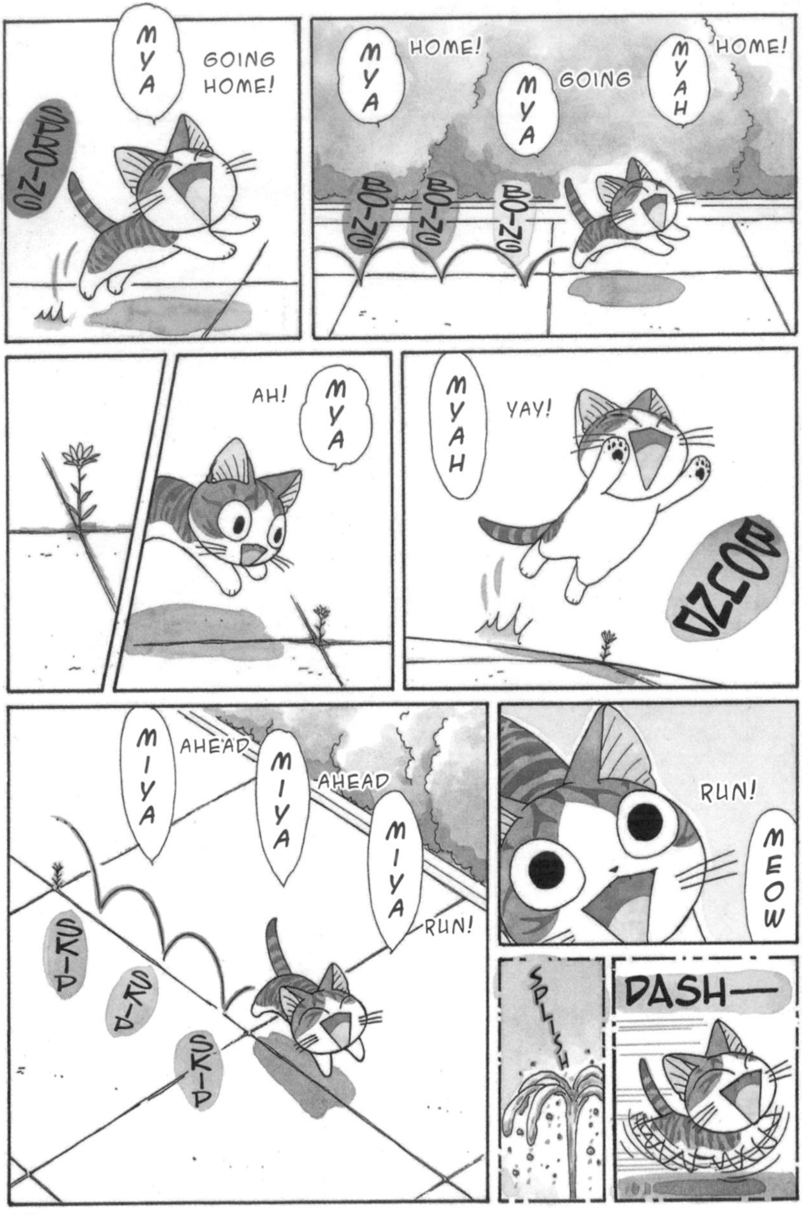
MYA
GOING HOME!
SPROING
MYA
HOME!
MYA
GOING
MYAH
HOME!
BOING
BOING
BOING
AH!
MYA
MYAH
YAY!
BOING
MIYA
AHEAD
MIYA
AHEAD
MIYA
RUN!
SKIP
SKIP
SKIP
RUN!
MEOW
SPLISH
DASH—

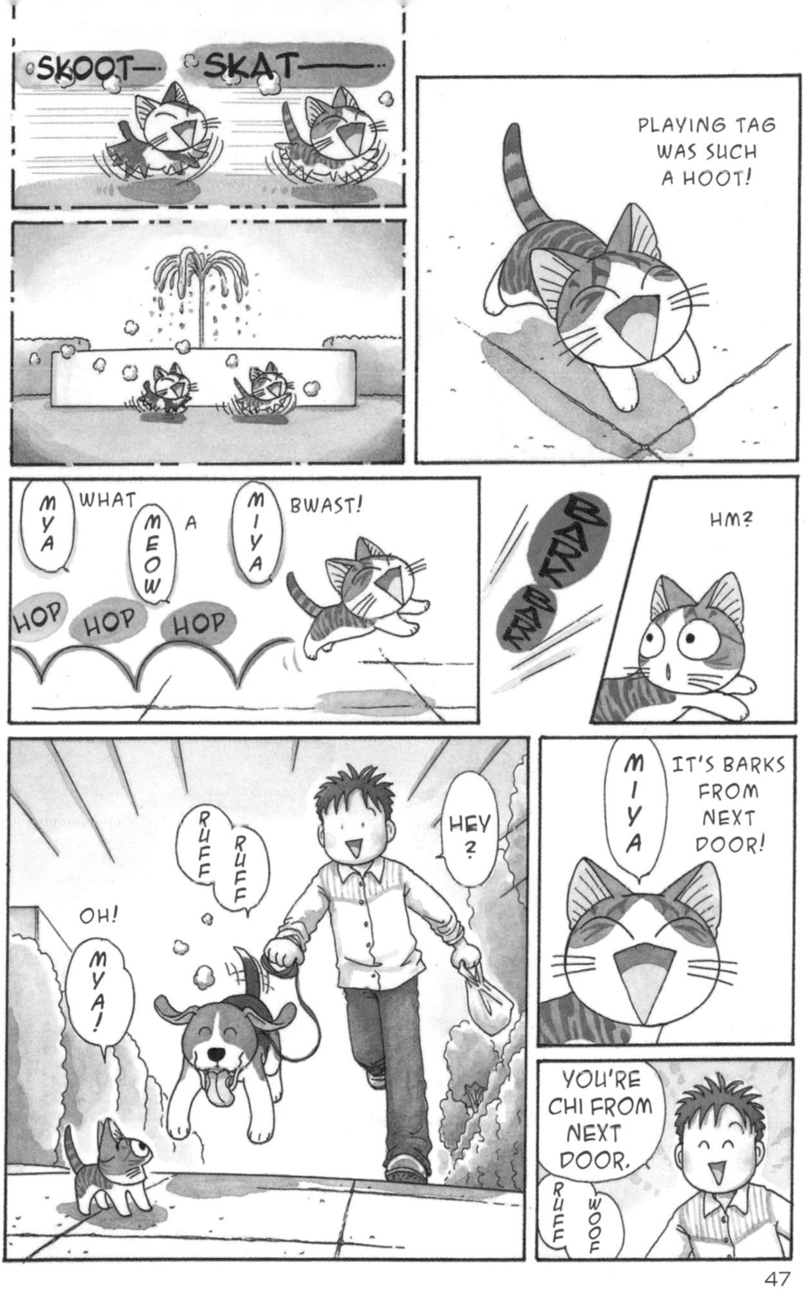
SKOOT—
SKAT—
PLAYING TAG WAS SUCH A HOOT!
MYA
WHAT
MEOW
A
MIYA
BWAST!
HOP
HOP
HOP
BARK
BARK
HM?
HEY?
RUFF RUFF
OH!
MYA!
MIYA
IT'S BARKS FROM NEXT DOOR!
YOU'RE CHI FROM NEXT DOOR.
RUFF
WOOF

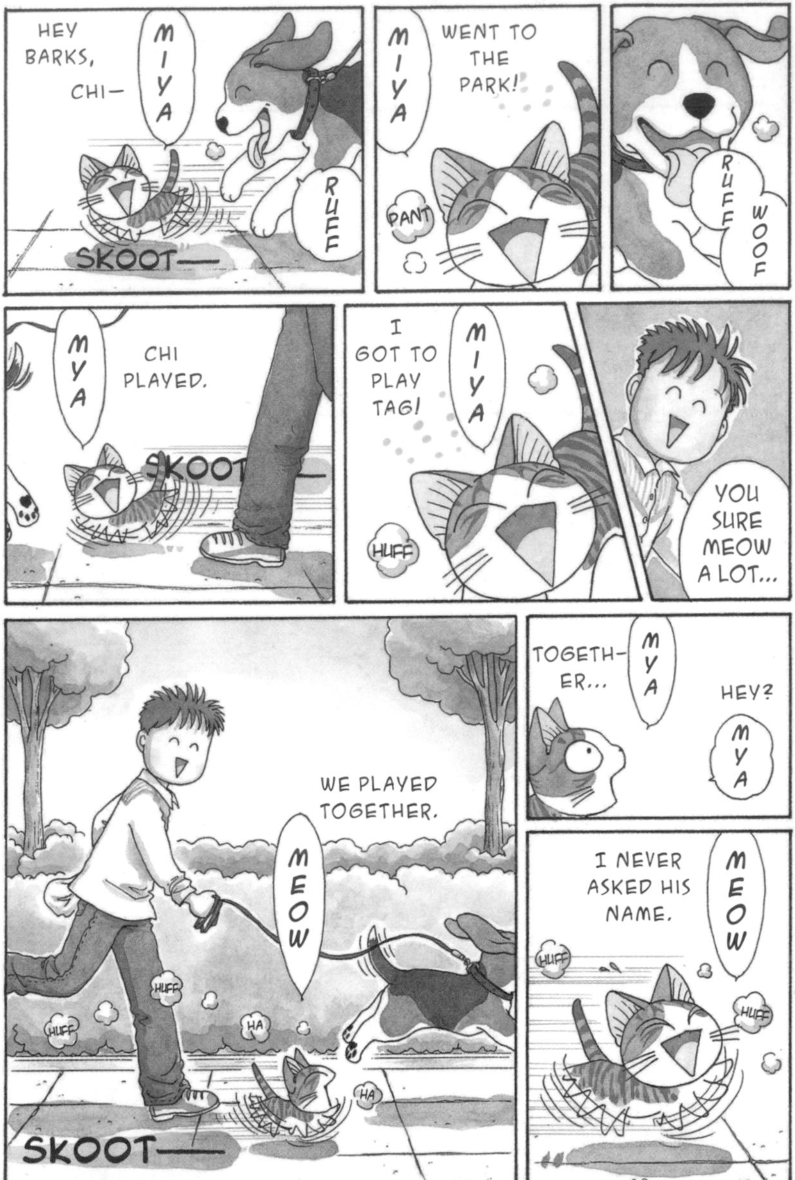
HEY BARKS, CHI—
MIYA
RUFF
SKOOT—
MIYA
WENT TO THE PARK!
PANT
RUFF
WOOF
MYA
CHI PLAYED.
SKOOT—
I GOT TO PLAY TAG!
MIYA
HUFF
YOU SURE MEOW A LOT...
WE PLAYED TOGETHER.
MEOW
HUFF
HUFF
HA
HA
SKOOT—
TOGETH-ER...
MYA
HEY?
MYA
I NEVER ASKED HIS NAME.
MEOW
HUFF
HUFF

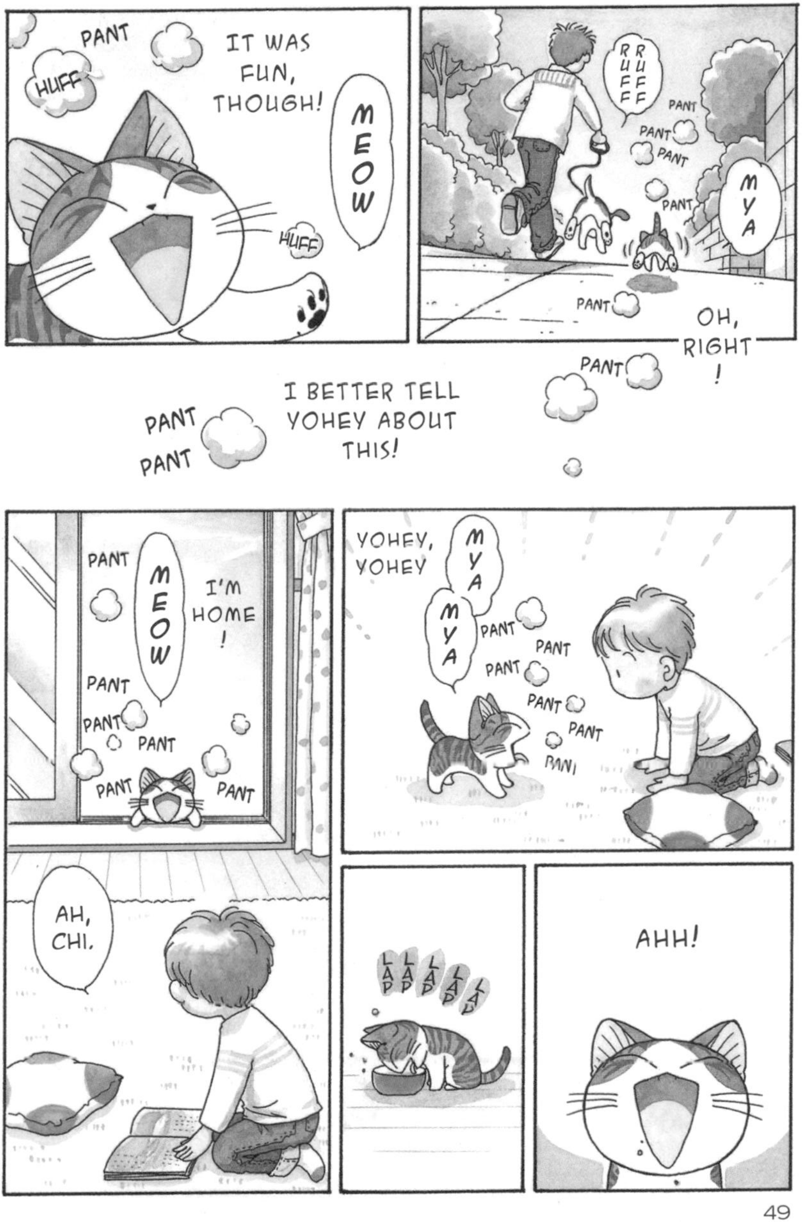
PANT
HUFF
IT WAS FUN, THOUGH!
MEOW
HUFF
RUFF RUFF
PANT
PANT
PANT
MYA
PANT
PANT
OH, RIGHT!
PANT
I BETTER TELL YOHEY ABOUT THIS!
PANT
PANT
PANT
MEOW
I'M HOME!
PANT
PANT
PANT
PANT
PANT
AH, CHI.
YOHEY, YOHEY
MYA
MYA
PANT
PANT
PANT
PANT
PANT
LAP LAP LAP LAP LAP
AHH!

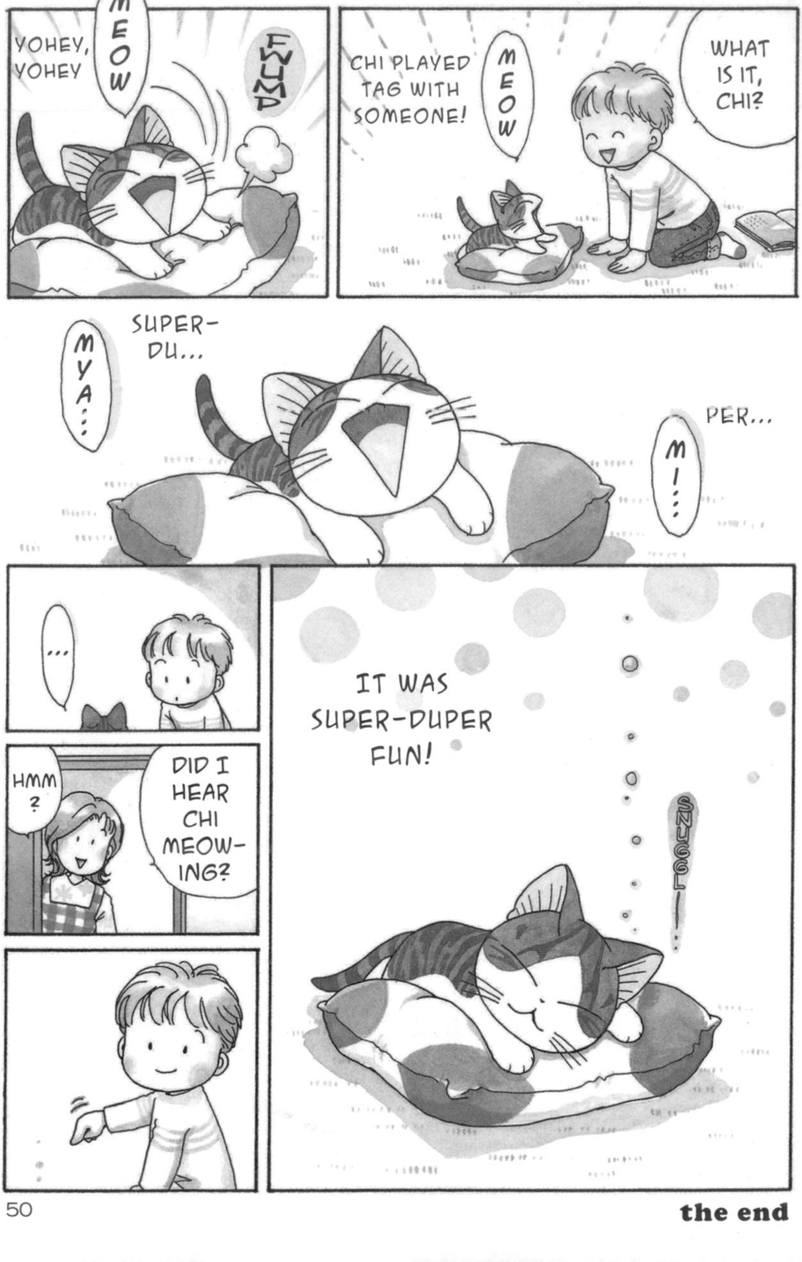
YOHEY, YOHEY
MEOW
FWUMP
CHI PLAYED TAG WITH SOMEONE!
MEOW
WHAT IS IT, CHI?
SUPER-DU...
MYA...
PER...
MI...
...
HMM?
DID I HEAR CHI MEOWING?
IT WAS SUPER-DUPER FUN!
SNUGGL...

**the end**

## homemade 99: a cat is pleased

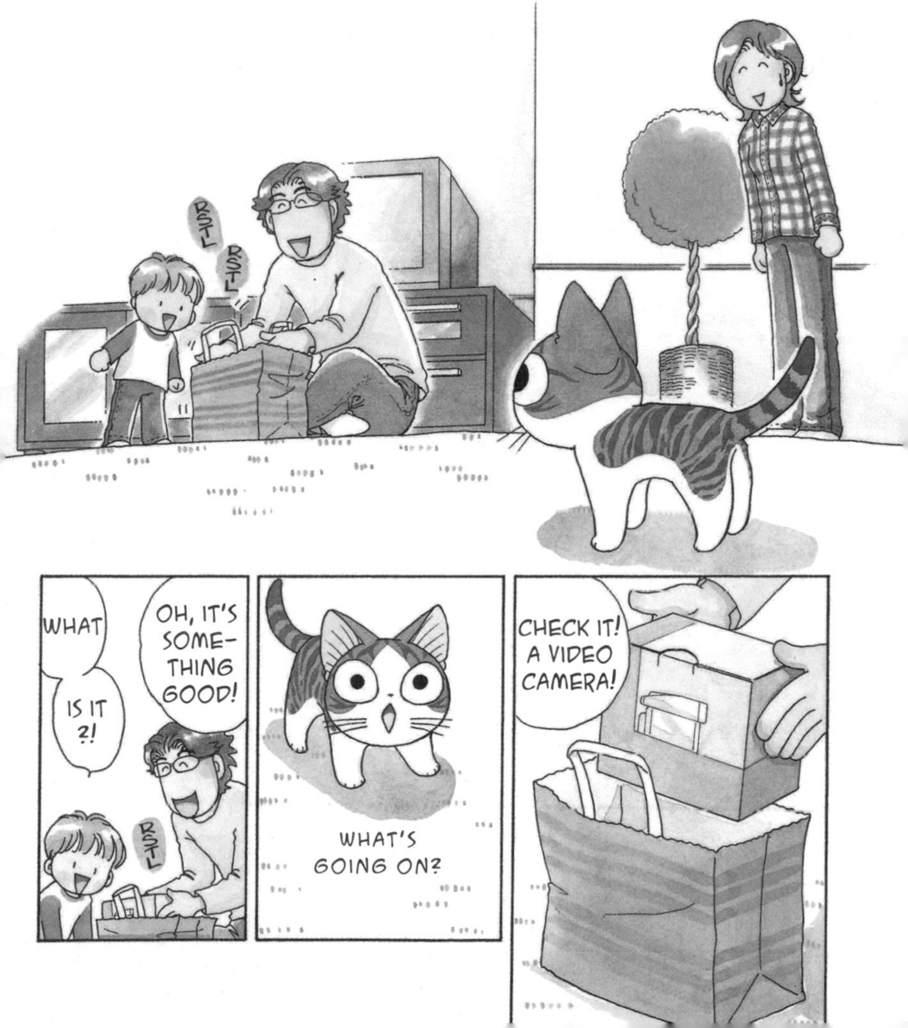
RSTL
RSTL
WHAT
IS IT ?!
OH, IT'S SOME-THING GOOD!
RSTL
WHAT'S GOING ON?
CHECK IT! A VIDEO CAMERA!

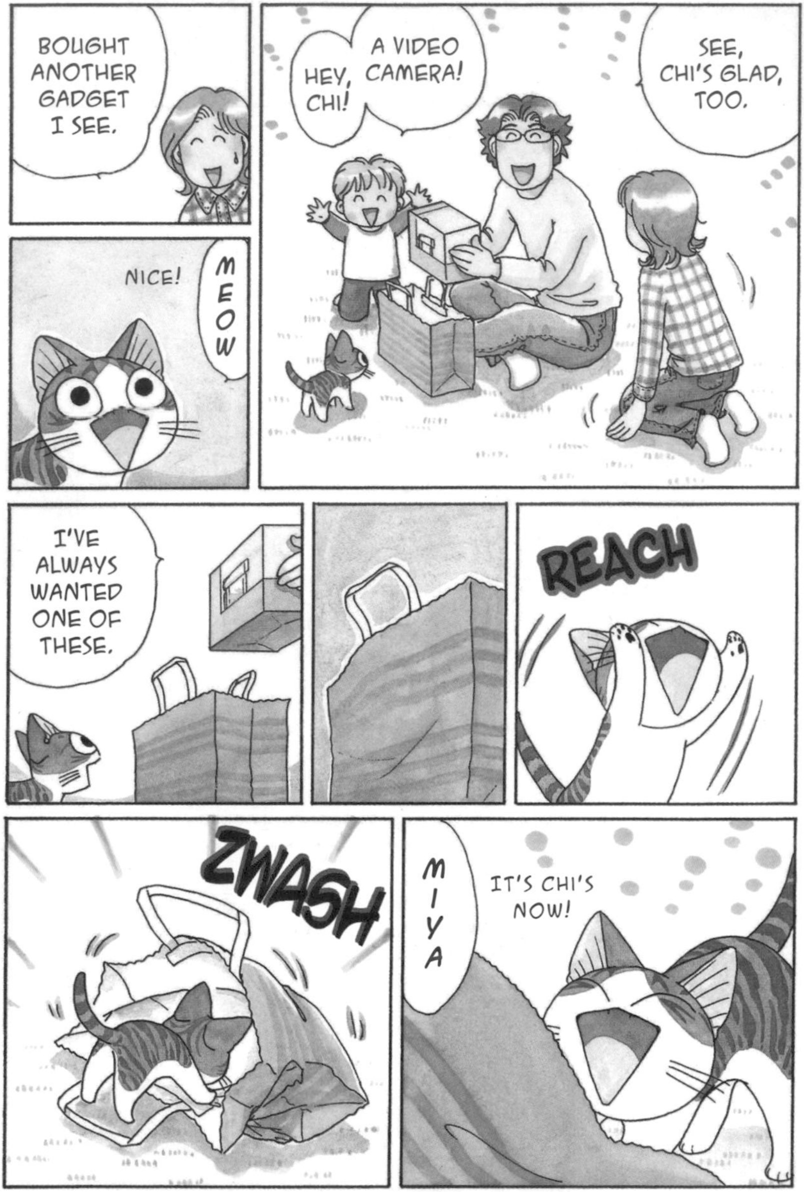
BOUGHT ANOTHER GADGET I SEE.
NICE!
MEOW
HEY, CHI!
A VIDEO CAMERA!
SEE, CHI'S GLAD, TOO.
I'VE ALWAYS WANTED ONE OF THESE.
REACH
ZWASH
MIYA
IT'S CHI'S NOW!

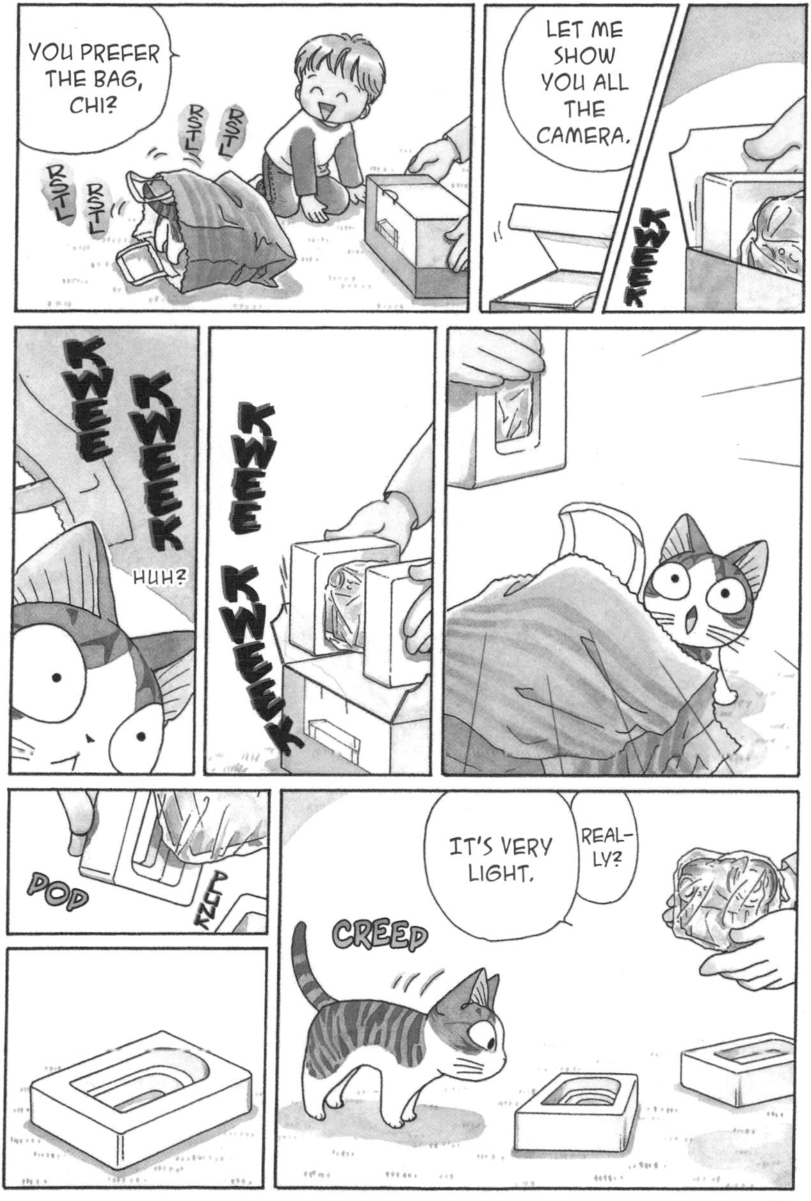
YOU PREFER THE BAG, CHI?
RSTL RSTL RSTL RSTL
LET ME SHOW YOU ALL THE CAMERA.
KWEEK
KWEE KWEEK
HUH?
KWEE KWEEK
POP
PLUNK
IT'S VERY LIGHT.
REAL-LY?
CREEP

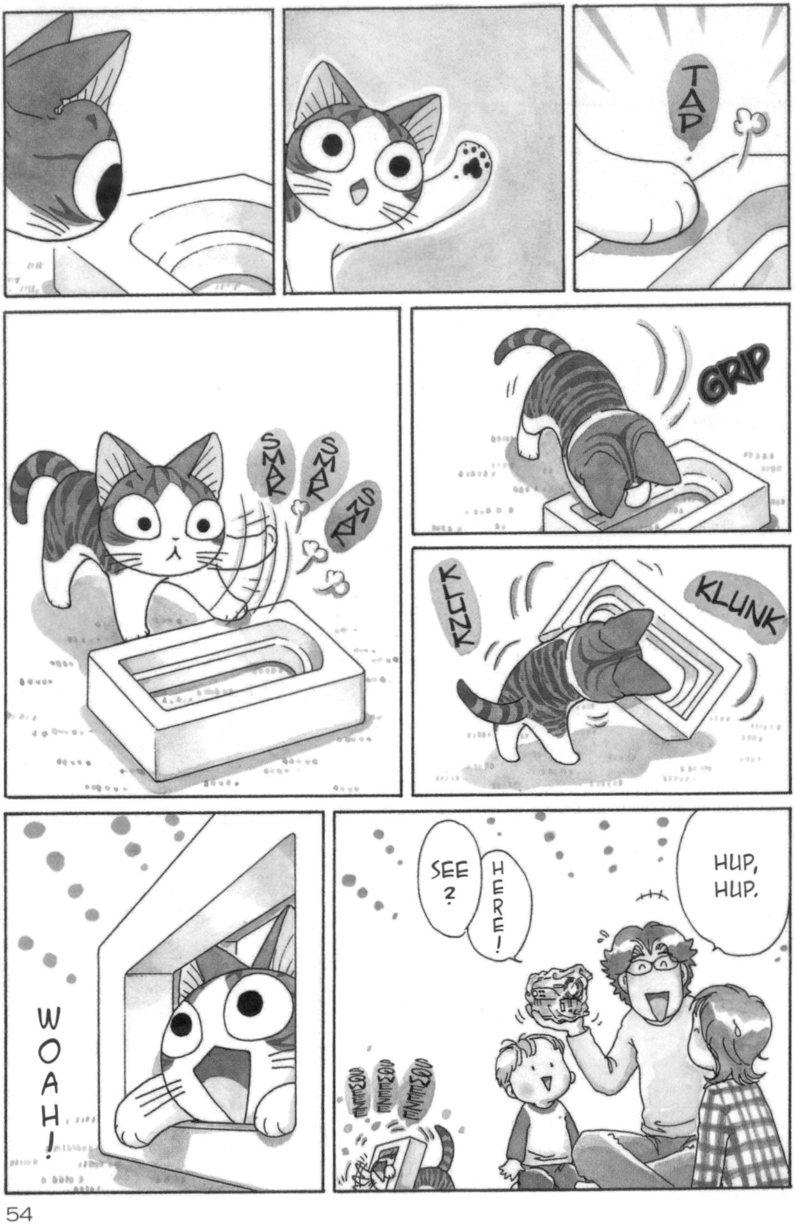
TAP
SMR
SMR
SMR
GRIP
KLUNK
KLUNK
WOAH!
SEE?
HERE!
HUP, HUP.

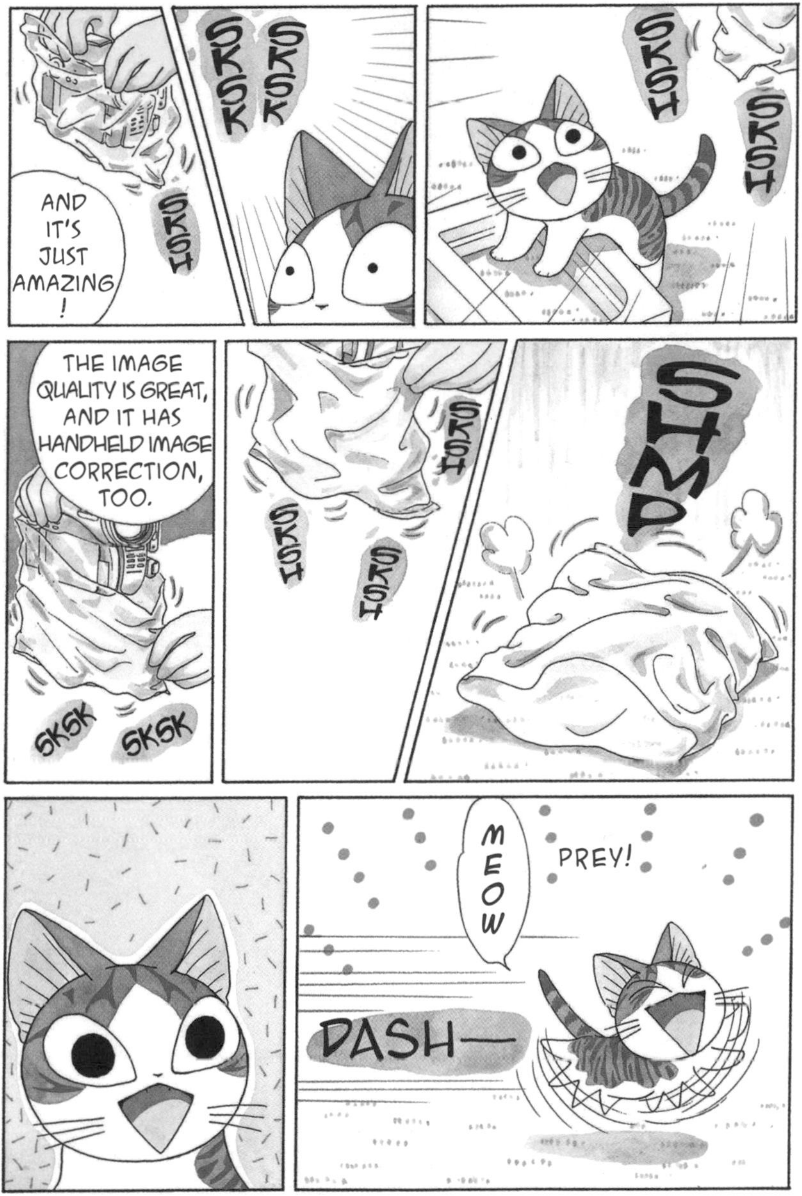
SKSH
AND IT'S JUST AMAZING!
SKSK
SKSK
SKSH
SKSH
THE IMAGE QUALITY IS GREAT, AND IT HAS HANDHELD IMAGE CORRECTION, TOO.
SKSK
SKSK
SKSH
SKSH
SKSH
SHMP
MEOW
PREY!
DASH—

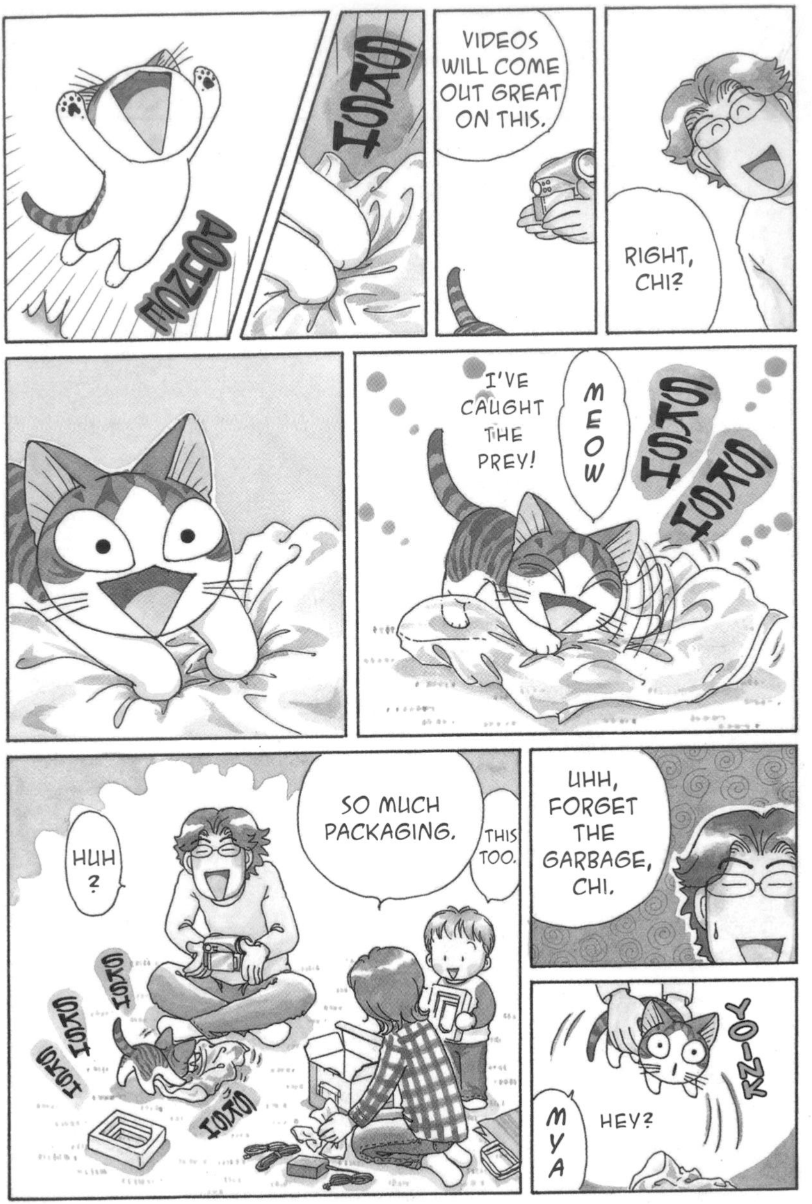
POUNCE
SKOSH
VIDEOS WILL COME OUT GREAT ON THIS.
RIGHT, CHI?
I'VE CAUGHT THE PREY!
MEOW
SKOSH
SKOSH
HUH?
SO MUCH PACKAGING.
THIS TOO.
SKOSH
SKOSH
SKOSH
SKOSH
UHH, FORGET THE GARBAGE, CHI.
YO-INK
MYA
HEY?

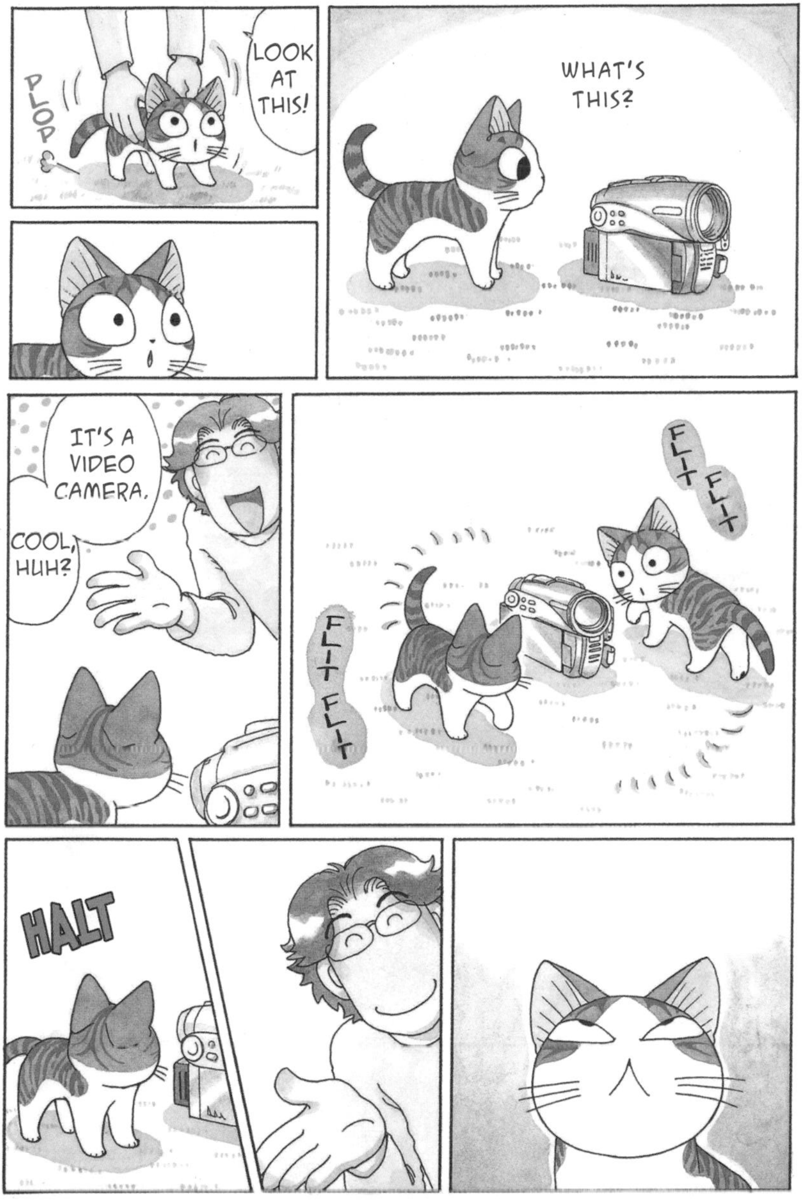
PLOP
LOOK AT THIS!
WHAT'S THIS?
IT'S A VIDEO CAMERA.
COOL, HUH?
FLIT FLIT
FLIT FLIT
HALT

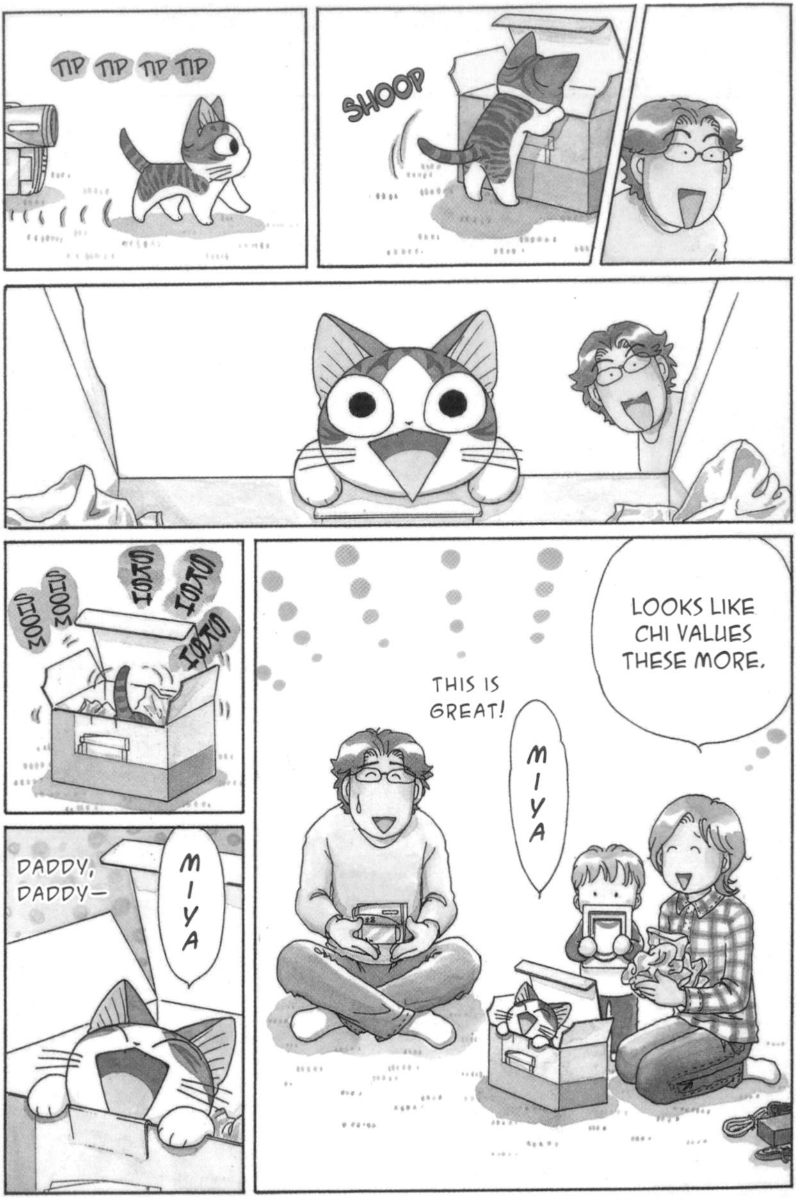
TIP TIP TIP TIP
SHOOP
SHOOM
SHOOM
DADDY, DADDY—
MIYA
THIS IS GREAT!
MIYA
LOOKS LIKE CHI VALUES THESE MORE.



**the end**

# homemade 100: a cat celebrates

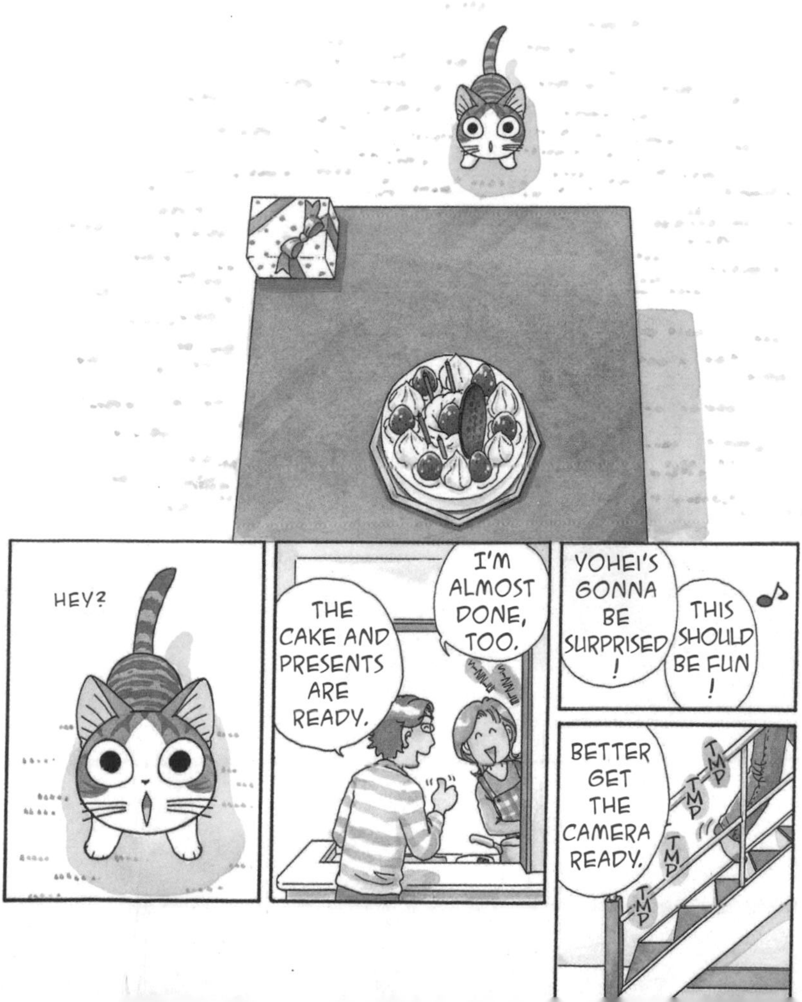

HEY?
THE CAKE AND PRESENTS ARE READY.
I'M ALMOST DONE, TOO.
YOHEI'S GONNA BE SURPRISED!
THIS SHOULD BE FUN!
BETTER GET THE CAMERA READY.
TMP
TMP
TMP
TMP

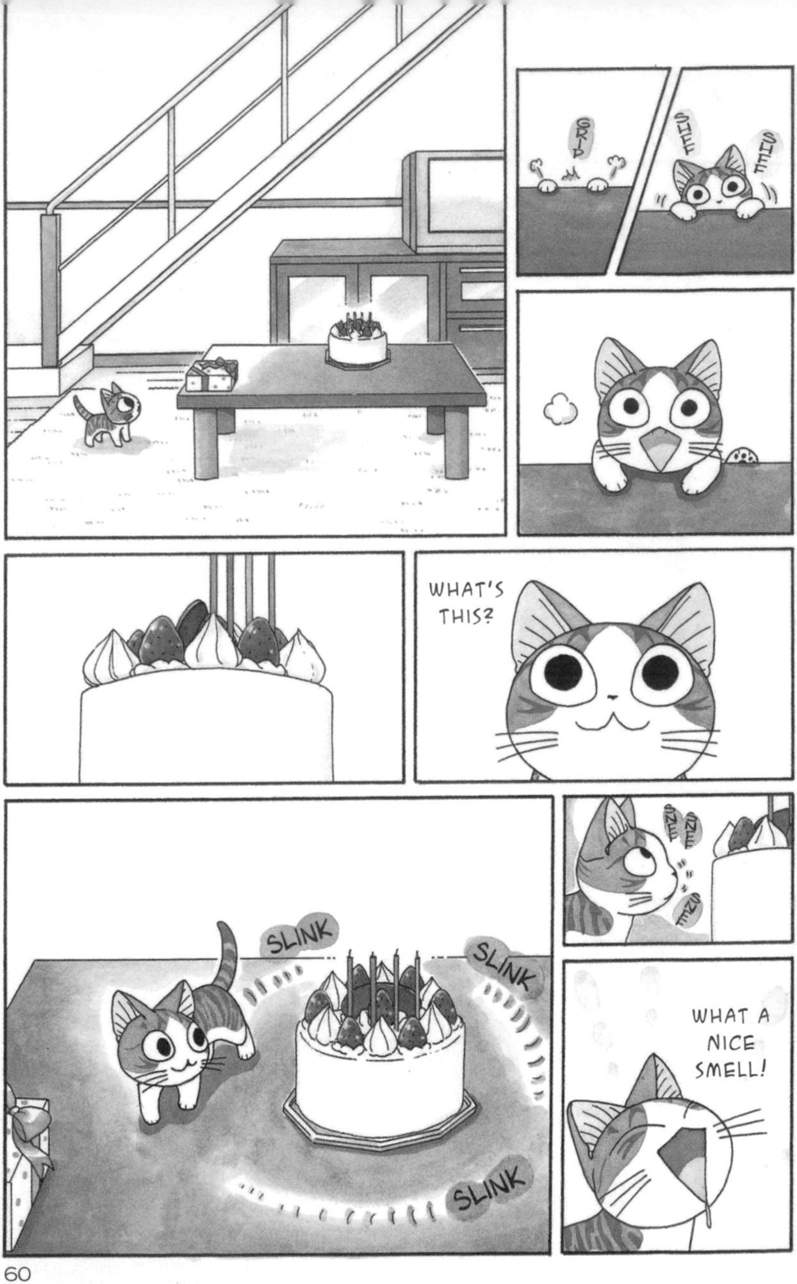
GRIP
SHFF
SHFF
WHAT'S THIS?
SLINK
SLINK
SLINK
SNIFF
SNIFF
SNIFF
WHAT A NICE SMELL!

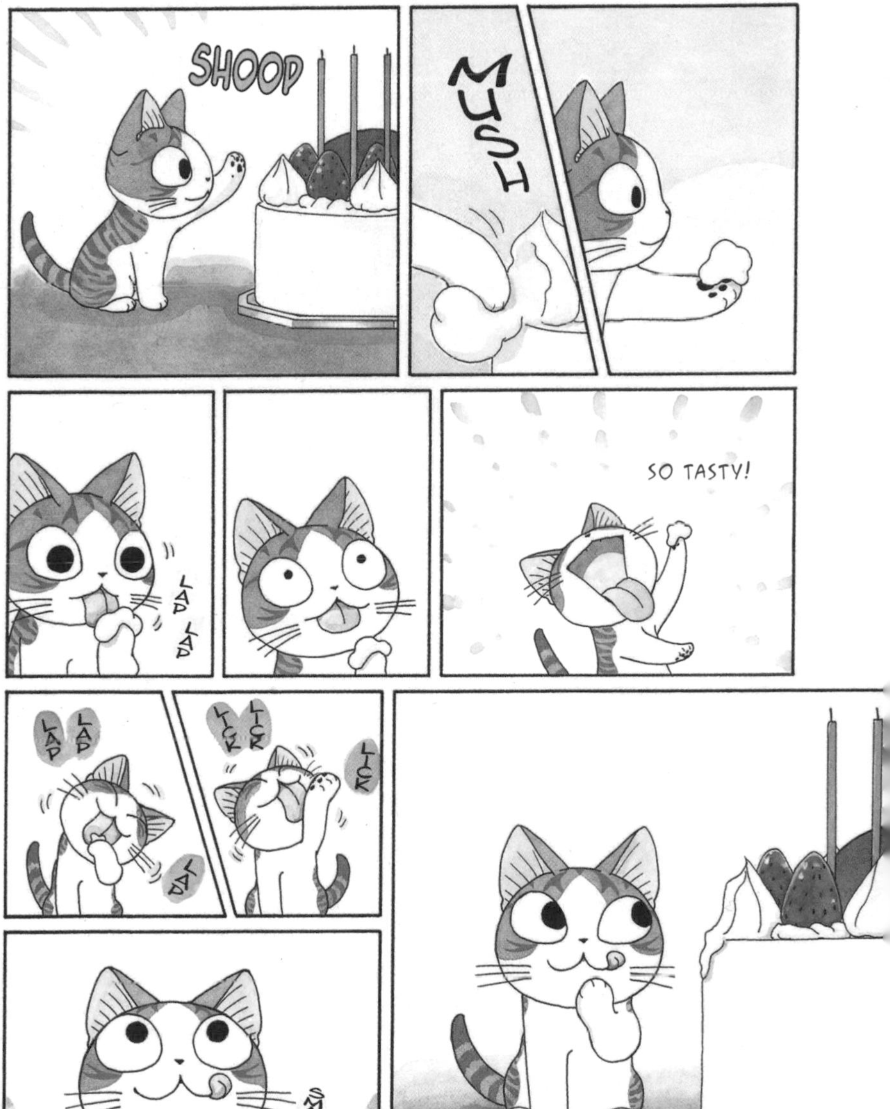
SHOOP
MUSH
LAP LAP
SO TASTY!
LAP LAP
LAP
LICK LICK
LICK
SMACK

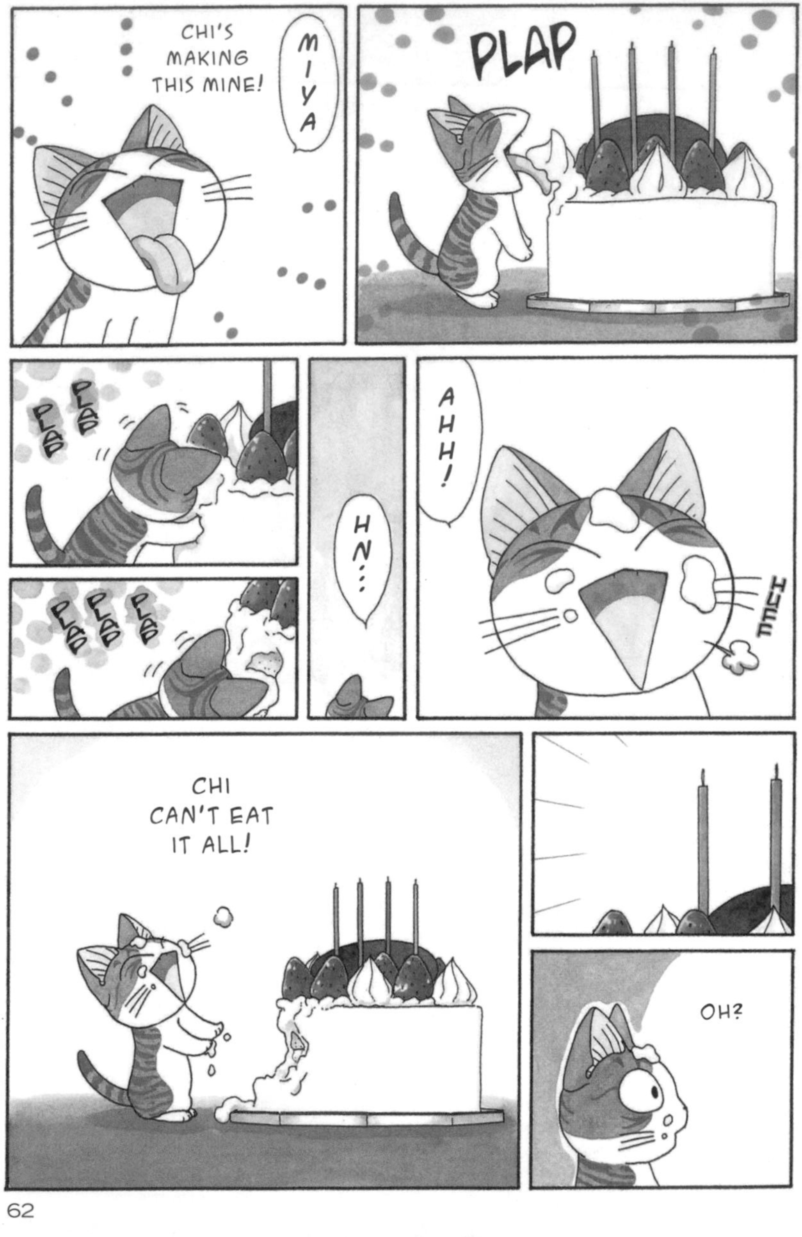
CHI'S MAKING THIS MINE!
MIYA
PLAP
PLAP PLAP
PLAP PLAP PLAP
HN...
AHH!
HUFF
CHI CAN'T EAT IT ALL!
OH?

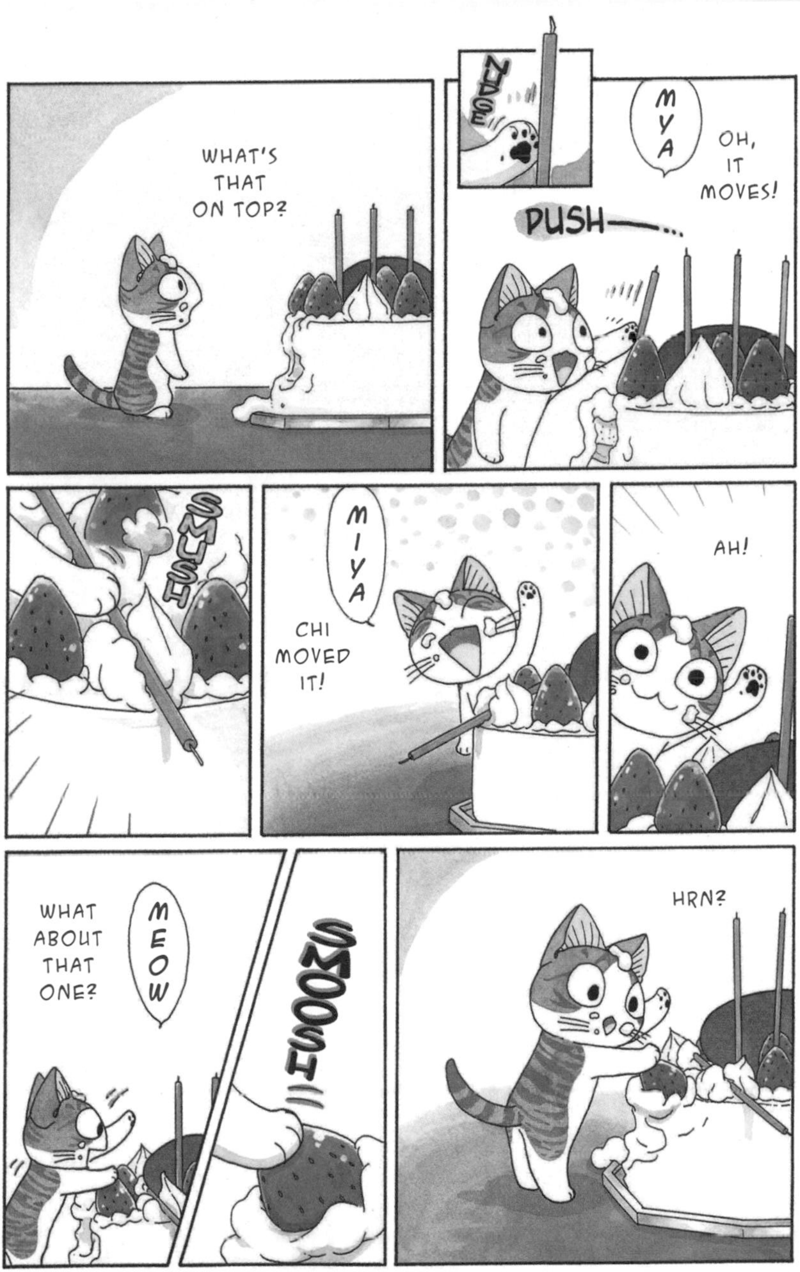
WHAT'S THAT ON TOP?
NUDGE
MYA
OH, IT MOVES!
PUSH—...
SMUSH
MIYA
CHI MOVED IT!
AH!
WHAT ABOUT THAT ONE?
MEOW
SMOOSH
HRN?

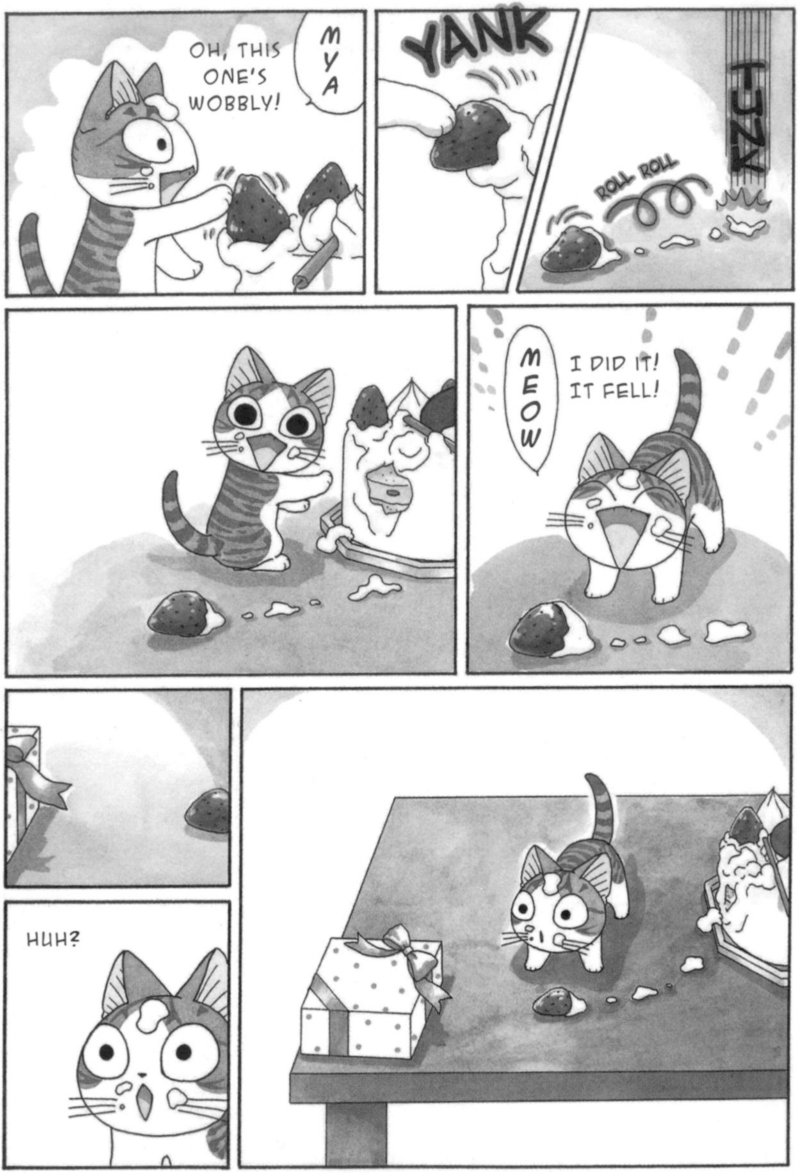
OH, THIS ONE'S WOBBLY!
MYA
YANK
TUNK
ROLL ROLL
MEOW
I DID IT! IT FELL!
HUH?

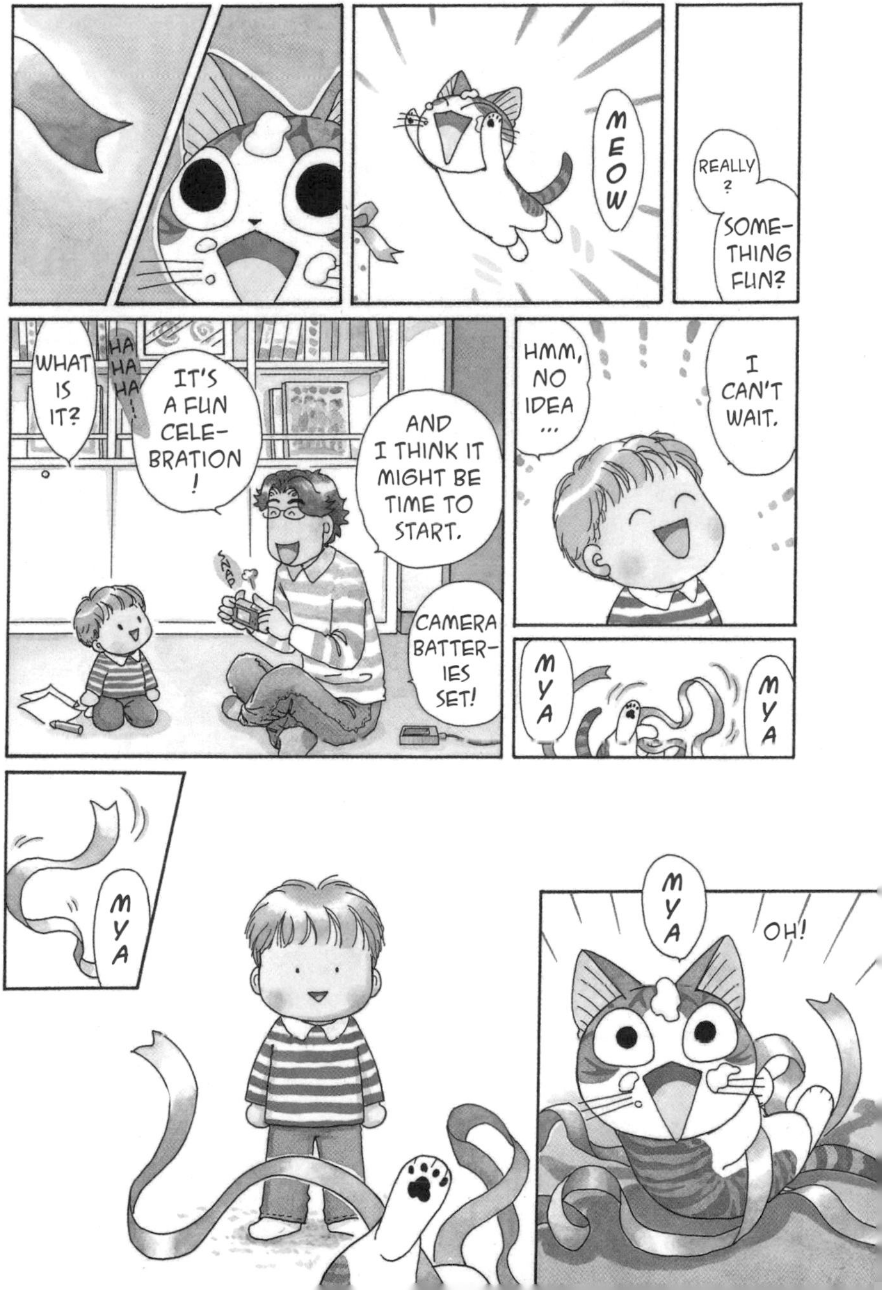
MEOW
REALLY?
SOME-THING FUN?
WHAT IS IT?
HA HA HA!!
IT'S A FUN CELE-BRATION!
AND I THINK IT MIGHT BE TIME TO START.
SNAP
CAMERA BATTER-IES SET!
HMM, NO IDEA...
I CAN'T WAIT.
MYA
MYA
MYA
MYA
OH!

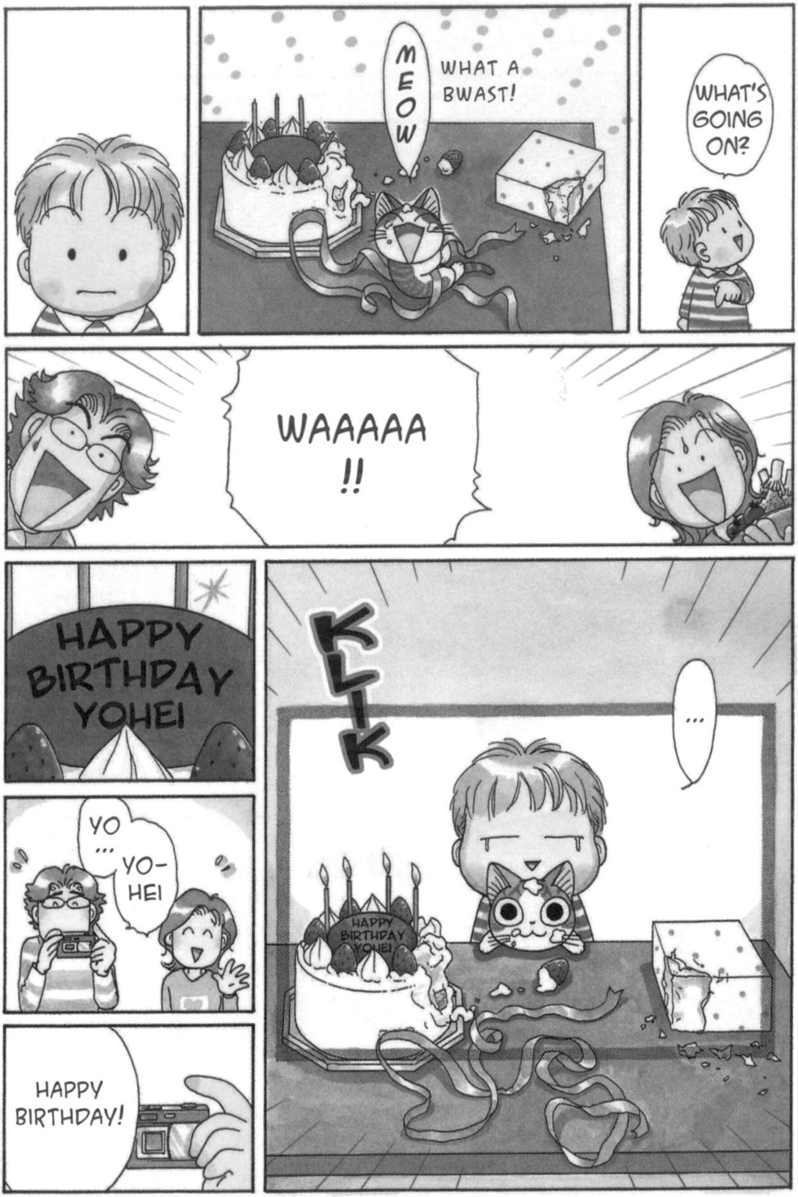
MEOW
WHAT A BWAST!
WHAT'S GOING ON?
WAAAAA!!
HAPPY BIRTHDAY YOHEI
YO... YO-HEI
HAPPY BIRTHDAY!
KLIK
...
HAPPY BIRTHDAY YOHEI

**the end**

# homemade 101: a cat shares

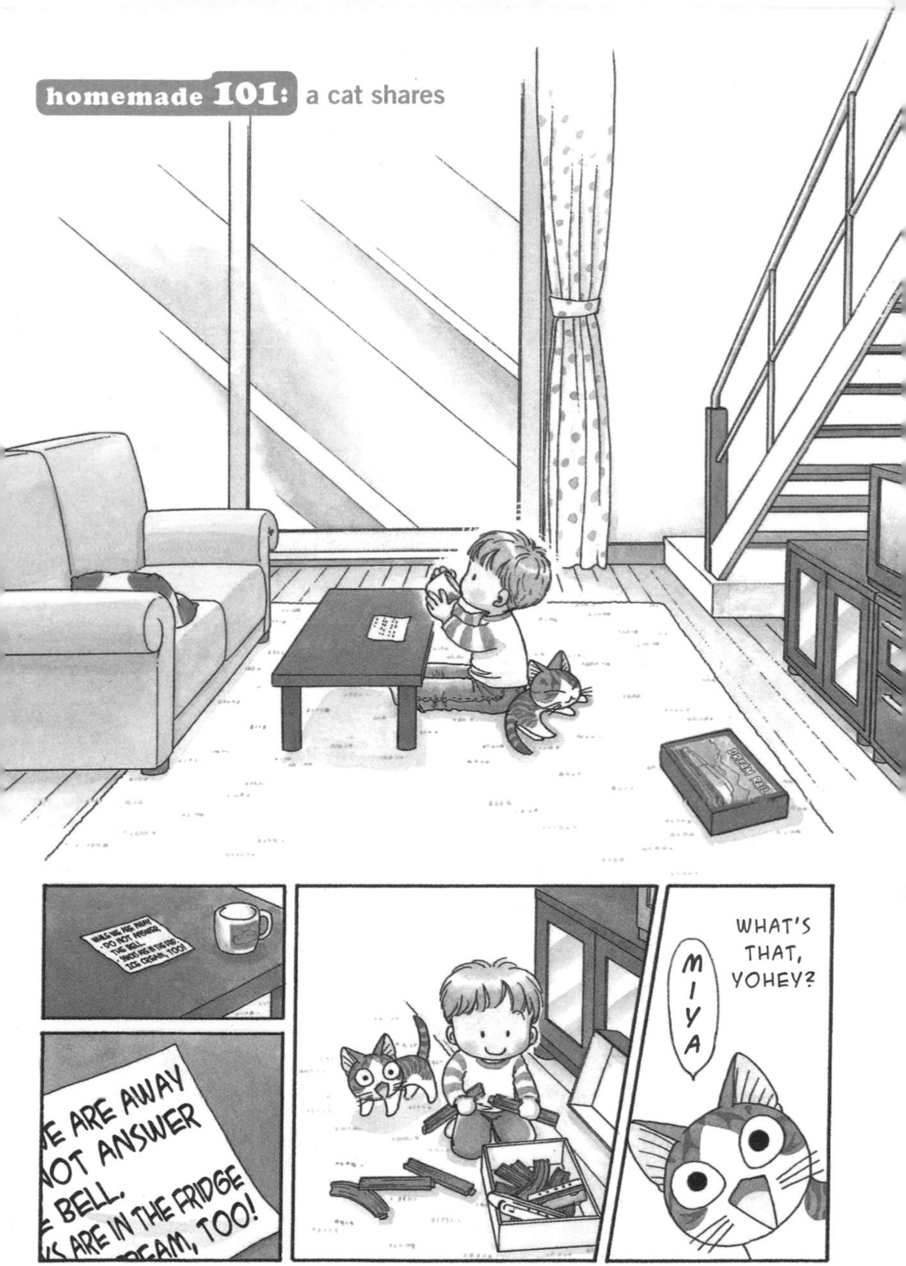
DREAM RAIL
· DO NOT ANSWER
THE BELL.
ICE CREAM, TOO!
ARE AWAY
NOT ANSWER
BELL.
ARE IN THE FRIDGE
TOO!
WHAT'S THAT, YOHEY?
MIYA

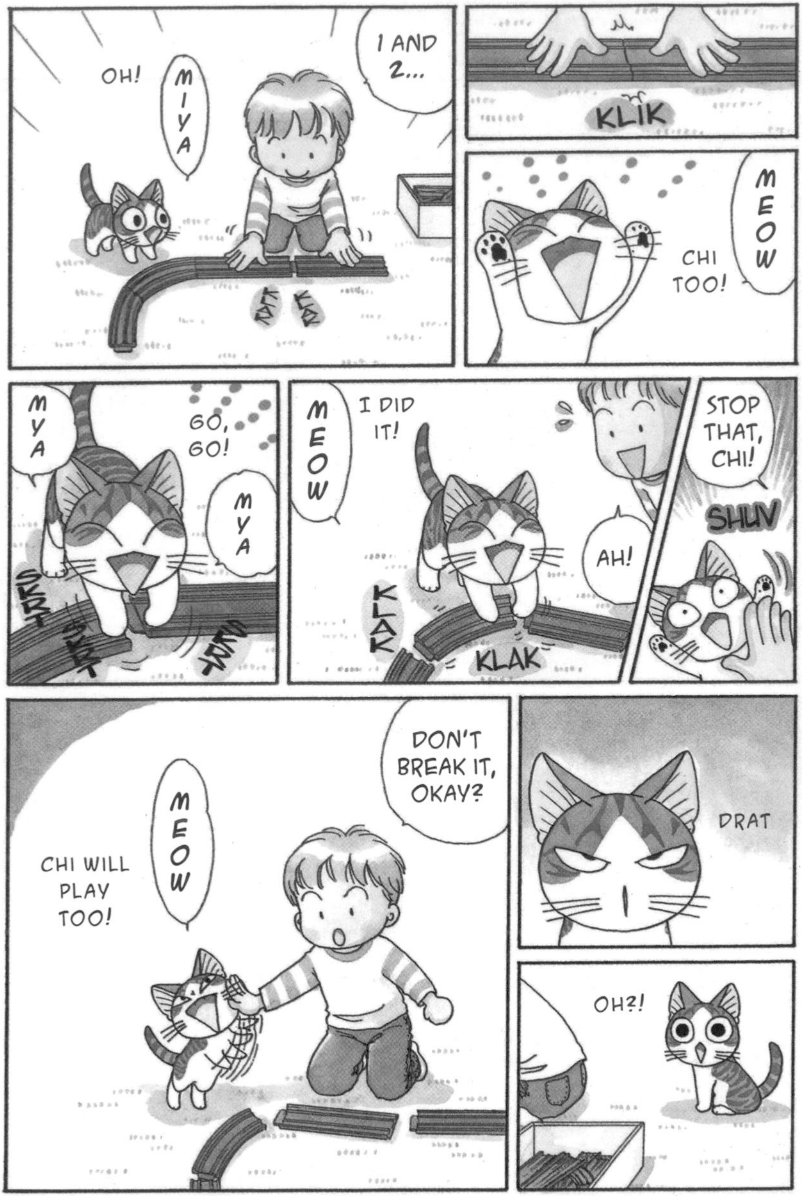
OH!
MIYA
1 AND 2...
KLAK KLAK
KLIK
MEOW
CHI TOO!
MYA
GO, GO!
MYA
SKRT SKRT SKRT
MEOW
I DID IT!
KLAK
KLAK
AH!
STOP THAT, CHI!
SHUV
DON'T BREAK IT, OKAY?
MEOW
CHI WILL PLAY TOO!
DRAT
OH?!

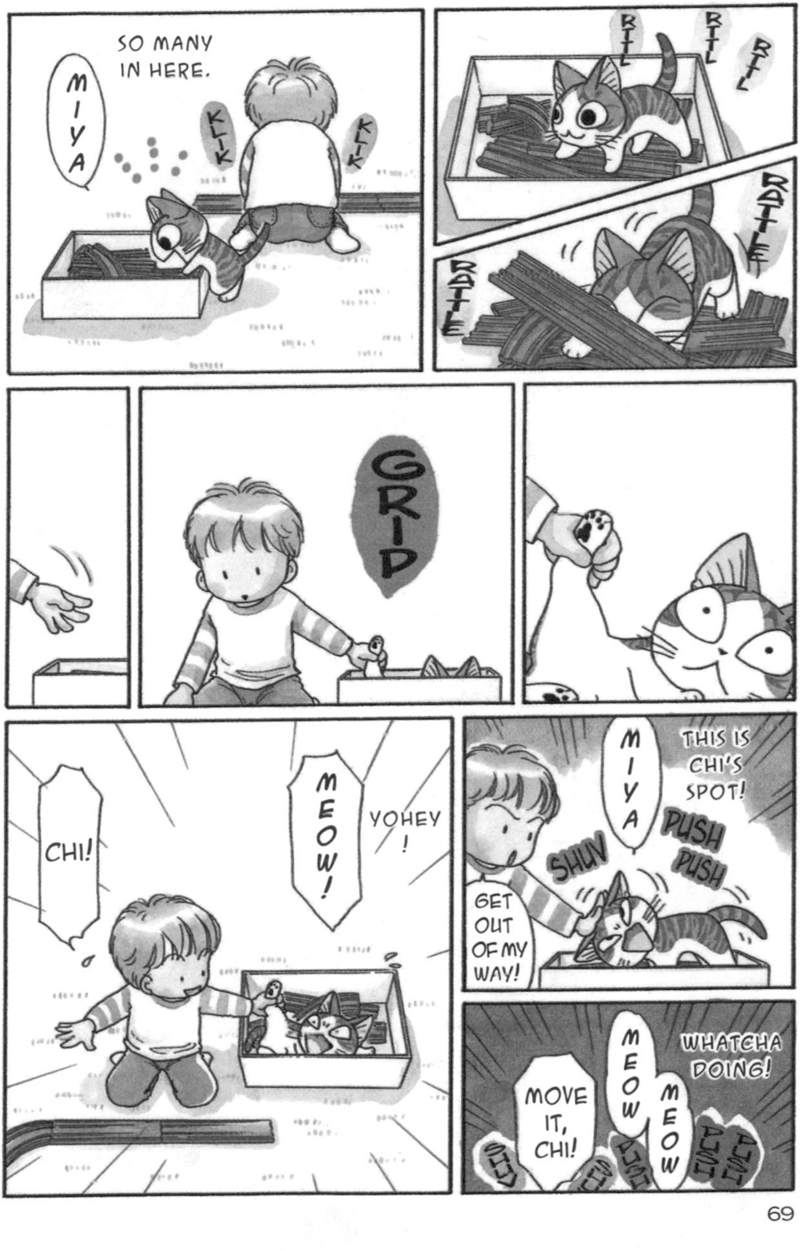
SO MANY IN HERE.
MIYA
KLIK
KLIK
RITL
RITL
RITL
RATTLE
RATTLE
GRIP
CHI!
MEOW!
YOHEY!
MIYA
THIS IS CHI'S SPOT!
SHUV
PUSH
PUSH
GET OUT OF MY WAY!
MEOW
WHATCHA DOING!
MOVE IT, CHI!
MEOW
SHUV
PUSH
PUSH
PUSH

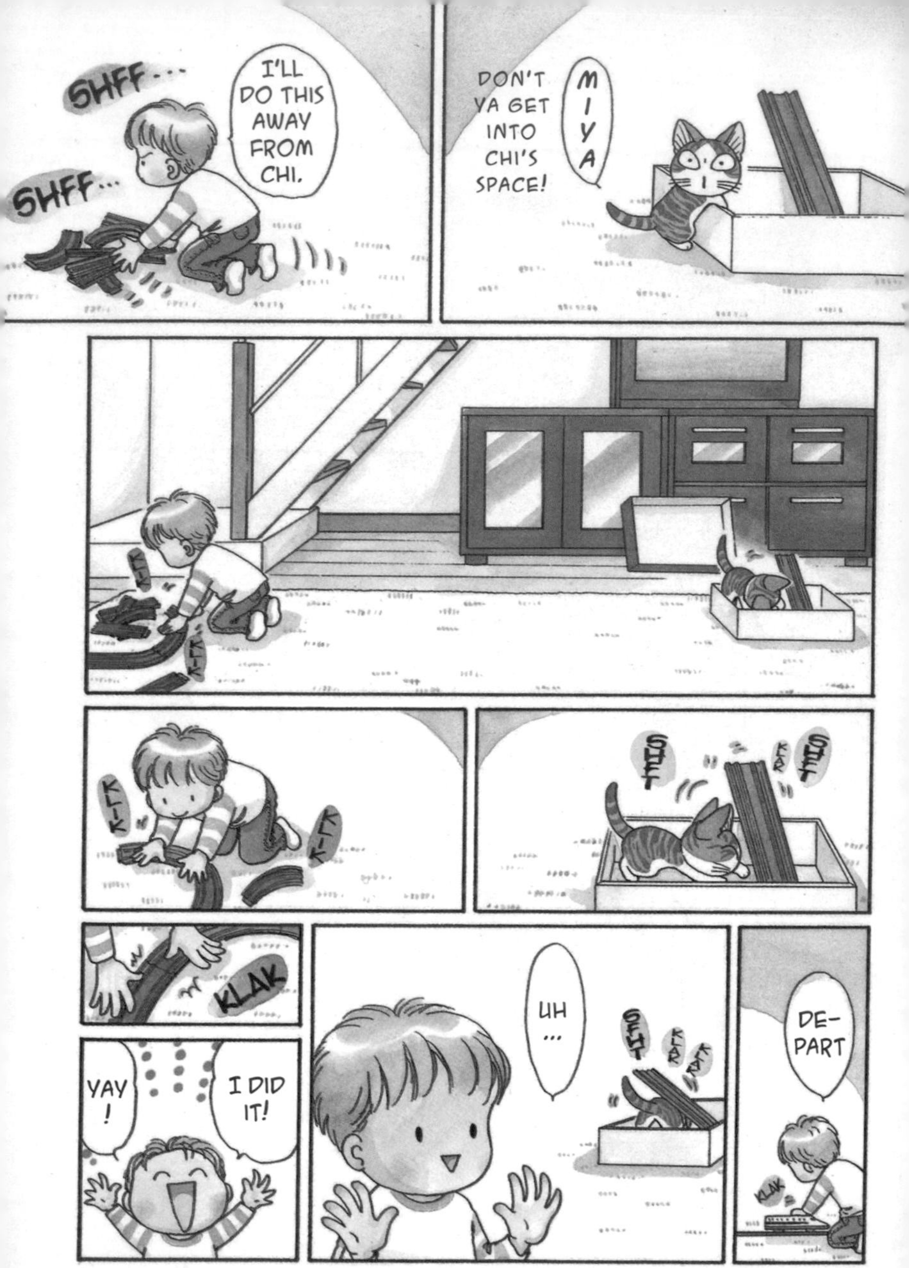
SHFF...
SHFF...
I'LL DO THIS AWAY FROM CHI.
DON'T YA GET INTO CHI'S SPACE!
MIYA
KLIK
KLIK
KLIK
KLIK
SHFT
KLAK
SHFT
KLAK
YAY!
I DID IT!
UH...
SHFT
KLAK
KLAK
DE-PART
KLAK

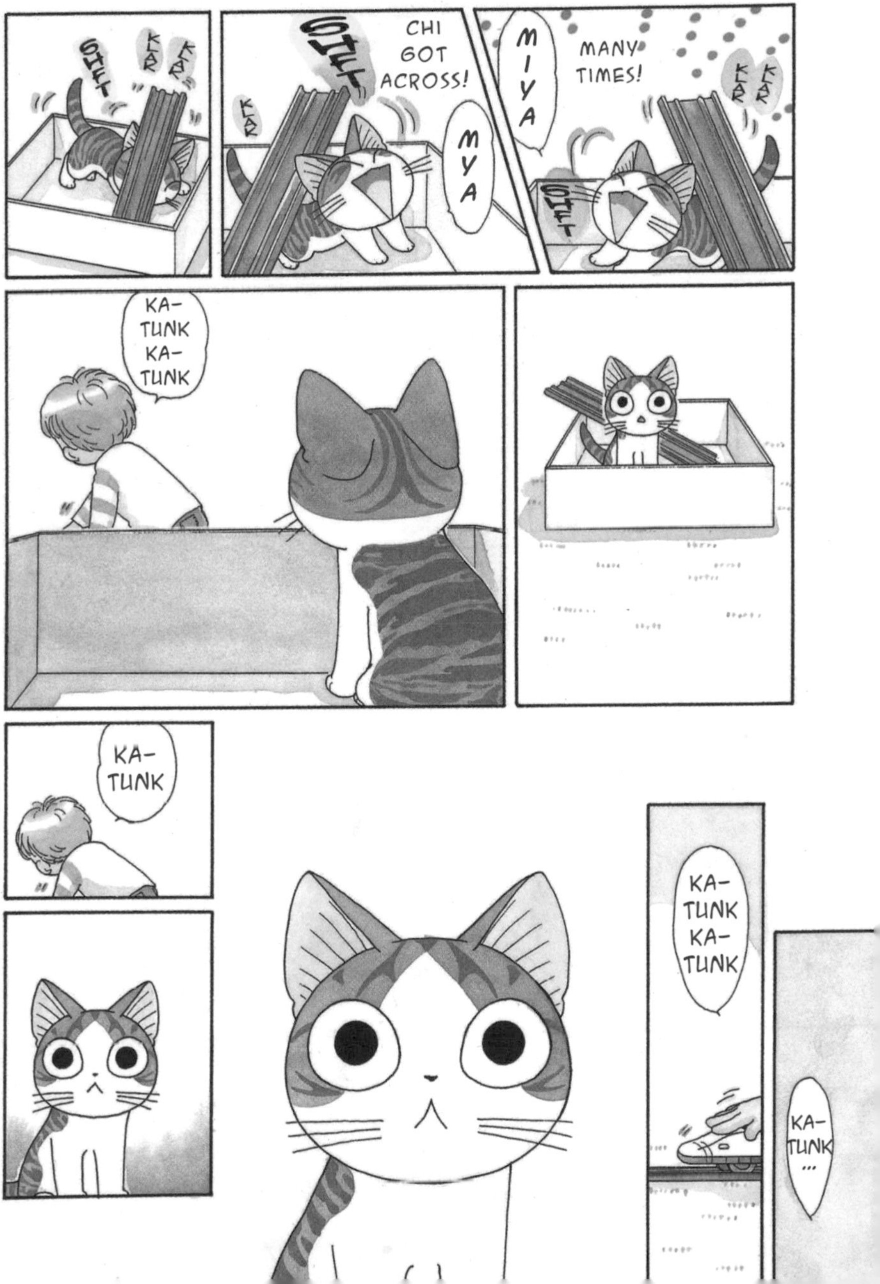
SHFT
KLAK KLAK
SHFT
KLAK
CHI GOT ACROSS!
MYA
MIYA
MANY TIMES!
KLAK KLAK
SHFT
KA-TUNK KA-TUNK
KA-TUNK
KA-TUNK KA-TUNK
KA-TUNK ...

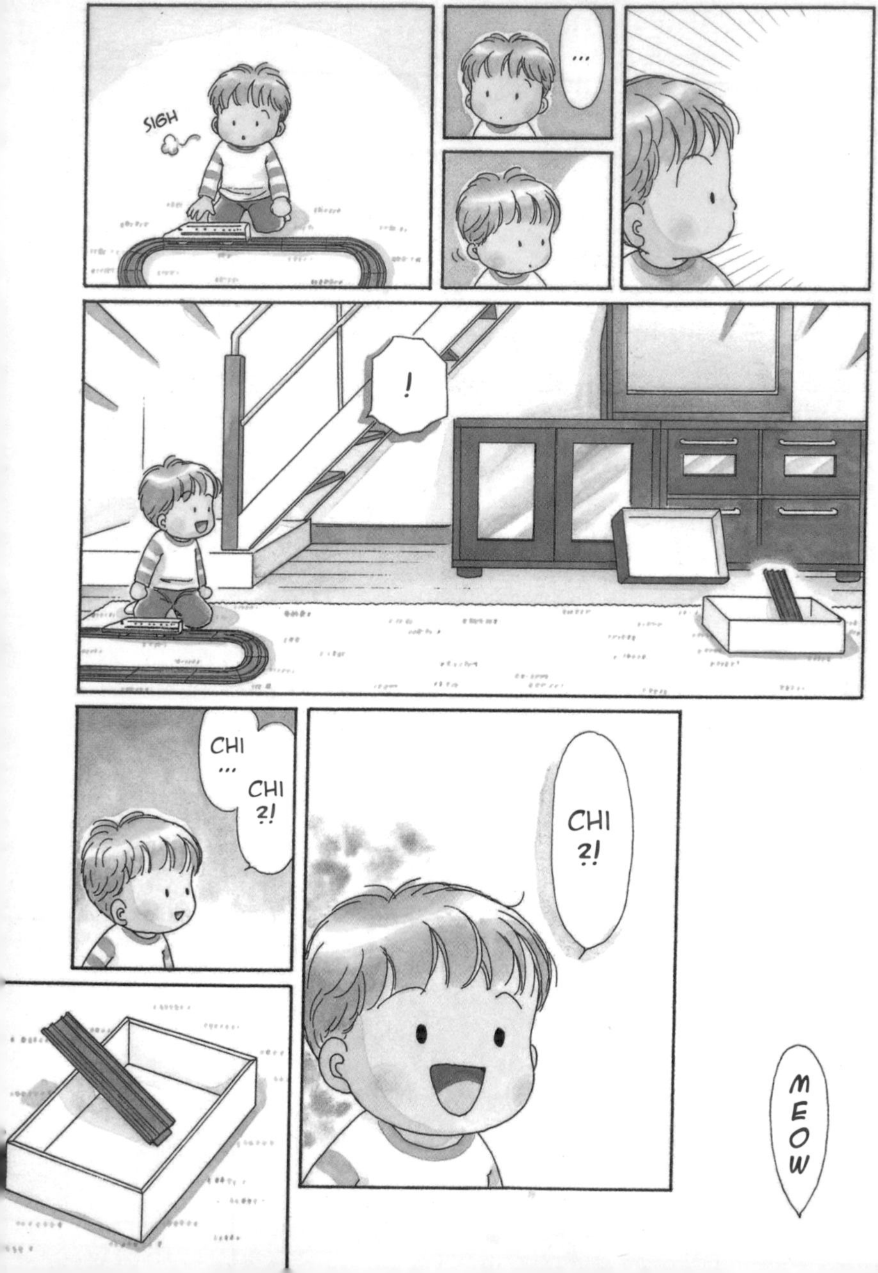
SIGH
...
!
CHI ... CHI ?!
CHI ?!
MEOW

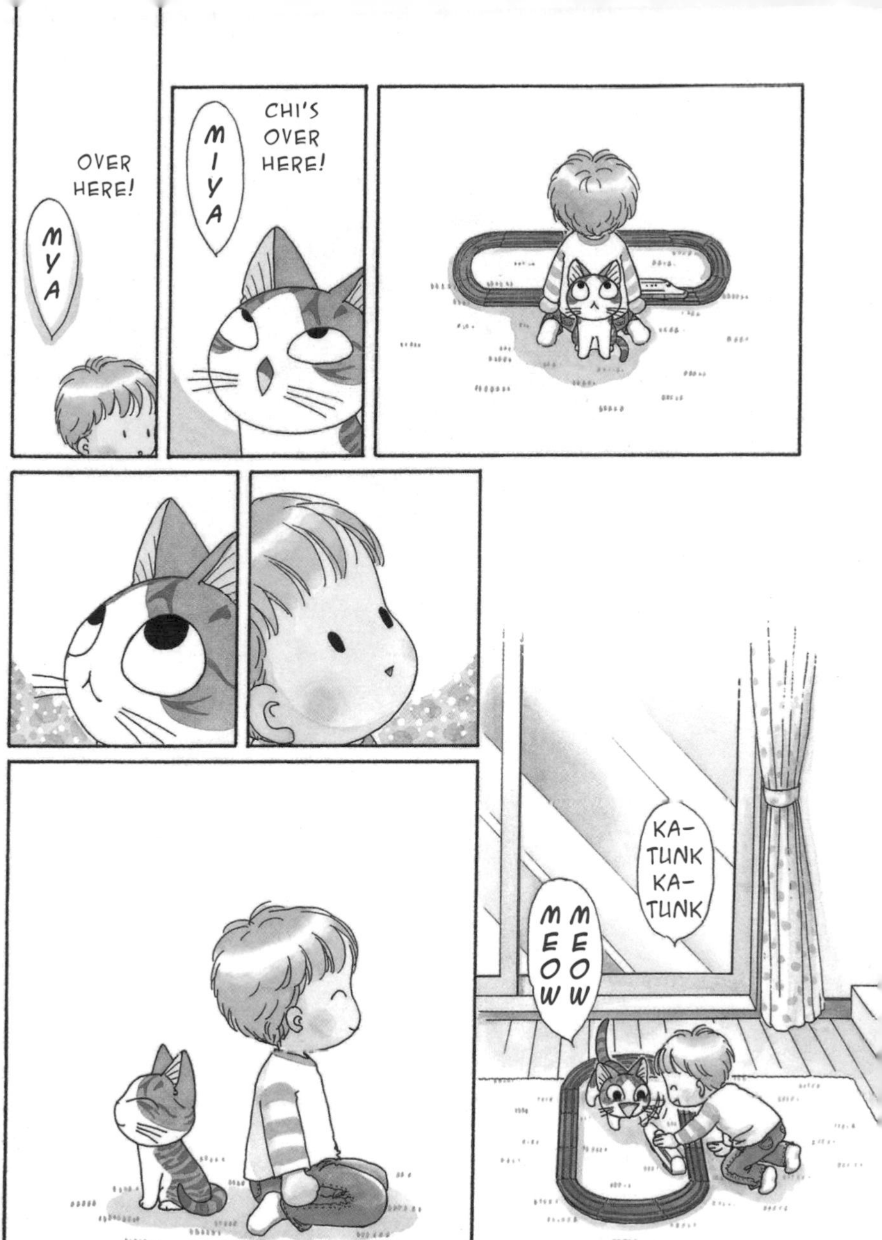
OVER HERE!
MYA
CHI'S OVER HERE!
MIYA
KA-TUNK KA-TUNK
MEOW MEOW

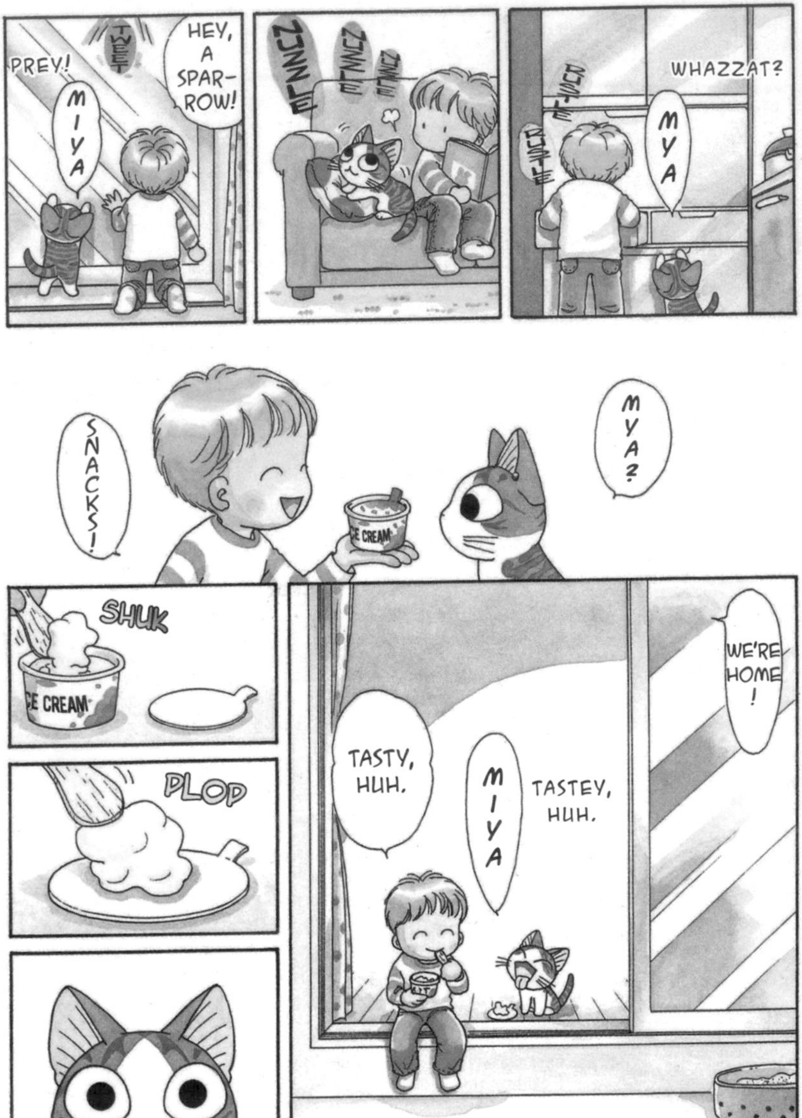
TWEET
HEY, A SPARROW!
PREY!
MIYA
NUZZLE
NUZZLE
NUZZLE
RUSTLE
WHAZZAT?
RUSTLE
MYA
SNACKS!
MYA?
ICE CREAM
SHUK
ICE CREAM
PLOP
WE'RE HOME!
TASTY, HUH.
MIYA
TASTEY, HUH.



**the end**

# homemade 102: a cat is sucked

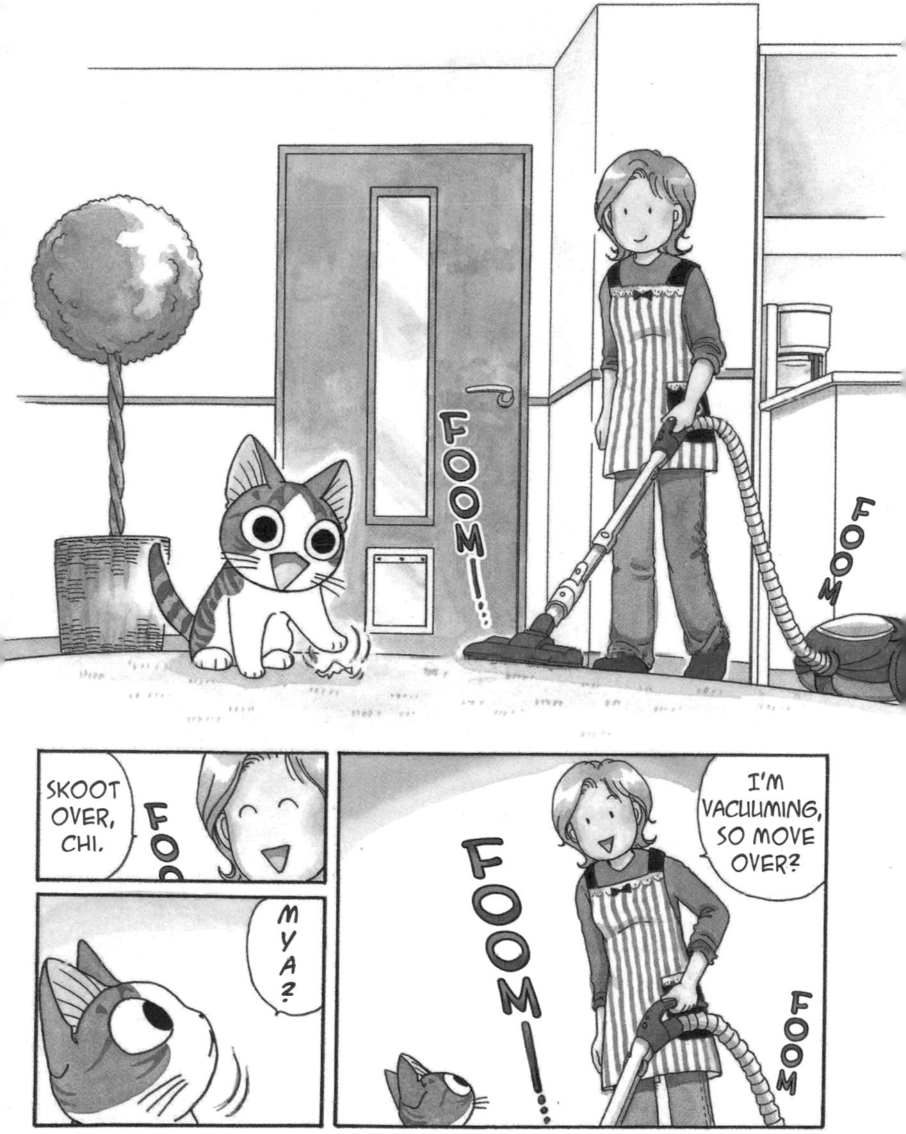
FOOM!...
FOOM
SKOOT OVER, CHI.
FOO
MYA?
I'M VACUUMING, SO MOVE OVER?
FOOM!...
FOOM

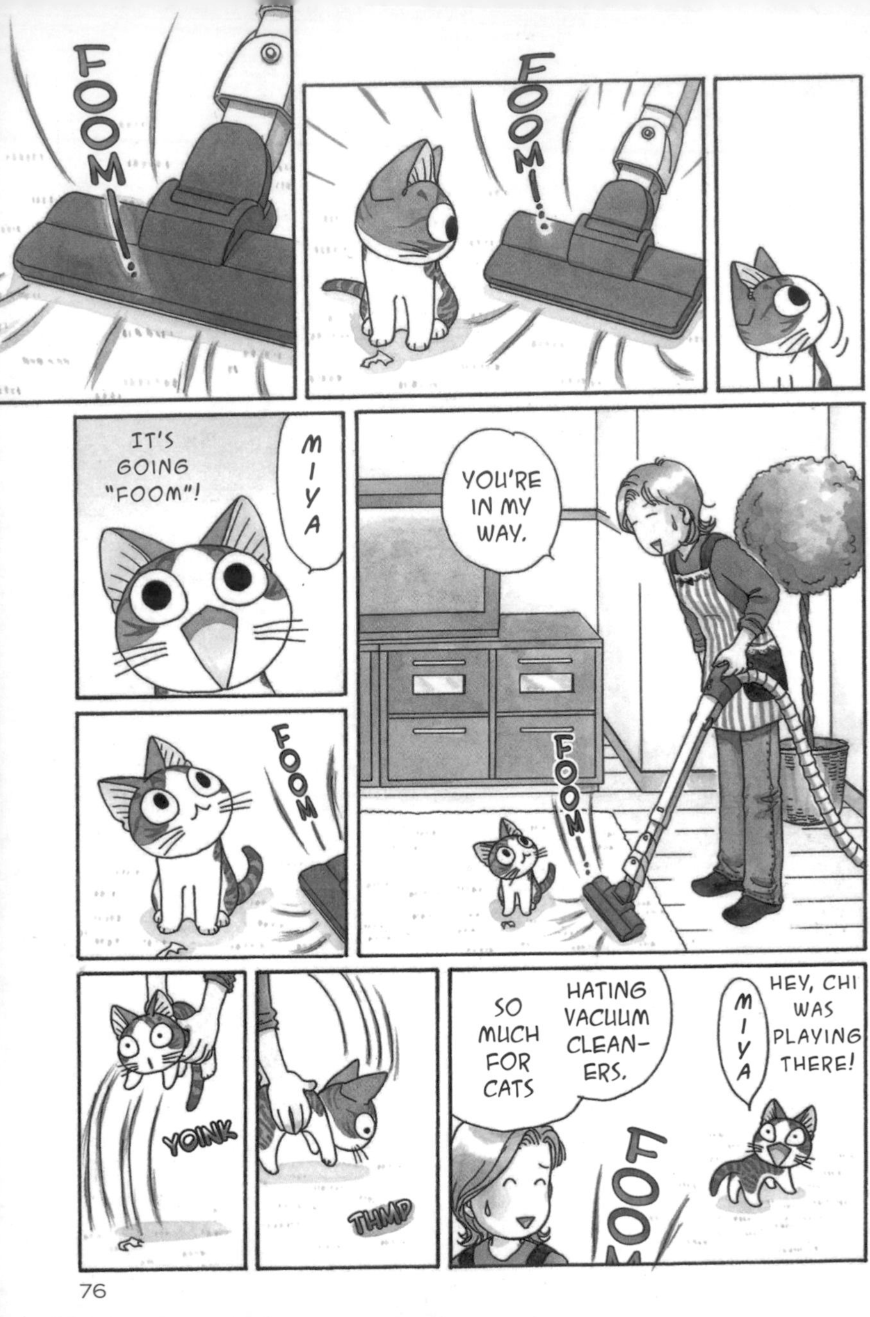
FOOM!
FOOM!...
IT'S GOING "FOOM"!
MIYA
FOOM
YOU'RE IN MY WAY.
FOOM!...
YOINK
THMP
SO MUCH FOR CATS HATING VACUUM CLEAN-ERS.
MIYA
HEY, CHI WAS PLAYING THERE!
FOOM

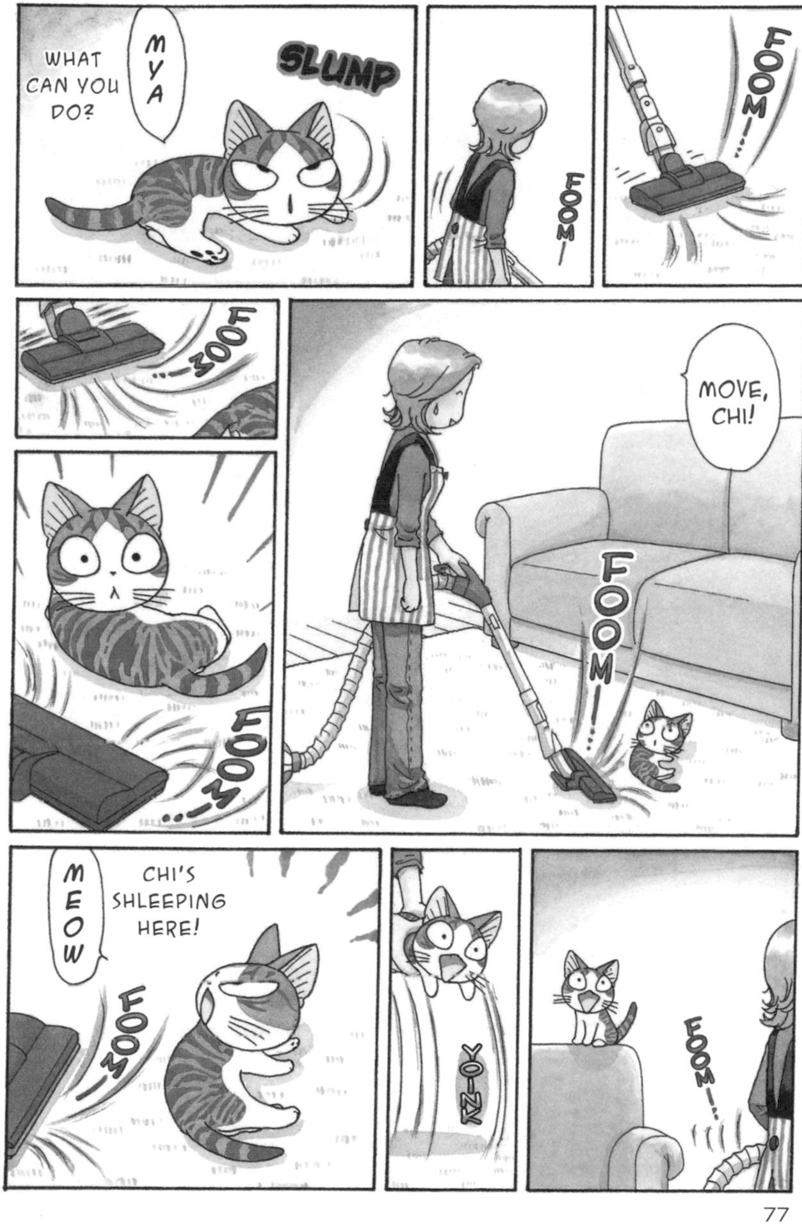
WHAT CAN YOU DO?
MYA
SLUMP
FOOM
FOOM...
FOOM...
MOVE, CHI!
FOOM...
FOOM...
MEOW
CHI'S SHLEEPING HERE!
FOOM
YOINK
FOOM...

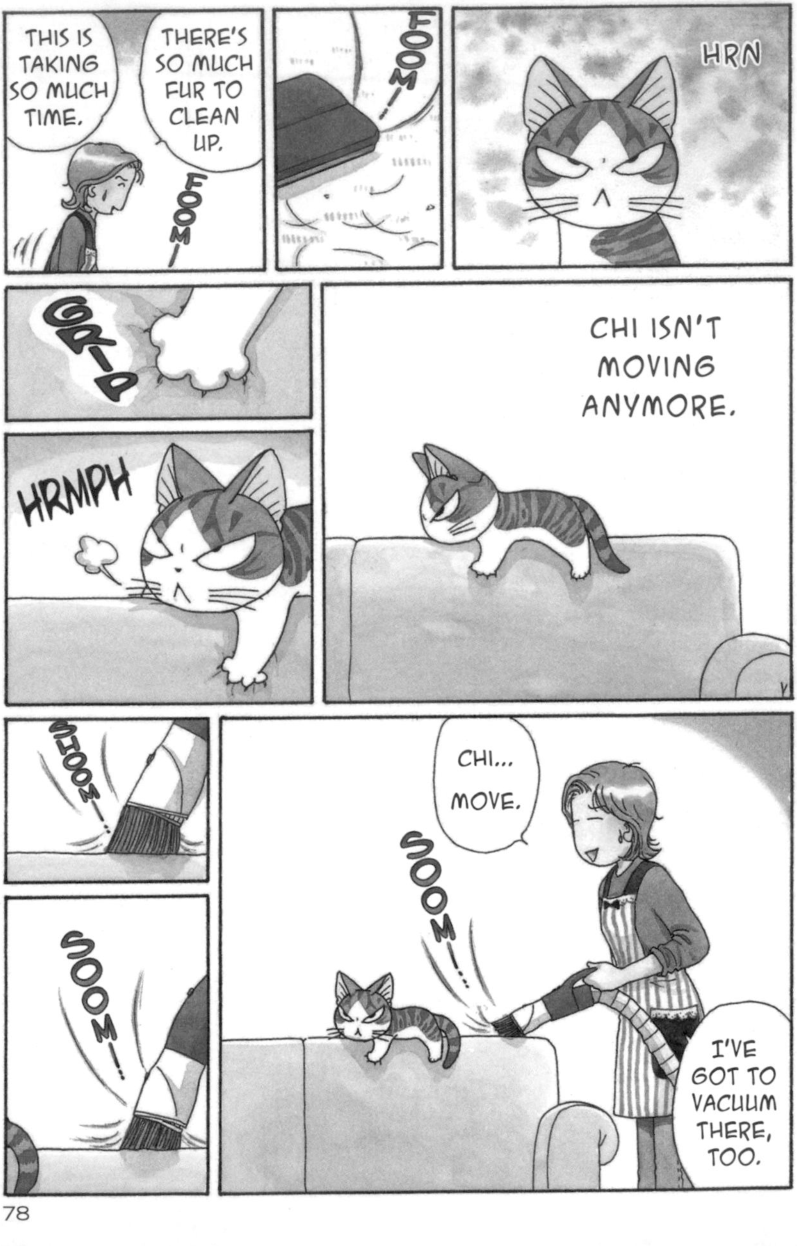
THIS IS TAKING SO MUCH TIME.
THERE'S SO MUCH FUR TO CLEAN UP.
FOOM!
FOOM!
HRN
GRIP
HRMPH
CHI ISN'T MOVING ANYMORE.
SHOOM!..
SOOM!..
CHI... MOVE.
SOOM!...
I'VE GOT TO VACUUM THERE, TOO.

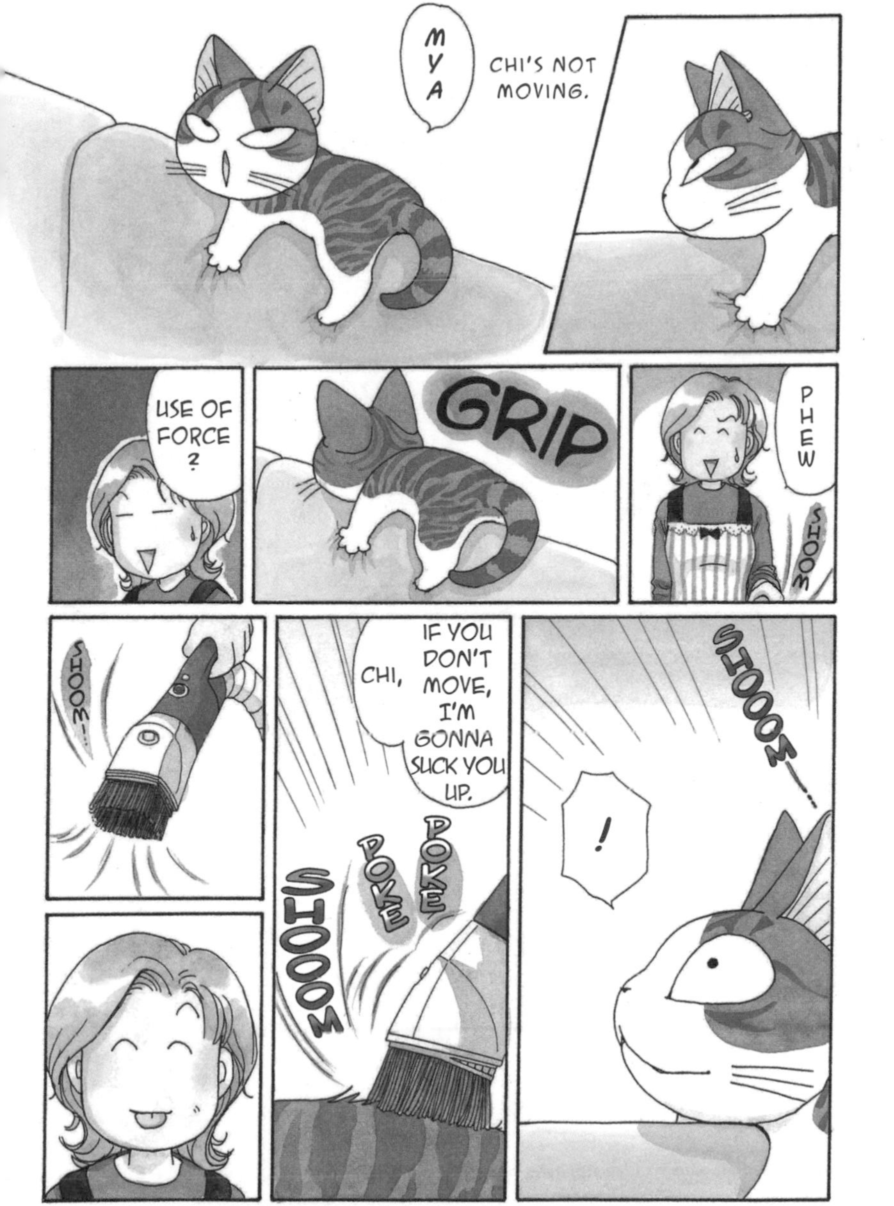
MYA
CHI'S NOT MOVING.
USE OF FORCE ?
GRIP
PHEW
SHOOM
SHOOM...
CHI, IF YOU DON'T MOVE, I'M GONNA SUCK YOU UP.
POKE
POKE
SHOOOM
SHOOOM...
!

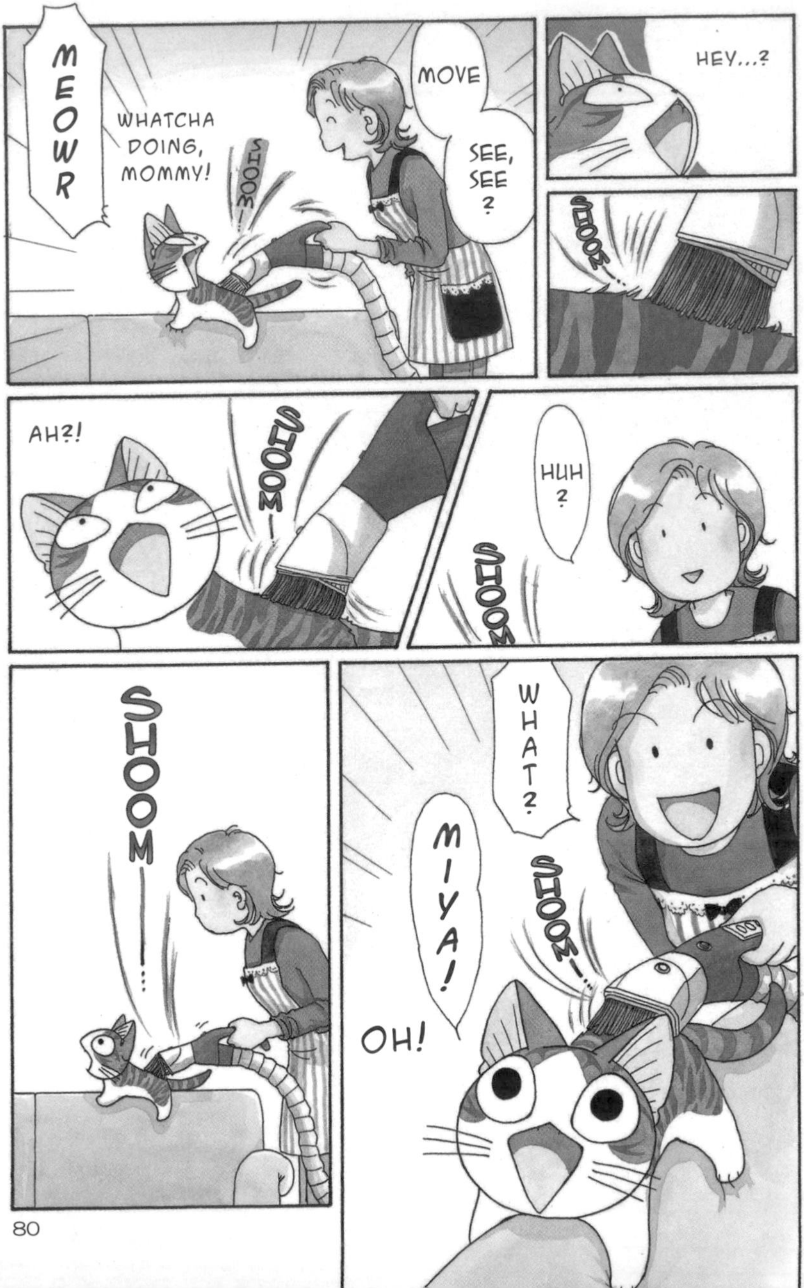
MEOWR
WHATCHA DOING, MOMMY!
SHOOM!
MOVE
SEE, SEE?
HEY...?
SHOOM...
AH?!
SHOOM!
HUH?
SHOOM
SHOOM!...
WHAT?
MIYA!
SHOOM!...
OH!

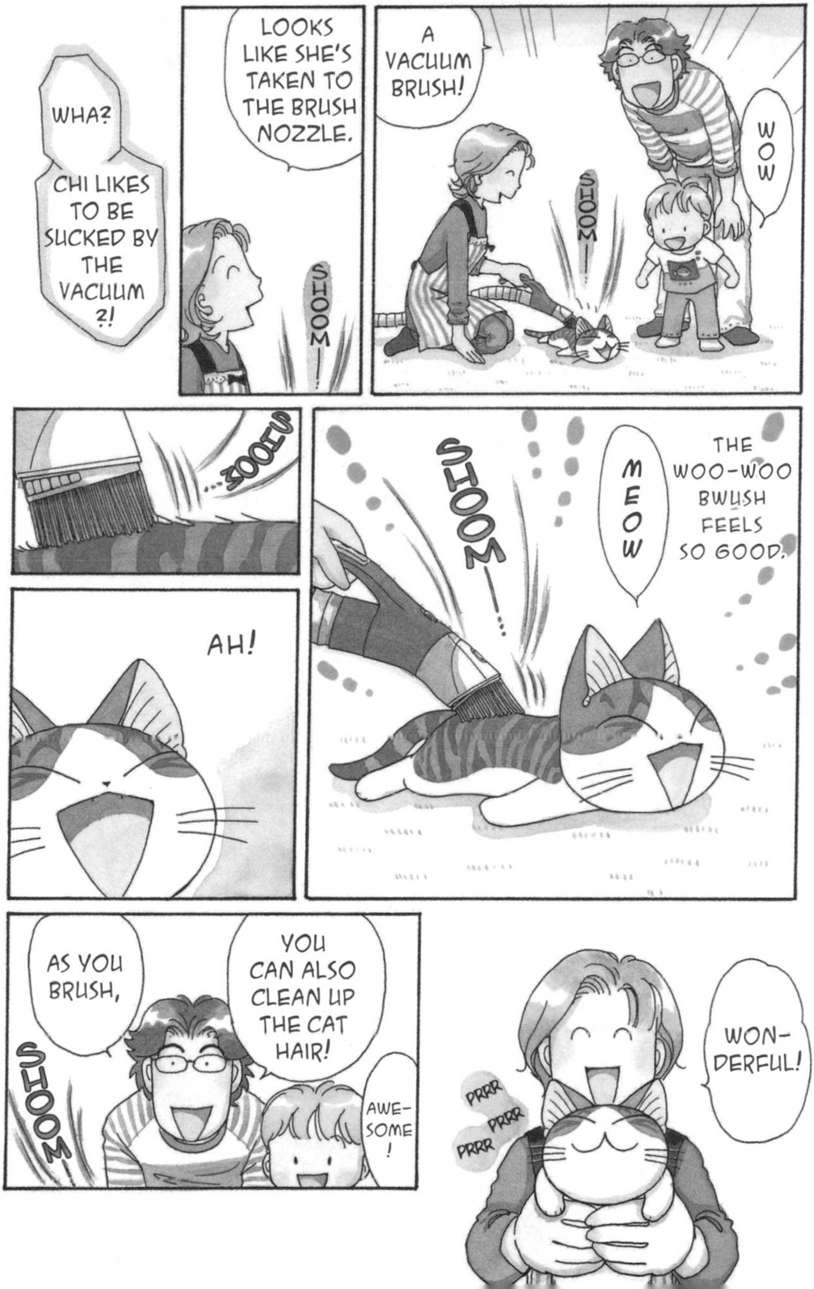
WHA?
CHI LIKES TO BE SUCKED BY THE VACUUM ?!
LOOKS LIKE SHE'S TAKEN TO THE BRUSH NOZZLE.
SHOOM—!
A VACUUM BRUSH!
SHOOM—!
WOW
AH!
SHOOM—...
MEOW
THE WOO-WOO BWUSH FEELS SO GOOD.
AS YOU BRUSH,
YOU CAN ALSO CLEAN UP THE CAT HAIR!
SHOOM
AWE-SOME!
WON-DERFUL!
PRRR
PRRR
PRRR

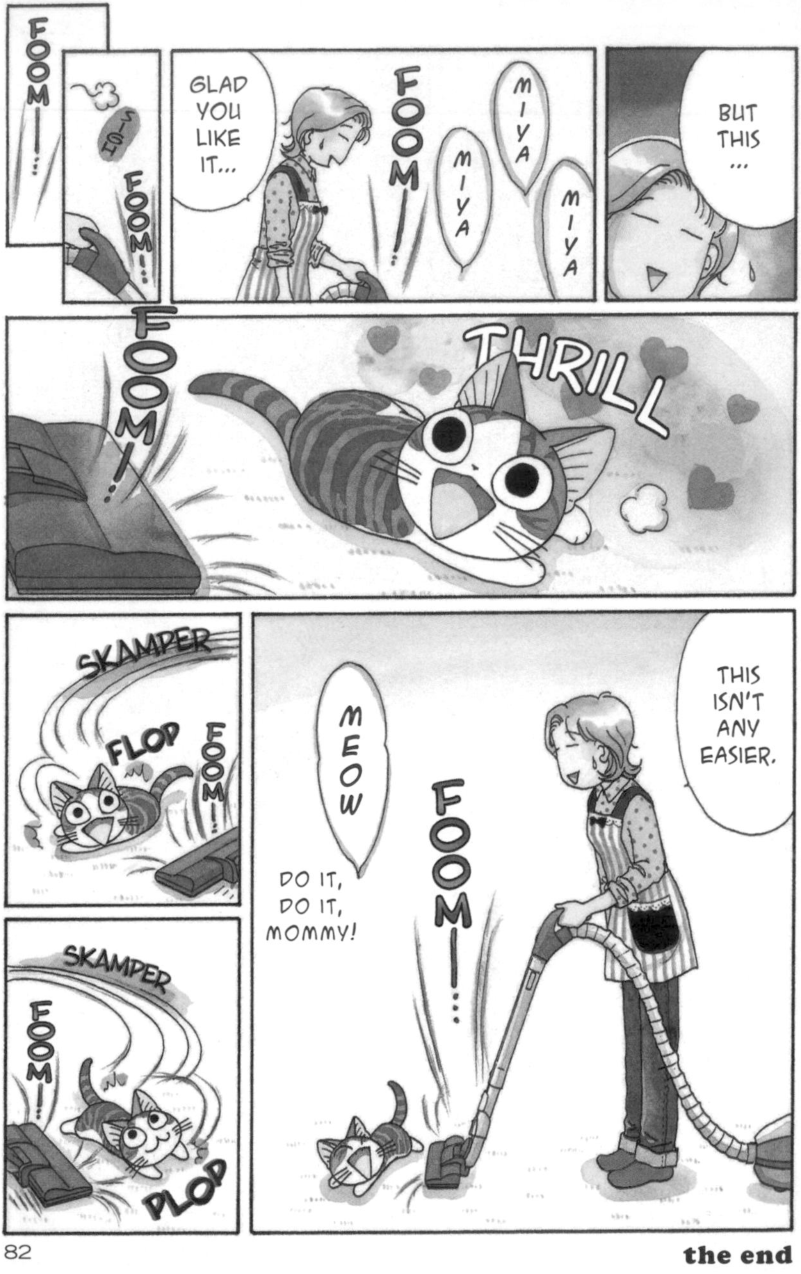
FOOM!...
SIGH
FOOM!...
GLAD YOU LIKE IT...
FOOM!...
MIYA
MIYA
MIYA
BUT THIS...
FOOM!...
THRILL
SKAMPER
FLOP
FOOM!
SKAMPER
FOOM!
PLOP
MEOW
DO IT, DO IT, MOMMY!
FOOM!...
THIS ISN'T ANY EASIER.

**the end**

# homemade 103: a cat tosses

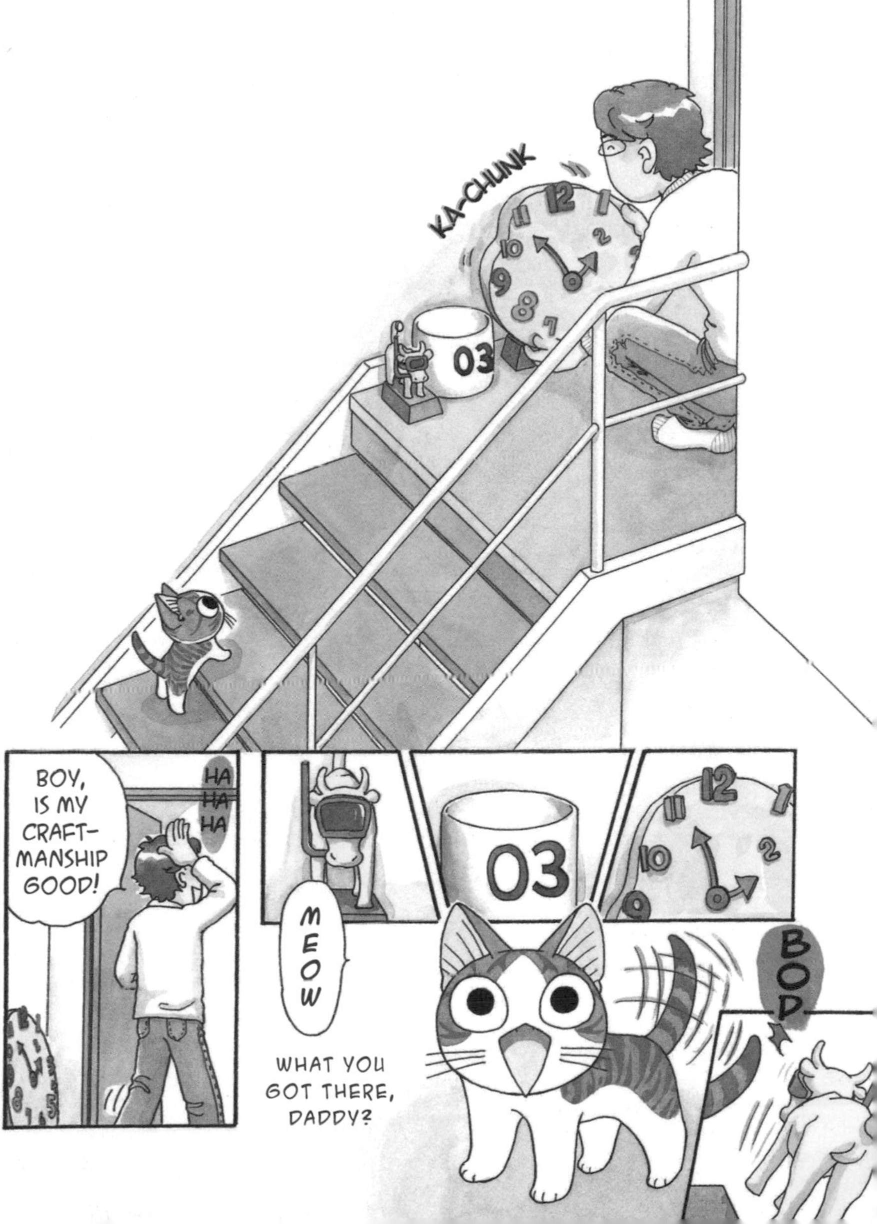
KA-CHUNK
03
BOY, IS MY CRAFT-MANSHIP GOOD!
HA HA HA
03
MEOW
WHAT YOU GOT THERE, DADDY?
BOD

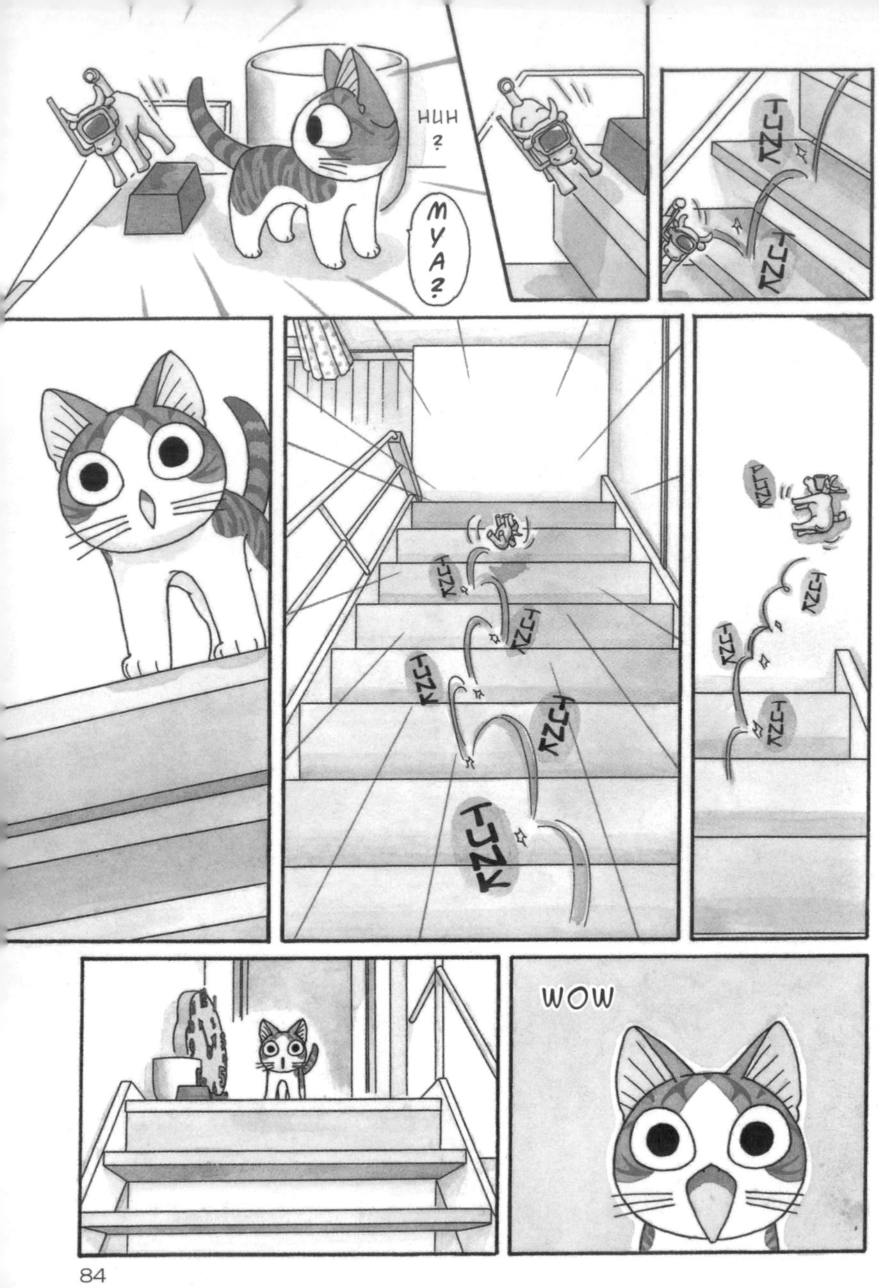
HUH?
MYA?
TJNK
TJNK
TJNK
TJNK
TJNK
TJNK
TJNK
TJNK
TJNK
TJNK
TJNK
WOW

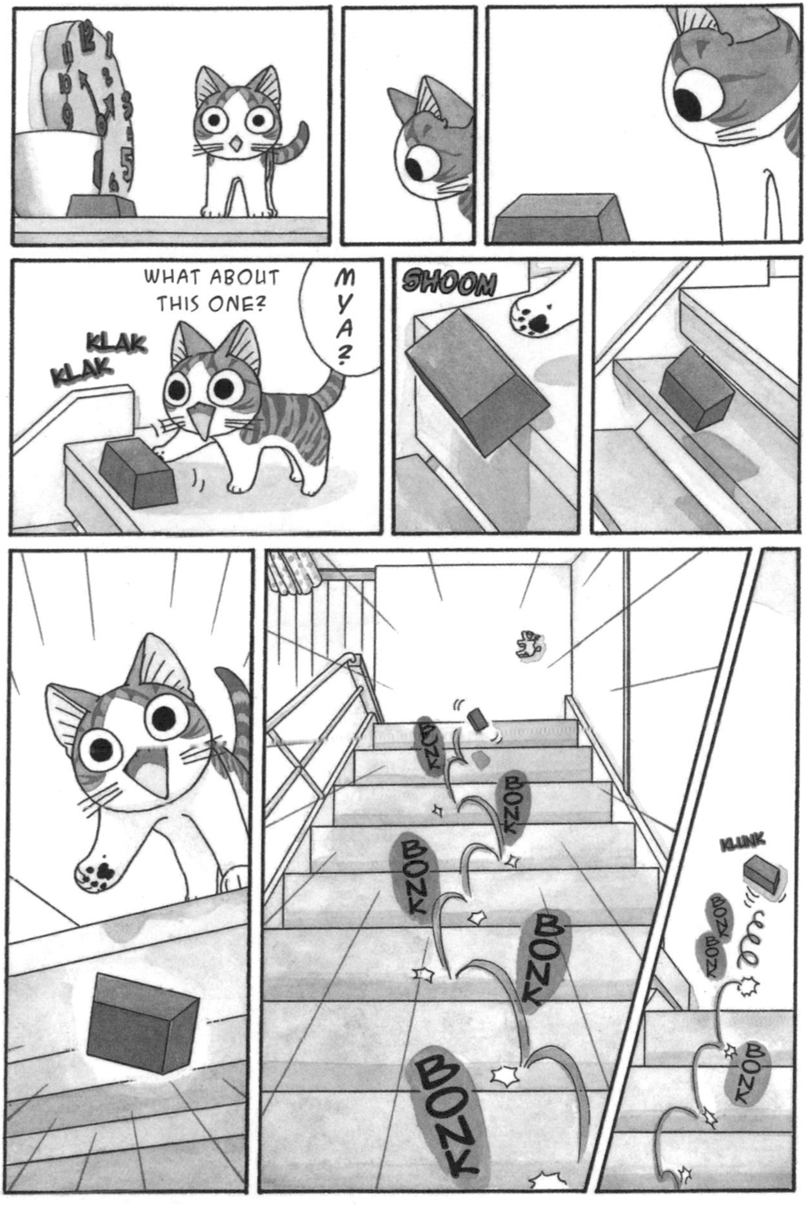
KLAK
KLAK
WHAT ABOUT THIS ONE?
MYA?
SHOOM
BONK
BONK
BONK
BONK
BONK
BONK
BONK
BONK
KLUNK

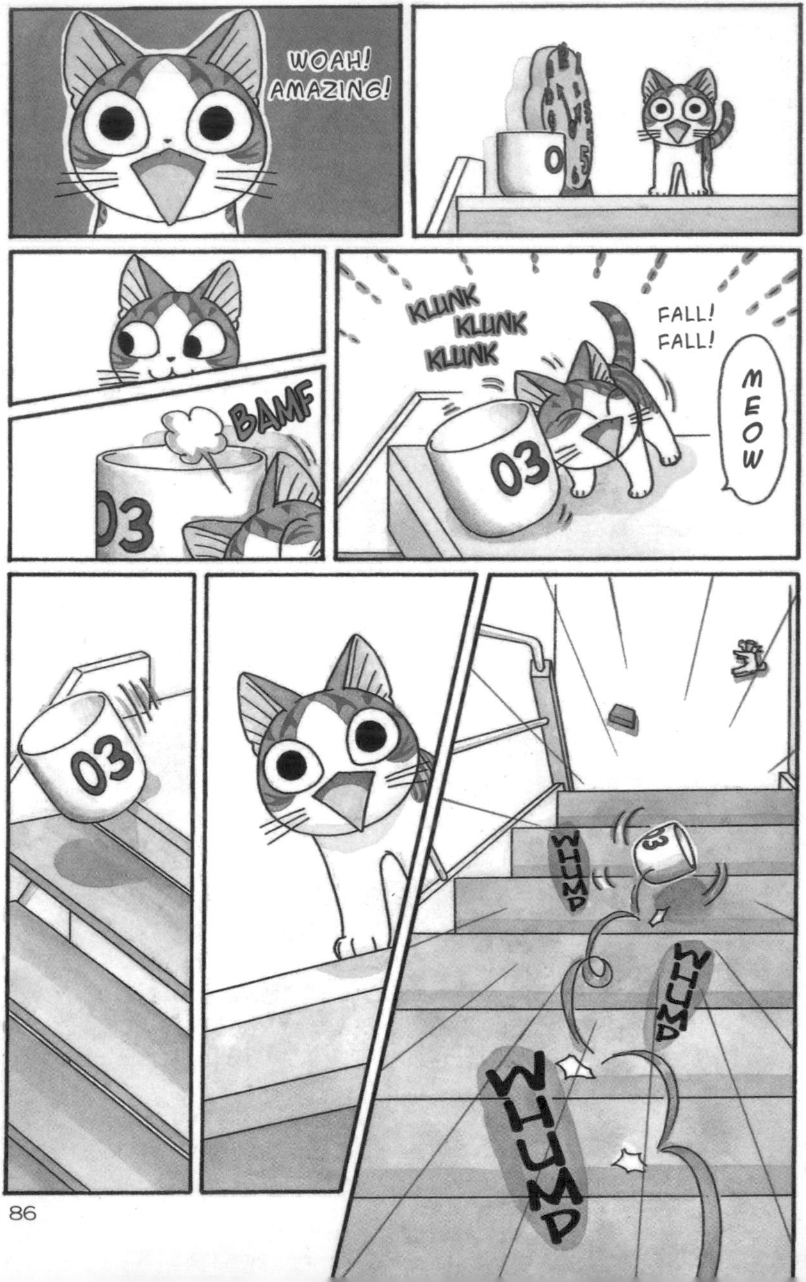
WOAH! AMAZING!
BAMF
03
KLUNK
KLUNK
KLUNK
FALL! FALL!
MEOW
03
03
WHUMP
03
WHUMP
WHUMP

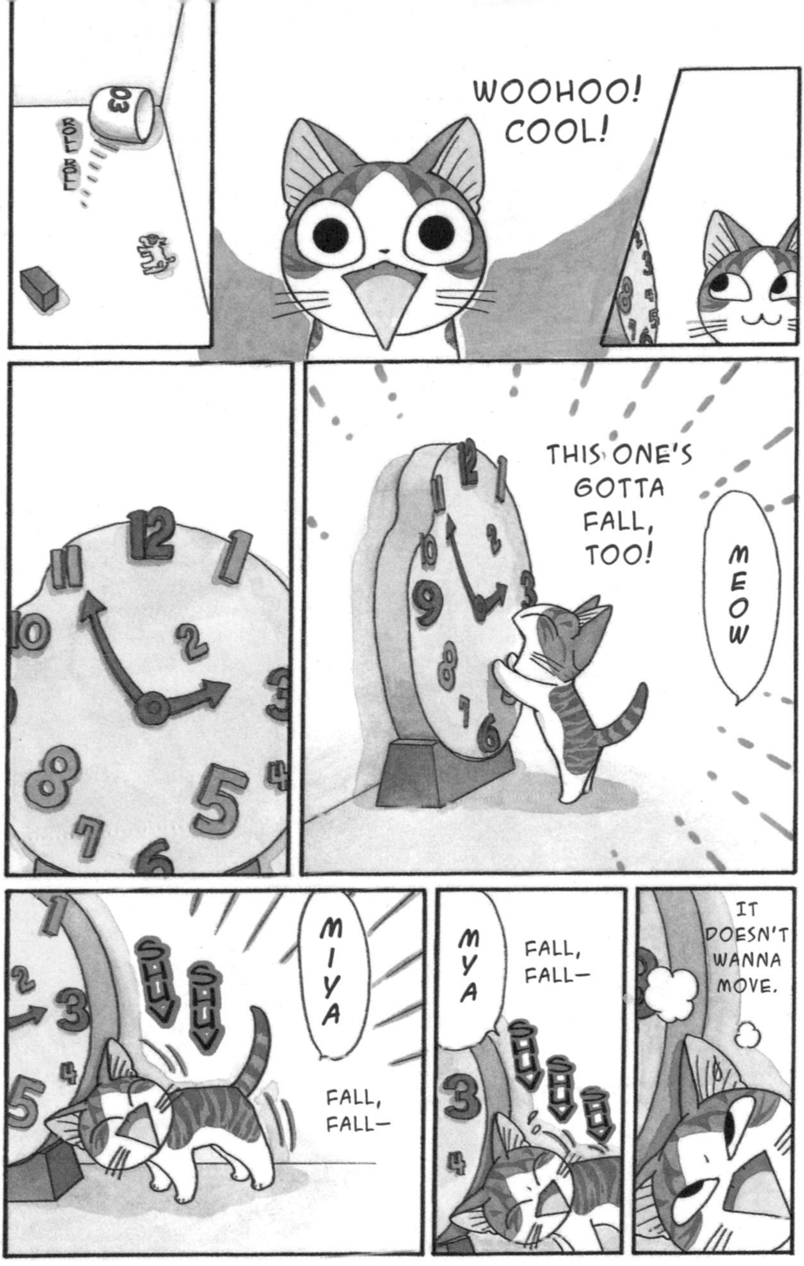
ROLL ROLL
WOOHOO! COOL!
THIS ONE'S GOTTA FALL, TOO!
MEOW
SHU SHU
MIYA
FALL, FALL–
MYA
FALL, FALL–
SHU SHU SHU
IT DOESN'T WANNA MOVE.

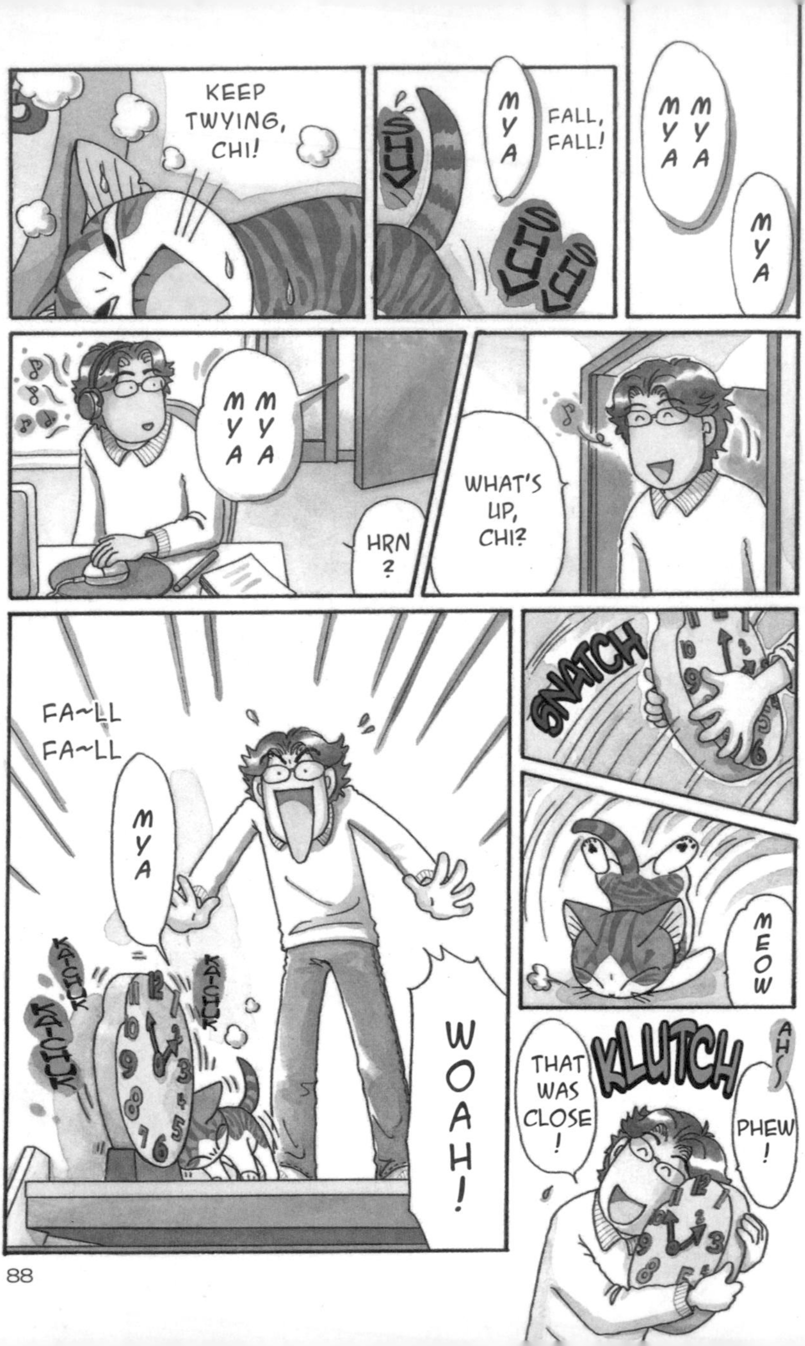
KEEP TWYING, CHI!
SHU
MYA
FALL, FALL!
SHU
SHU
MYA MYA
MYA
MYA MYA
HRN?
WHAT'S UP, CHI?
SNATCH
FA~LL FA~LL
MYA
KA-CHUK
KA-CHUK
KA-CHUK
WOAH!
MEOW
KLUTCH
AH~
THAT WAS CLOSE!
PHEW!

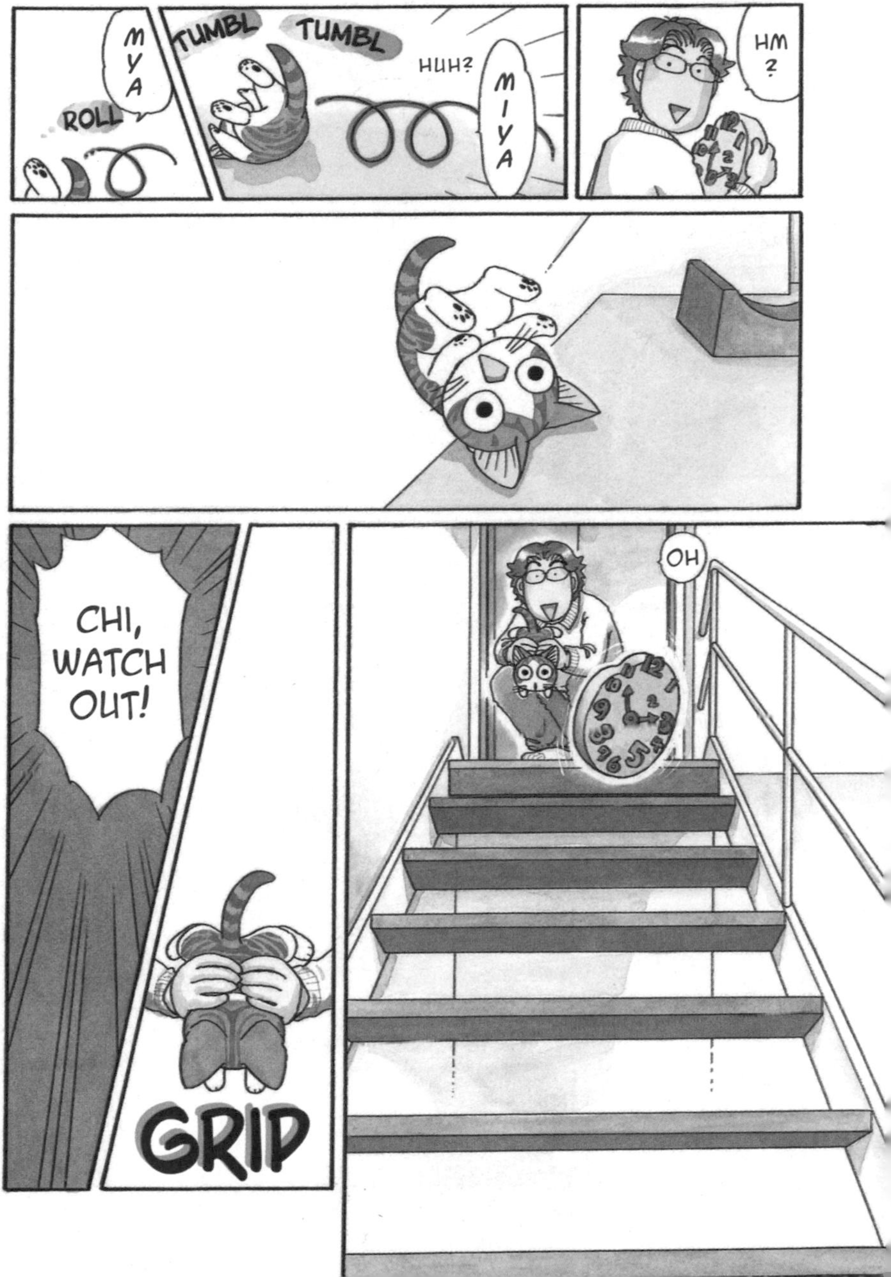
MYA
ROLL
TUMBL
TUMBL
HUH?
MIYA
HM?
CHI, WATCH OUT!
GRIP
OH

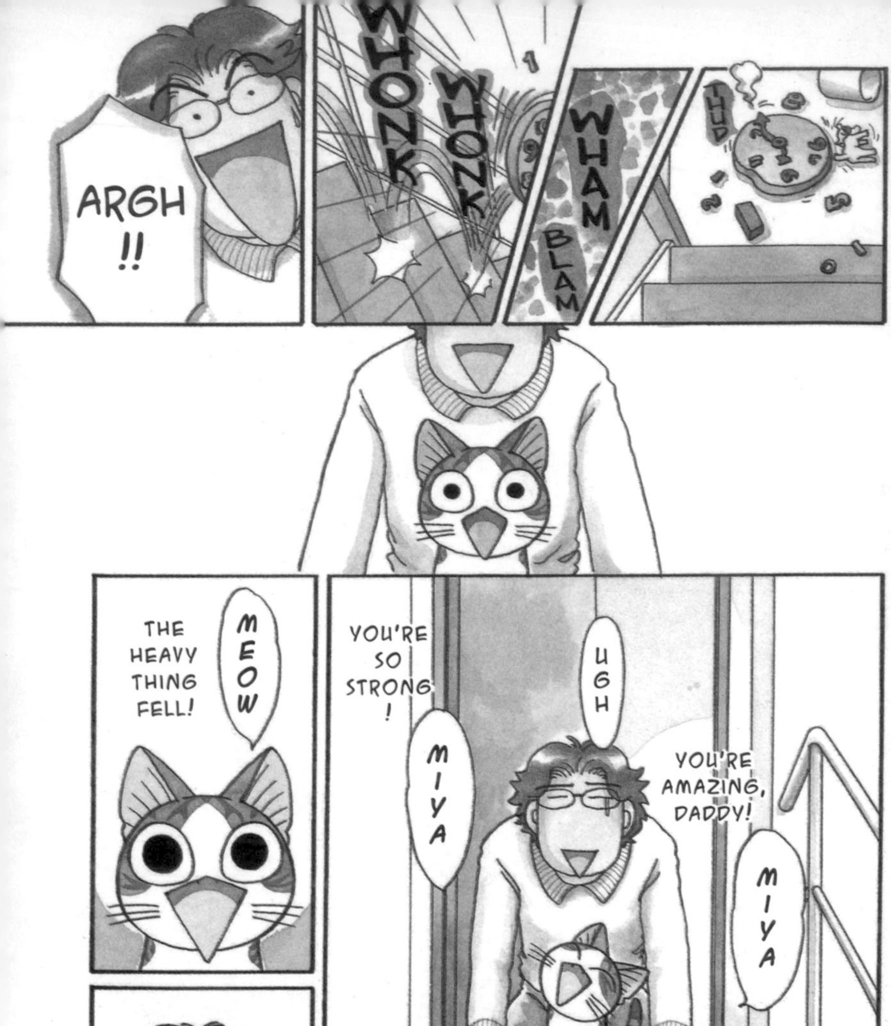
ARGH!!
WHONK
WHONK
WHAM
BLAM
THUD
THE HEAVY THING FELL!
MEOW
YOU'RE SO STRONG!
MIYA
UGH
YOU'RE AMAZING, DADDY!
MIYA



**the end**

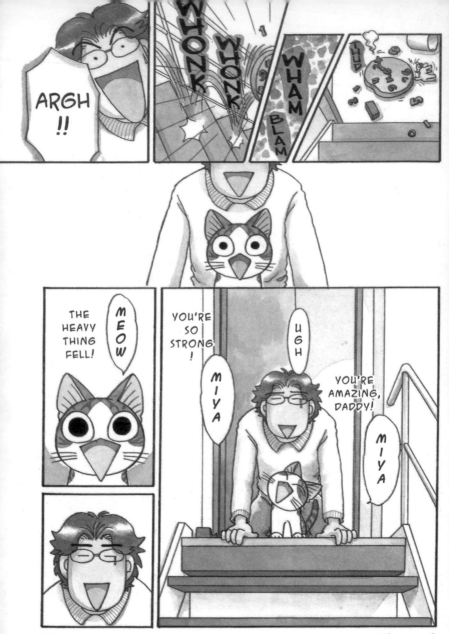

# homemade 104: a cat peeks

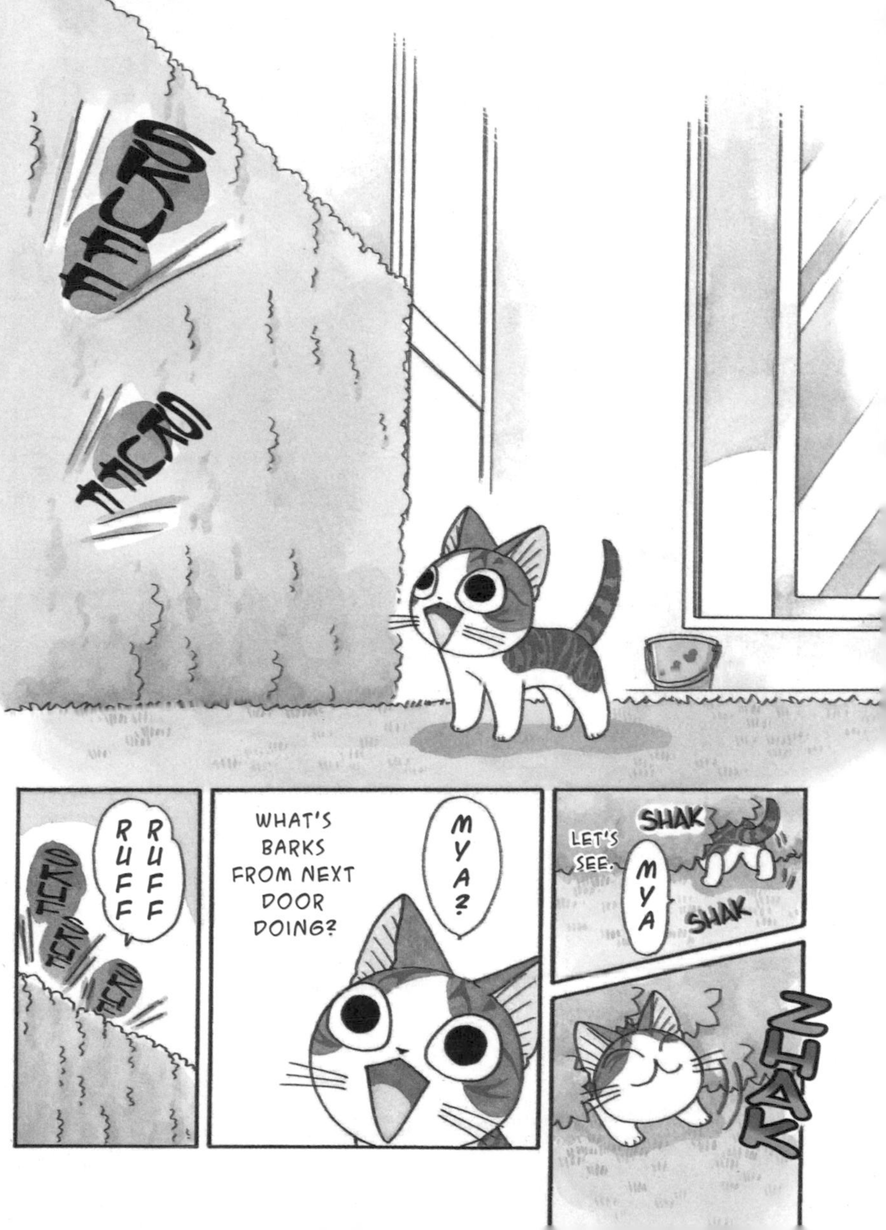
RUFF RUFF
WHAT'S BARKS FROM NEXT DOOR DOING?
MYA?
LET'S SEE.
SHAK
MYA
SHAK
ZHAK

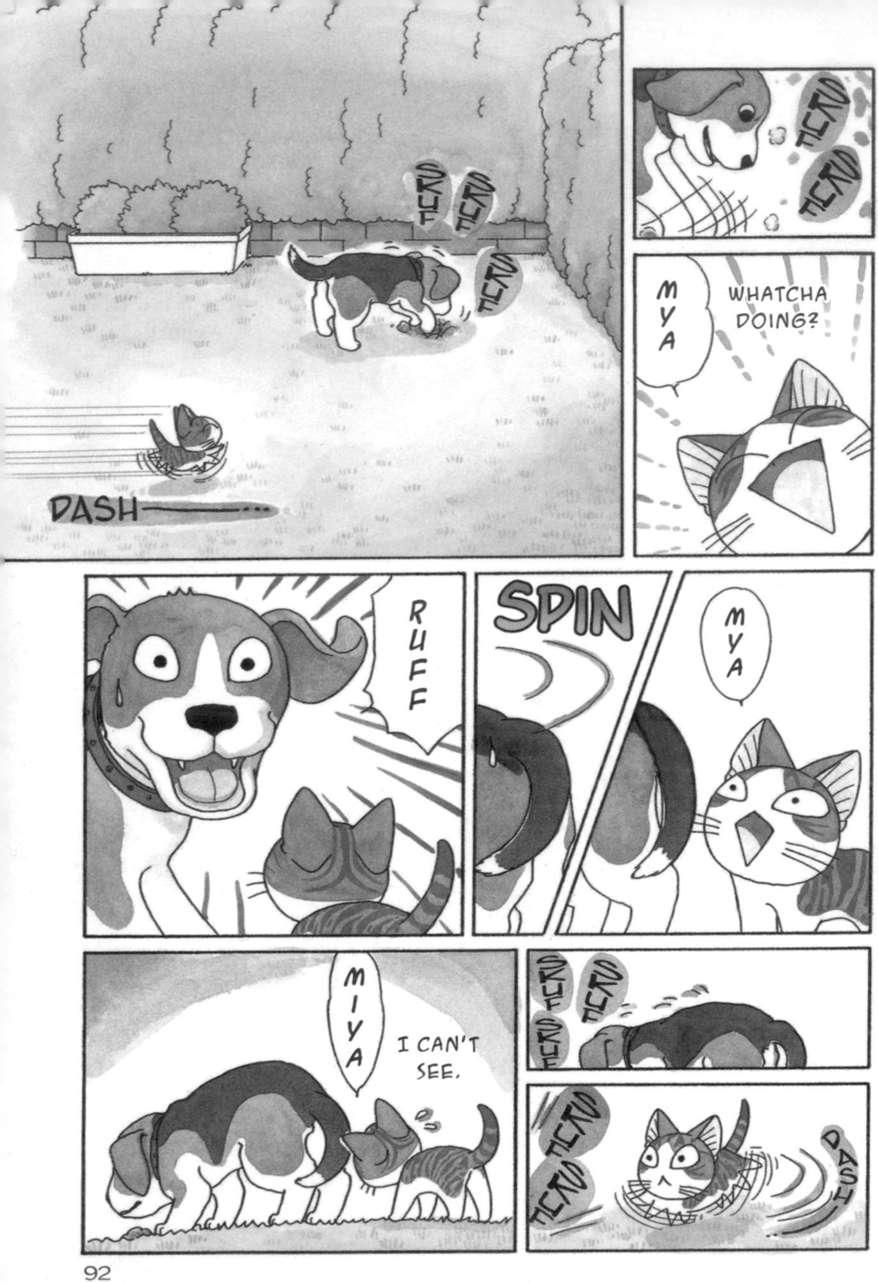
SCRUF
SCRUF
SCRUF
DASH
SCRUF
SCRUF
MYA
WHATCHA DOING?
RUFF
SPIN
MYA
MIYA
I CAN'T SEE.
SCRUF
SCRUF
SCRUF
SCRUF
SCRUF
DASH

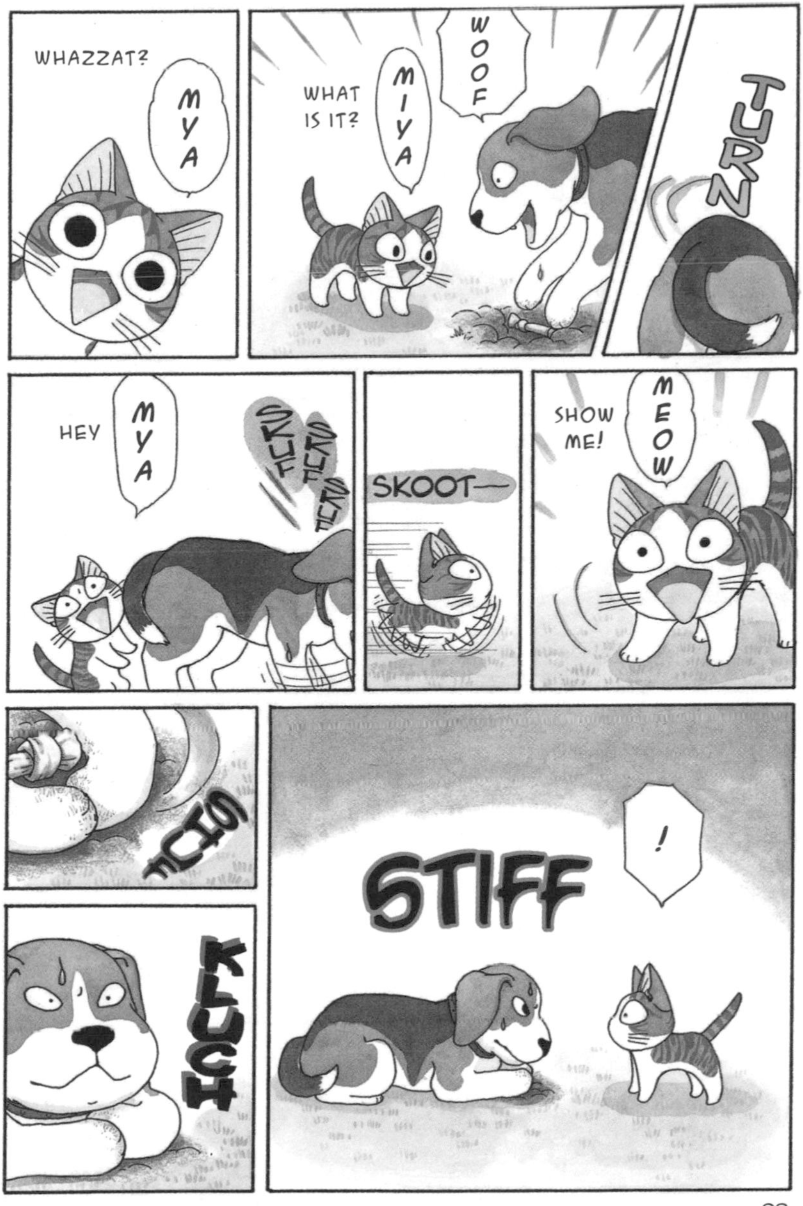
WHAZZAT?
MYA
WHAT IS IT?
MIYA
WOOF
TURN
HEY
MYA
SKUF SKUF SKUF
SKOOT—
SHOW ME!
MEOW
KLUCH
!
STIFF

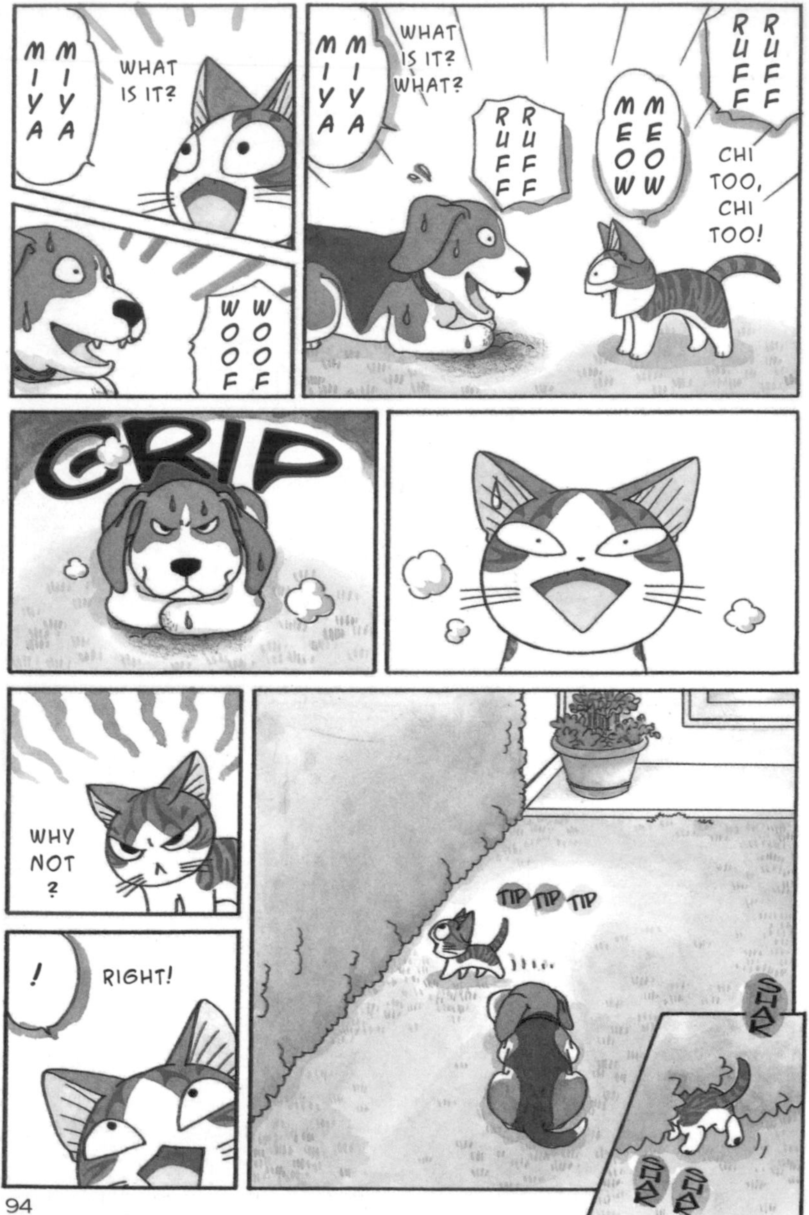
MIYA MIYA
WHAT IS IT?
WOOF WOOF
MIYA MIYA
WHAT IS IT? WHAT?
RUFF RUFF
MEOW MEOW
RUFF RUFF
CHI TOO, CHI TOO!
GRIP
WHY NOT ?
!
RIGHT!
TIP TIP TIP
SHAR
SHAR SHAR

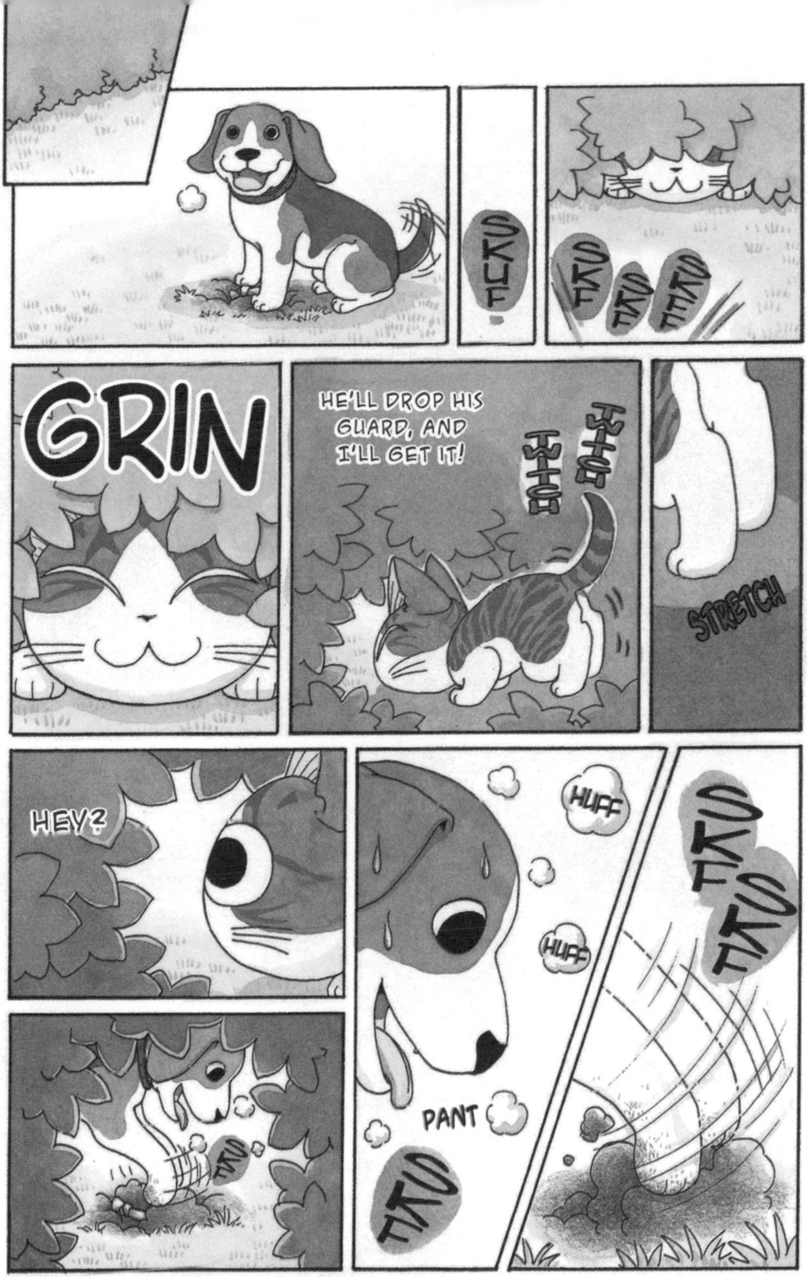
SKUF
SKF SKF SKFF
GRIN
HE'LL DROP HIS GUARD, AND I'LL GET IT!
TWITCH TWITCH
STRETCH
HEY?
HUFF
HUFF
PANT
TKUS
SKF SKF TKU TKU
TKUS

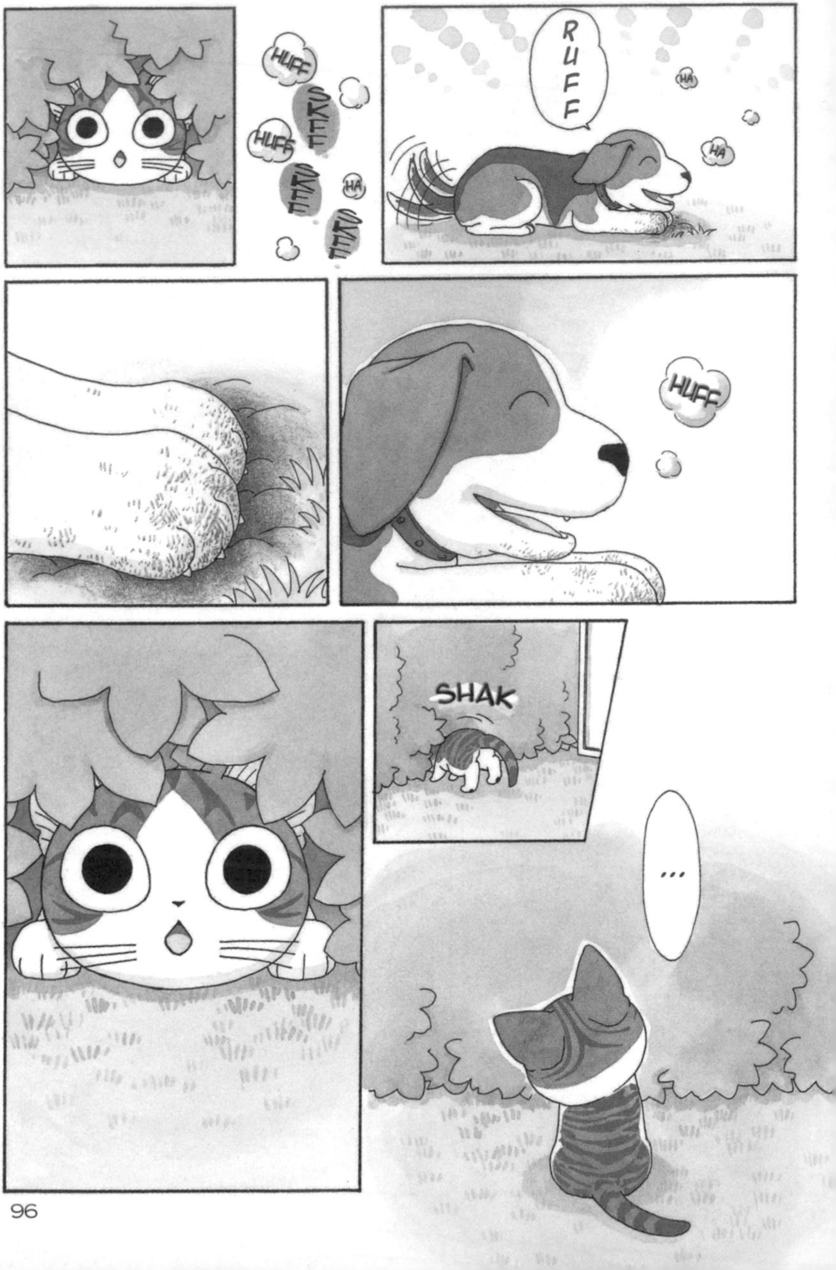
HUFF
SKFF
HUFF
SKFF
HA
SKFF
RUFF
HA
HA
HUFF
SHAK
...

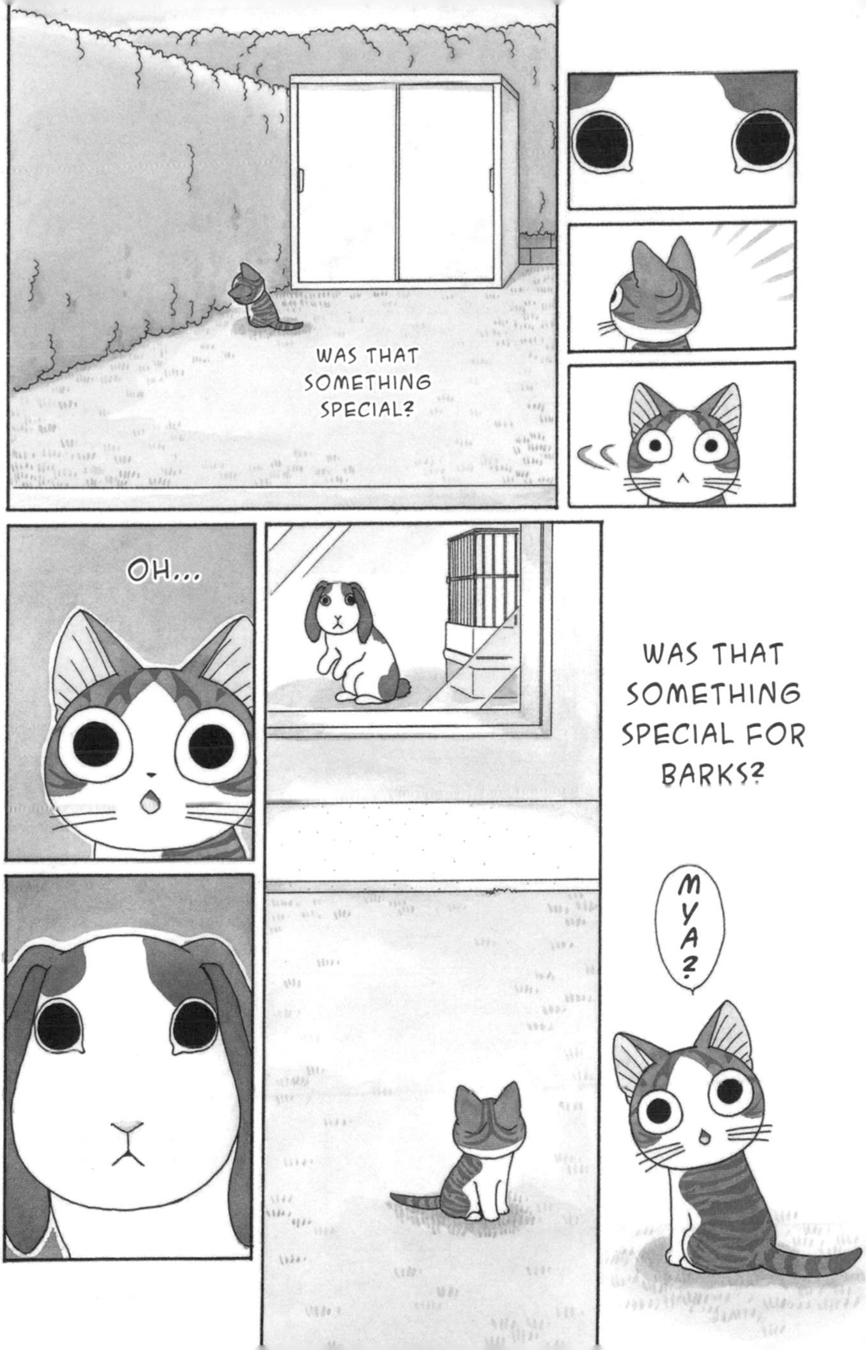
WAS THAT SOMETHING SPECIAL?
OH...
WAS THAT SOMETHING SPECIAL FOR BARKS?
MYA?

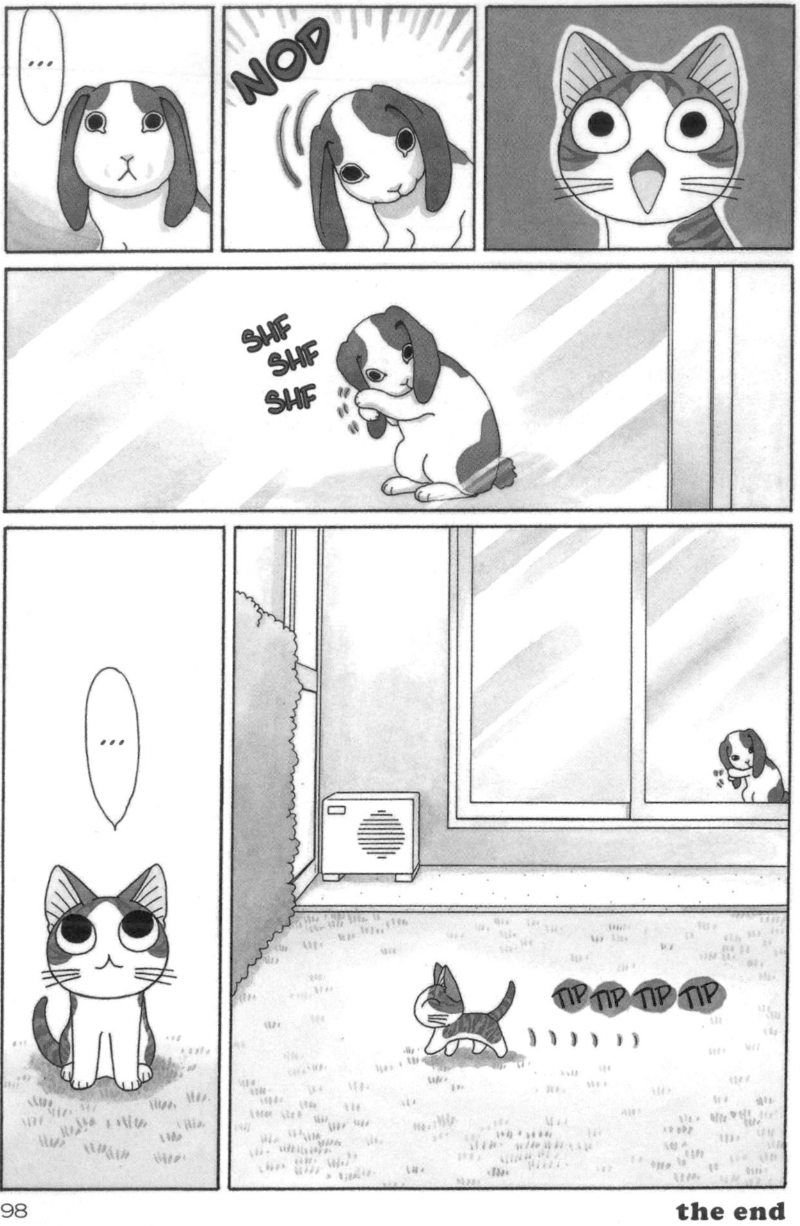
...
NOD
SHF
SHF
SHF
...
TIP TIP TIP TIP



**the end**

## homemade 105: a cat opens her heart

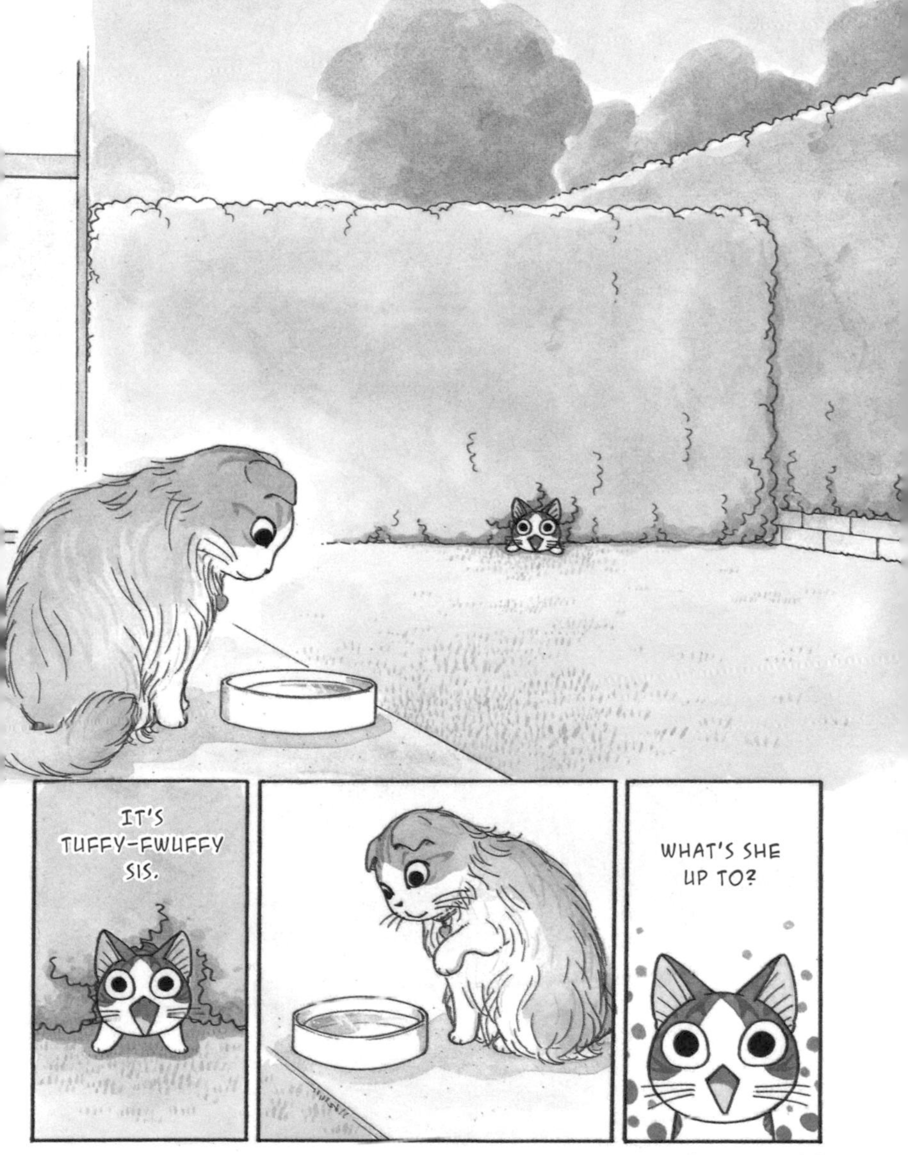
IT'S TUFFY-FWUFFY SIS.
WHAT'S SHE UP TO?

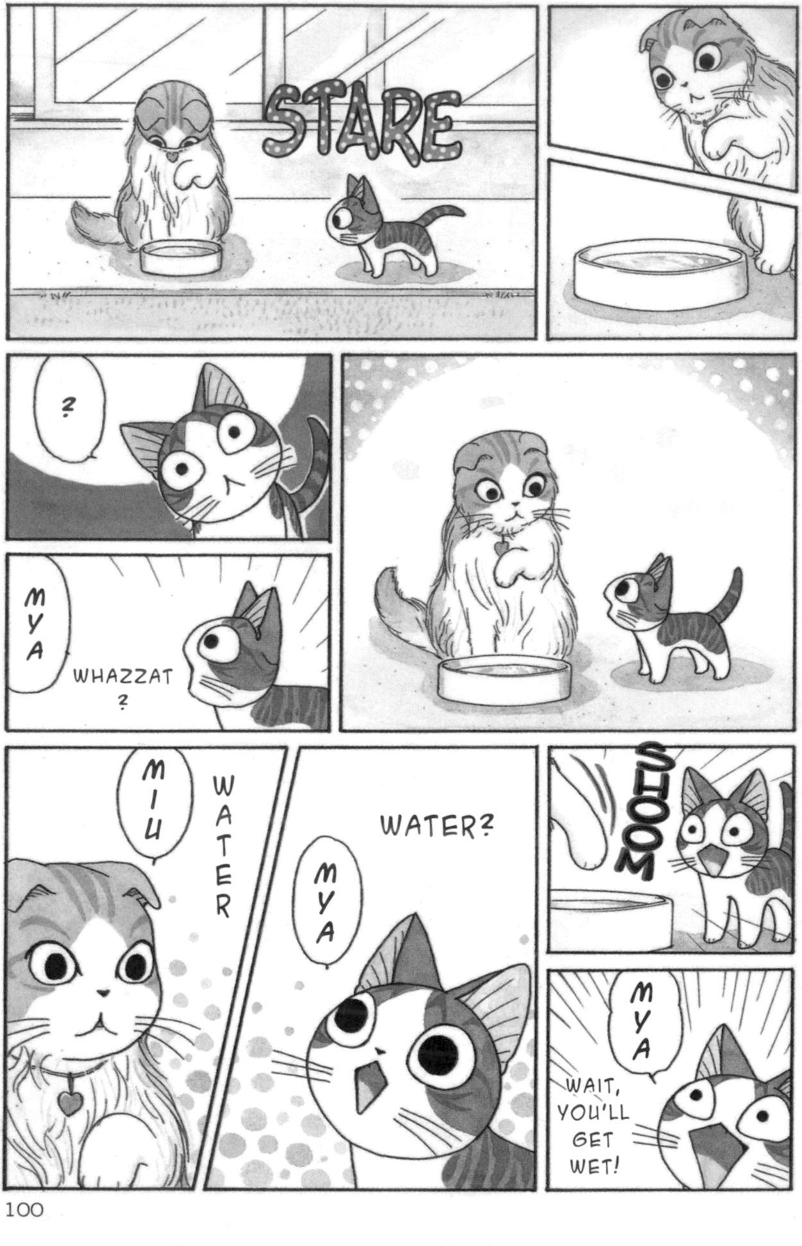
STARE
?
MYA
WHAZZAT?
MIU
WATER
MYA
WATER?
SHOOM
MYA
WAIT, YOU'LL GET WET!

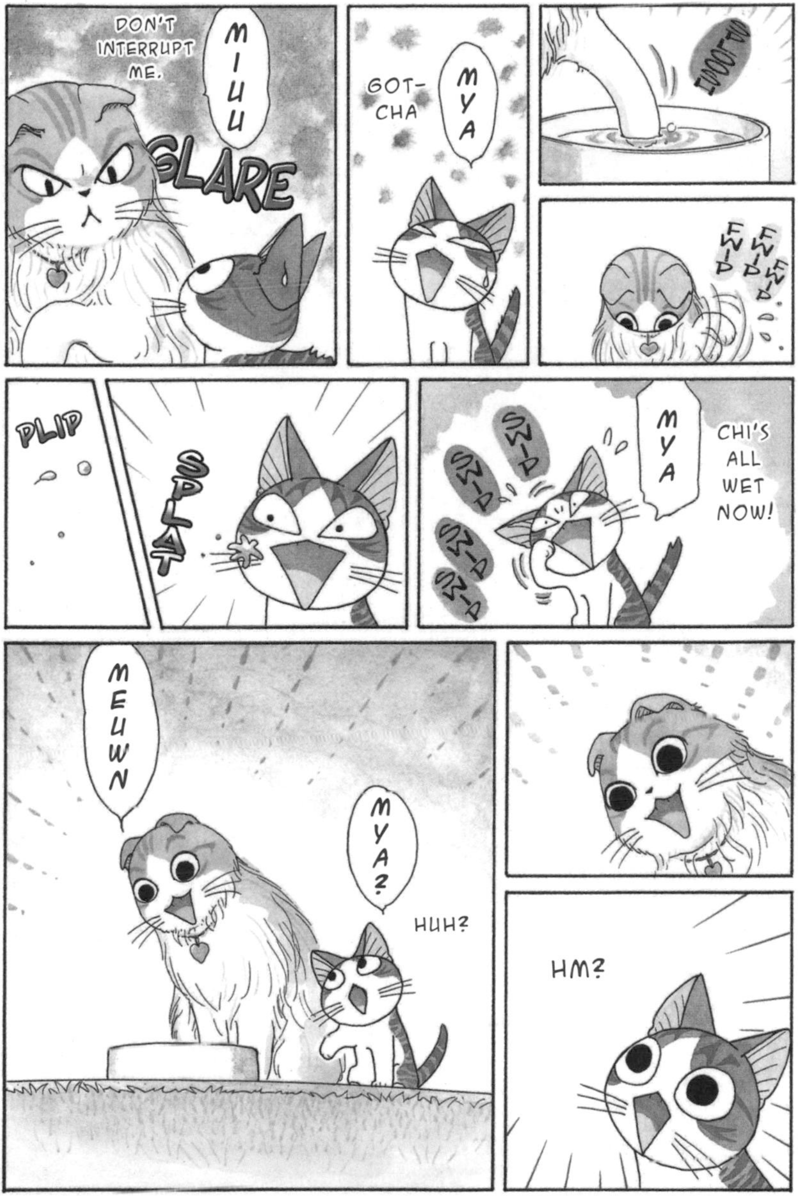
DON'T INTERRUPT ME.
MIUU
GLARE
GOT-CHA
MYA
GLOOP!
FWIP FWIP FWIP
PLIP
SPLAT
SWIP SWIP SWIP SWIP
MYA
CHI'S ALL WET NOW!
MEUWN
MYA?
HUH?
HM?

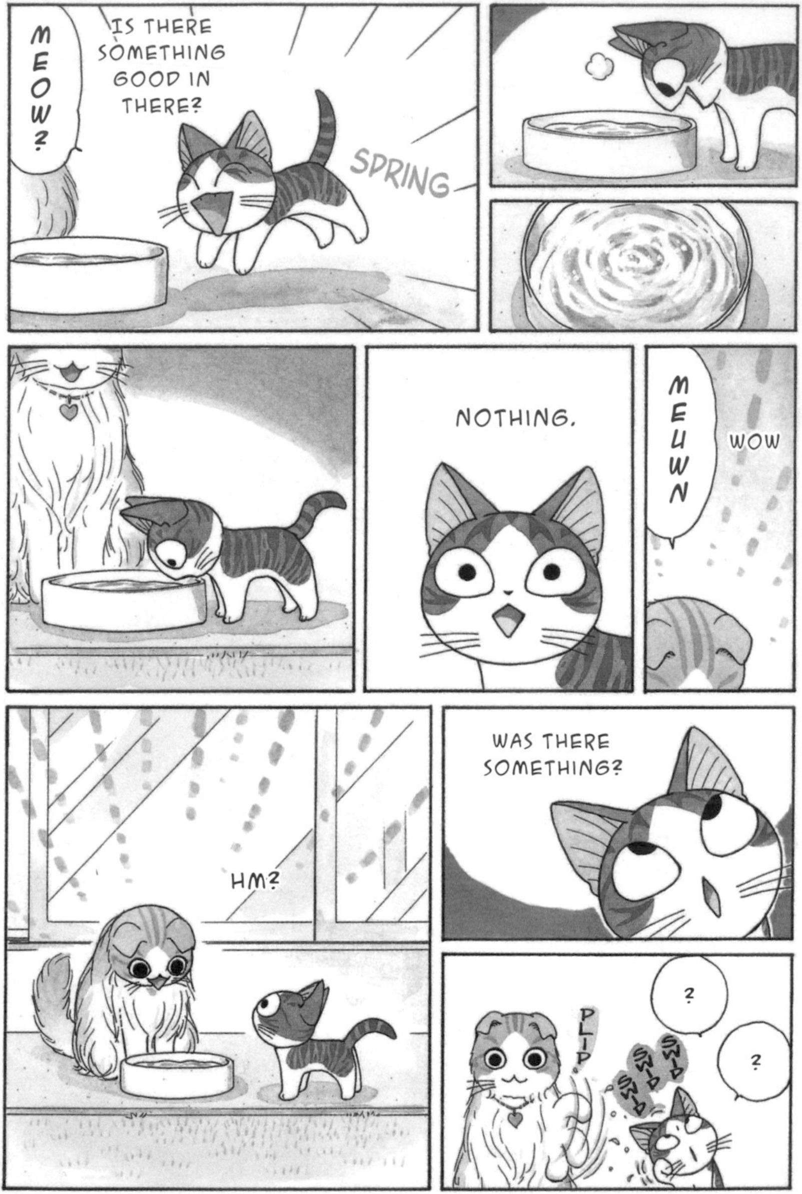
MEOW?
IS THERE SOMETHING GOOD IN THERE?
SPRING
NOTHING.
MEUWN
WOW
HM?
WAS THERE SOMETHING?
PLIP
SWIP SWIP
SWIP SWIP
?
?

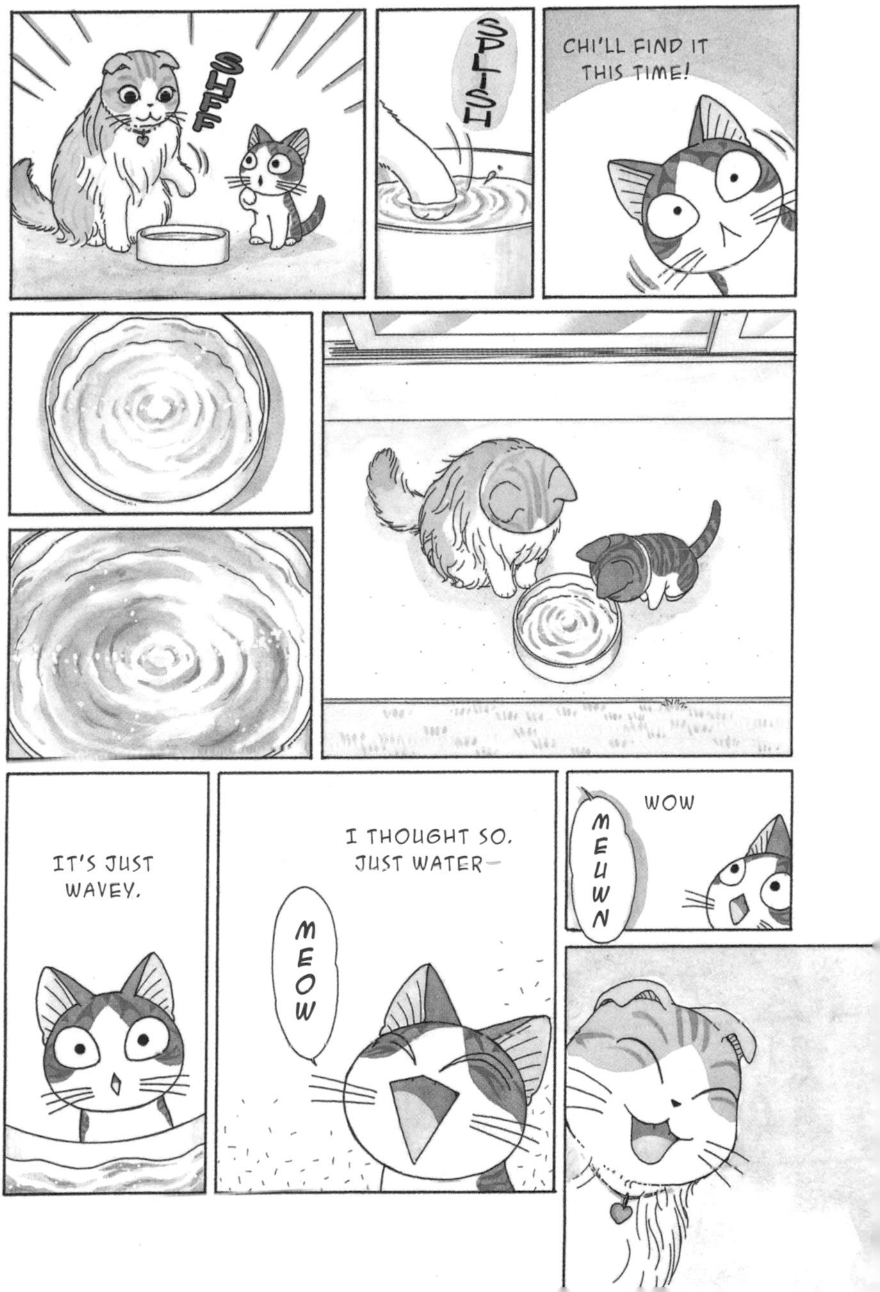
SHFF
SPLISH
CHI'LL FIND IT THIS TIME!
IT'S JUST WAVEY.
I THOUGHT SO. JUST WATER—
MEOW
WOW
MEUWN

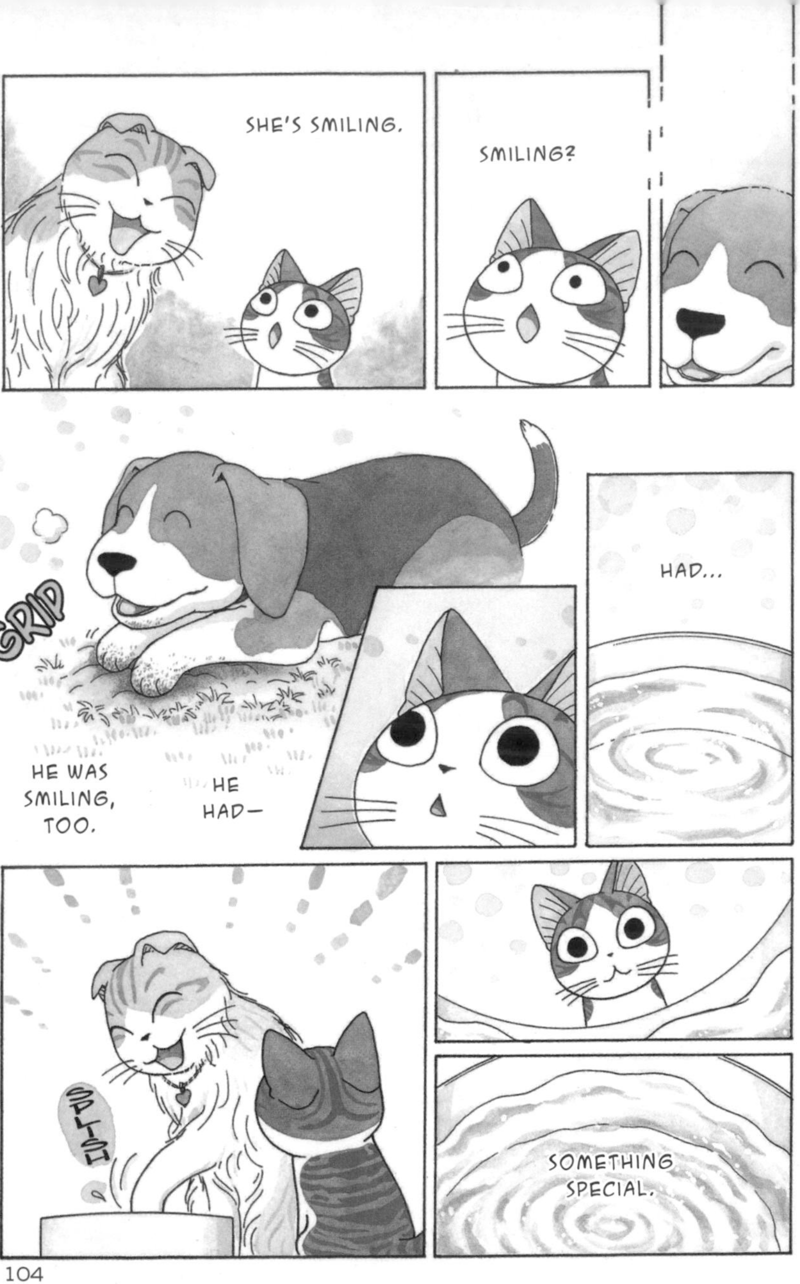
SHE'S SMILING.
SMILING?
GRIP
HE WAS SMILING, TOO.
HE HAD—
HAD...
SPLISH
SOMETHING SPECIAL.

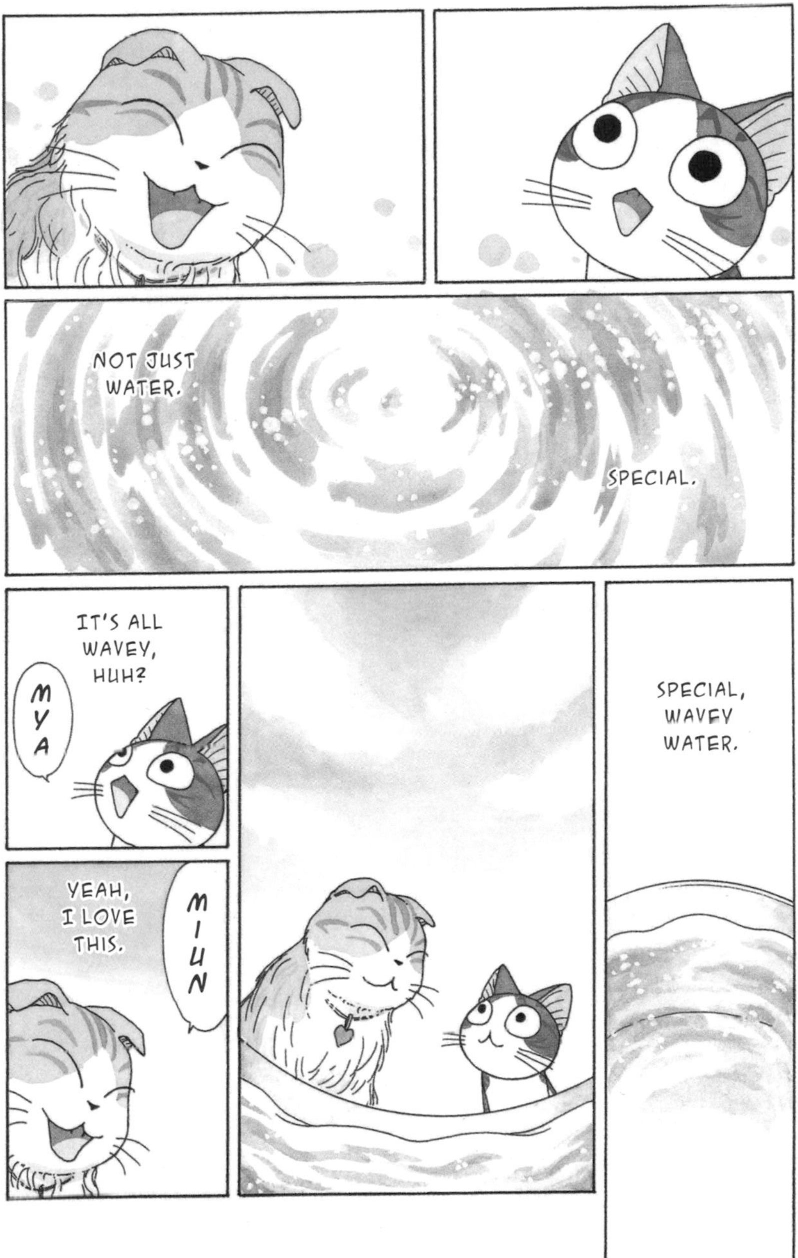
NOT JUST WATER.
SPECIAL.
IT'S ALL WAVEY, HUH?
MYA
YEAH, I LOVE THIS.
MIUN
SPECIAL, WAVEY WATER.

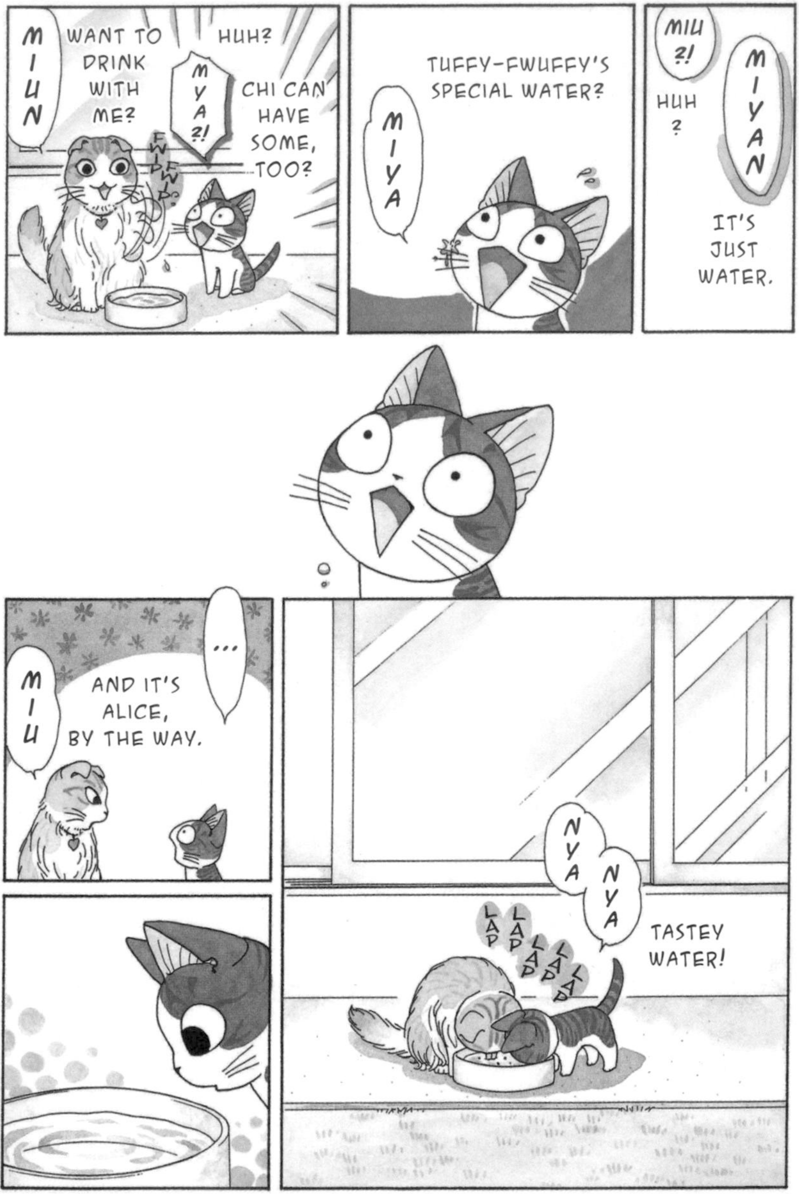
MIUN
WANT TO DRINK WITH ME?
HUH?
MYA?!
FWIP FWIP
CHI CAN HAVE SOME, TOO?
TUFFY-FWUFFY'S SPECIAL WATER?
MIYA
MIU?!
HUH?
MIYAN
IT'S JUST WATER.
MIU
AND IT'S ALICE, BY THE WAY.
...
NYA
NYA
LAP LAP LAP LAP LAP
TASTEY WATER!



**the end**

# homemade 106: a cat is copied

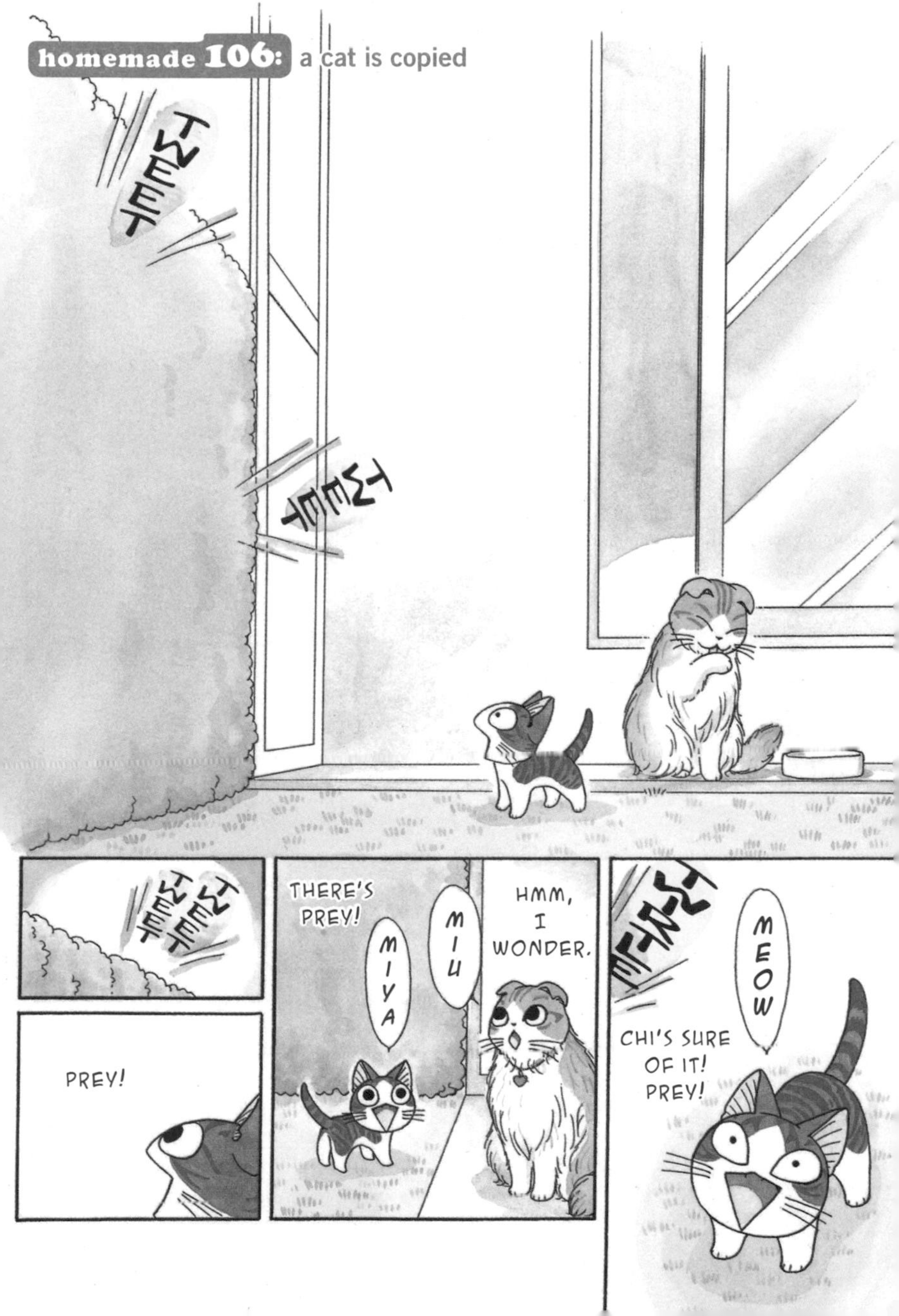
TWEET
TWEET
TWEET
TWEET
PREY!
THERE'S PREY!
MIYA
MIU
HMM, I WONDER.
TWEET
MEOW
CHI'S SURE OF IT! PREY!

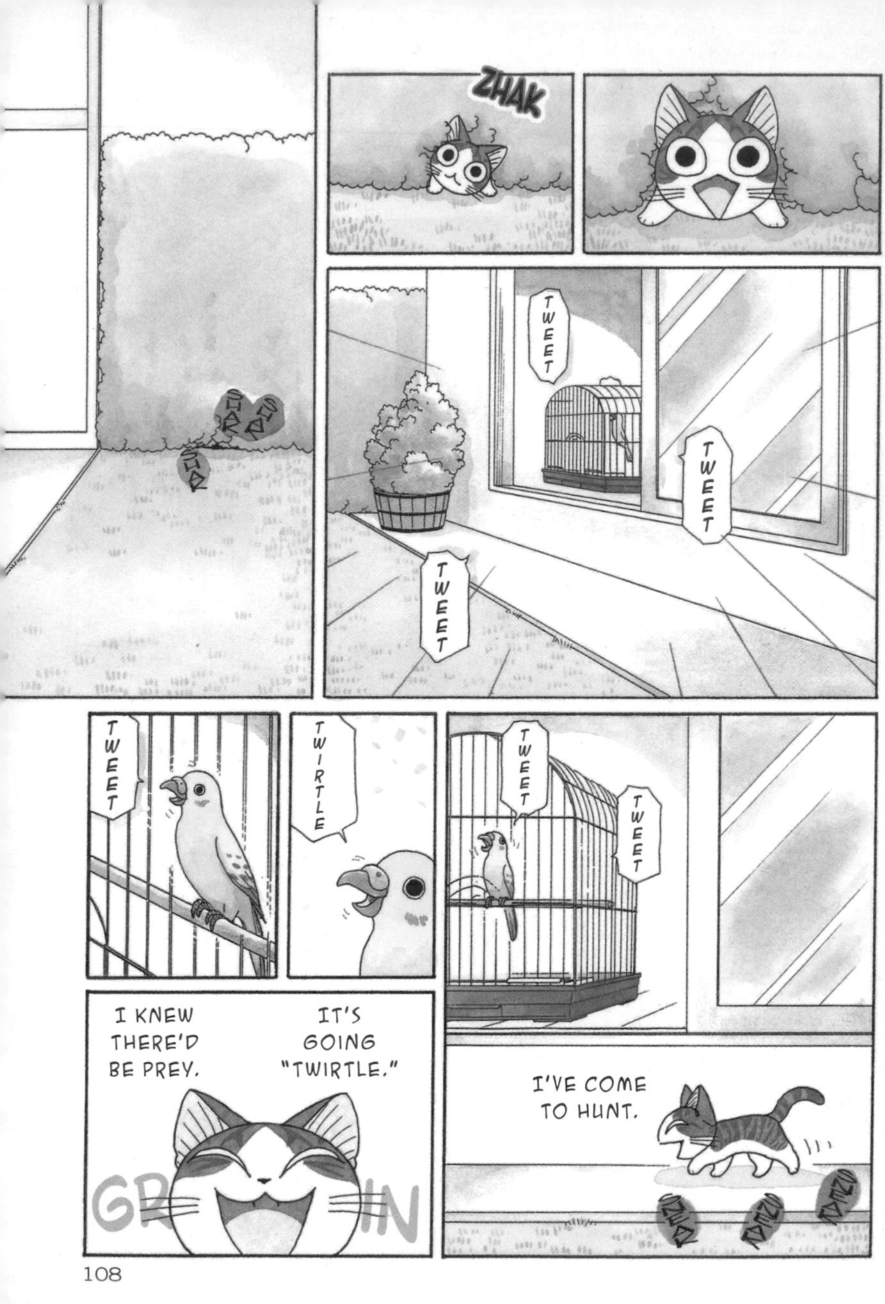
SHAK
SHAK
SHAK
ZHAK
TWEET
TWEET
TWEET
TWEET
TWIRTLE
TWEET
TWEET
I KNEW THERE'D BE PREY.
IT'S GOING "TWIRTLE."
GRIN
I'VE COME TO HUNT.
SNEAK
SNEAK
SNEAK

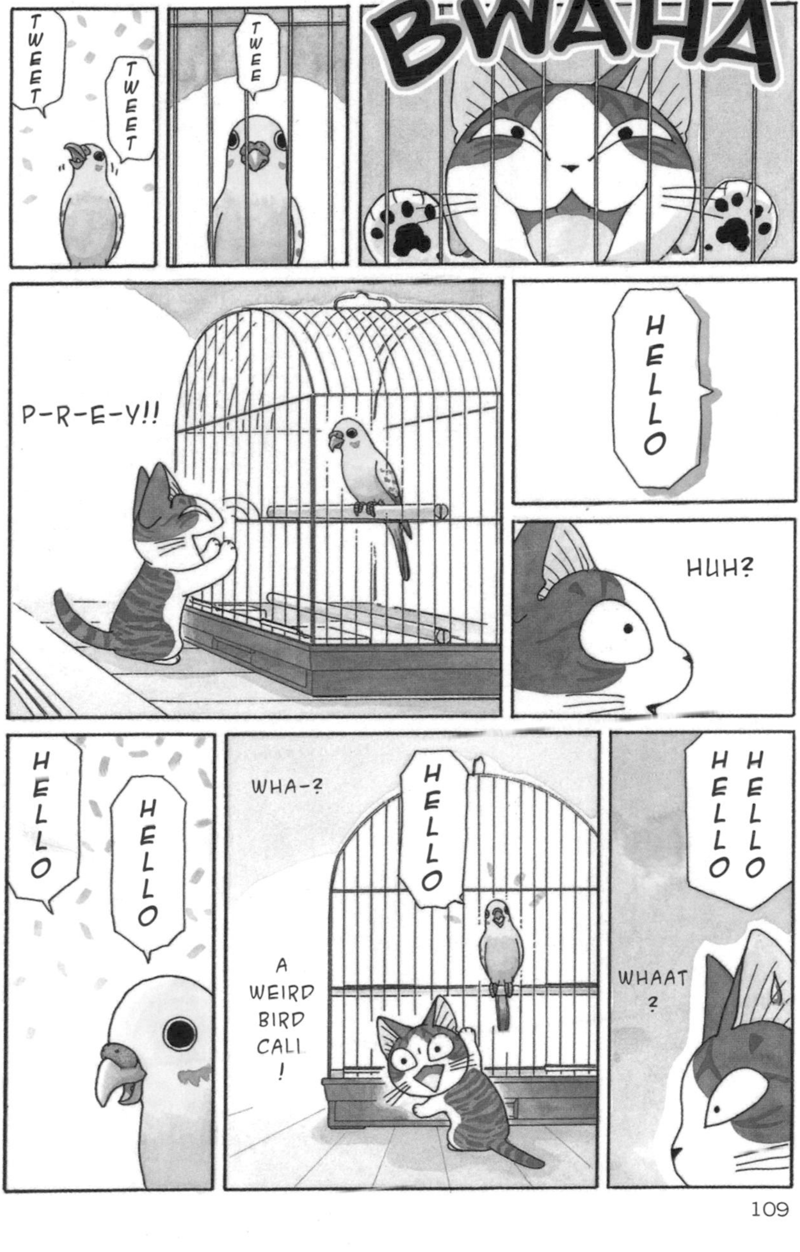
BWAHA
TWEE
TWEET
TWEET
HELLO
HUH?
P-R-E-Y!!
HELLO
HELLO
WHAAT?
HELLO
WHA-?
A WEIRD BIRD CALL!
HELLO
HELLO

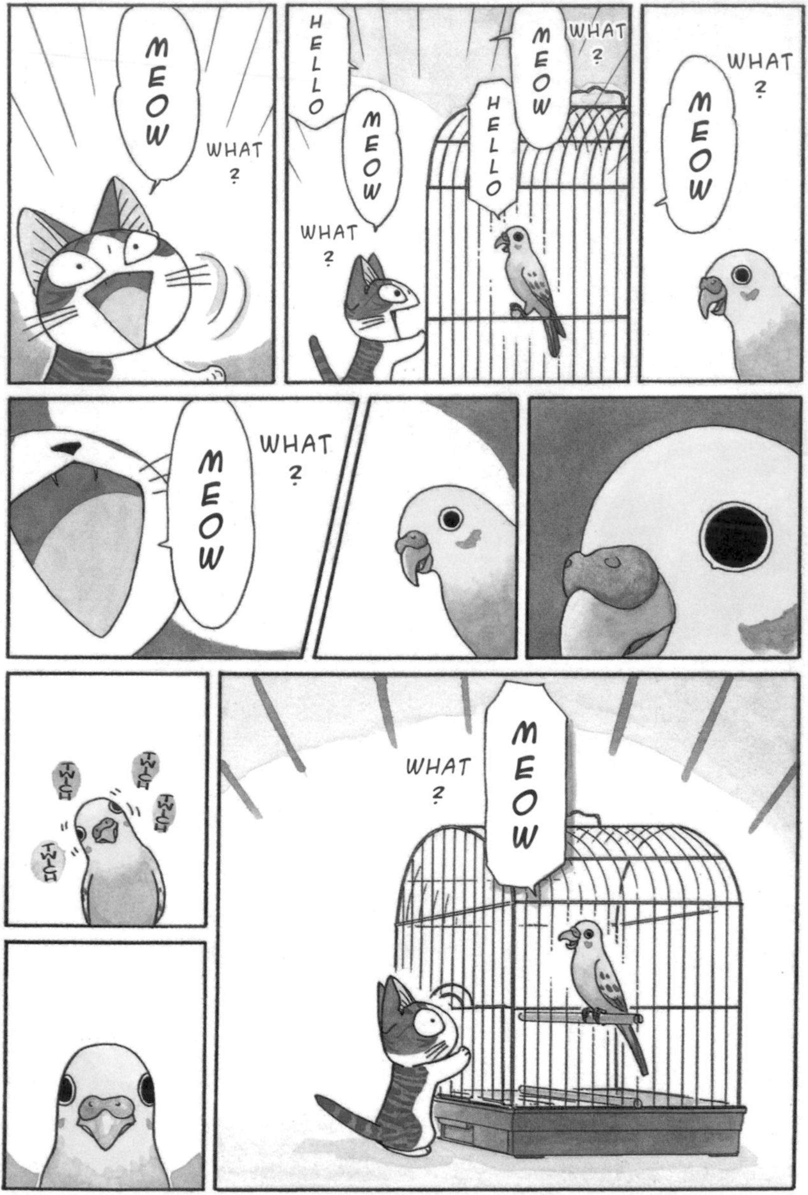
MEOW
WHAT ?
HELLO
MEOW
WHAT ?
HELLO
MEOW
WHAT ?
WHAT ?
MEOW
MEOW
WHAT ?
TWICH
TWICH
TWICH
TWICH
WHAT ?
MEOW

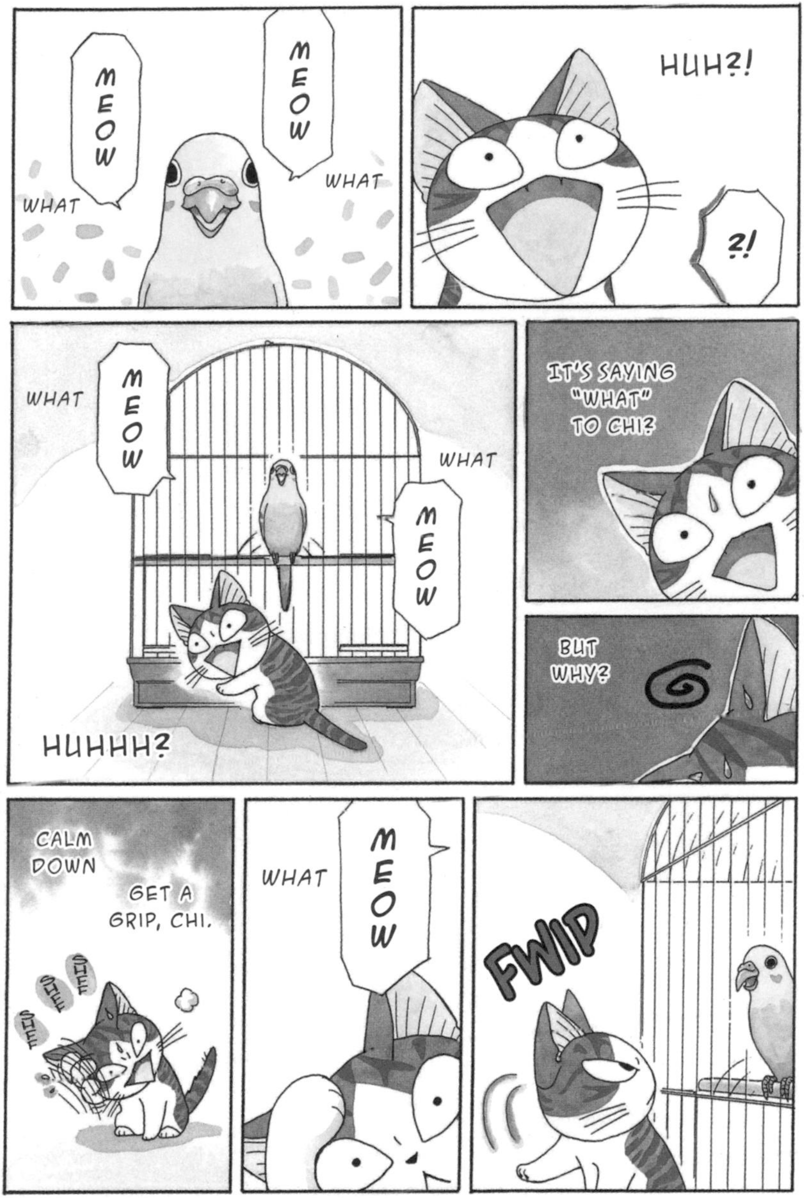

MEOW
WHAT
MEOW
WHAT
HUH?!
?!
WHAT
MEOW
WHAT
MEOW
HUHHH?
IT'S SAYING "WHAT" TO CHI?
BUT WHY?
CALM DOWN
GET A GRIP, CHI.
SHEF
SHEF
SHEF
WHAT
MEOW
FWIP

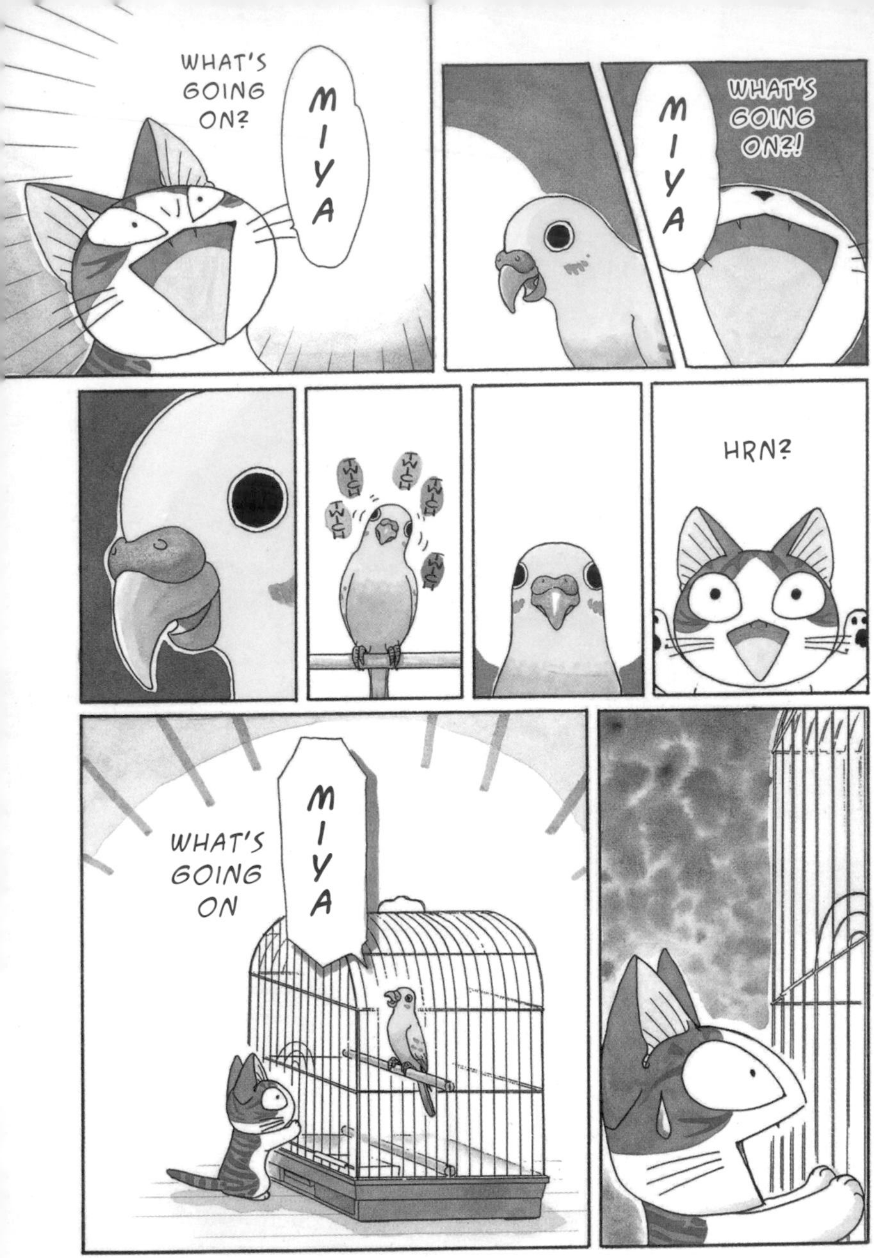
WHAT'S GOING ON?
MIYA
MIYA
WHAT'S GOING ON?!
TWICH
TWICH
TWICH
TWICH
TWICH
HRN?
WHAT'S GOING ON
MIYA

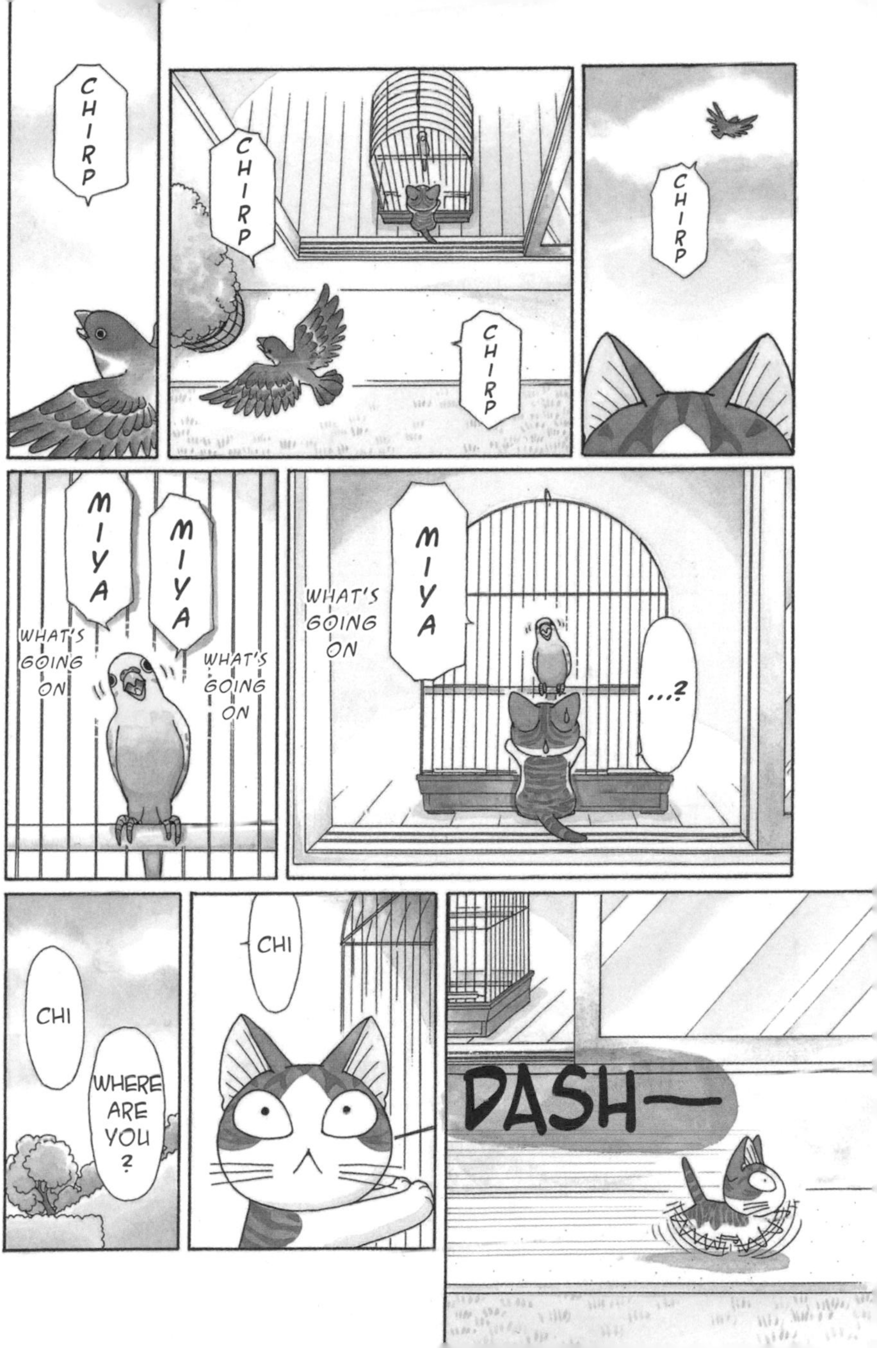
CHIRP
CHIRP
CHIRP
CHIRP
MIYA
MIYA
WHAT'S GOING ON
WHAT'S GOING ON
WHAT'S GOING ON
MIYA
...?
CHI
WHERE ARE YOU?
CHI
DASH—

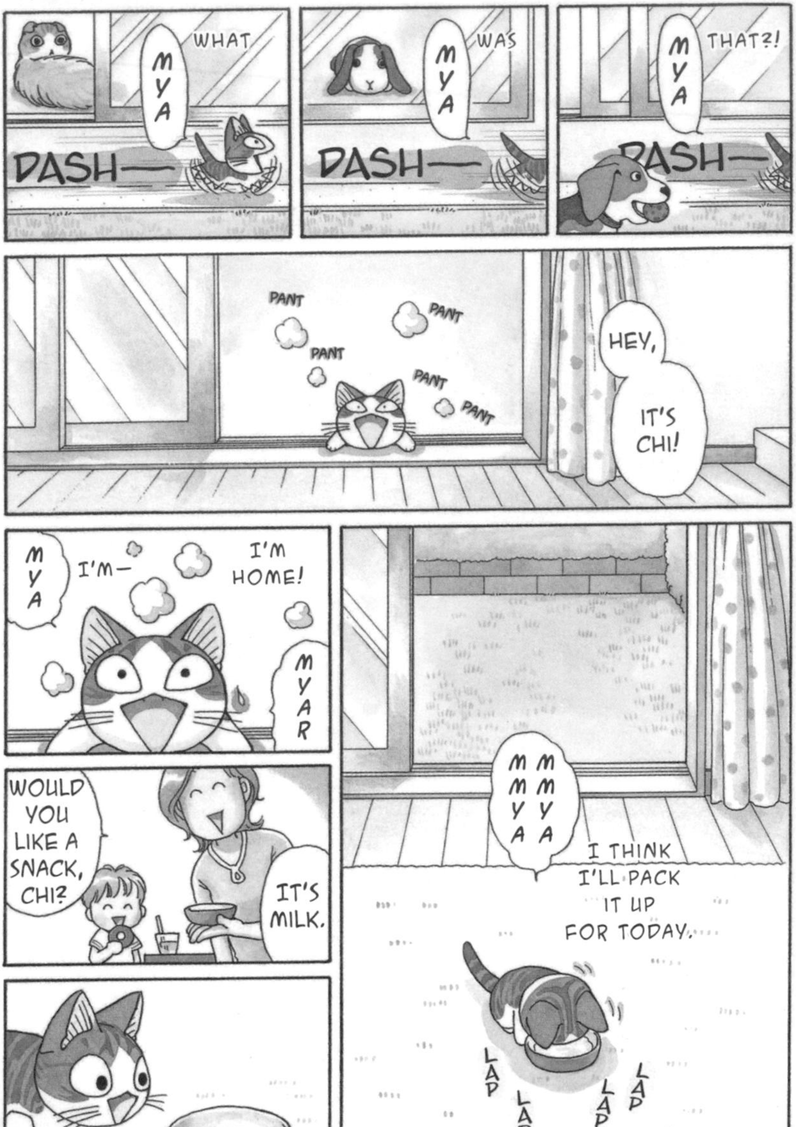
MYA
WHAT
DASH—
MYA
WAS
DASH—
MYA
THAT?!
DASH—
PANT
PANT
PANT
PANT
PANT
HEY,
IT'S CHI!
MYA
I'M—
I'M HOME!
MYAR
WOULD YOU LIKE A SNACK, CHI?
IT'S MILK.
MMYA
MMYA
I THINK I'LL PACK IT UP FOR TODAY.
LAP
LAP
LAP
LAP



**the end**

## homemade 107: a cat accepts

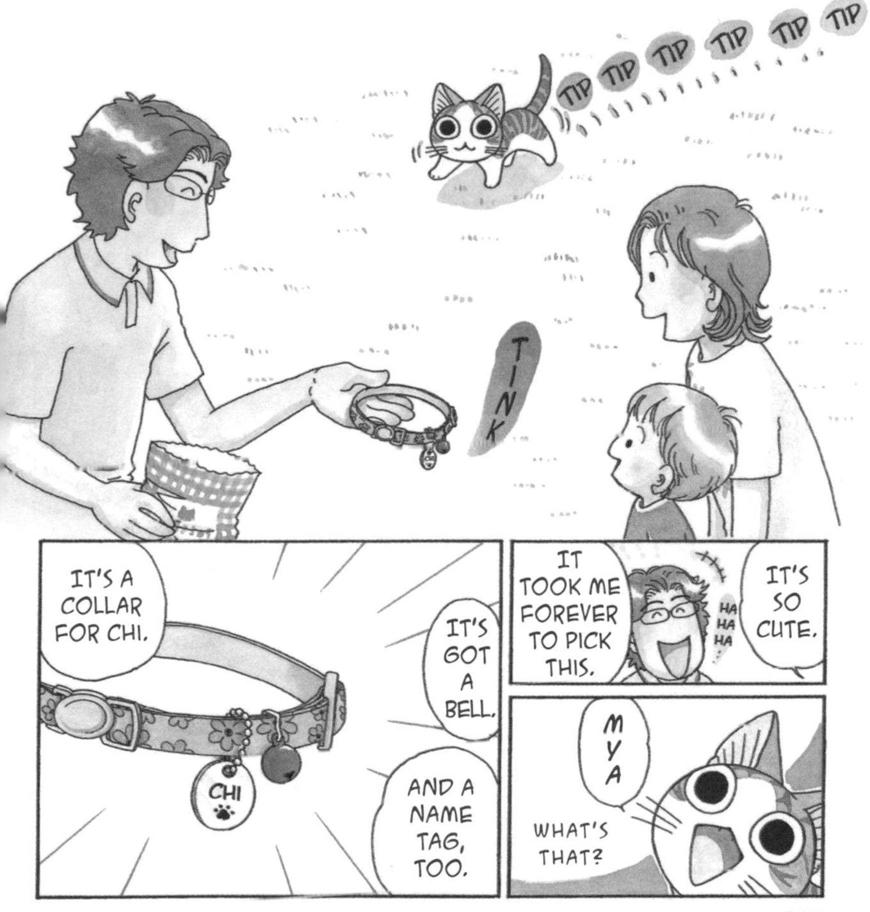
TIP TIP TIP TIP TIP TIP
TINK
IT'S A COLLAR FOR CHI.
IT'S GOT A BELL.
CHI
AND A NAME TAG, TOO.
IT TOOK ME FOREVER TO PICK THIS.
HA HA HA
IT'S SO CUTE.
MYA
WHAT'S THAT?

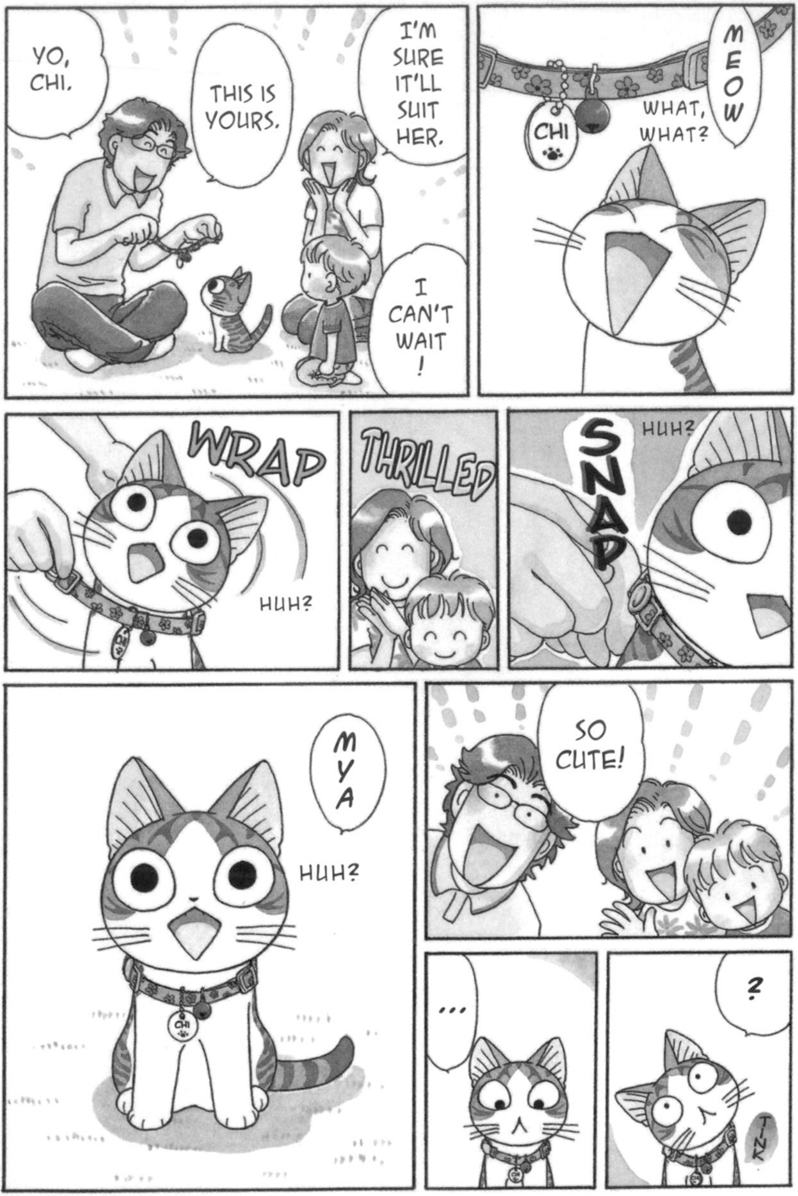
YO, CHI.
THIS IS YOURS.
I'M SURE IT'LL SUIT HER.
I CAN'T WAIT!
MEOW
CHI
WHAT, WHAT?
WRAP
HUH?
THRILLED
SNAP
HUH?
MYA
HUH?
SO CUTE!
...
?
TINK

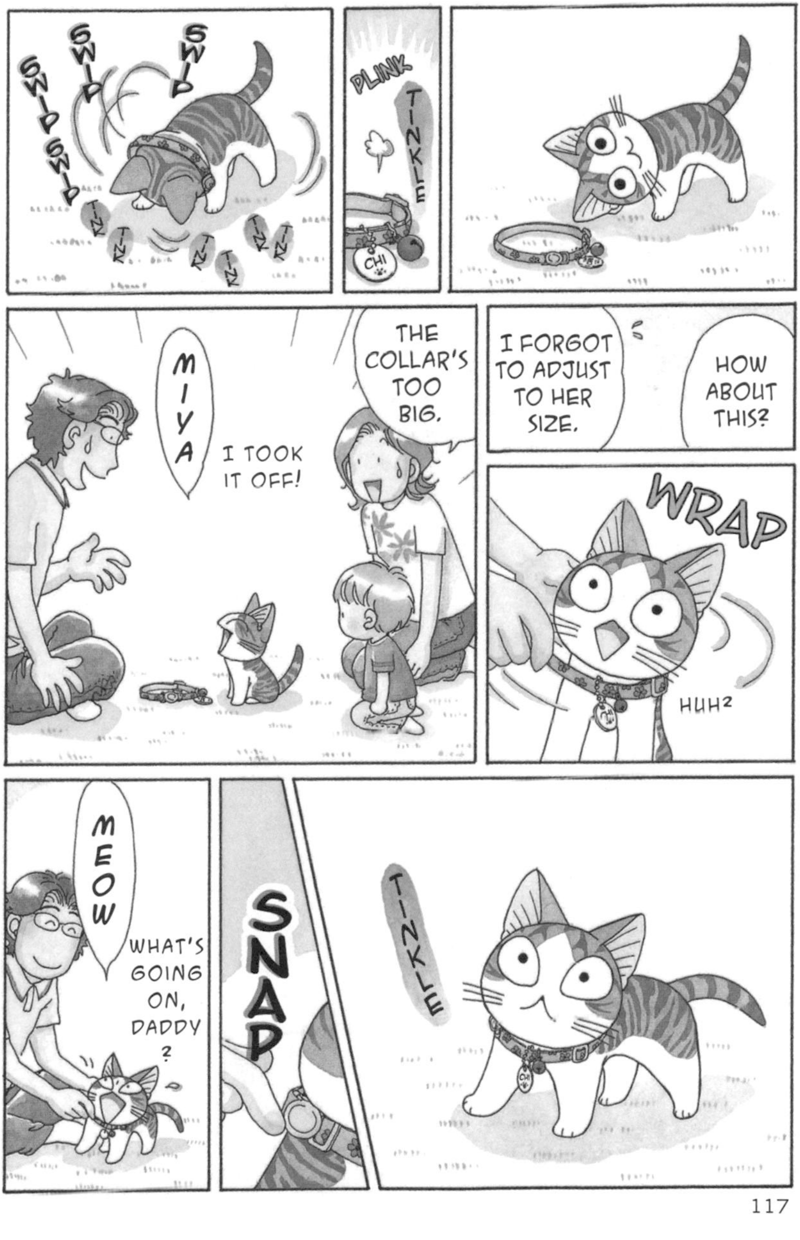
SWIP SWIP
SWIP
SWIP
SWIP
TINK
TINK
TINK
TINK
TINK
TINK
PLINK
TINKLE
CHI
MIYA
I TOOK IT OFF!
THE COLLAR'S TOO BIG.
I FORGOT TO ADJUST TO HER SIZE.
HOW ABOUT THIS?
WRAP
HUH?
MEOW
WHAT'S GOING ON, DADDY?
SNAP
TINKLE

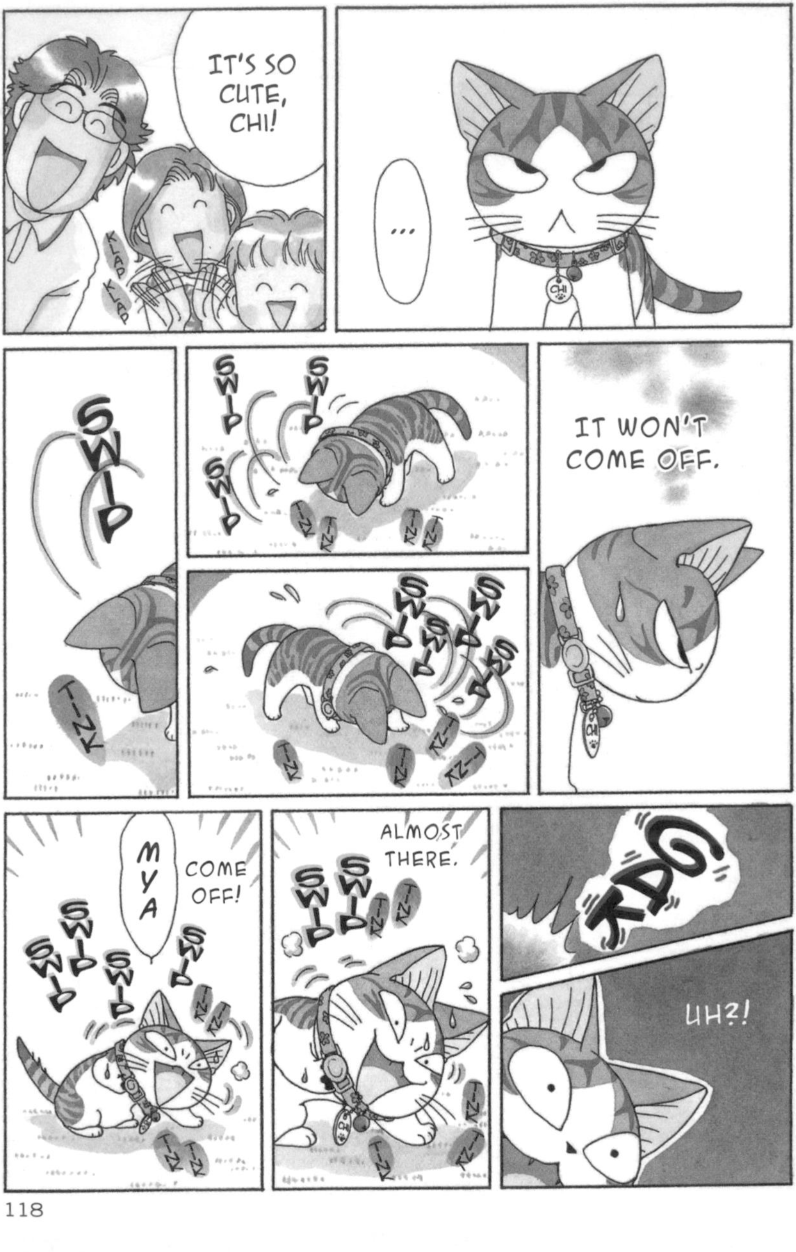
IT'S SO CUTE, CHI!
KLAP KLAP
...
CHI
SWIP
TINK
SWIP SWIP SWIP
TINK TINK TINK TINK
SWIP SWIP SWIP SWIP
TINK TINK
TZZ-- TZZ--
IT WON'T COME OFF.
CHI
MYA
COME OFF!
SWIP SWIP SWIP SWIP
TINK TINK
TINK TINK
ALMOST THERE.
SWIP SWIP
TINK TINK
TINK TZZ-- TZZ--
KDG
UH?!

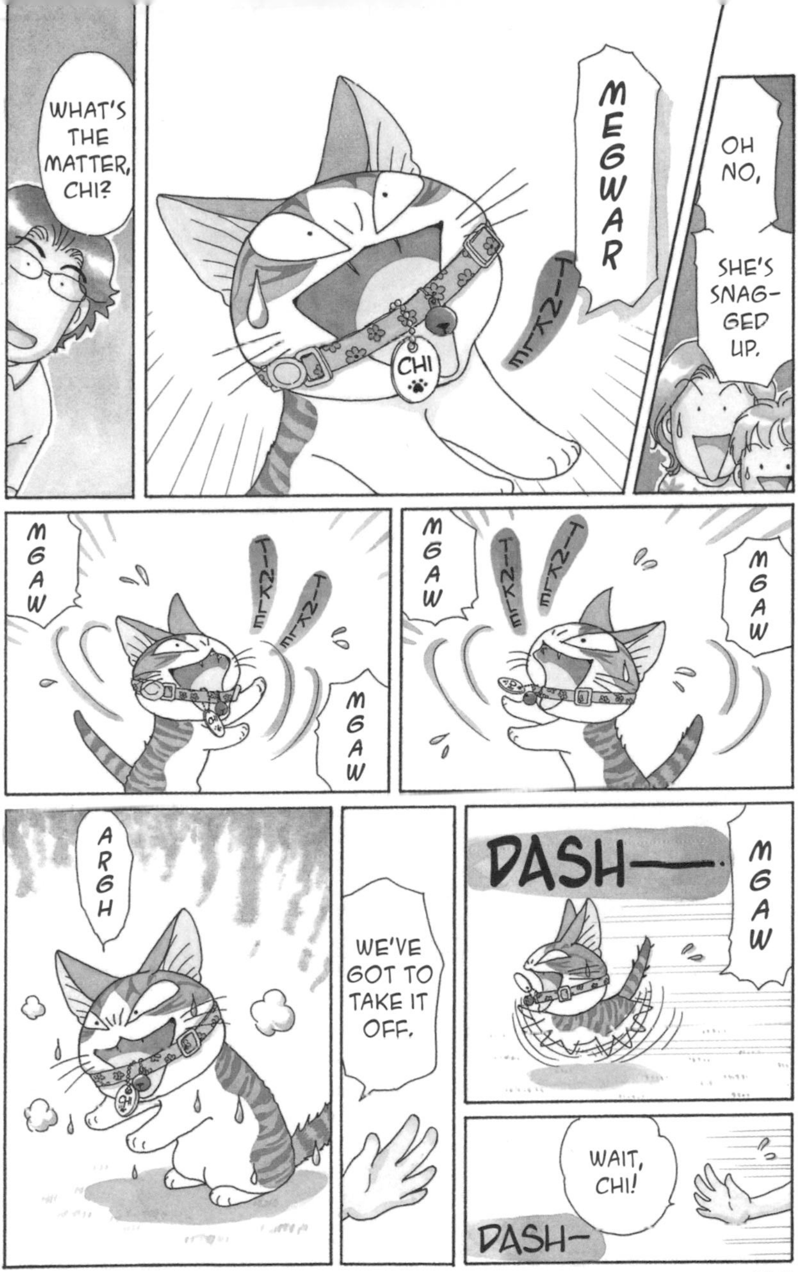

WHAT'S THE MATTER, CHI?
MEGWAR
TINKLE
OH NO,
SHE'S SNAG-GED UP.
MGAW
TINKLE
TINKLE
MGAW
MGAW
TINKLE
TINKLE
MGAW
ARGH
WE'VE GOT TO TAKE IT OFF.
DASH——
MGAW
WAIT, CHI!
DASH-

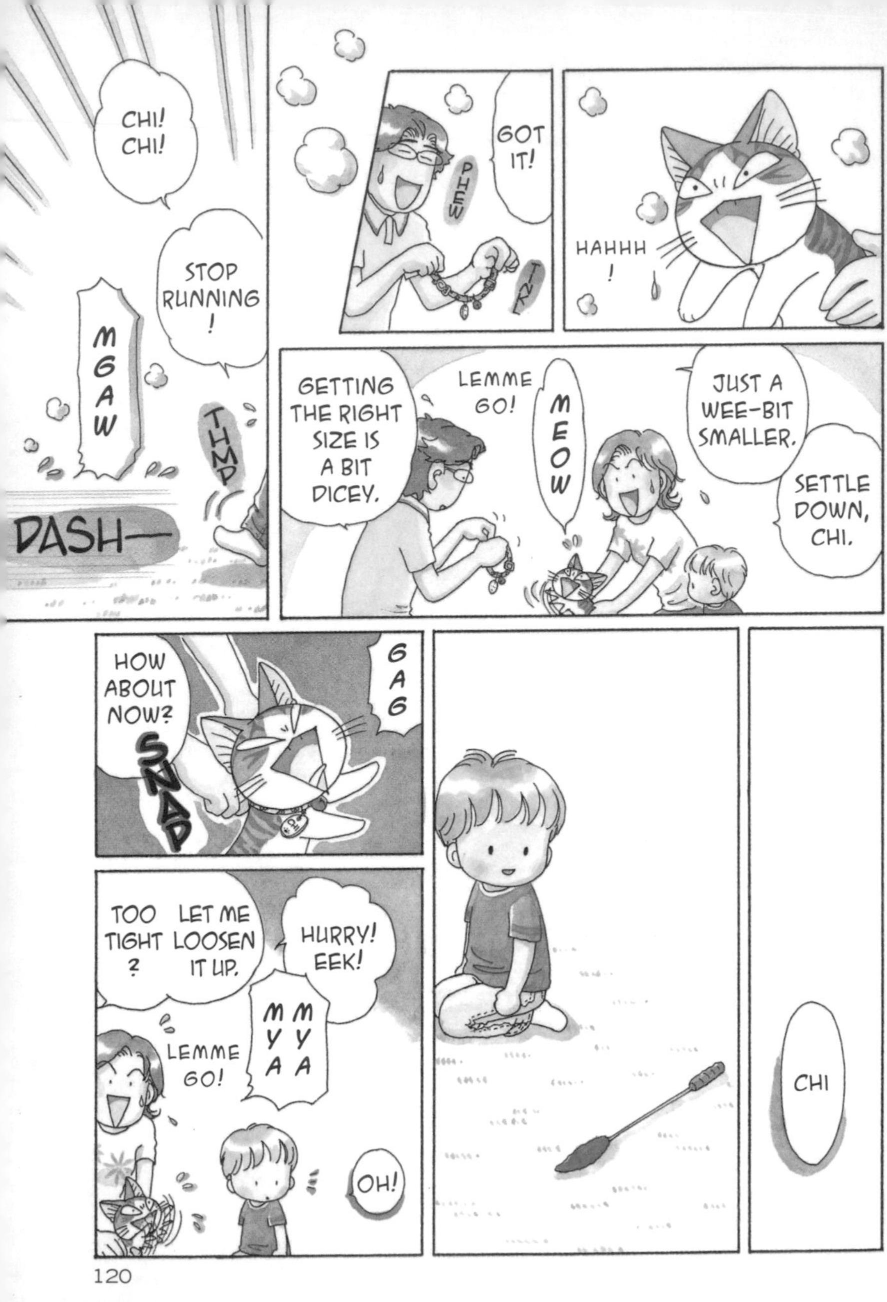
CHI! CHI!
STOP RUNNING!
MGAW
THMP
DASH—
GOT IT!
PHEW
TINKL
HAHHH!
GETTING THE RIGHT SIZE IS A BIT DICEY.
LEMME GO!
MEOW
JUST A WEE-BIT SMALLER.
SETTLE DOWN, CHI.
HOW ABOUT NOW?
GAG
SNAP
TOO TIGHT?
LET ME LOOSEN IT UP.
HURRY! EEK!
MYA MYA
LEMME GO!
OH!
CHI

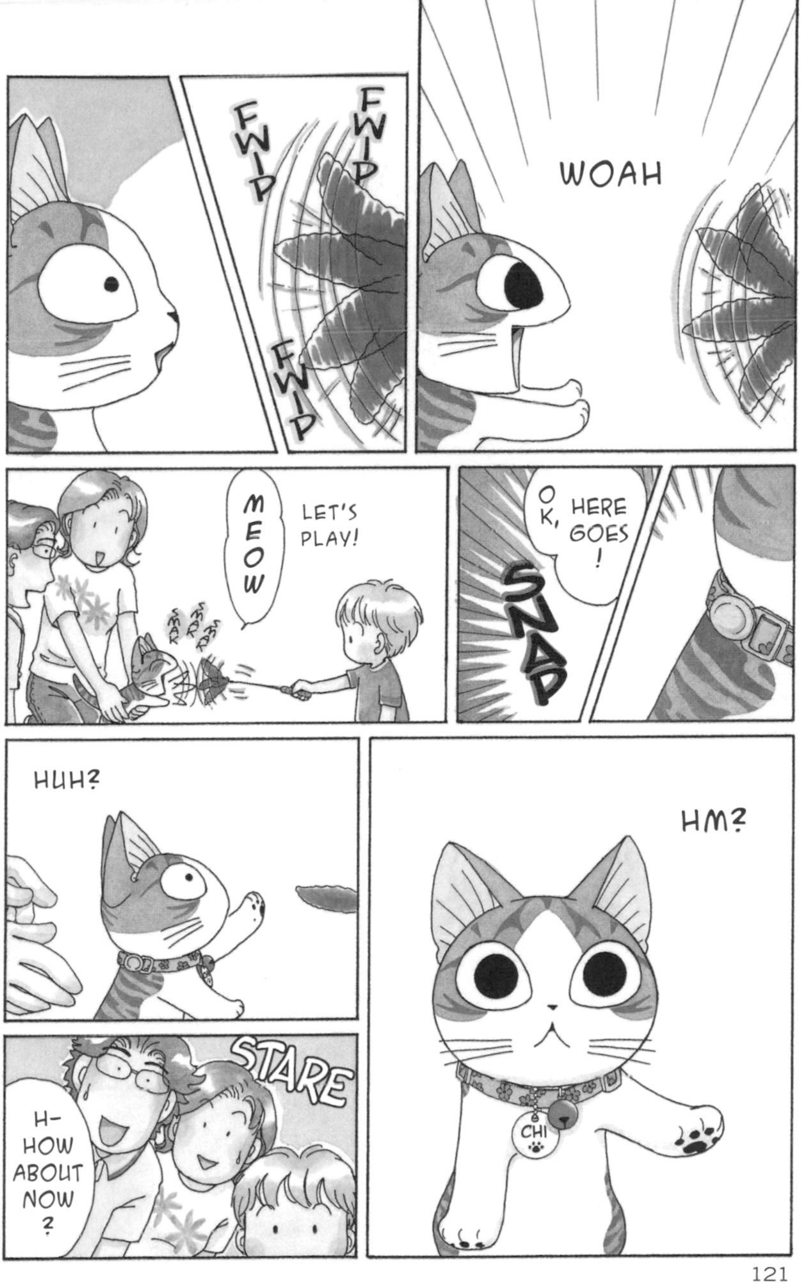
FWIP
FWIP
FWIP
WOAH
MEOW
LET'S PLAY!
OK, HERE GOES!
SNAP
HUH?
STARE
H-HOW ABOUT NOW?
HM?
CHI

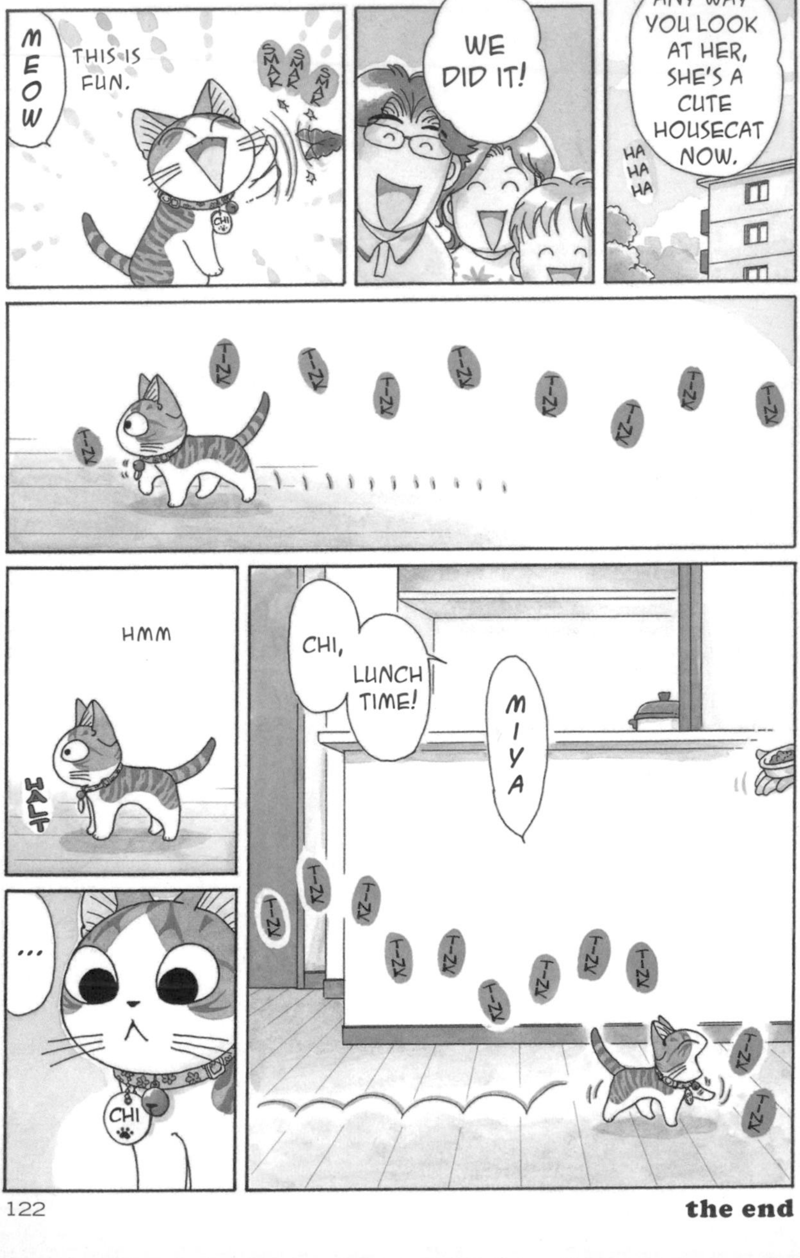
MEOW
THIS IS FUN.
SMAK SMAK SMAK
WE DID IT!
ANY WAY YOU LOOK AT HER, SHE'S A CUTE HOUSECAT NOW.
HA HA HA
TINK TINK TINK TINK TINK TINK TINK TINK TINK
HMM
HALT
...
CHI, LUNCH TIME!
MIYA
TINK TINK TINK TINK TINK TINK TINK TINK TINK TINK TINK TINK



**the end**

homemade 108: a cat saunters

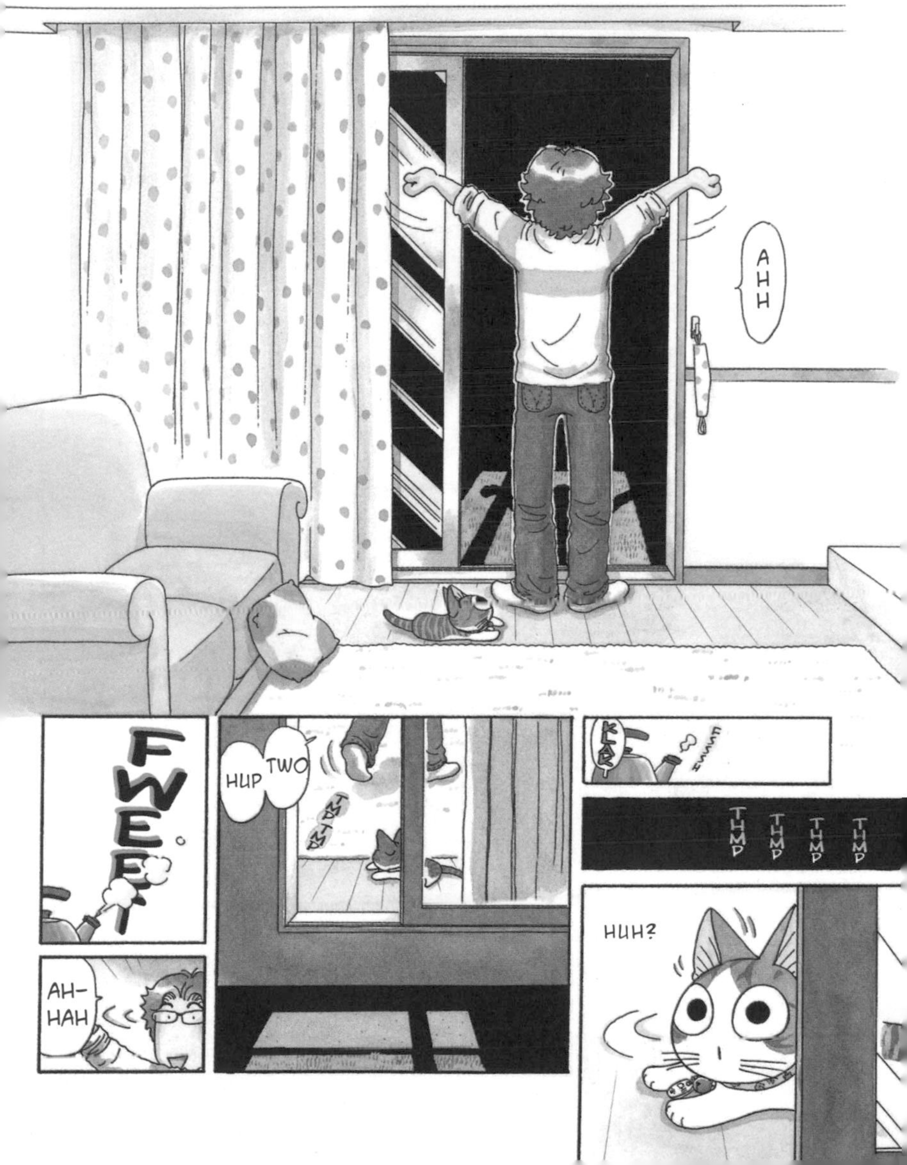
AHH
FWEEE
AH-HAH
HUP TWO
TMP TMP
KLAK
THMP THMP THMP THMP
HUH?

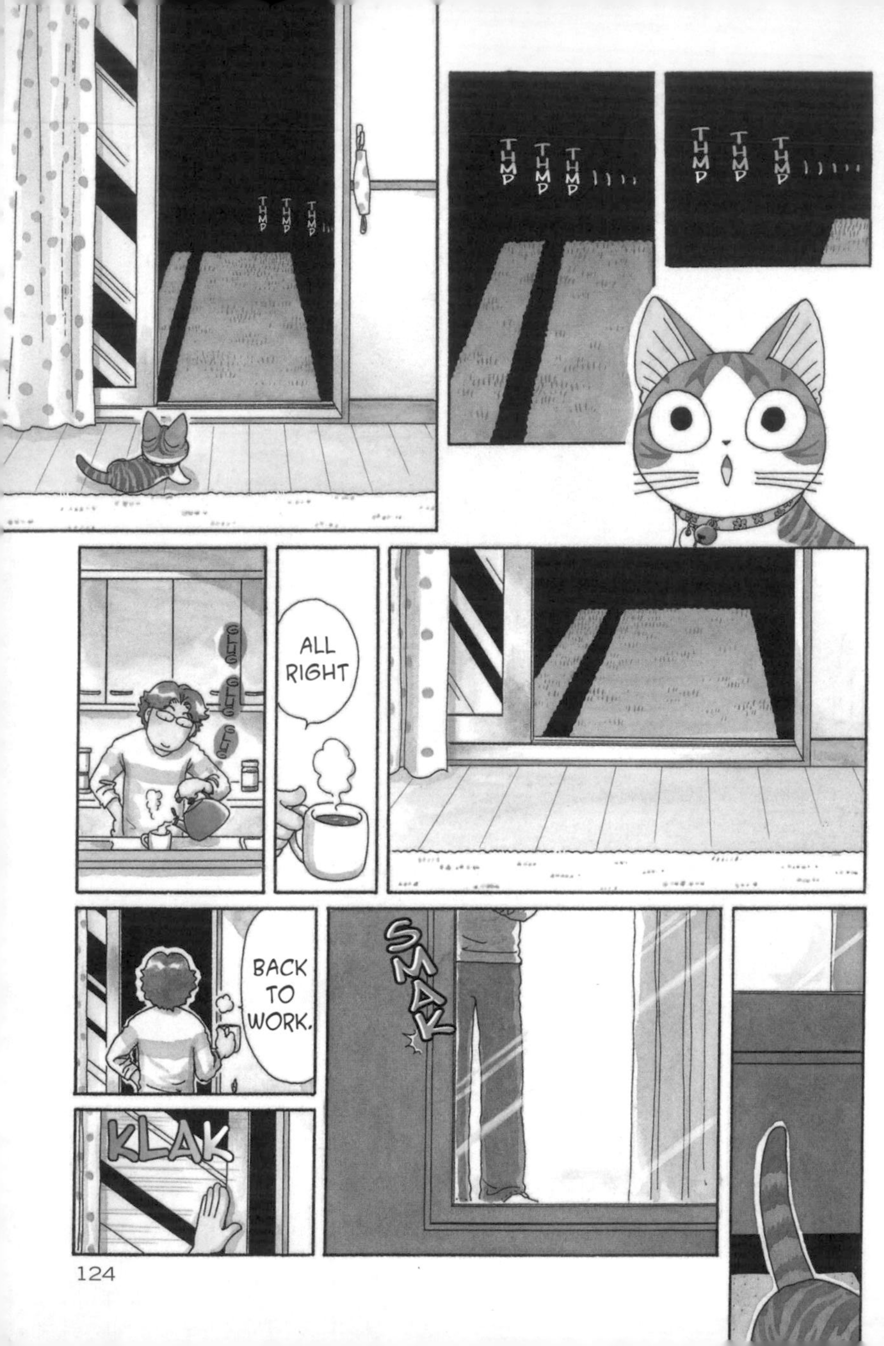
THMP THMP THMP
THMP THMP THMP
THMP THMP THMP
GLUG GLUG GLUG
ALL RIGHT
BACK TO WORK.
KLAK
SMAK

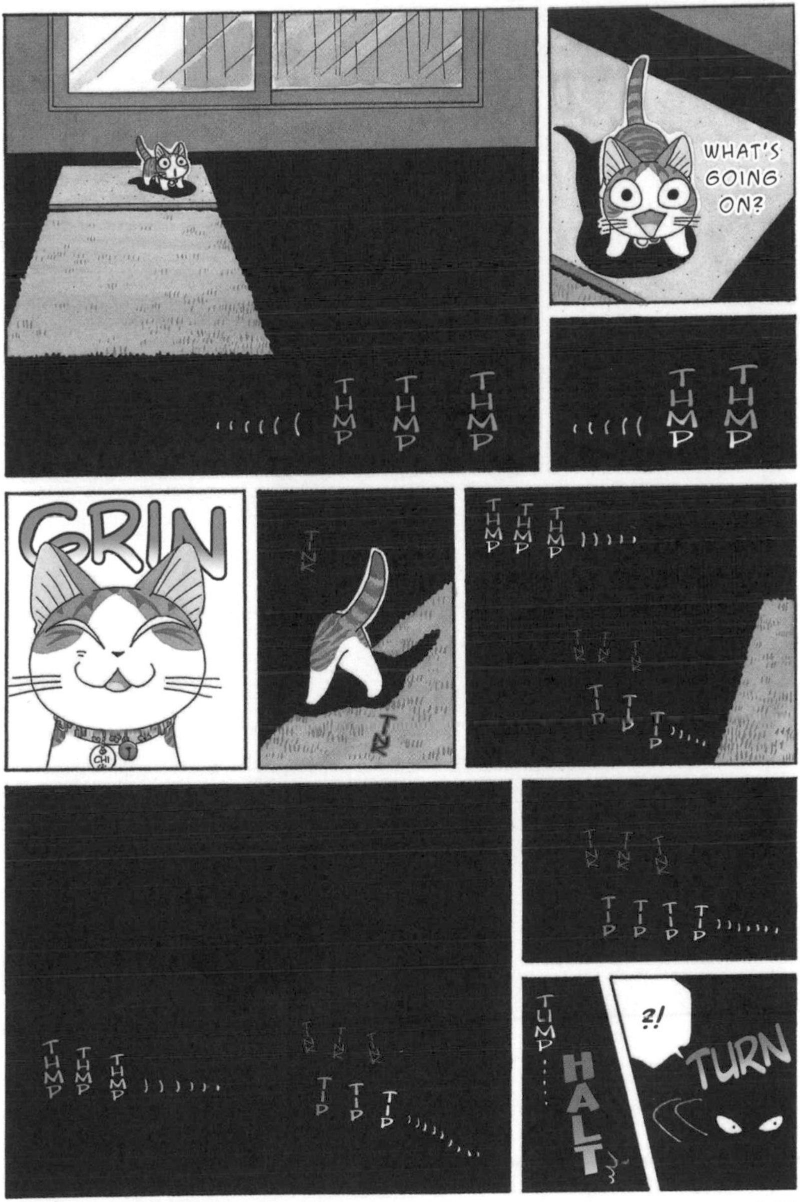

THMP THMP THMP
WHAT'S GOING ON?
THMP THMP
GRIN
TINK
TINK
THMP THMP THMP
TINK TINK TINK
TIP TIP TIP
THMP THMP THMP
TINK TINK TINK
TIP TIP TIP
TINK TINK TINK
TIP TIP TIP TIP
TUMP.....
HALT
?!
TURN

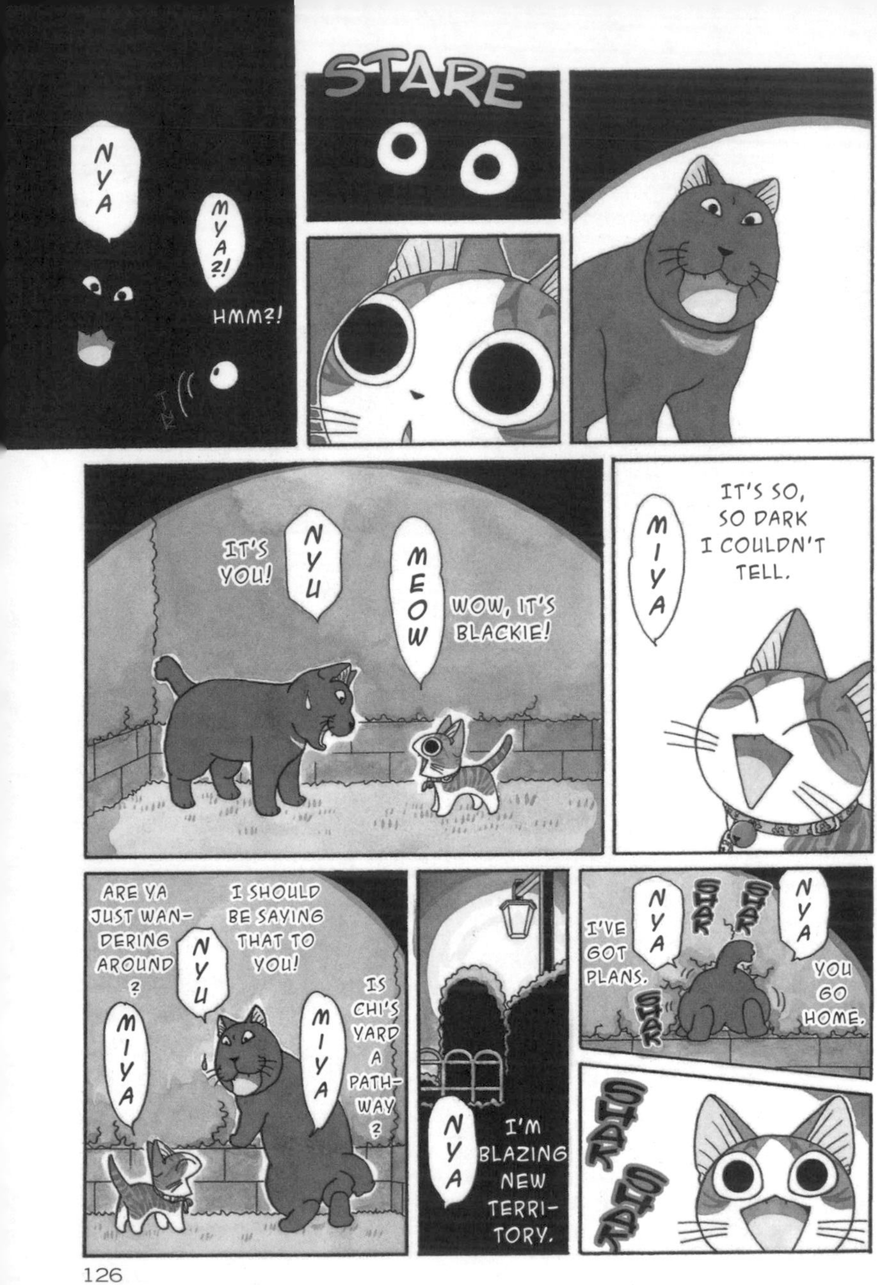
NYA
MYA?!
HMM?!
STARE
IT'S YOU!
NYU
MEOW
WOW, IT'S BLACKIE!
MIYA
IT'S SO, SO DARK I COULDN'T TELL.
ARE YA JUST WANDERING AROUND?
I SHOULD BE SAYING THAT TO YOU!
NYU
MIYA
IS CHI'S YARD A PATHWAY?
MIYA
NYA
I'M BLAZING NEW TERRITORY.
NYA
I'VE GOT PLANS.
SHAR
SHAR
SHAR
NYA
YOU GO HOME.
SHAR
SHAR
SHAR

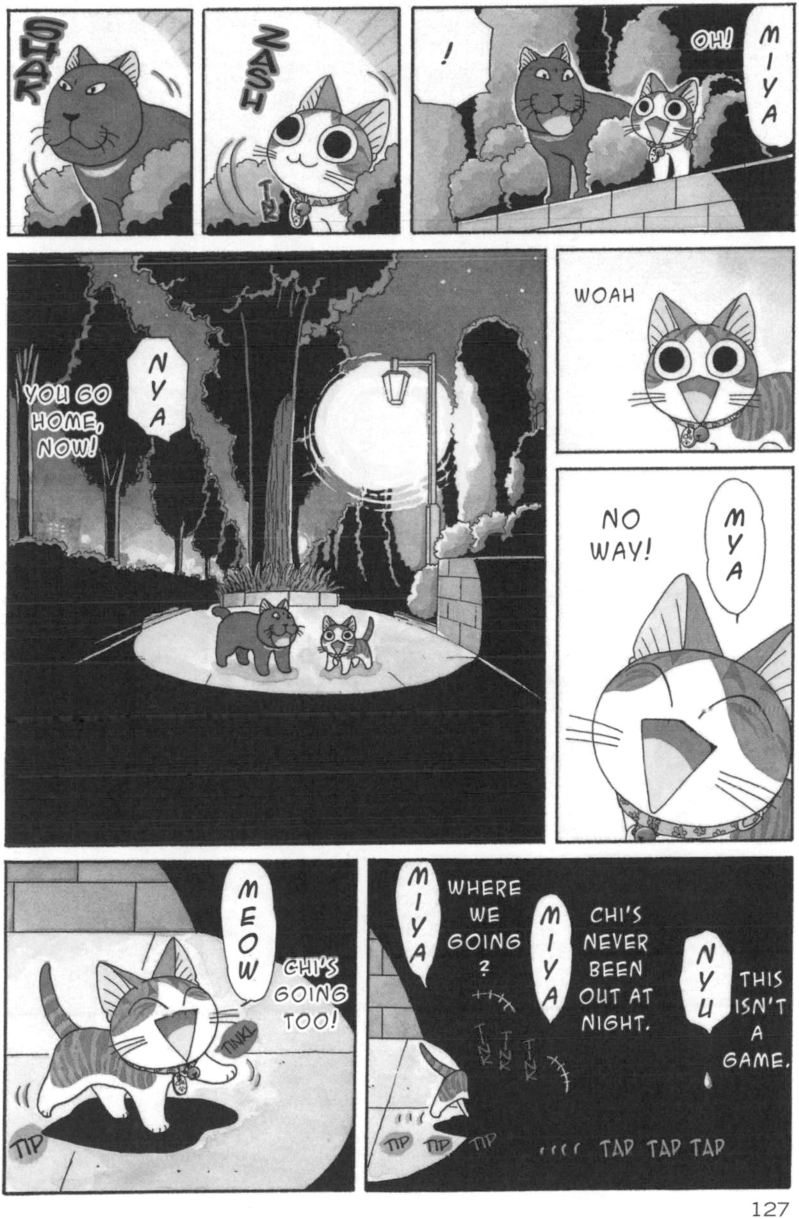
SHAK
ZASH
TIN
!
OH!
MIYA
YOU GO HOME, NOW!
NYA
WOAH
NO WAY!
MYA
MEOW
CHI'S GOING TOO!
TINKL
TIP
MIYA
WHERE WE GOING?
MIYA
CHI'S NEVER BEEN OUT AT NIGHT.
NYU
THIS ISN'T A GAME.
TINK TINK TINK
TIP TIP TIP
TAP TAP TAP

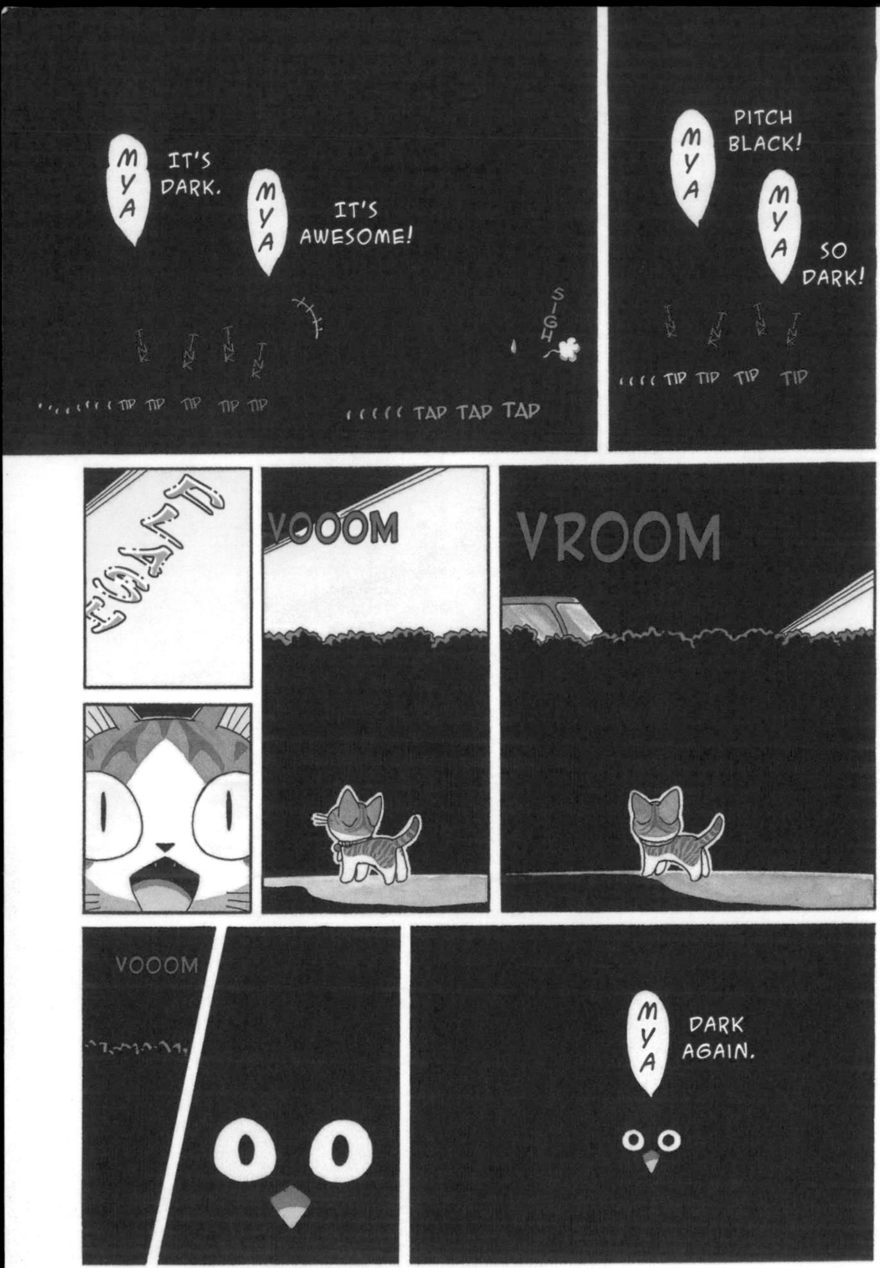
MYA
IT'S DARK.
MYA
IT'S AWESOME!
TINK TINK TINK TINK
TIP TIP TIP TIP TIP
SIGH
TAP TAP TAP
MYA
PITCH BLACK!
MYA
SO DARK!
TINK TINK TINK TINK
TIP TIP TIP TIP
FLASH
VOOOM
VROOM
VOOOM
MYA
DARK AGAIN.

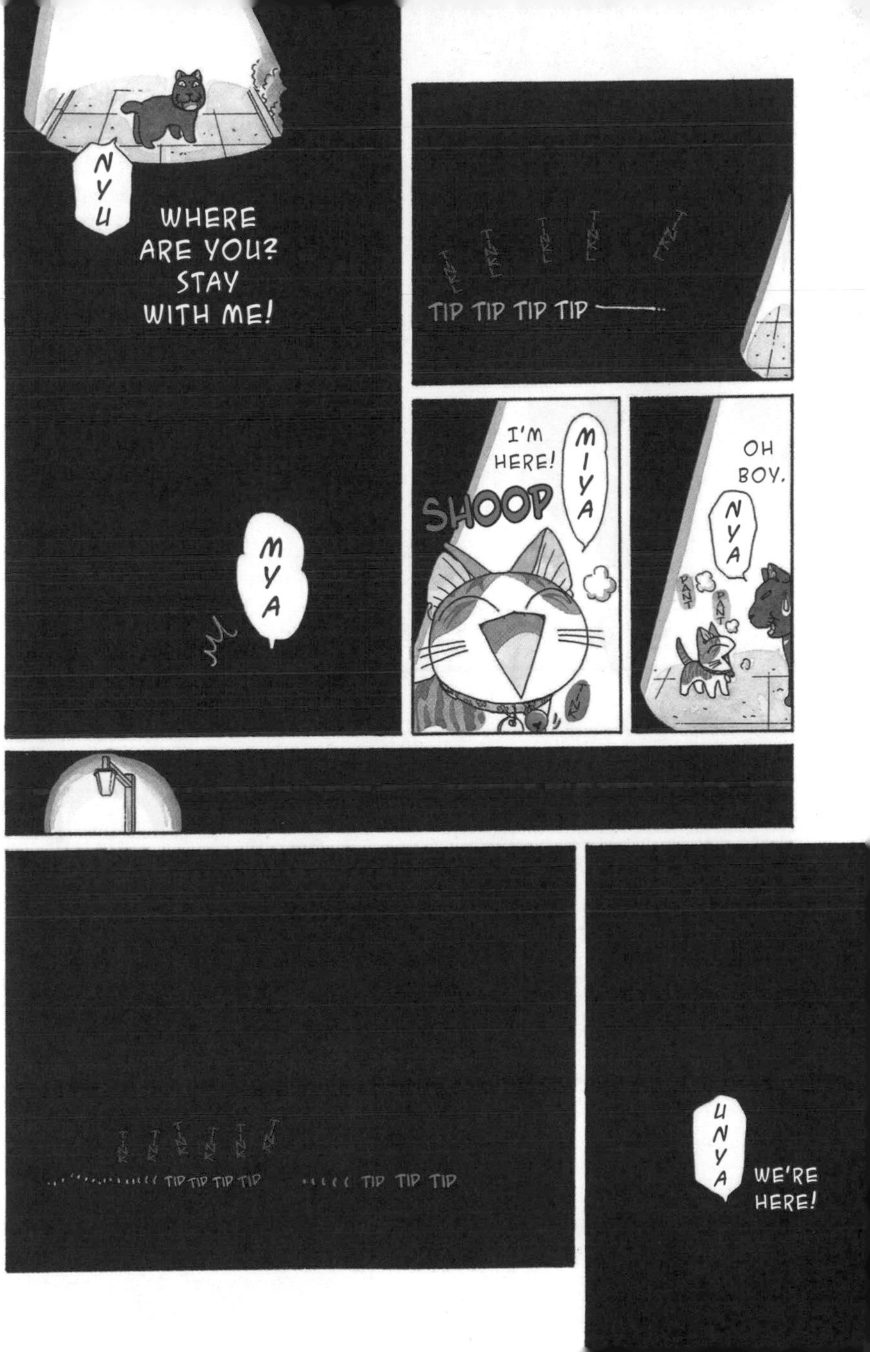
NYU
WHERE ARE YOU? STAY WITH ME!
MYA
TINKL TINKL TINKL TINKL TINKL
TIP TIP TIP TIP
I'M HERE!
MIYA
SHOOP
TINK
OH BOY.
NYA
PANT PANT
TINK TINK TINK TINK TINK TINK
TIP TIP TIP TIP
TIP TIP TIP
UNYA
WE'RE HERE!

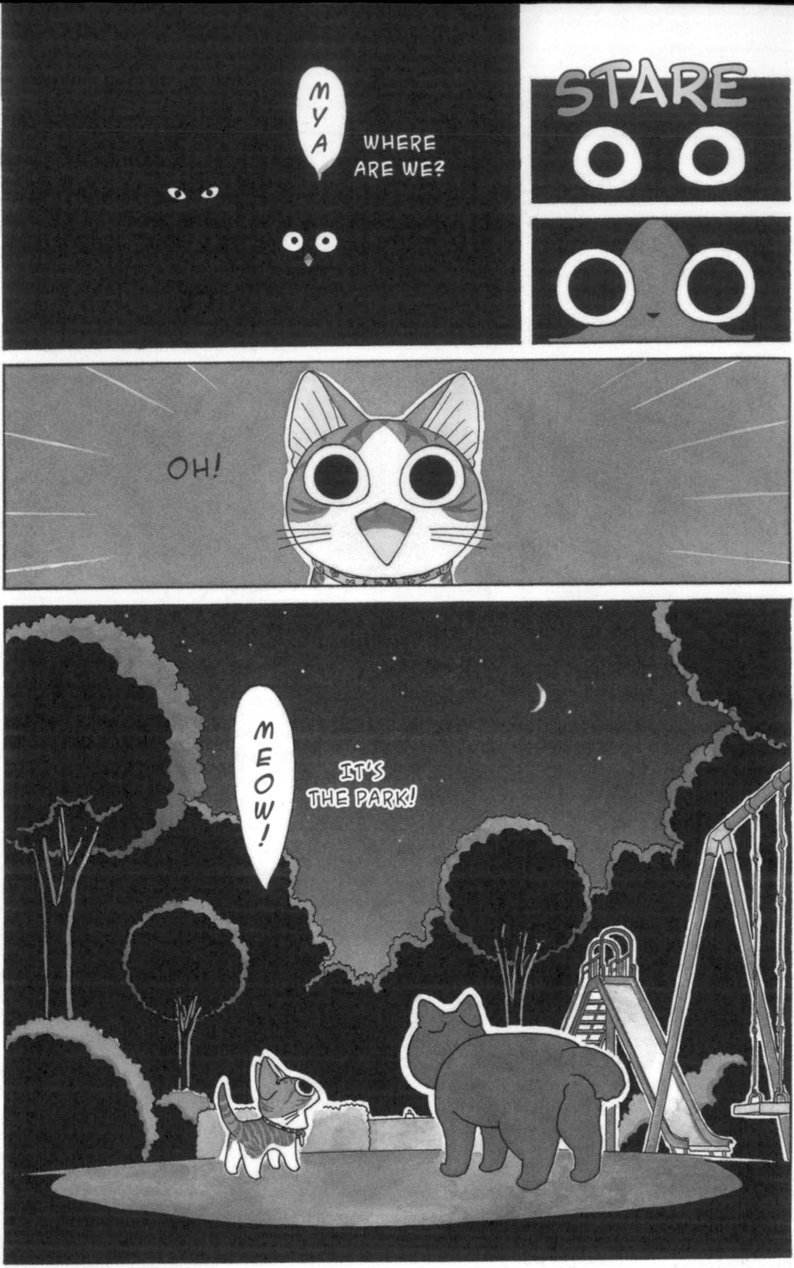
MYA
WHERE ARE WE?
STARE
OH!
MEOW!
IT'S THE PARK!



**the end**

# homemade 109: a cat continues to saunter

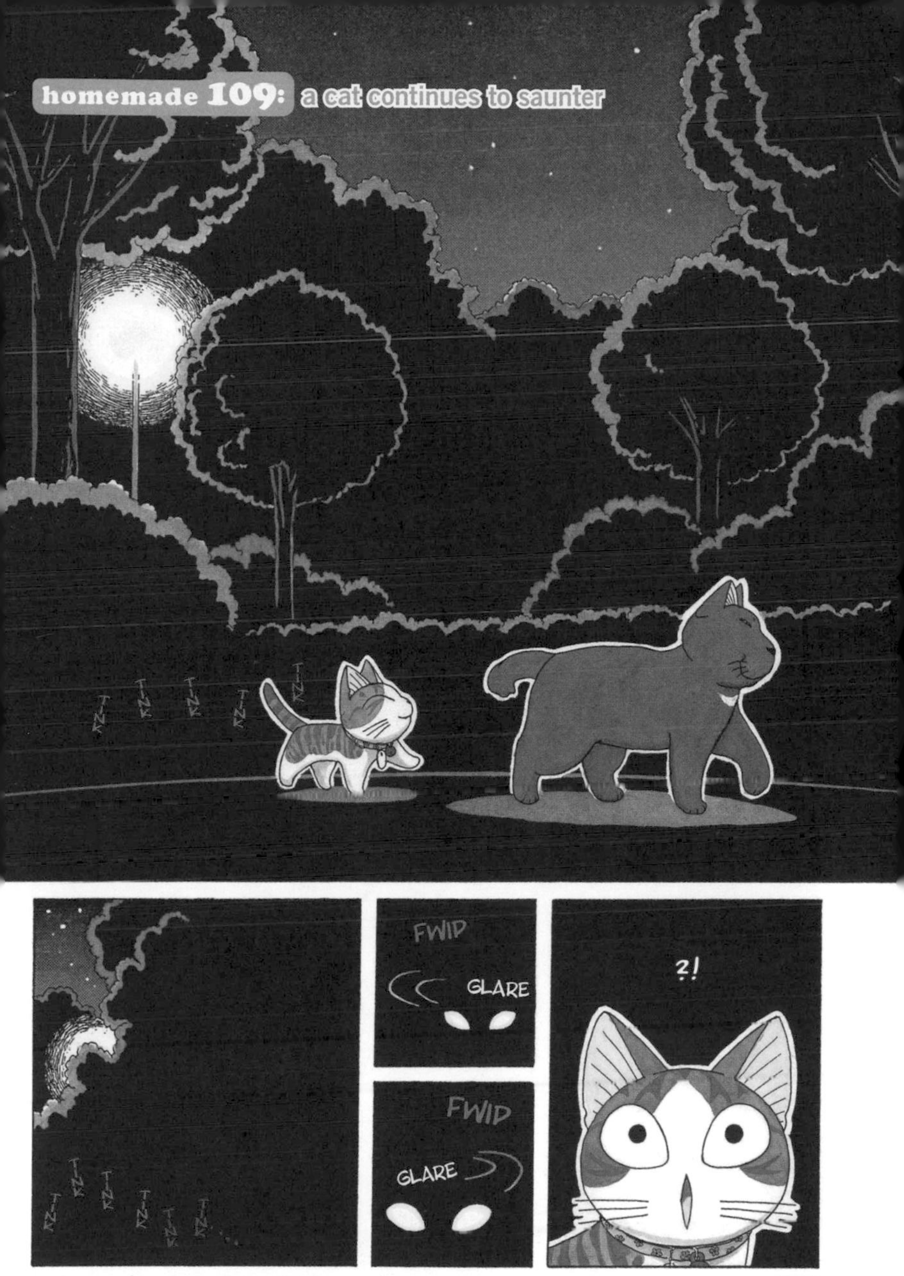
TINK
TINK
TINK
TINK
TINK
TINK
TINK
TINK
TINK
TINK
TINK...
FWIP
GLARE
FWIP
GLARE
?!

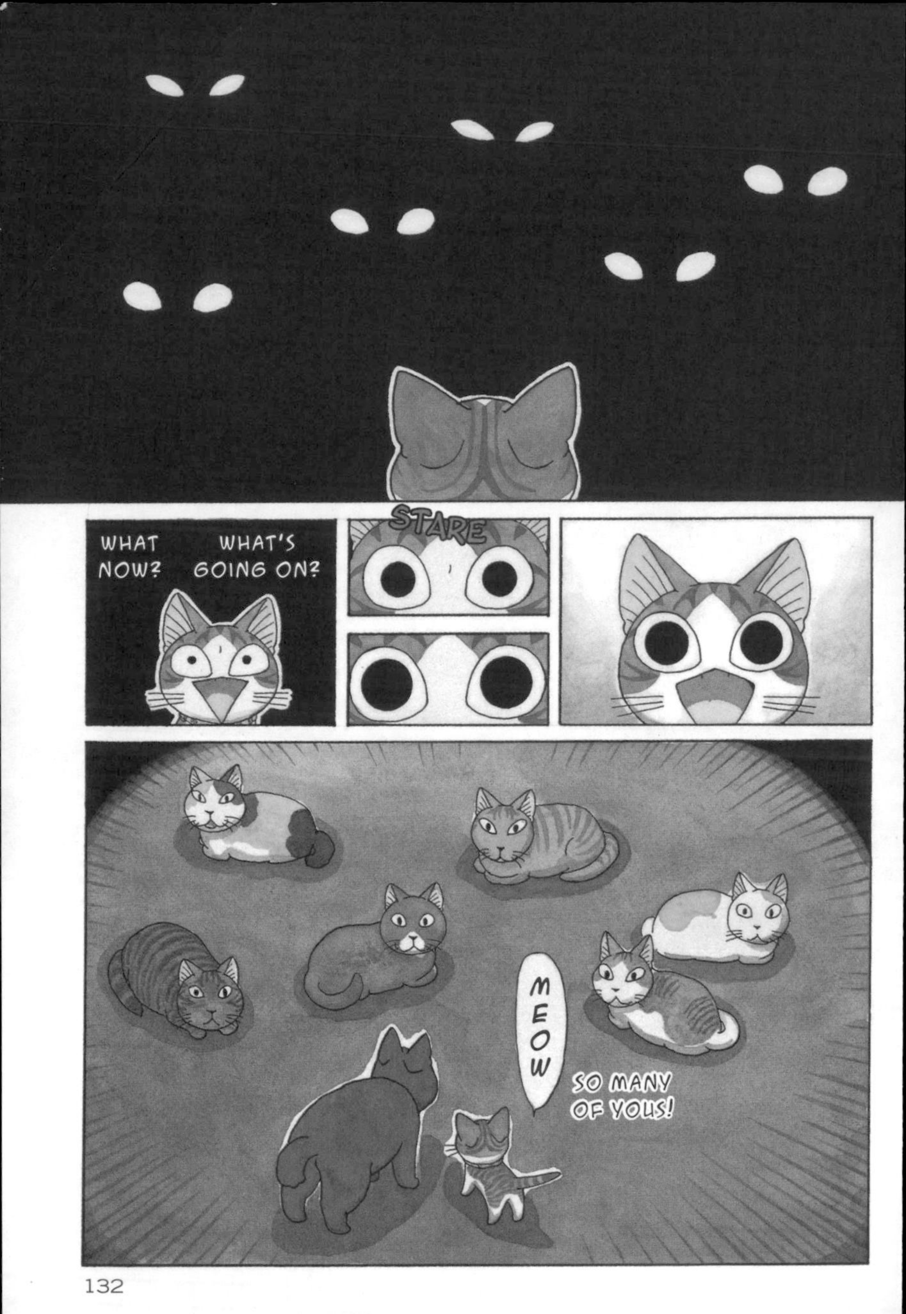
WHAT NOW?
WHAT'S GOING ON?
STARE
MEOW
SO MANY OF YOUS!

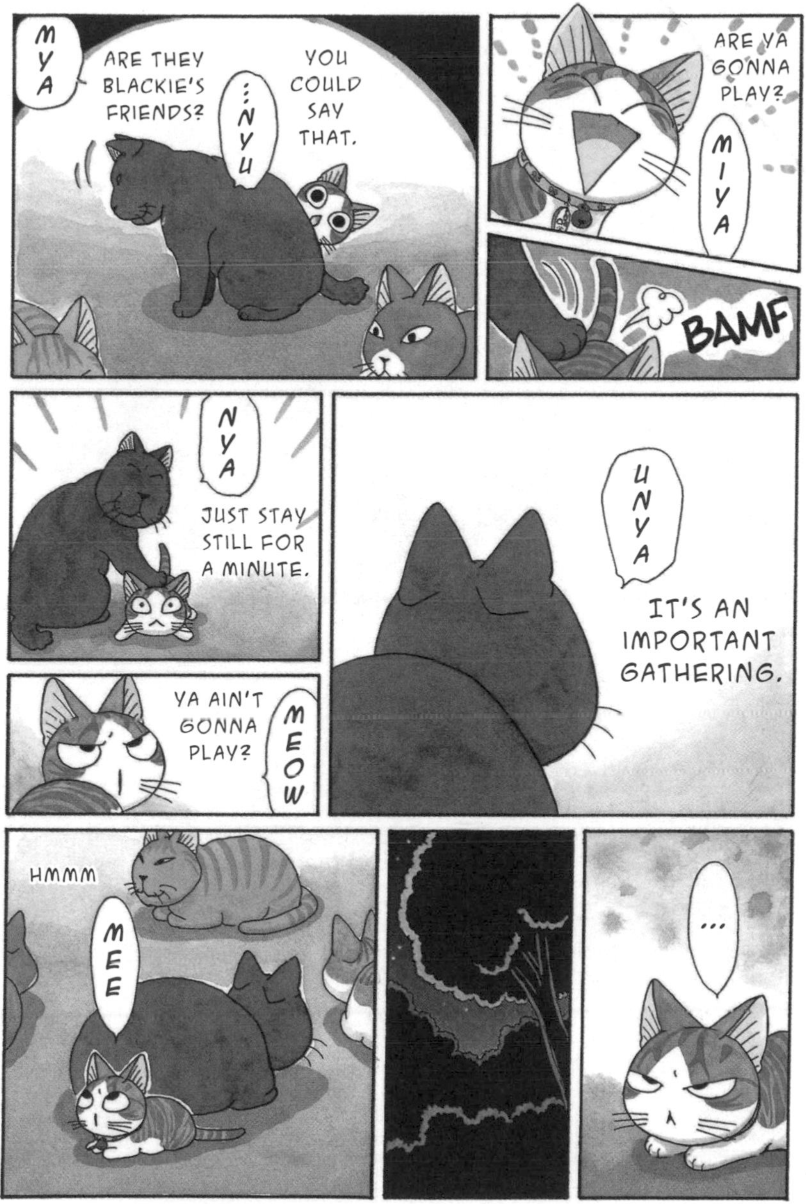
MYA
ARE THEY BLACKIE'S FRIENDS?
...NYU
YOU COULD SAY THAT.
ARE YA GONNA PLAY?
MIYA
BAMF
NYA
JUST STAY STILL FOR A MINUTE.
UNYA
IT'S AN IMPORTANT GATHERING.
YA AIN'T GONNA PLAY?
MEOW
HMMM
MEE
...

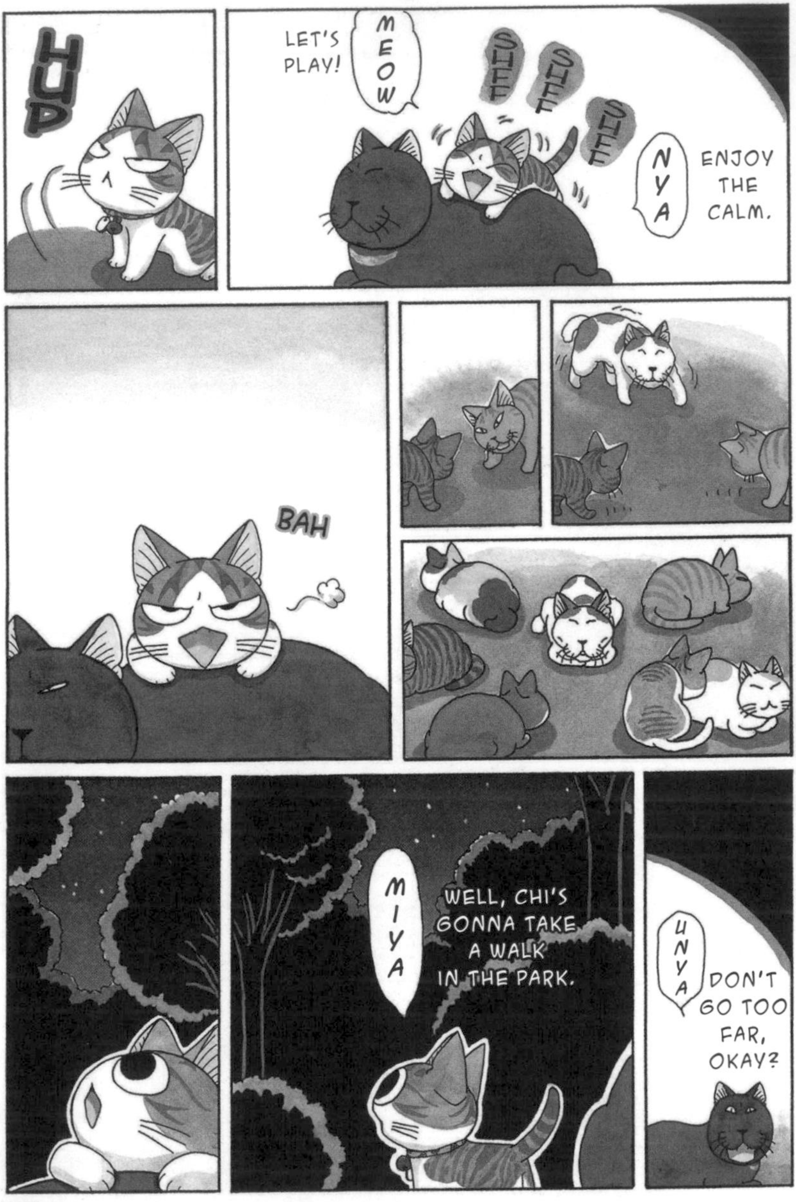
HUP
LET'S PLAY!
MEOW
SHFF
SHFF
SHFF
NYA
ENJOY THE CALM.
BAH
MIYA
WELL, CHI'S GONNA TAKE A WALK IN THE PARK.
UNYA
DON'T GO TOO FAR, OKAY?

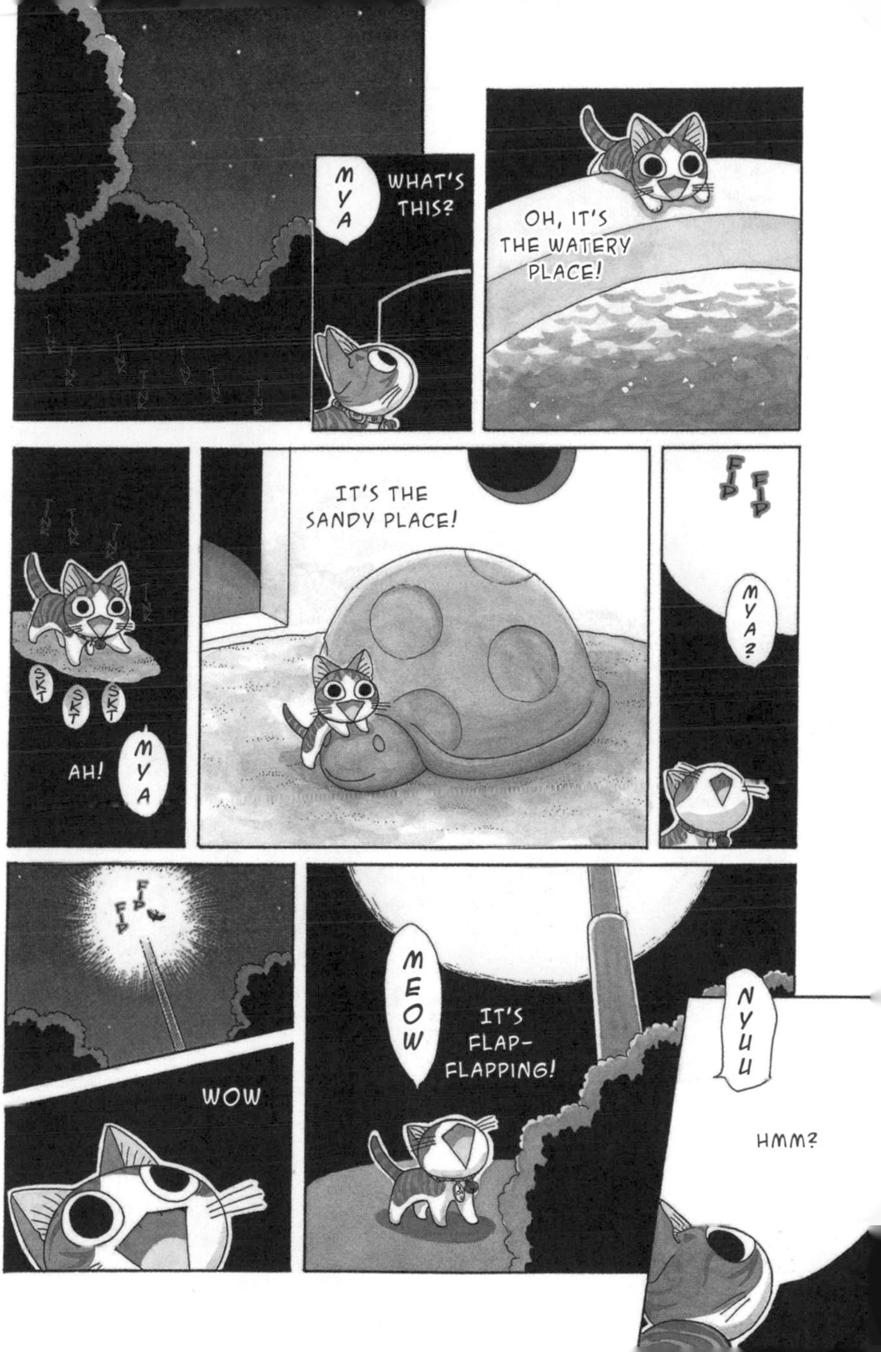
TINK TINK TINK TINK TINK TINK TINK
MYA
WHAT'S THIS?
OH, IT'S THE WATERY PLACE!
TINK TINK TINK TINK
SKT SKT SKT
AH!
MYA
IT'S THE SANDY PLACE!
FIP FIP
MYA?
FIP FIP
WOW
MEOW
IT'S FLAP-FLAPPING!
NYUU
HMM?

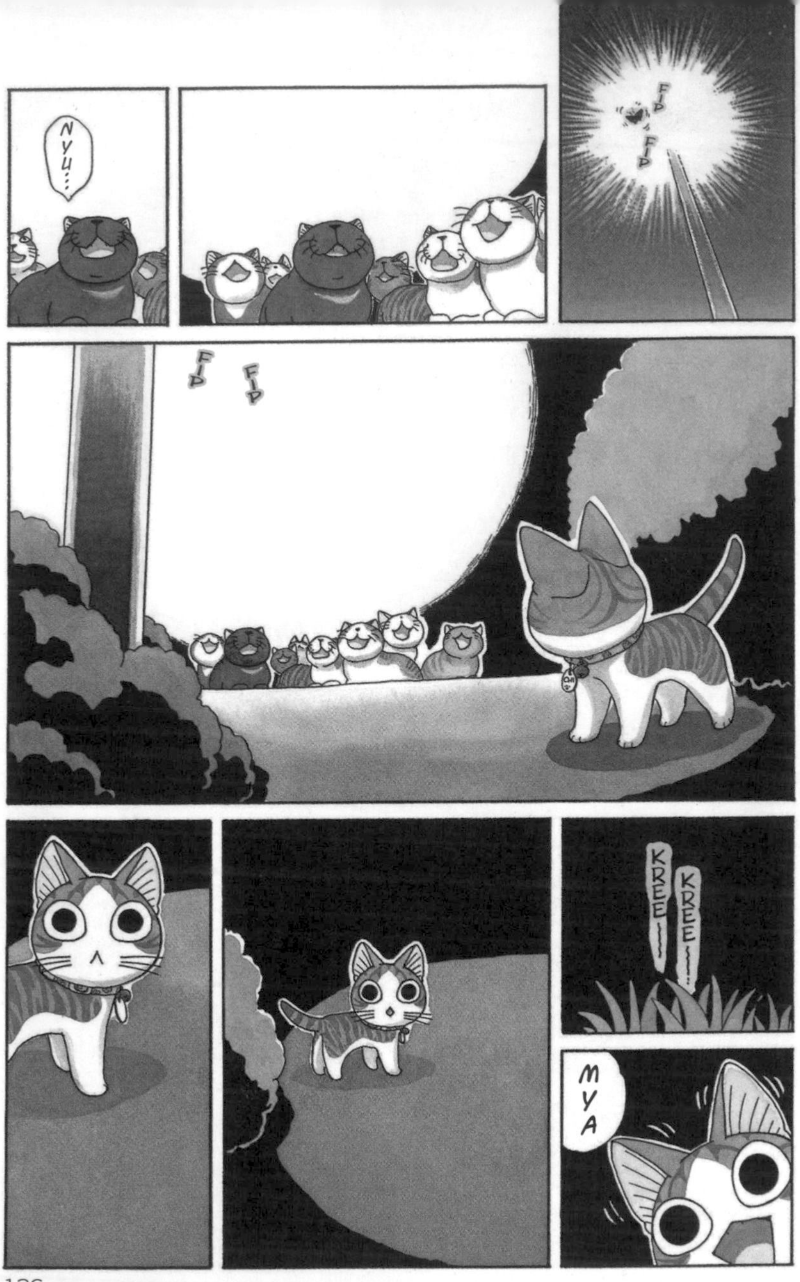
NYU...
FIP
FIP
FIP
FIP
KREE...
KREE...
MYA

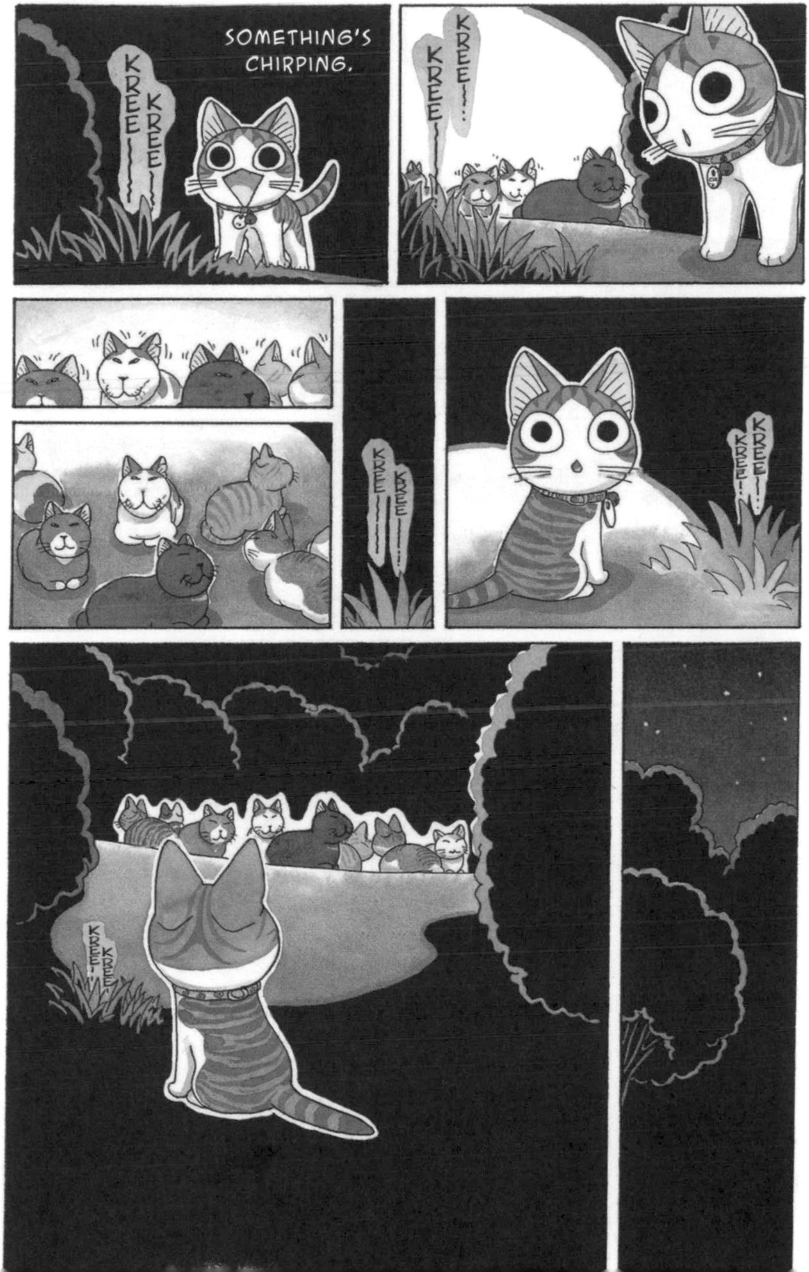
KREE KREE
SOMETHING'S CHIRPING.
KREE KREE...
KREE KREE
KREE! KREE!
KREE! KREE

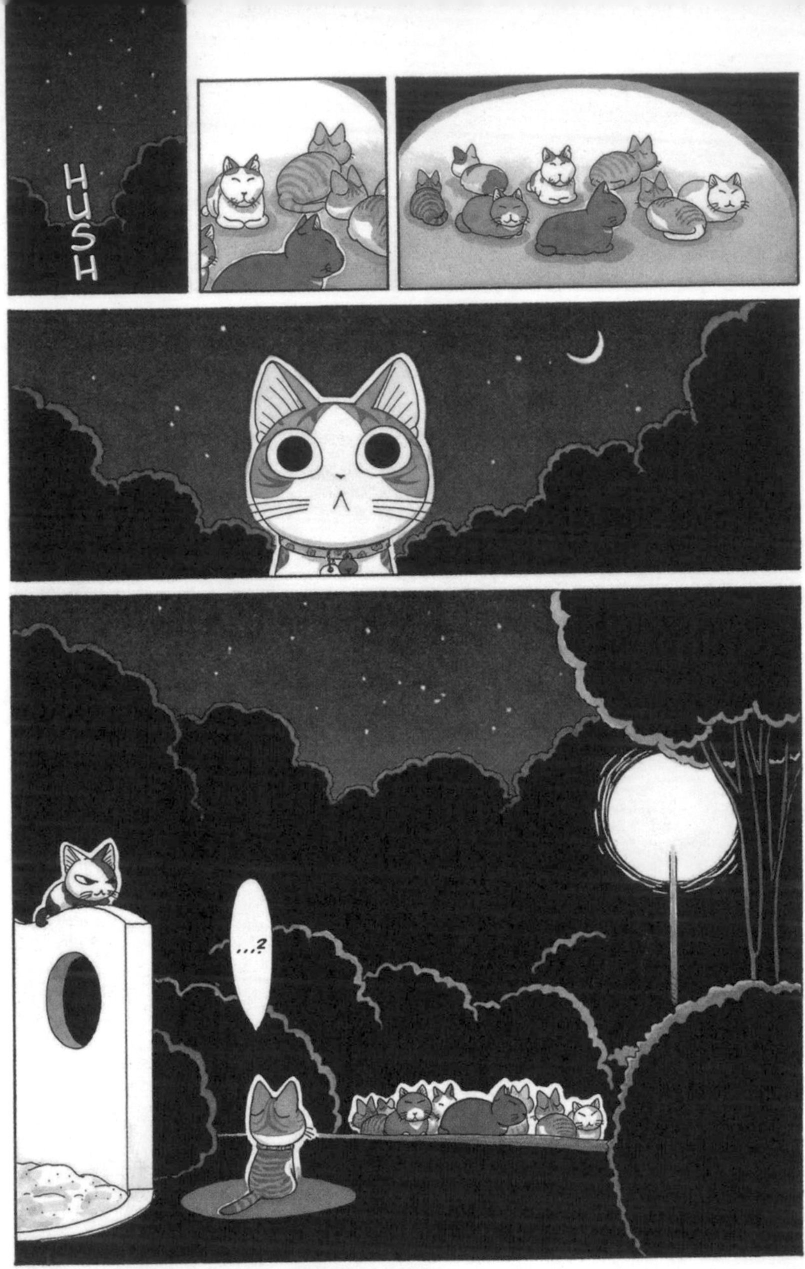
HUSH
...?

**the end**

# homemade 110: a cat steps forth

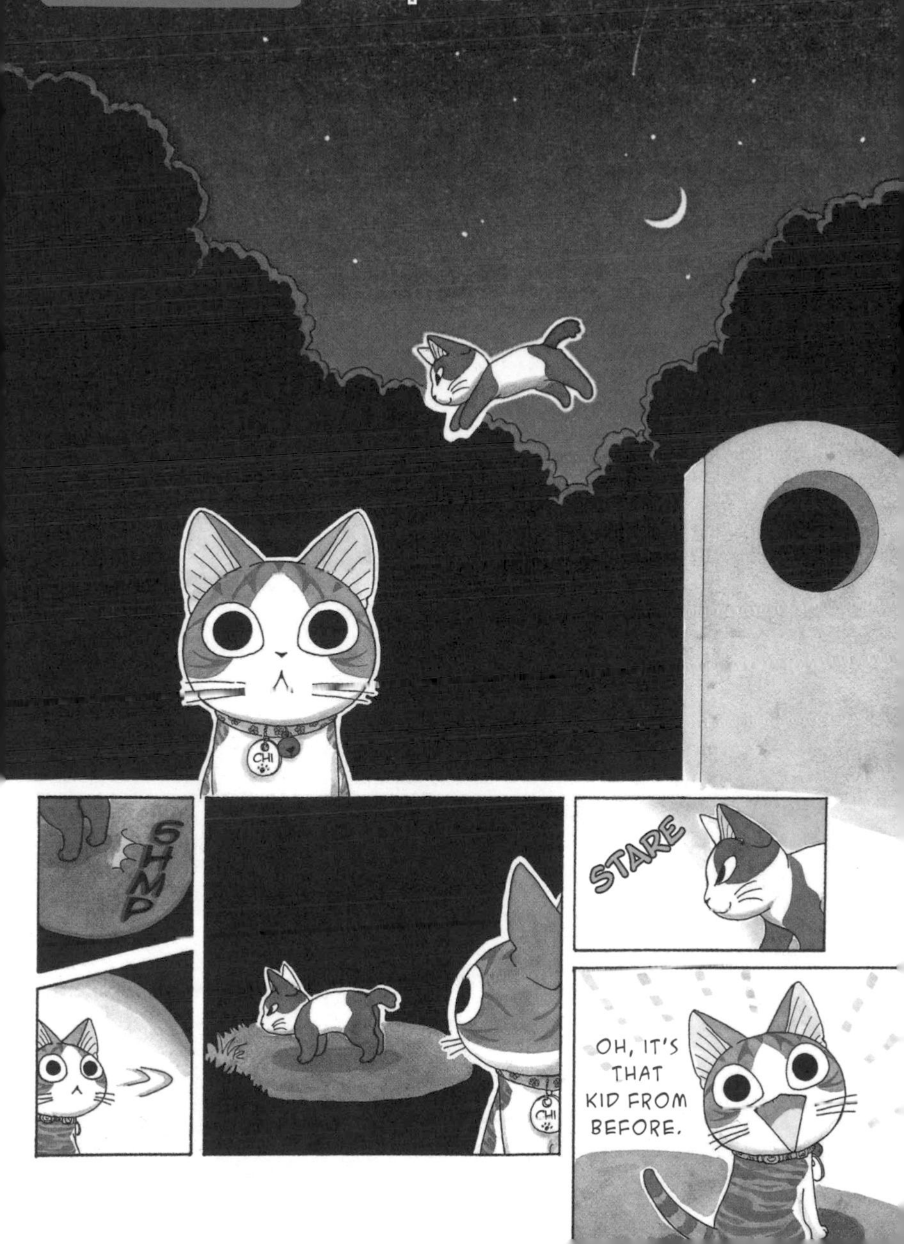
CHI
SHMP
CHI
STARE
OH, IT'S THAT KID FROM BEFORE.

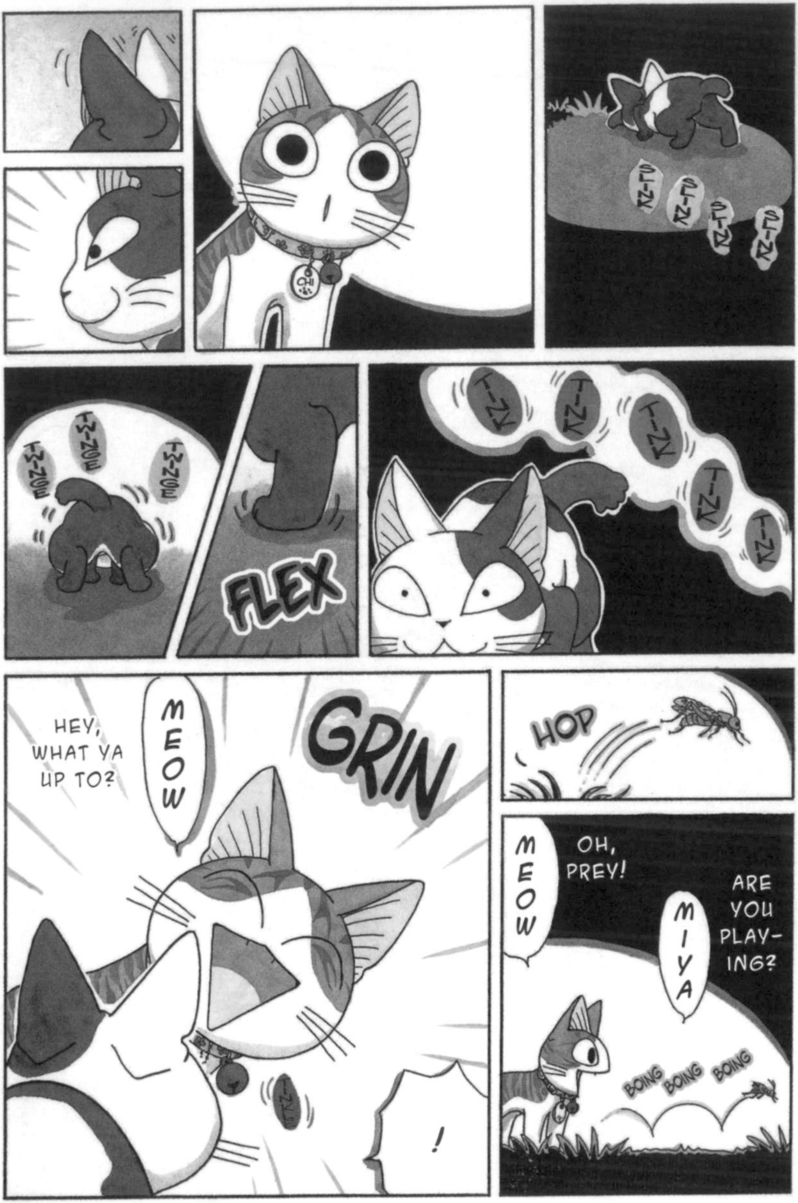
CHI
SLINK SLINK SLINK SLINK
TWINGE TWINGE TWINGE
FLEX
TINK TINK TINK TINK TINK
HEY, WHAT YA UP TO?
MEOW
GRIN
!
HOP
MEOW
OH, PREY!
MIYA
ARE YOU PLAYING?
BOING BOING BOING

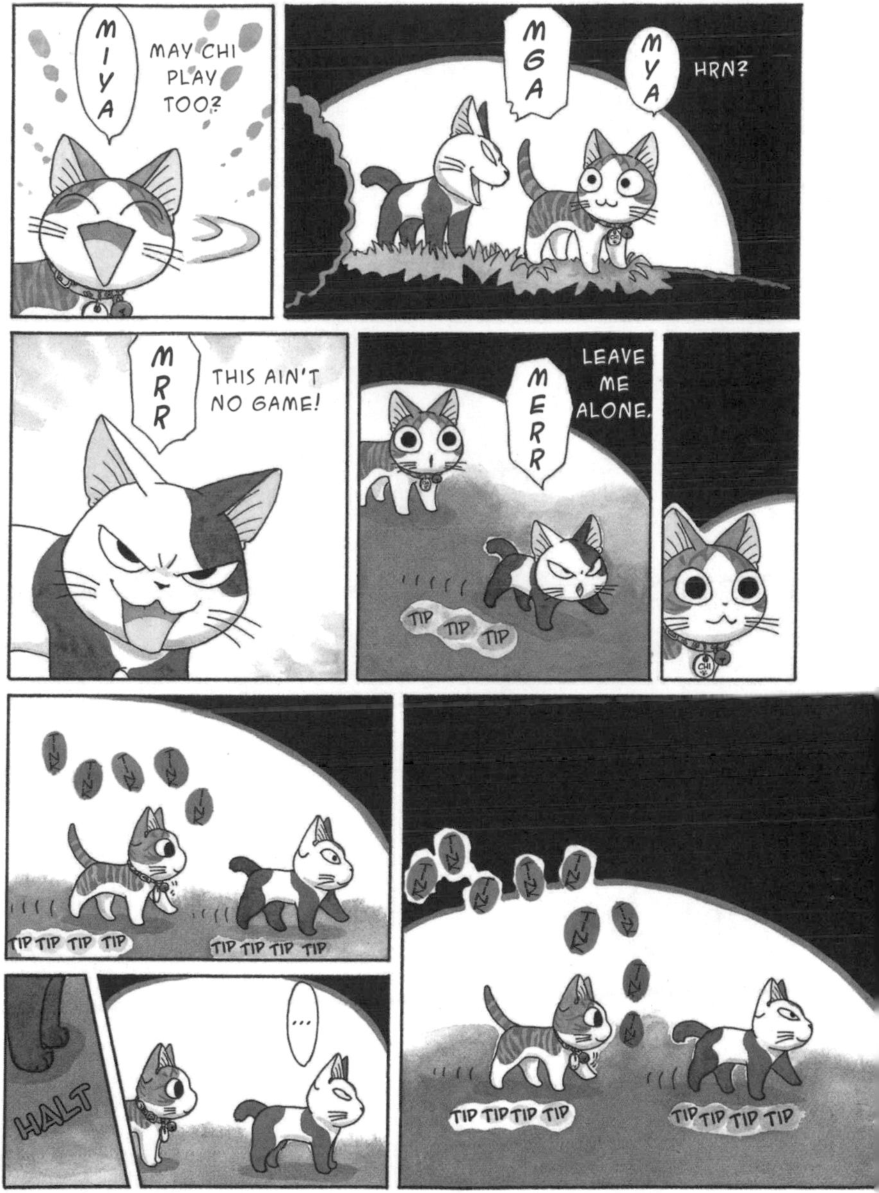
MIYA
MAY CHI PLAY TOO?
MGA
MYA
HRN?
MRR
THIS AIN'T NO GAME!
MERR
LEAVE ME ALONE.
TIP TIP TIP
TINK TINK TINK TINK TINK
TIP TIP TIP TIP
TIP TIP TIP TIP
HALT
...
TINK TINK TINK TINK TINK TINK TINK TINK TINK TINK
TIP TIP TIP TIP
TIP TIP TIP TIP

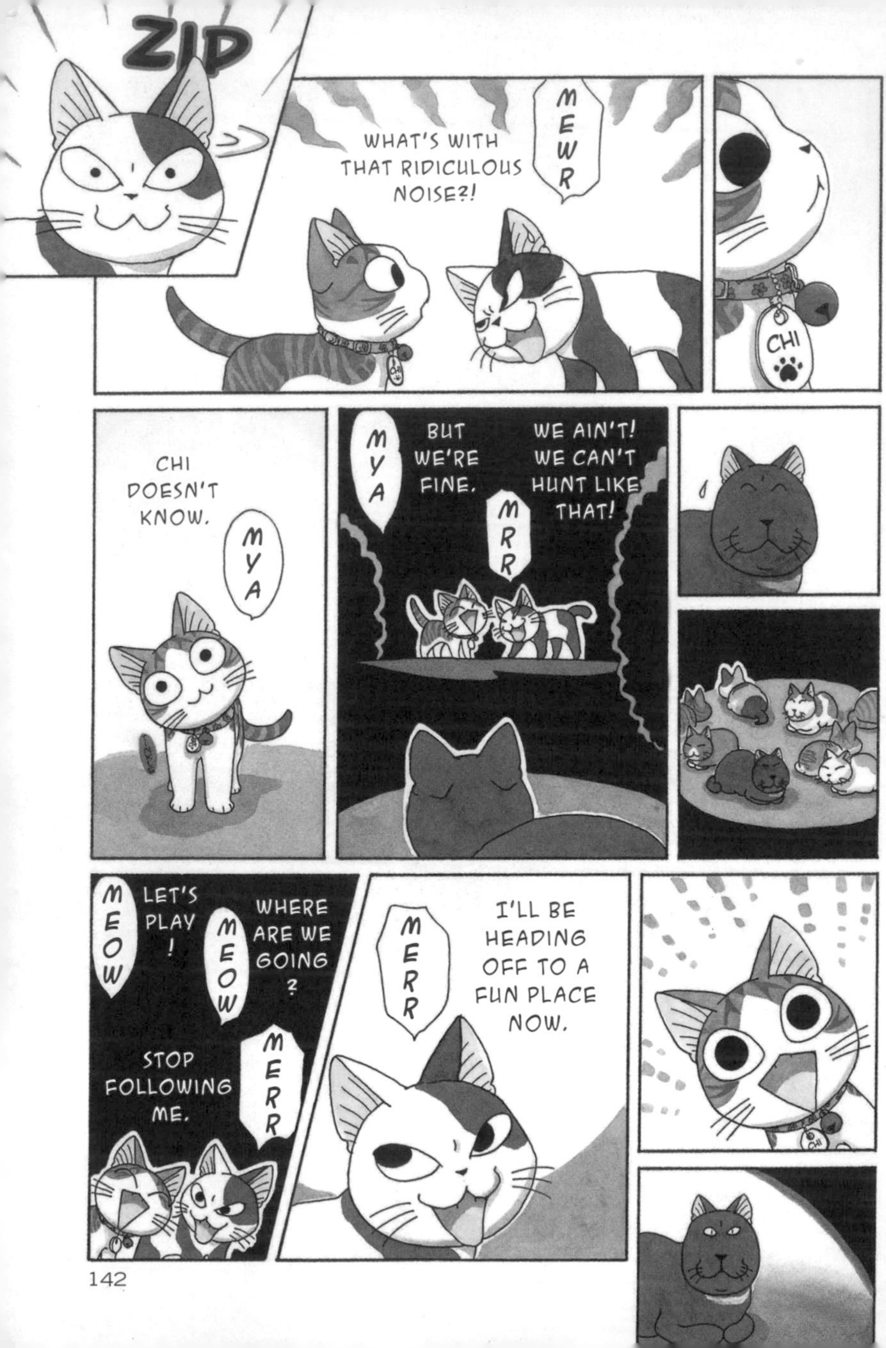
ZIP
WHAT'S WITH THAT RIDICULOUS NOISE?!
MEWR
CHI
CHI DOESN'T KNOW.
MYA
MYA
BUT WE'RE FINE.
MRR
WE AIN'T! WE CAN'T HUNT LIKE THAT!
MEOW
LET'S PLAY!
MEOW
WHERE ARE WE GOING?
STOP FOLLOWING ME.
MERR
MERR
I'LL BE HEADING OFF TO A FUN PLACE NOW.
CHI

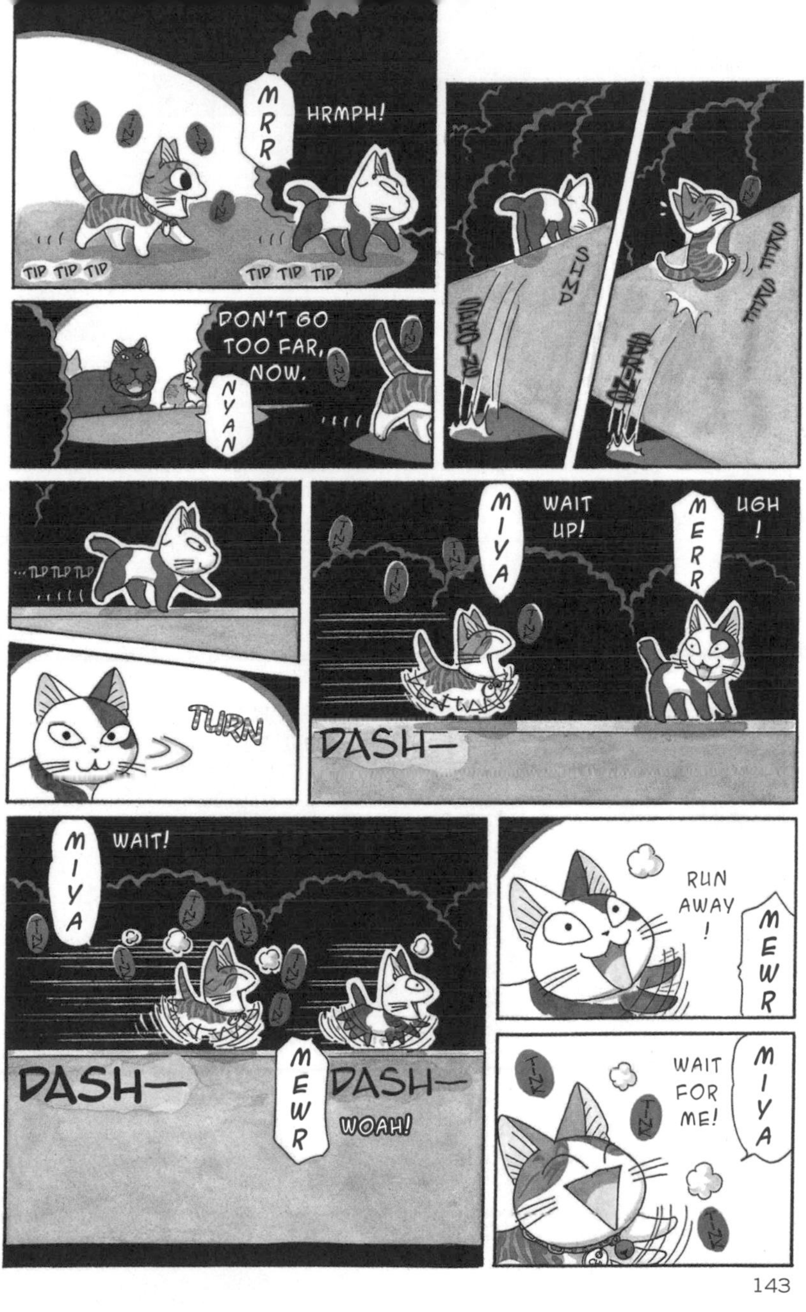
MRR
HRMPH!
TIP TIP TIP
TIP TIP TIP
DON'T GO TOO FAR, NOW.
NYAN
SHMP
...TIP TIP TIP
TURN
MIYA
WAIT UP!
MERR
UGH!
DASH—
MIYA
WAIT!
DASH—
MEWR
DASH—
WOAH!
RUN AWAY!
MEWR
WAIT FOR ME!
MIYA

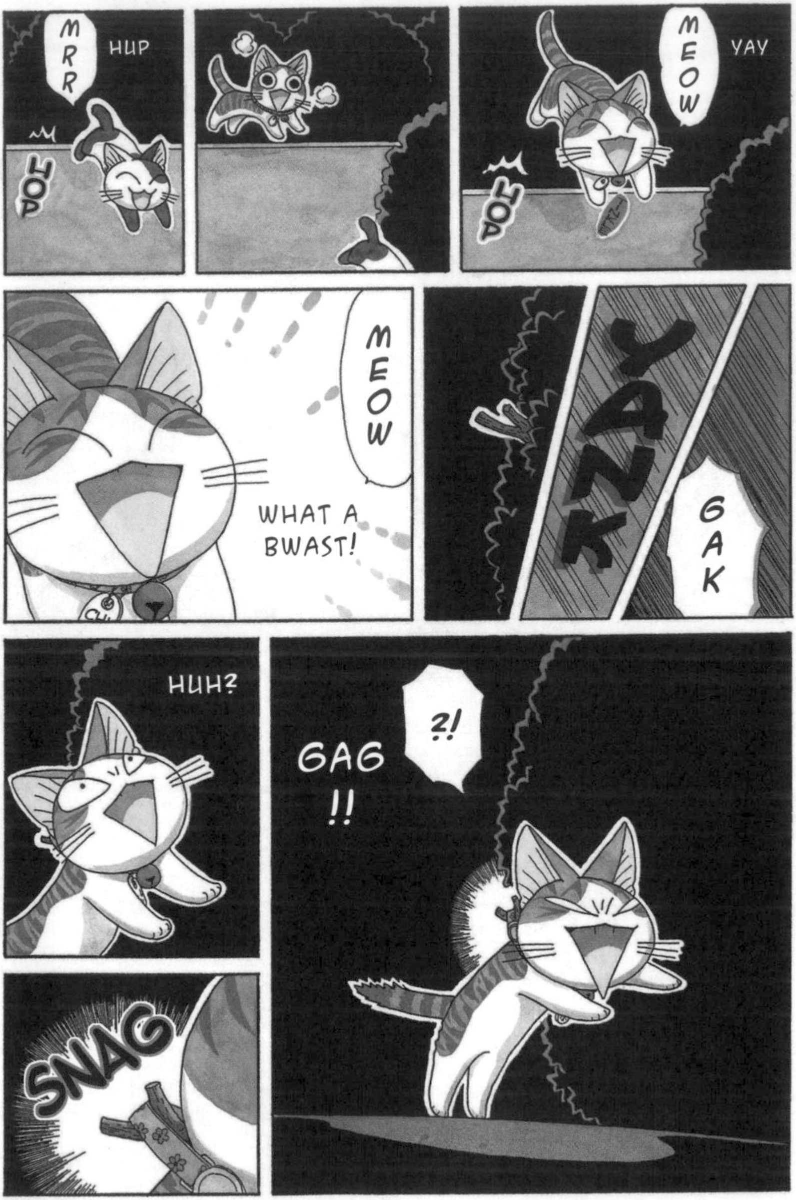
MRR
HUP
HOP
MEOW
YAY
HOP
MEOW
WHAT A BWAST!
YANK
GAK
HUH?
SNAG
?!
GAG !!

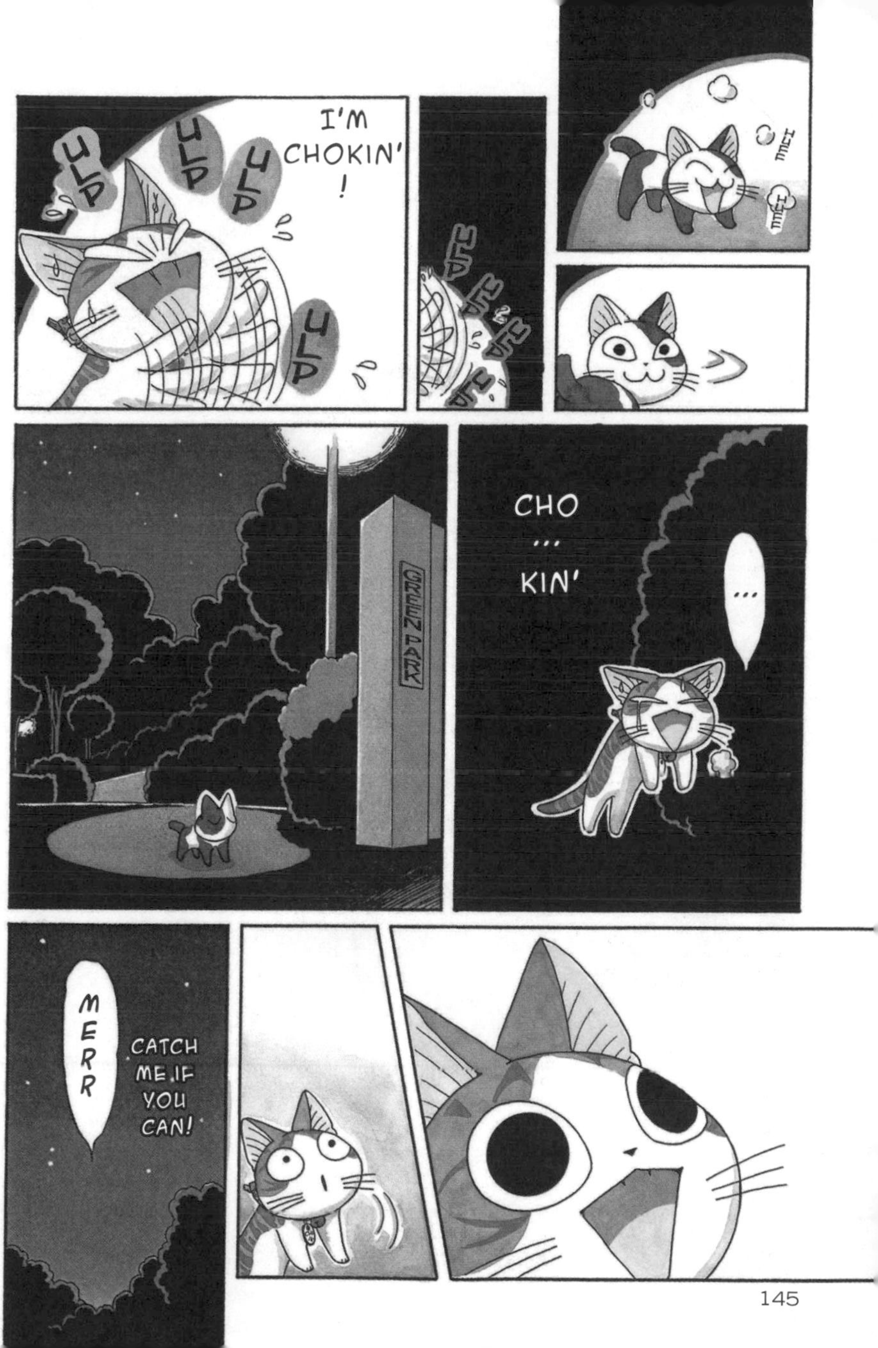
ULP
ULP
ULP
I'M CHOKIN'!
ULP
GREEN PARK
CHO... KIN'
...
MERR
CATCH ME IF YOU CAN!

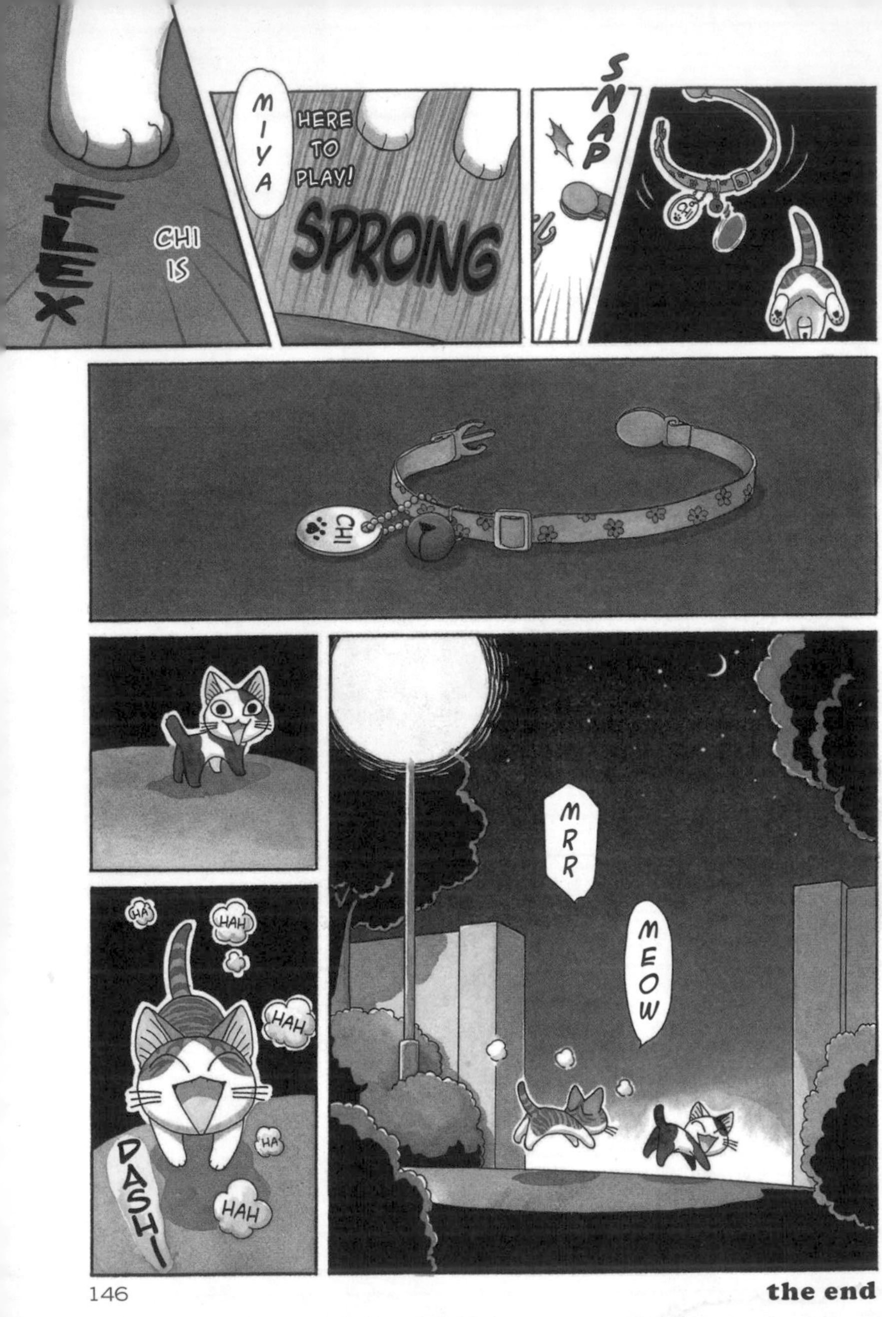
FLEX
CHI IS
MIYA
HERE TO PLAY!
SPROING
SNAP
CHI
CHI
HA
HAH
HAH
HA
HAH
DASHI
MRR
MEOW



**the end**

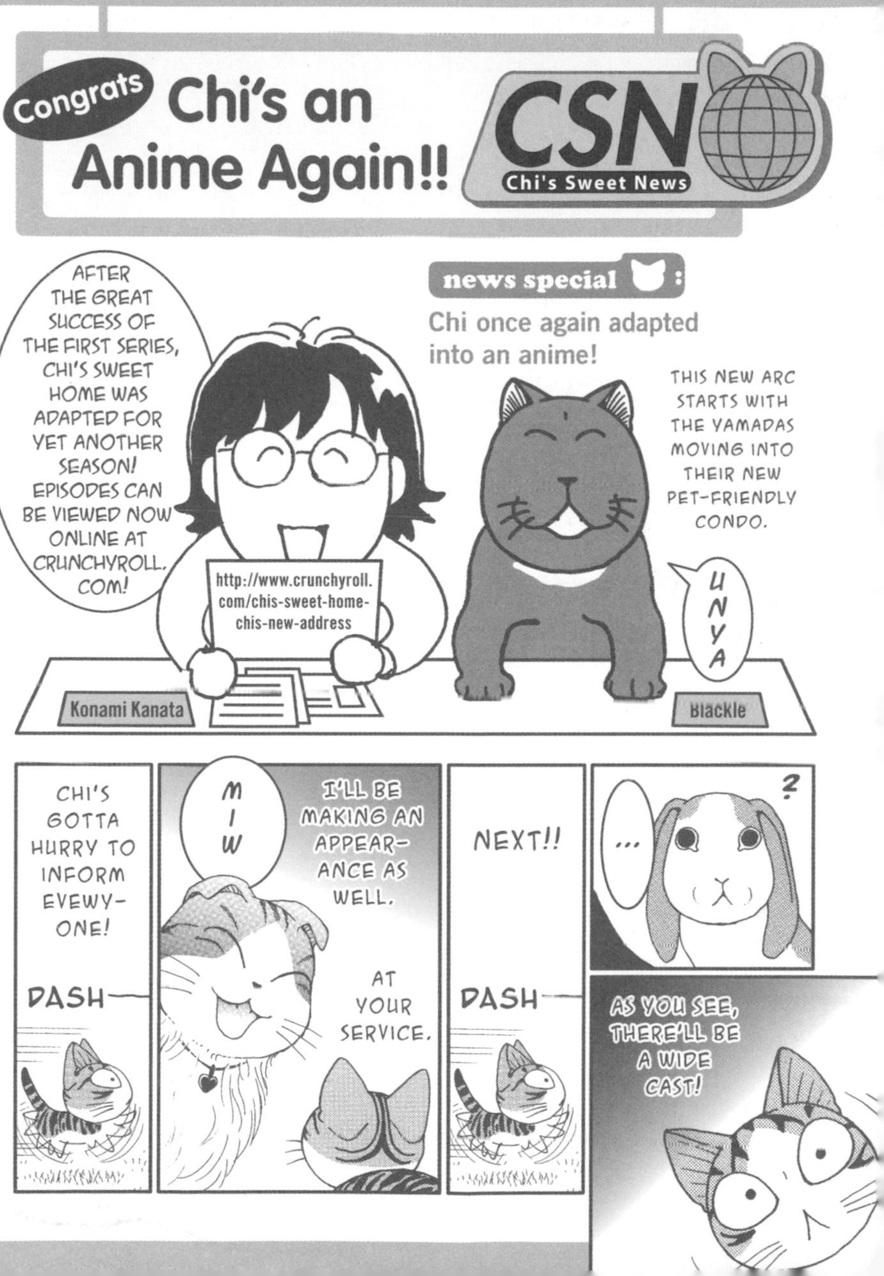
Congrats
Chi's an Anime Again!!
CSN
Chi's Sweet News
news special:
Chi once again adapted into an anime!
AFTER THE GREAT SUCCESS OF THE FIRST SERIES, CHI'S SWEET HOME WAS ADAPTED FOR YET ANOTHER SEASON! EPISODES CAN BE VIEWED NOW ONLINE AT CRUNCHYROLL.COM!
http://www.crunchyroll.com/chis-sweet-home-chis-new-address
THIS NEW ARC STARTS WITH THE YAMADAS MOVING INTO THEIR NEW PET-FRIENDLY CONDO.
UNYA
Konami Kanata
Blackle
CHI'S GOTTA HURRY TO INFORM EVEWY-ONE!
DASH
MIW
I'LL BE MAKING AN APPEAR-ANCE AS WELL.
AT YOUR SERVICE.
NEXT!!
DASH
?
...
AS YOU SEE, THERE'LL BE A WIDE CAST!

# Who knew these characters had such backgrounds...

**In the anime's second season we get to meet many of Chi's new neighbors. So in this extra we'd like to share some character designs as well as profiles created for the anime. Once you know their personalities better, you might discover something new when you watch the anime.**

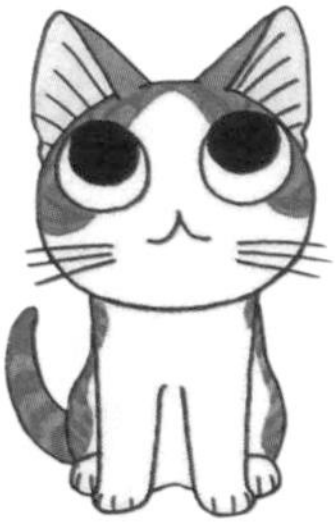

**Name:** Yuki Kusano
**Age:** 12 years old
**Family Structure:** Lives with his mom ar dad and older sister.
**Personality:** Energetic and good at spor (especially those involving a ball).

## David and the Kusano Boy

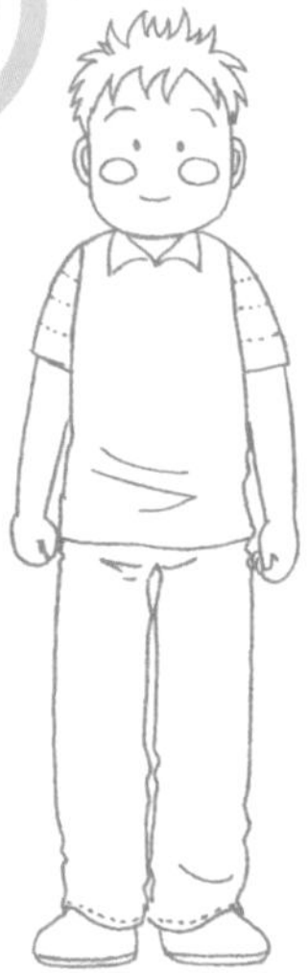

**Name:** David
**Gender:** Male
**Breed:** Beagle
**Age:** About 6 months old
**Caretakers:** the Kusano family
**Personality:** Always full of spunk. And while he's got a silly side, he always loyally listens to the Kusano boy.

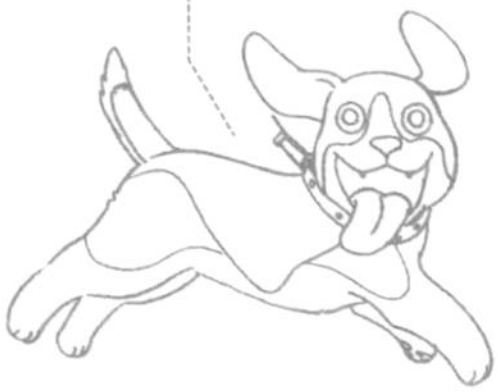

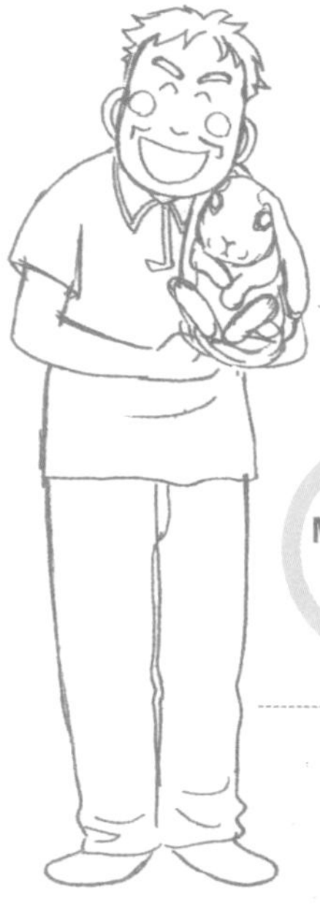

## Mee and Mr. Furukawa

**Name:** Mee
**Age:** Unknown
**Gender:** Unknown
**Breed:** Holland Lop
**Caretaker:** Mr. Furukawa
**Personality:** Mysterious and always silent, Mee lives life at its own pace.

**Name:** Kazuya Furukawa
**Age:** 51 years old
**Occupation:** Advertising firm employee
**Personality:** Always heard laughing heartily. Enjoys traveling abroad with his wife, where he often purchases strange souvenirs.

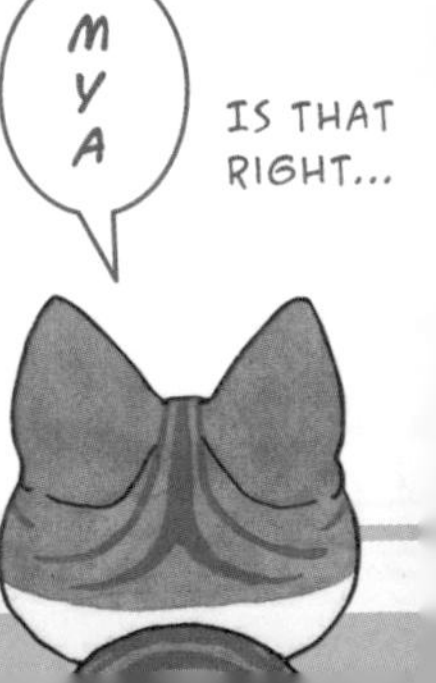
MYA
IS THAT RIGHT...

## Auntie Cali

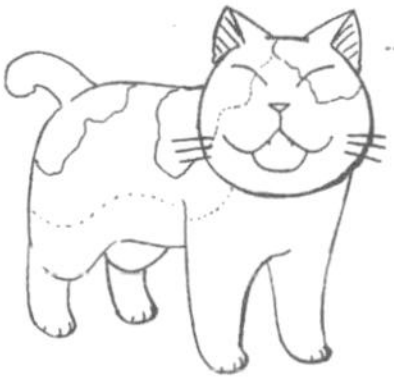

**Name:** Cali
**Gender:** Female
**Breed:** Calico
**Age:** About 40 in human years
**Caretakers:** She lives in a large traditional Japanese home.
**Personality:** Often seen smiling, but she's also a little forgetful.

## Alice and Saori

**Name:** Saori Ijuuin
**Age:** 26 years old
**Occupation:** Picture book author; her pen name is Yume Hanabatake
**Personality:** Gentle and calm, yet kinda ditzy.

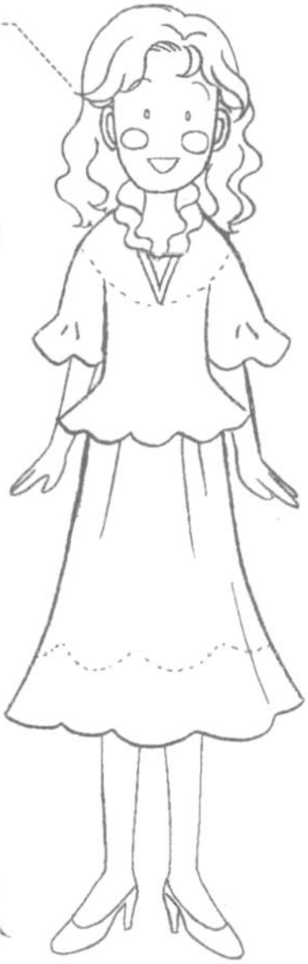

**Name:** Alice
**Gender:** Female
**Breed:** Scottish Fold Longhair
**Personality:** Gentle and calm, yet kinda ditzy.
**Age:** 12 to 18 months
**Caretaker:** Saori
**Personality:** Very proud, but occasionally she succumbs to her feline nature.

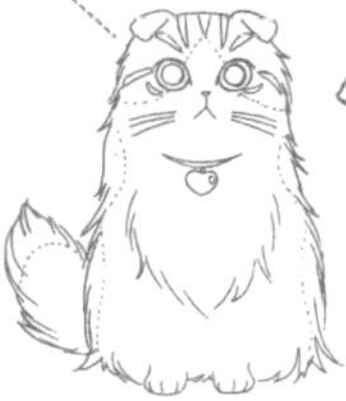

## Lucky & Mrs. Akashi

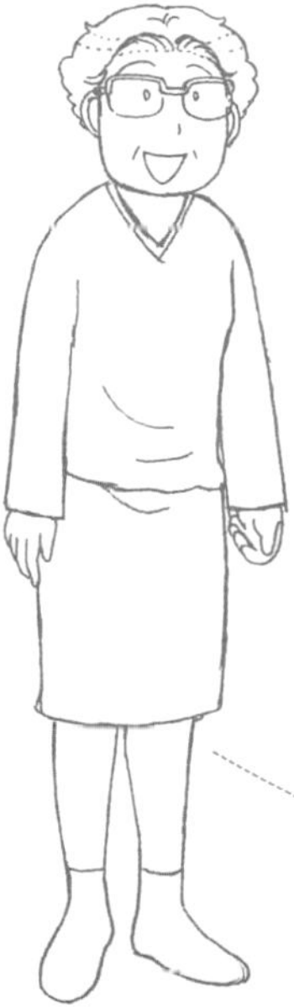

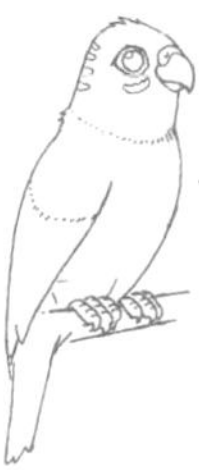

**Name:** Lucky
**Gender:** Male
**Age:** About 18 in human years
**Caretaker:** the Akashi family
**Talents:** He can mimic words.
**Personality:** He lacks the nervousness of other small birds and is quite bold.

**Name:** Yasuko Akashi
**Age:** In her 60's
**Occupation:** Housewife
**Personality:** Composed and big-hearted.

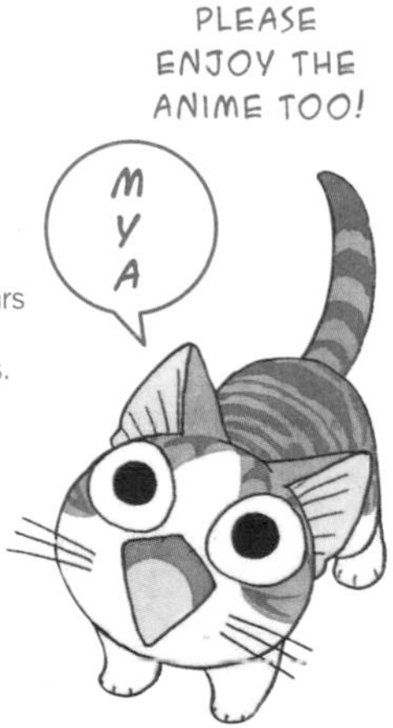
PLEASE ENJOY THE ANIME TOO!
MYA

# TWIN SPICA

## Kou Yaginuma

### Space has never seemed so close and yet so far!

Asumi has passed her exams and been accepted into the Tokyo Space School. Now even greater challenges await in the metropolis. It's clear she is made of the right stuff, but can her little body put all those talents to use under the mental and physical rigors of astronaut training?

**"*Twin Spica* is a pleasantly unexpected tear-jerker that hits the nostalgia key for those of us of a certain age who wanted desperately to go to space camp, even after the Challenger explosion."**
**—Erin Finnegan, Zero-Gravity Bride &**
***Anime News Network* writer**

© Kou Yaginuma

# Chi's Sweet Home, volume 6

Translation - Ed Chavez
Production - Hiroko Mizuno
            Tomoe Tsutsumi

Translation provided by Vertical, Inc., 2011
Published by Vertical, Inc., New York

Originally published in Japanese as *Chiizu Suiito Houmu* by Kodansha, Ltd., 2007-2008
*Chiizu Suiito Houmu* first serialized in *Morning*, Kodansha, Ltd., 2004-

*Chiizu Suiito Houmu: Atarashii O-Uchi* animation character designs
© Konami Kanata Kodansha / TV Tokyo Chi's Sweet Home Production Committee

This is a work of fiction.

ISBN: 978-1-935654-14-8

Manufactured in the United States of America

First Edition

Third Printing

Vertical, Inc.
451 Park Avenue South 7th Floor
New York, NY 10016
www.vertical-inc.com

Special thanks to: K. Kitamoto